The Book of Fabulous Beasts

The Book of

Edited by

Joseph Nigg

A Treasury
of Writings
from Ancient
Times to
the Present

Fabulous Beasts

New York   Oxford   ⁀   Oxford University Press   ⁀   1999

Oxford University Press

Oxford   New York
Athens   Auckland   Bangkok   Bogotá   Buenos Aires
Calcutta   Cape Town   Chennai   Dar es Salaam   Delhi   Florence
Hong Kong   Istanbul   Karachi   Kuala Lumpur   Madrid
Melbourne   Mexico City   Mumbai   Nairobi   Paris   São Paulo
Singapore   Taipei   Tokyo   Toronto   Warsaw

and associated companies in
Berlin   Ibadan

Published by Oxford University Press, Inc.
198 Madison Avenue, New York, NY 10016

Oxford is a registered trademark of Oxford University Press

Cataloging-in-Publication Data
The book of fabulous beasts : a treasury of writings from ancient times
to the present / edited by Joseph Nigg.
p.   cm.
A collection of writings about fabulous creatures, arranged
chronologically by writer, with section introductions by the editor
and accompanying illustrations.
Includes bibliographical references and index.
ISBN 0-19-509561-8
1. Animals, Mythical.   I. Nigg, Joe.
GR820.B66   1998   808.8'0374—dc21   97-52944

1 3 5 7 9 8 6 4 2
Printed in the United States of America
on acid free paper

For Esther,
her gray eyes glinting

and

In honor and memory
of Michael

Fresh spirit fills me, face to
face with these—
Grand are the Forms, and
grand the Memories!

—Goethe, *Faust*

Contents

III. STRANGE AND DUBIOUS CREATURES 200

Preface

Animals that never lived upon earth exist in images and words all around us. Representations of dragons, unicorns, griffins, the phoenix, and other fantastic shapes appear in multiple materials and forms—from gift-shop figures to business logos. These animals we now term "fabulous" are also widespread in fantasy fiction, and shelves of books about them further attest to the fascination we still have with such ancient creatures' dreamlike shapes and mysterious powers.

Most books dealing with multiple imaginary beasts arrange the material by animal, the standard structure of bestiaries and natural histories. Also, these books usually cite earlier authorities such as the Bible, Herodotus, Pliny, Marco Polo, Sir John Mandeville, Shakespeare, and Edward Topsell. While passages are referred to and frequently quoted, readers interested in the larger contexts of the material must seek out often difficult-to-find original sources on their own.

This book is, first of all, a source book of representative writings about fabulous beasts, collected in a single volume to make primary sources and their contexts readily accessible to the general reader as well as to specialists on the subject.

This collection offers an alternative approach to the usual bestiary/natural history order of the material. Chronological order by writer rather than classification by animal first establishes a historical context for the subject as a whole. This arrangement consolidates the contribution of each author, placing individual passages within works, works within their own time, and finally works within the total literary tradition. By representing that tradition, writings in this collection comprise a composite history of fabulous animals themselves.

The parts of the book—Part I, Ancient Animals; Part II, Beasts of God; Part III, Strange and Dubious Creatures; and Part IV, Recurring Images—roughly correspond to the classical, medieval, Renaissance and "modern" periods of Western history. Within this broad historical framework, medieval and Renaissance sections are loosely grouped by genres that represent distinct areas of the literary development of fabulous animals. In Part II, Chapters 5–7, "A Fabulous Bestiary," "Storied Menagerie," and "Travelers' Tales," are sometimes concurrent with each other or chronologically overlap sections preceding and following them. The same is true of the subsections in Part III. Works that developed over centuries, such as the Bible, *The Romance of Alexander*, and *The Arabian Nights*, can be placed in time only arbitrarily, but with consideration for contexts of influence.

An overall chronological order of the material precludes self-contained histories of individual beasts. Readers seeking descriptions or development of particular animals should consult the glossary, general index, and the cross-references to individual authors or works included elsewhere in the collection which are cited in the introductions to entries. Recent books on both individual or multiple animals are listed in the bibliography for further reading.

While the dragon, phoenix, and unicorn in particular have Asian counterparts, the writings in this anthology are Western in origin or influence, representing a distinctly Western literary tradition. Besides ancient Egyptian and Middle Eastern texts, however, entries include writings about the roc (rukh) from *The Arabian Nights* and the journal of the Moslem traveler, Ibn Battuta. Sindbad's adventures are well known throughout the West through countless editions, illustrations, and cinematic versions, and Battuta's tale of the roc has been cited in many books of animal lore. The Indian Garuda, the Chinese Ki-Lin, and other Asian animals appear in entries composed by Western authors.

My selection of entries from the vast body of writings about fabulous creatures began, of course, with standard expository accounts and literary works essential to the tradition, and then extended to lesser-known writings. From the nineteenth century on, books in which these animals are either objects of study or fictional characters become so widespread that selections can only represent typical treatments of the subject. Given space limitations, J. R. R. Tolkien's *Hobbit*, for example, is the lone representative of the vast body of recent fantasy fiction — collected in numerous anthologies — in which fantastic creatures play important roles.

The lengths of entries vary, from brief references in the Bible and the works of Shakespeare to extended selections from narrative poetry and treatises. Earlier authors' accounts of individual creatures tend to be shorter and more self-contained than later writings, particularly those from the sixteenth century and later. When length restrictions prevented inclusion of complete entries, I was faced with the unhappy choice of selecting parts or omitting the work altogether. I have usually chosen to excerpt in order to present material important to a fuller understanding of the subject.

While most of the entries are expository, poetic and fictional uses of the animals are highlights of the creatures' literary history, such as Ovid's phoenix, Dante's griffin, Spenser's dragon, Shakespeare's beast images, and the phantasmagorical menageries of Goethe and Flaubert.

Most of the entries are translations, some of them in archaic English. Some translations of poetry are in prose. Overall, standard nineteenth- and twentieth-century academic translations are used here for classical and medieval texts. With the exceptions of modernized versions of Mela and Solinus (Part I) and Caxton's own translation of Jacobus de Voragine (Part III), I use Renaissance translations in their own period. Except for Mela and Solinus, I have retained the original spelling and punctuation in archaic works, including *v* for *u* and *i* for *j*. I have, however, omitted ligatures, the long *s*, and pervasive Renaissance italics. I have retained in texts and accompanying titles the various spellings of creatures' names by authors and translators, but have used the most common spelling in general editorial. My own bracketed words in texts are preceded by "ed."

References accompanying the entries include both page numbers from particular editions and, in the case of standard texts, book and line numbers within parentheses.

Titles of entries — added to individualize the pieces and indicate their content — are my own. When appropriate, the title is either the author's own or is a phrase taken from the passage; in other cases, the title simply describes the subject. Bracketed and italicized subheadings are also mine.

Most — but not all — of the authors referred to in editorial introductions are represented in this anthology.

A collection of writings about fabulous animals would hardly be complete without samples of the other major source of the beasts' cultural existence: art. Imaginary creatures have been depicted globally in all mediums and styles. The representive graphic works in this collection are generally contemporaneous with the writings they accompany. Many of the woodcuts in Chapter 10 originally appeared with the corresponding texts, and some of the illustrations from modern books were created by the authors themselves. And then there is the icon that appears throughout the book. This hybrid creature with the beak, wings, and front feet of a bird and the body of a lion is a 5000-year-old griffin figure from ancient Susa. Like other imaginary animals in this collection, it moves through time, from one epoch to another.

I am indebted not only to modern fabulous-beast scholarship in general, but to three sources in particular that have pointed the way to a chronological approach to the material: the text and charts of literary development in P. Ansell Robin's *Animal Lore in English Literature* (1932) and T. H. White's *Book of Beasts* (1954), and the introduction and annotations in Margaret Robinson's bibliography, *Fictitious Beasts* (1961).

In addition to the publishers, libraries, and museums acknowledged elsewhere in this collection, many people have contributed significantly to the production of this book. I would like to express my deep appreciation to the following in particular: Oxford University Press executive editor Helen McInnis, specialist readers David A. Leeming and the late Stephen Lonsdale, my editor Susan Chang, her editorial assistant Susan Barba, copy editor Stephanie Saxon, designer Jeff Hoffman, and production editor Joellyn Ausanka, for shaping this book into its published form; Frances Howard-Gordon for her helpful suggestions at the outset of this project; Dr. Raymond P. Tripp, Jr., for his translations of the Old English *Phoenix*, *Beowulf*, and the *Anglo-Saxon Chronicle* and for his review of portions of the manuscript; Dr. Mary Margolies DeForest for her translation of Hildegard of Bingen and her review of portions of the manuscript; Dr. Gregory K. Jember for his translation of the Old English Riddle No. 10; Jeff VanderMeer for his interest and review of the manuscript; Joseph Hutchison for recommending poetry translations; Don Waite for biblical research; Albert Smith for mythological resources; Gary Reilly for technological support; Jim Nelson for discussion of ideas, book suggestions, and proofing; and Marjorie Muzzillo for proofing. And on the personal side: my father, for a hybrid animal figure on an antique lamp, the image that many years ago led me to this subject; and for all my family and friends, particularly my late mother and my elder son, Joey, for moral support and encouragement.

In addition, I honor with loving remembrance my son Michael, whom our family lost during the production of this book. And I specially thank my wife, Esther, who not only shared with me her books, classical knowledge, and literary skills, but provided unlimited emotional support from the first day of this project to the last.

The Book of Fabulous Beasts

Introduction

A History of Fabulous Beasts

escendants of monstrous figures of ancient mythologies, imaginary animals of a newer generation emerged from the ocean of oral story and spread through tales of Greek and Roman travelers, historians, geographers, and poets. On the basis of written authority, accounts of these creatures were repeated and varied by writer after writer, leading to general acceptance of their place in the animal kingdom. Following the decline of the classical world, the creatures returned in the Christian epoch through the Bible, homilies of the Church Fathers, and the medieval bestiaries. Encyclopedias included them among living creatures. Some of them figured in the tales of saints, heroes, and travelers who journeyed to the edges of the earth. They entered printed books through classical texts and new literature, joined actual animals in handbooks of heraldry, and became allegories of alchemy. Doubts about the creatures' existence were expressed in medical treatises and natural histories and increased with the development of seventeenth-century science — until the creatures were challenged and discredited as "fabulous." After centuries of literary hiatus, they returned to books as "mythical" beasts, often in the company of their mythological ancestors, and they thrive again — in scholarly works, popular nonfiction, children's literature, and adult fantasy.

Writings about animals that the human imagination has shaped from nature form a millennia-long literary tradition. These writings also comprise a composite history, even epic, of the creatures themselves. Spanning millennia and a variety of genres, works of both major and less well-known authors present the protean creatures' literary transformations from one historical age to another. Portrayals of them necessarily reflect the ideas dominant in the times and places in which they were produced. The history of fabulous animals ultimately, then, reflects the development of the Western imagination itself.

Originally derived from immemorial oral lore, these creatures were established in authoritative writings and perpetuated through transmission from writer to writer. (See T. H. White's charts of the literary development and influence of animal lore in Part IV, Recurring Images.) From ancient times up through the 1600s, most of the writings in which these animals appear are expository, and most of them confirm a widespread acceptance of the animals' existence. Even when major authorities themselves remained unconvinced of the tale they had heard or read, and other authors rejected the alleged existence or powers and attributes of a given creature, the willingness of later authors and their readers to believe led to transmission of the information.

In the second century A.D., Pausanias explained one of the channels through which erroneous facts are perpetuated: "Those who like to listen to the miraculous are themselves apt to add to the marvel," he said, "and so they ruin truth by mixing it with falsehood." The writings that present imaginary creatures as actual represent the efforts of Western authors to extend knowledge of the known world. In doing so, they often reported (sometimes with reservations) what they had heard and often repeated what they had read, thus producing a body of writings that are about fact and fiction, belief and disbelief—writings that dramatize how fantasies are developed and are rationally challenged—and how, if the creatures written about are elemental enough in the human psyche, they continue to be transformed into other shapes of meaning.

BEGINNINGS

A few early writers suspected that certain creatures were "fabulous," but it was primarily after the New Science of the seventeenth century rejected traditional authority that many such animals, "dubious" at first, were deemed "fabulous," "mythical," "fictitious," "fantastic," and "imaginary." In common usage, these terms are largely equivalent, as are the accompanying "beast," "animal," "being," and "creature." "Monster" is also often used in reference to the more grotesque figures and to mixed creatures in heraldry.

The earliest hybrid creatures—which can be regarded as the ancestors, the first generation—also arose from the oral tradition, but as monsters in the oldest mythological poetry. In the Babylonian epic of creation, *Enuma Elish*, the mother goddess Tiamat (traditionally regarded as a dragon) gives birth to a nightmare brood of horned serpents, demons, and scorpion-men. Hesiod's succession myth in his *Theogony* records that the offspring of the gods Ceto and Phorcys included the Gorgons, Medusa, and the nymph-snake Echidna, who bore three-headed Cerberus, the Hydra of Lerna, the Chimera, and other fearsome shapes. Part of Hesiod's description of the fire-breathing composite Chimera (perhaps an interpolation) is repeated from Homer, whose *Odyssey* in particular represents the beginnings of the Western literary tradition of monsters. Among those creatures that confront Odysseus on his homeward journey from Troy are the deadly Sirens and many-headed Scylla. In one of the hymns originally attributed to Homer, the god Apollo slays Python, the dragon guarding the sacred spring of the Delphic oracle. All these may be considered among the earliest generation of fantastic creatures.

With the development of early Greek science, philosophy, prose, and historical writing in the fifth century B.C., the monsters of mythology were rationalized as fables and regarded as marvels. In their place arose a new generation of animals, exotic creatures reported to be living in the distant lands of Egypt, Ethiopia, Arabia, Persia, India, and Scythia. Herodotus told in his *History* tales of the Arabian phoenix that appeared in Egypt every 500 years and great birds in Arabia that built their nests of precious cinnamon. He repeated from the epic poet Aristeas that in northern Scythia, griffins guarded their gold from a race of one-eyed men; in India, he said, ants larger than foxes dug up gold from the desert. Also in India, according to Ctesias the Cnidian, lived a ferocious wild ass whose single horn had magical curative powers, and the *martikhora* (manticore), a red lion-sized monster with a man's face, ears, and eyes, and a tail like a scorpion.

Later, from the first Roman geographer, Pomponius Mela, came tales of exotic birds — the horned *tragopomones* and horse-eared *pegasies*—and the lethargic *catoplepe* (catoblepas) with a gaze fatal to any who looked into his eyes. And all the earlier beasts joined the noxious basilisk, the yale with the movable horns, and other bizarre creatures in the menagerie of Pliny the Elder's first-century A.D. *Natural History*.

The fabulous animals that dominate this collection are members of this later group: creatures that, while not existing in nature, have been referred to in expository prose as animals that either do exist or might exist. (The dragon, griffin, and a few others span the two categories.) Also included here are actual animals with fabulous characteristics, such as the salamander, that lives in fire, the barnacle goose born from barnacles on sea-rotted wood, and the legless and wingless *manucodiata* (bird of paradise). In this book, then, "fabulous animal" includes a wide variety of creatures, from the barnacle goose to the phoenix, animal composites such as the basilisk and griffin, and even creatures with human parts, such as the manticore and the mermaid. With rare exceptions, this collection does not include the primarily human-formed vampires and werewolves, aliens, or the legion of individually created literary cousins.

Twelfth-century St. Bernard, contemplating a composite figure in monastic sculpture, scornfully asked: "What is that ridiculous monstrosity doing, an amazing kind of deformed beauty and yet a beautiful deformity?" Bernard goes on to describe a quadruped with a serpent's tail, a fish with the head of a quadruped, a horse–goat hybrid and a horned horse, "everywhere so plentiful and astonishing a variety of contradictory forms." Given nature's bounty of about a million insect species alone, and the giraffe, elephant, and other actual animals whose shapes are as fantastic as any created by the imagination, we well may wonder why human beings have since ancient times created their own animals.

Writers in different epochs offer widely varying scientific and artistic theories about the nature of hybrid beasts. The Roman atomist Lucretius described the composite process in mechanical terms, explaining that flimsy films of atoms fly off the surface of objects and that when they meet in the mind, they form images of creatures that never before existed, as when a film of the image of a horse combines with the image-film of a man, creating a centaur. Leonardo da Vinci proposed that the way to make imaginary animals appear natural in art was to incorporate in the figures realistic parts of other animals. (Tudor heralds introduced into coats of arms combinations of animals as fantastic as those in the religious art St. Bernard described.) The alchemist Paracelsus wrote of unnatural unions in the sea and on land, of sperm dropping from the stars and being carried by the winds, leading to random impregnation and producing hybrid monsters. Twentieth-century art scholar Heinz Mode notes in *Fabulous Beasts and Demons* that the imagination fuses into a single form the powers of multiple animals, which are represented in prominent parts such as wings, horns, fangs, and claws. In his *Lives of a Cell*, twentieth-century microbiologist Lewis Thomas compares microorganisms to imaginary animals, maintaining that living things tend to combine with each other, and that any living cell, under the right conditions, can fuse with any other.

The writings also lead to a variety of other answers.

First, there is eyewitness testimony. "I have often seen with my own eyes more than a thousand minute embryos of birds of this species on the seashore, hanging from one piece of timber," the twelfth-century ecclesiastic Giraldus Cambrensis said of the unnatural birth of barnacle geese, and four centuries later, the botanist John Gerard echoed the claim, saying, "What our eies have seene, and hands have touched we shall declare." While the story they reported was debated as late as the eighteenth century, what both Giraldus and Gerard described were actually shellfish. Aristotle's reference to a unicorn in his *Historia Animalium* is also credited to inaccurate observation — either his or someone else's. His labeling of the oryx as a single-horned quadruped has led many to conclude that this two-horned animal, seen from a distance, had broken off one of its horns or was viewed in profile. The most famous firsthand accounts of unicorns are Ludovico de Varthema's early sixteenth-century descriptions of small, single-horned animals in the Temple of Mecca and in the city of Zeila, in ancient Ethiopia. Later discoveries of the "unicornization" of young animals, practiced in diverse parts of the world, gave credence to his report. The father of Renaissance artist Benvenuto Cellini showed his children "a little animal, resembling a lizard," that was running around in the hottest part of the fire. He then beat his son so he would remember being among the first to see the fabled salamander, an actual amphibian that has no resistance to flame. Richard Whitbourne's encounter with a "Mermaide"-like creature is one of many such accounts during the Age of Exploration.

Then there is hearsay, the oral tradition, the major conduit of accounts of early fabulous beasts. Faulty observation, inaccurate reporting, storytellers' love of exaggeration, and the imagination of the listener hearing something described and then passing it on in turn could all contribute to the reshaping of actual animals into fantastic creatures: the Indian rhinoceros into the equine or goatlike unicorn of the imagination, or a constrictor such as the python into an even larger dragon, perhaps one with crocodile legs, scales and head, and even wings and fiery breath. Rationalistic hypotheses linking living prototypes to beasts of the imagination have been advanced from ancient times up to the present school of "cryptozoology," the science of unknown animals.

There are travelers' and others' literary descriptions of exotic animals. Authors from Herodotus to the seventeenth-century natural history compiler Edward Topsell used a composite technique to describe exotic creatures in terms of animals familiar to their readers. The phoenix that Herodotus saw pictures of in Egypt was "in size almost that of an eagle," and his gold-digging ants were "in size somewhat less than dogs, but bigger than foxes." Far more elaborate, Pliny's unicorn has the body of a horse, a head like a stag, feet like an elephant, a tail like a boar, and a three-foot-long black horn protruding from its forehead. The giraffe is an example of an animal whose hybrid characteristics are reflected in its early name: "cameleopard." What fantastic images composite descriptions must have created in the imaginations of readers.

Bestiary and natural history artists rendered these described creatures into images that then took on their own reality and served as later graphic models of the animals. (See the illustrations in Chapters 5 and 10.)

Art itself is sometimes a source of a literary animal, as in the pictures that Herodotus saw of the phoenix.

There is the confusion of translation and etymology. It has been proposed that the Persian word for "marmot" is equivalent to "mountain ant" and generated the tale of the giant, gold-digging ants of India. In Job, *phoenix* is variously rendered as "palm tree," "phoenix" (the bird), and even "sand" (Job 29:18); and *mermicoleon*, a Greek word meaning "a lion among ants" (Job 4:11), becomes the composite ant–lion.

There are hoaxes: the distant kingdom of marvels described in the spurious twelfth-century *Letter of Prester John* and for centuries sought by explorers, and the *Travels* of the fictitious Sir John Mandeville, whose compendium of classical and medieval lore helped shape early Renaissance maps. As Pliny reported,

Roman records attested that a bird exhibited in Rome was said to be a phoenix that appeared in Egypt. The tusk of the northern narwhal was displayed in cathedrals as the horn of a unicorn, and it was powdered and sold as alicorn for exorbitant sums in apothecary shops. Aristotle had stated there was no such thing as a footless bird, but when Ferdinand Magellan's only surviving ship returned to Spain with the bodies of two beautifully plumed birds of paradise, stories spread of the birds being footless, living in air and feeding on dew. The truth was, the natives traditionally prepared the birds' skins for drying by removing the wings and legs. In our own time, faked photographs and other hoaxes have contributed to questions about the existence of the Loch Ness Monster, the Abominable Snowman (Yeti) of the Himalayas, and the American Sasquatch (Bigfoot).

OBSTACLES TO DEVELOPMENT

Creatures with such questionable beginnings could be expected to face a variety of obstacles to their literary development as animals that existed in nature.

Foremost of possible enemies to belief in marvelous creatures is the study of living animals. What would eventually evolve into the science of zoology had its beginnings in the fourth century B.C., with Aristotle's *Historia Animalium*. Although the pioneering book established concepts that later proved to be erroneous, and either inadvertently or through interpolation included a few creatures that were fabulous, it set for natural histories a scientific standard that was not to be matched until Conrad Gesner's sixteenth-century work of the same name. The natural histories of Pliny and Aelian were influential as well, but these freely admitted fabulous creatures along with actual animals. Aristotle's imaginary beasts were assured of literary longevity by power of his authority, and creatures not included in the *Historia Animalium* received attention elsewhere.

In the thirteenth century, Albertus Magnus appended his own natural history to his translation and commentaries of Aristotle's work. Albertus questioned the authenticity of many creatures, but in spite of, or because of, its innovative approach, his natural history had little demonstrable effect upon continued acceptance of fantastic creatures.

Three centuries after Albertus, Gesner compiled his massive four-volume *Historia Animalium*. Considered the starting point of modern zoology, Gesner's volumes are a comprehensive documentation of the animal world. He does include a small number of imaginary creatures, most of them treated with qualification. While he sanctions the unicorn, the barnacle goose, and the extant fable of the bird of paradise, he places dragons among the serpents and presents the basilisk as a snake, dismissing beliefs in the creature's noxious powers and that it was hatched by a toad from a cock's egg. Gesner's volumes remained the zoological standard for centuries, and variations of the work's hundreds of woodcut illustrations appeared in several natural histories.

Gesner's books, along with other sixteenth-century natural histories such as those of Ulisse Aldrovandi, expressed doubts about the credibility of several animals of the imagination. Yet to come, however, was the English version of Gesner's mammal volume, Edward Topsell's *Historie of Foure-Footed Beastes* (1607), an attested translation with additional pictures, stories, and opinions of the compiler. Topsell freely accepted and commented on the unicorn, lamia, manticore, winged dragon, and so many other fantastic creatures that his work became, in general, an encyclopedia of animal lore up to his time.

Besides the implicit and sometimes explicit discrediting of imaginary animals in natural histories, the creatures had other critics from classical times on. Aristotle's teacher, Plato, had already made his fictional Socrates refuse to rationalize the monsters of mythology, electing instead to study the human self, and the poet Lucretius later explained away mythological hybrids with atomic theory. Pausanias and Philostratus both discounted the manticore of Ctesias as fabulous, Pausanias identifying the monster with the Indian tiger. Strabo scoffed at the fabrications of India. As already mentioned, St. Bernard denounced fantastic figures in monastic art. Marco Polo, a reliable naturalist overall, stated that the unicorn and the griffin were not what Europeans thought they were but were, respectively, a beast that lives in mud (the rhinoceros) and the gigantic "Ruc" (roc—actually another fabulous bird) of Madagascar. He also rejected the salamander, concluding it was a fire-resistant material, not an animal at all. In spite of the charges made against imaginary creatures, common belief in them was so strong that critics up to Sir Thomas Browne had little effect upon their development.

What posed the biggest threat to the literary survival of such creatures were changing epochs. With the fall of classical Rome, the phoenix and other traditional imaginary animals also reached the end of an era. But the concurrent rise of Christianity brought with it the holy scriptures—to believers, the ultimate authority—and different versions of the Bible included the phoenix, the unicorn, the dragon, and the cockatrice (basilisk) as well as mythical monsters. Granted divine authority, the phoenix, unicorn, and other imaginary creatures were subjects of homilies by the Church Fathers. Lore of creatures both actual and imaginary also came from a heterogeneous collection of animal tales known as the *Physiologus* ("The Naturalist" or "The Book of Nature"), thought to have been composed in Egypt around the second century A.D. While the original no longer exists, Greek and later Latin versions were allegorized into Christian lessons, typically containing scripture, a description of the animal, and a moral. Homilies of the Church Fathers being structurally similar to *Physiologus* entries, St. Basil, St. Ambrose, and other churchmen were traditionally credited with composing versions of the work. While the majority of the creatures are based on actual animals, the phoenix, unicorn, siren, onocentaur, and animals with fantastic attributes, such as the salamander and the whale, appear in most versions. The yale, manticore, and other fantastic classical beasts from Pliny, Solinus, and Aelian in particular crowded into the later bestiaries, which flourished in the twelfth and thirteenth centuries. Many of the same fabulous figures gained entry into thirteenth-century encyclopedias, which derived much of their natural history from the bestiaries. During the later development of the *Physiologus* and the flourishing of the bestiaries, imaginary animals appeared in a variety of literary genres, including saint's lives, epics, riddles, chronicles, and monks' tales. Also appearing in these stories are the heroes Beowulf, King Arthur, St. George, Alexander the Great, and even the Norse god Thor. The dominant beast in these tales is the dragon of legend.

The importance of the bestiaries and other allegorical Christian writings decreased along with the monolithic power of the Church. Writings about animals gradually changed with the invention of the printing press and global exploration. William Caxton, the first English printer, rendered into English a thirteenth-century French version of a compilation of classical works in Latin. Caxton's *Mirrour of the World* presented the griffin, manticore, unicorn, and other fantastic beasts as though they were still living in the remote parts of the earth. Also, the works of Pliny, Solinus, and Mela were all honored with print in the English translations of Philemon Holland and Arthur Golding. Printing, though, led not only to a revival of classical learning but to new knowledge. The spread of learning in all directions — looking both to the past and to the expanding natural world — would eventually lead to reassessment of traditional authority.

Created in literature by classical writers, imaginary animals could not be discredited until the authors of the works in which the animals appeared were discredited. By the time Herodotus, Pliny, and other authorities came under the scrutiny of rationalism, imaginary animals were already established in a medieval graphic form that continued to develop during the Renaissance and has remained imagistically vital in Western culture to this day: the art and science of heraldry.

Heavily influenced by Christian iconography from bestiaries and sculpture, heraldry infused new symbolic life into the depiction of animals, using their characteristics to represent the qualities of individual families and institutions. Just as creatures of the imagination had joined actual animals in their movement from oral tradition into the writings of the ancients and from those books into the bestiaries, so did they join real creatures in coats of arms and in handbooks of heraldry.

Growing doubts about the credibility of authorities inevitably culminated in a rationalistic confrontation with tradition. Sir Thomas Browne's *Pseudodoxia Epidemica* (1646, known as "Vulgar Errors") targeted erroneous assumptions established by authorities and perpetuated through the ages. Among the false opinions he singled out in the empirical spirit of the New Science were ideas about the phoenix, griffin, basilisk, unicorn, and other "dubious" creatures. His discrediting of traditional authority did not go unanswered. Alexander Ross, a schoolmaster and prolific author known in his time as "Champion of the Ancients," came to the defense of authority and tradition. Browne's denial of certain animals and Ross's affirmation constitute a climactic debate over the existence of these — and by extension, other — animals of the imagination. While Ross's own book was never reprinted, Browne's was expanded up to its fifth edition years after Ross's death. In the new scientific age, George Caspard Kirchmeyer and Oliver Goldsmith were among those who denounced discredited creatures.

It was not the first time that animals of the imagination had faced literary extinction, but from ancient times up to the 1600s, they had enjoyed a widespread belief in their existence. Now, for virtually the first time since their inception, many were no longer considered members of the animal kingdom.

The names of the basilisk, dragon, griffin, phoenix, and others were adopted as the scientific names of actual creatures in the zoological classification created by the Swedish botanist Carolus Linnaeus in the eighteenth century. Some — namely the dragon, phoenix, and unicorn — had already become immortalized in the names of constellations.

AUTHORITY AND TRANSMISSION

The second-century satirist Lucian prefaces his burlesque of travelers' tales with: "Well, on reading all these authors, I did not find much fault with them for lying, as I saw that this was already a common practice even among men who profess philosophy."

Lucian's charge notwithstanding, authority and the transmission of statements from sources such as Herodotus, Ctesias, Aristotle, Pliny, and the Bible were repeated and varied across millennia. Adding to the cultural stature of animals of the imagination is their presence in the works of some of the most revered literary figures, including Dante, Shakespeare, Milton, and Goethe.

Several passages in this collection are generally acknowledged as the first major accounts of a given animal, particularly the phoenix of Herodotus, the manticore and unicorn of Ctesias, and Pliny's basilisk. Ever since Herodotus referred to griffins in the *Arimaspia* of Aristeas, writers have cited, repeated, or varied other writers' descriptions of animals we now call fabulous.

Once authority has been established with an extensive account of a given creature in a major source — whether it is actually the first time the animal is mentioned or not — the animal's complex literary development can be glimpsed through various genres. While most of the traditional creatures would serve as an example, Herodotus's single-paragraph description of the Arabian phoenix dramatically demonstrates the establishment of authority and the overall process of literary transmission of knowledge. With its transformations through its continual reappearances, the phoenix represents the literary lives of other imaginary animals as well. Although the phoenix is different from most of the others in not being a composite creature, its fabulous nature is amply manifested in its powers to regenerate itself throughout eternity. With the exception of the references to Hecataeus, the phoenix accounts below are from entries in this collection.

Three centuries before Herodotus, Hesiod had said in a riddle concerning longevity that "the phoenix outlives nine ravens" but the divine Nymphs "out-live ten phoenixes." The well-known tale that Herodotus relates originated in Egypt, where ancient religious beliefs held that their sacred *benu*, worshipped in Heliopolis, was identified with gods from Atum to Osiris and with the ever-reborn sun itself. While Herodotus is generally credited with introducing the Egyptian phoenix story to the West, scholars concur that he actually derived his tale from an earlier account by the historian and geographer Hecataeus. In his version, Herodotus states he had never seen their phoenix "except in pictures," which portrayed a red and golden plumaged bird in shape and size of an eagle. It was not the hieroglyphic *benu*, a heron, but nonetheless, like the *benu* (both names meaning "date palm"), it was an eternal bird appearing in the City of the Sun. The story Herodotus tells — which he did not find credible — is that the bird, flying from Arabia every 500 years, "brings the parent bird, all plastered over with myrrh, to the temple of the Sun, and there buries the body."

The outline of Herodotus's phoenix story is the basis of the standard Western tradition of the bird. Aristotle did not include the phoenix in his *Historia Animalium*, but Ovid, Pomponius Mela, Pliny, and others repeated the tale, adding the building of a nest of spices and elaborating on the bird's colorful plumage. Tacitus is credited with being the first to mention that other birds honor the phoenix's triumphal flight to Egypt. Aelian and his friend Philostratus both recounted the phoenix tale, with variations from different traditions. Aelian jauntily satirized the priests who could not determine when the 500-year cycle would end, and the bird in Philostratus's life of the mystic Apollonius of Tyana lives in India and while dying sings its own funeral dirge like the fabled swan. By the fourth century A.D., fire becomes a central element in the phoenix's death and rebirth. Flames reduce the bird to ashes in Lactantius's influential *Carmen de ave phoenice*, which served as the basis of another extensive phoenix poem by Claudian and — four or more centuries later — the Old English *Phoenix* with its Christian allegory. Around the time of Claudian in the fourth century, the phoenix, as sacred to the sun, returned to its Egyptian source in the only surviving ancient work on Egyptian hieroglyphs; the treatise, attributed to Horapollo, became a major Renaissance handbook on the writing of ancient Egypt.

Even before enjoying such literary attention at the end of the classical era, the phoenix had evolved into a Christian allegory of resurrection. In his first-century A.D. *Epistle to the Corinthians*, St. Clement declared: "Let us look at the strange phenomenon which takes place in the East, that is, in the regions near Arabia.

There is a bird which is called the phoenix." While varied in detail, the story he relates is identical in outline to the phoenix of Herodotus, predating the fire element in Lactantius. Among other Church Fathers who developed the phoenix as a Christian symbol, St. Ambrose, three centuries after Clement, included the phoenix (still without the fire, uninfluenced by the earlier Lactantius version) in his *Hexameron* series of sermons. In the Latin *Physiologus*, however, the bird (from India) burns on its pyre in Heliopolis. From the *Physiologus*, the phoenix became a standard animal in the bestiaries and in Christian iconography, where it still remains. In a Judaic text attributed to Baruch, a phoenix from a different tradition accompanies the chariot of the sun through the sky, absorbing its heat to protect mankind.

Skeptical Albertus Magnus said that the phoenix, "according to some authors who devoted more attention to mystical themes than to the natural sciences, is supposed to be an Arabian bird found in parts of the East." Notwithstanding such doubts about the story, the phoenix appears in the spurious but influential works *The Letter of Prester John* and Sir John Mandeville's *Travels*. In the letter, the phoenix lives 100 years and dies after flying so high that the sun's heat ignites its wings; Mandeville's account, in which the phoenix both expires and is reborn on the altar in the Egyptian City of the Sun, parallels the story in the Latin *Physiologus*.

The bird was adopted as an emblem of renewal in heraldry and, in alchemy, an allegory of the transmutation of metals. François Rabelais satirizes travelers, authors, and fabulous beasts alike in the voyage of Gargantua, Pantagruel, and company to the fantasy island of Satinland, where all figures are made of tapestry. Although Pantagruel had read that the phoenix was supposed to be the only one of its kind in the world at any one time, he sees fourteen of them on the island. He thinks that "those who have written on the subject — even Lactantius Firmianus — have never seen one anywhere except in Tapestry-land." Soon after Rabelais, the phoenix regains its majesty in Guillaume de Salluste du Bartas's religious epic of creation, *The Divine Weeks*. In this work, the immortal creature is firstborn of birds, followed by a thousand others, including the griffin and the bird of paradise. The phoenix was metaphorically rich in Elizabethan speech and in the plays of Shakespeare, signifying itself, rebirth, a paragon, and even Queen Elizabeth I.

Amid increasing skepticism of the phoenix and other traditional animals, clergyman John Swan, for one, reasoned from biblical authority that the bird, one of a kind, could not follow God's command to multiply nor enter the Ark. He concludes: "As for the Phoenix, I (and not I alone) think it is a fable. . . ." The doubts grew into Sir Thomas Browne's reasoned discrediting of the phoenix and other imaginary animals. Browne supports his position regarding the phoenix with reference to Herodotus, who even when he "led the story unto the Greeks," considered it improbable. Alexander Ross defended the phoenix against Browne's attack, saying in the case of Herodotus that what the Greek historian doubted was not the existence of the phoenix but the details of the story he was told in

Heliopolis. Only nine years after the publication of Ross's *Arcana Microcosmi*, George Caspard Kirchmeyer declared the story of the phoenix "impossible, absurd, and openly ridiculous."

Shortly after Kirchmeyer's pronouncement, Milton compared the angel Raphael's flight to Eden with the phoenix's flight to Egypt. Milton's simile is poetic, classical, unrelated to questions of literal belief. Nearly two centuries later, the literary phoenix returned to the world of books as a distinctly fabulous creature. Thomas Bulfinch reviews the literary sources of the bird (including Milton's passage) in the "Modern Monsters" chapter of his *Age of Fable*. In the *Zoological Mythology* of Angelo de Gubernatis, typical of the solar and lunar mythological theories of the time, the phoenix is identified with the rising and setting sun, thus completing a symbolic cycle beginning with the bird's Egyptian source. At the beginning of the twentieth century, the phoenix is reborn in a London fireplace to the amazement of English children in E. Nesbit's *The Phoenix and the Carpet*. The mythopoeic D. H. Lawrence was so attracted by the symbolic regeneration of the bird that he chose it as his own personal emblem. In Barbara Wersba's children's book, *The Land of Forgotten Beasts*, the griffin sings that, someday,

> A Phoenix will be seen on the horizon
> And all forgotten creatures shall belong.

Following Herodotus's establishment of the story in the West, perpetuation of the tale was effected by its literary transmission across nearly two-and-a-half millennia.

All this was generated from a story of which not only the first major writer, Herodotus, was himself uncertain, but also other classical authorities, Pliny and Tacitus, and later, Albertus Magnus. The inevitable question arises: Given skepticism from its Western beginning, how could such a fantastic story have gained and maintained such credence for so long? The same question applies to many other creatures we now regard as fabulous.

The credibility of a story should be expected to depend on the credibility of the writer. That such an assumption is erroneous, however, is evident in the influence of Herodotus, Ctesias, Pliny, Philostratus, Solinus, and others consistently criticized for their weakness for the marvelous. Nor would authority explain why a tale of which even the teller is openly doubtful is repeated with variation but without qualification by writer after writer. As Pausanias said, those who enjoy tales of the marvelous perpetuate the lies. Many eighteenth- and nineteenth-century writers attributed acceptance of such tales to ignorant superstition.

But there is more at work here than ignorance and superstition. First, given a world filled with such a diversity and abundance of animal life, how could anyone be expected to distinguish between actual animals and fabulous ones, particularly when authoritative authors compared the parts of exotic creatures to animals with which one was familiar? Second, there is the power of authority and the prevailing beliefs in different epochs. Both classical authorities and medieval Christianity generally accepted the existence of many animals we now regard as fabulous, and after such creatures' rejection by seventeenth-century rationalism, the Age of Reason was, itself, found wanting by Romanticism. And so, protean in nature, fabulous animals returned to books in a variety of forms. Elemental expressions of the human imagination, they resurfaced through the Romantic period's emphasis upon the value and truth of the imagination as expressed in folklore and mythology. Interest in these traditional Western creatures expanded globally to include their mythical counterparts and relatives from around the world: Arabian "wonder birds," the Indian Garuda and Ganesha, the Chinese dragon, Feng-Huang (phoenix), and Ki-Lin (unicorn), and a host of others.

The varied fictional forms and scholarship in which fabulous animals appeared in the nineteenth century increased throughout the twentieth. An extensive body of scholarship has now made them a distinct area of study. And now, too, their enduring images and forms are found throughout contemporary culture, from coats of arms and business logos to antiques and mail-order gifts.

Pausanias may well be closer to the truth than later detractors of those who had accepted animals of the imagination as members of the animal kingdom. There must first be a desire for — even a human need for — the imagination's transformation of the everyday into something apart from nature's making. Our own animal creations, in particular, are dwarfed by nature's, but ours are, after all, our own. Shapes of the mind and the soul, our fantastic animal forms are expressions of human wonder, fears, desire for eternal life, joy in creation itself.

At the end of another millennium, animals of the imagination are, then, still with us. As Goethe's Faust said upon seeing mythical creatures on the Pharsalian Plain:

> Fresh spirit fills me, face to face with these —
> Grand are the Forms, and Grand the Memories!

Part

Ancient Animals

1

Greek drinking cup with three fabulous creatures: a griffin, a siren, and a sphinx. Made in Corinth. GRA 1958.7–21.1. By permission of the British Museum.

"When skies above were not yet named," the first fantastic creatures emerge from primal chaos. Mesopotamian dragons and demons, an Egyptian sun-bird, and the Greek Scylla, Hydra, and Chimera are among the brood of unnatural beasts that are transformed from oral tradition into the oldest mythological poetry in cuneiform characters, Egyptian hieroglyphs, and preclassical Greek writing.

While Greek science and philosophy rationalize away the powers of most of these creatures, expository works of travelers, historians, and geographers introduce a new generation of exotic animals said to live in distant Scythia, India, Arabia, Ethiopia, and Libya. Authors including Herodotus and Pliny the Elder describe them by comparing parts of the creatures to animals familiar to their readers, and others repeat and vary their reports. In spite of isolated doubts about individual animals, accounts of the phoenix, griffin, manticore, unicorn, basilisk, and other curious beasts multiply throughout the classical era.

Mythic Beginnings

ENUMA ELISH
(2ND MILLENNIUM B.C.)

In the writings of one of the world's earliest civilizations, the universe is formed from an imaginary creature. As the story is told in the Babylonian epic of creation, Tiamat, a mother goddess traditionally regarded as a she-dragon, gives birth to a brood of monsters, and after slaying her, the god Marduk creates heaven and earth from her body.

Apsu was the fresh water and Tiamat the salt water of the primal abyss. The mingling of the waters produced pairs of offspring, and from them generations of gods. The aging Apsu became so annoyed with the raucous younger gods disturbing his repose that he plotted to destroy them, but after they learned of his plan, the exalted Ea (Nudimmud) bound Apsu with a spell of words and killed him. Incited by her older children to avenge the murder of Apsu, Tiamat (Mother Hubur) bore dragons, demons, and hybrid men with scorpion, fish, and bull bodies. She formed an alliance with Kingu (Qingu) and presented him with the prized Tablet of Destinies. The frightened younger gods proclaimed Marduk, Ea's son, king and sent him to do battle with the terrible Tiamat. Victorious, Marduk divided the monster's body into earth and sky. Later, from the blood of Kingu, he created mankind.

The mother goddess Tiamat has generally been interpreted as a cosmic serpent and Marduk considered one of the earliest and most renowned of monster slayers. Tiamat, the mother of dragons, opens her

Gorgons, and Hydras, and Chimaeras dire.

—John Milton, *Paradise Lost*

cavernous mouth to devour the warrior god, and in Mesopotamian art, Marduk is represented with a horned dragon at his feet. A Babylonian cylinder seal depicts a lightning-bearing god attacking a serpentine dragon with two short legs. In his *Babylonian Genesis*, Alexander Heidel questions that Tiamat is actually a dragoness, contending that nowhere in the poem is the goddess explicitly described as a dragon and the cylinder seal and similar Mesopotamian art portraying monster battles do not specifically represent Marduk and Tiamat. Regardless of Tiamat's identity, Marduk girds himself for battle with a monster that threatens the community, travels to its lair, and in a battle to the death, kills it by striking it in its vulnerable spot — quintessential dragon-slayer motifs.

Named after its opening words (variously translated as, "When skies above," "When above," "When on high," and so on), the *Enuma Elish* was transcribed in cuneiform on seven clay tablets. The poem of the young god creating order out of primordial chaos exalted Marduk as the king of the Babylonian gods and was recited and perhaps even dramatized yearly at the New Year's festival in early spring. Written in the Akkadian script of Babylonian and Assyrian dialects, the *Enuma Elish* is thought to have been transcribed by the twelfth century B.C. and to have derived from Sumerian stories dating back to 3000 B.C.

A nineteenth-century team of British archeologists excavated the first fragments of tablets from the ruins of King Ashurbanipal's library at Nineveh (seventh century B.C.). The first modern account of the poem, by translator George Smith, appeared in the London *Daily Telegraph* in 1875. The earliest translators of the cosmological poem were struck by the resemblances they found to the later Old Testament book of Genesis. Later scholars cite fundamental differences between the two works while acknowledging the transmission of traditional story throughout the Middle East.

The *mushussu*-dragon (sirrush) offspring of Tiamat is one of the animal figures on the Ishtar Gate of Babylon. It is a scaly creature with four legs, long neck and tail, fangs, curved horn, feline forefeet and raptor hind feet, the sacred animal of Marduk.

See Hesiod's succession myth of Greek gods and monsters, and apocalyptic beasts in Revelation. See dragon battles, notably *Beowulf*, Jacob de Voragine, and Edmund Spenser.

Birth of the Gods *

When skies above were not yet named
Nor earth below pronounced by name,

---

* *The Epic of Creation*, in *Myths from Mesopotamia*, trans. Stephanie Dalley (New York: Oxford University Press, 1991), 233, 237, 251–55 (Tablets 1 and 4).

Babylonian cylinder seal depicting a god battling a dragon. The god is commonly identified with Marduk and the dragon with Tiamat. By permission of the British Museum.

Apsu, the first one, their begetter
And maker Tiamat, who bore them all,
Had mixed their waters together,
But had not formed pastures, nor discovered reed-beds;
When yet no gods were manifest,
Nor their names pronounced, nor destinies decreed,
Then gods were born within them.

Tiamat's Monstrous Brood

They crowded round and rallied beside Tiamat.
They were fierce, scheming restlessly night and day.
They were working up to war, growling and raging.
They convened a council and created conflict.
Mother Hubur, who fashions all things,
Contributed an unfaceable weapon: she bore giant
    snakes,
Sharp of tooth and unsparing of fang.
She filled their bodies with venom instead of blood.
She cloaked ferocious dragons with fearsome rays,
And made them bear mantles of radiance, made them
    godlike.
    (*chanting this imprecation*)
"Whoever looks upon them shall collapse in utter
    terror!

Their bodies shall rear up continually, and never turn away!"
She stationed a horned serpent, a *mushussu*-dragon, and a
    lahmu-hero,
An *ugallu*-demon, a rabid dog, and a scorpion-man,
Aggressive *umu*-demons, a fish-man, and a bull-man
Bearing merciless weapons, fearless in battle.
Her orders were so powerful, they could not be
    disobeyed.
In addition she created eleven more likewise.

Marduk's Battle with Tiamat

The gods his fathers thus decreed the destiny of the
    lord
And set him on the path of peace and obedience.
He fashioned a bow, designated it as his weapon,
Feathered the arrow, set it in the string.
He lifted up a mace and carried it in his right hand,
Slung the bow and quiver at his side,
Put lightning in front of him,
His body was filled with an ever-blazing flame.
He made a net to encircle Tiamat within it,
Marshalled the four winds so that no part of her could
    escape:
South Wind, North Wind, East Wind, West Wind,
The gift of his father Anu, he kept them close to the
    net at his side.
He created the *imhullu*-wind (evil wind), the tempest,
    the whirlwind,
The Four Winds, the Seven Winds, the tornado, the
    unfaceable facing winds.
He released the winds which he had created, seven of
    them.
They advanced behind him to make turmoil inside Tiamat.
The lord raised the flood-weapon, his great weapon,
And mounted the frightful, unfaceable storm-chariot.

. . .

Clothed in a cloak of awesome armour,
His head was crowned with a terrible radiance.

The Lord set out and took the road,
And set his face towards Tiamat who raged out of
    control.

. . .

Face to face they came, Tiamat and Marduk, sage of the
    gods.
They engaged in combat, they closed for battle.
The Lord spread his net and made it encircle her,
To her face he dispatched the *imhullu*-wind, which had
    been behind:
Tiamat opened her mouth to swallow it,
And he forced in the *imhullu*-wind so that she could not
    close her lips.
Fierce winds distended her belly;
Her insides were constipated and she stretched her mouth
    wide.
He shot an arrow which pierced her belly,
Split her down the middle and slit her heart,
Vanquished her and extinguished her life.
He threw down her corpse and stood on top of her.
When he had slain Tiamat, the leader,
He broke up her regiments; her assembly was scattered.

. . .

The Lord trampled the lower part of Tiamat,
With his unsparing mace smashed her skull,
Severed the arteries of her blood,
And made the North Wind carry it off as good news.
His fathers saw it and were jubilant: they rejoiced,
Arranged to greet him with presents, greetings gifts.
The Lord rested, and inspected her corpse.
He divided the monstrous shape and created marvels from it.
He sliced her in half like a fish for drying:
Half of her he put up to roof the sky,
Drew a bolt across and made a guard hold it.
Her waters he arranged so that they could not escape.
He crossed the heavens and sought out a shrine;
He levelled Apsu, dwelling of Nudimmud.
The Lord measured the dimensions of Apsu

And the large temple (Eshgalla), which he built in its
    image, was Esharra:
In the great shrine Esharra, which he had created as the sky,
He founded cult centres for Anu, Ellil, and Ea.
He fashioned stands for the great gods.

THE BOOK OF THE DEAD
(2ND MILLENNIUM B.C.)

Called "phoenix" by the Greeks, the Egyptian *benu* (*bennu*) was a sacred bird associated with the worship of the Sun God at Heliopolis. The *benu* was hieroglyphically depicted as a heron, sometimes standing upon a pyramid. The Sun God was said to have appeared as a phoenix upon the pyramidal "ben" stone in the Temple of the Sun on the hill that rose from the waters of creation. The gods Atum, Rā, and later Osiris, as well as the *benu*, the Pharaoh, and the pyramid form, which represented the sun's rays, were all symbolically identified with the sun. All were eternal, like the sun reborn each day after its voyage through night.

The Book of the Dead, also known as *The Coming Forth by Day*, is a collection of hymns, prayers, and magical spells to guide the soul of the deceased on its passage through the underworld to its judgment by Osiris. Funerary texts were inscribed in hieroglyphs on the chamber walls of pyramids, on coffins, and on papyrus. Pyramid Texts, Coffin Texts, and *The Book of the Dead* roughly correspond to the Old Kingdom (c. 2700–2100 B.C.), Middle Kingdom (c. 2100–1600 B.C.), and New Kingdom (c. 1600–1200 B.C.) periods of Egyptian history, with later texts being derived from earlier ones. Religious tradition attributed authorship of the writings to Thoth, the divine ibis- or baboon-headed scribe. Texts of *The Book of the Dead* speak for the deceased, uniting the dead with the gods through eternity.

Two important *benu* texts in the Egyptian *Book of the Dead* are Chapter 17 and "The Chapter of Changing into a *Bennu*." In the excerpt from the former, the bird is one of the many forms of the eternal gods. While the *benu* is not named in the second entry, the entire chapter concerns the transfiguration of the deceased into immortal form.

Egyptian hieroglyph of a *benu*. From E.A. Wallis Budge, *The Egyptian Book of the Dead*.

Despite its hieroglyphic depiction as a heron, the *benu* is usually considered the source of the classical phoenix. Both the Greek word, *phoenix*, and the Egyptian word, *benu*, referred not only to the bird but also to the date palm, which continually renews itself, and both are immortal birds of the sun, figures of rebirth and regeneration. The Egyptian identification of the *benu* with the gods, and the Greek phoenix with eternal rebirth, both prefigure the Christian association of the phoenix with Christ and resurrection.

The best-known Western account of the phoenix of Heliopolis is that of Herodotus. For the phoenix in Egypt, see also Pliny, Tacitus, Aelian, Horapollo, the Latin *Physiologus*, and Sir John Mandeville.

Chapter 17*

Here begin the praises and glorifyings of coming out from and going into the glorious Neter-Khert in the beautiful Amenta, of coming out by day in all the forms of existence which praise him, of playing at draughts and sitting in the Seh hall, and of coming forth as a living soul. Behold Osiris, the scribe Ani, after he hath come to his haven of rest. That which hath been done upon earth by Ani being blessed, all the words of the god Tmu come to pass. "I am the god Tmu in my rising; I am the only One. I came into existence in Nu. I am Rā who rose in the beginning. He hath ruled that which he made."

Who then is this? It is Rā, who rose for the first time in the city of Suten-henen crowned as a king in his rising. The pillars of Shu were not as yet created, when he was upon the high place of him who is in Khemennu.

"I am the great god who gave birth to himself, even Nu, who created his name *Paut Neteru* as god."

Who then is this? It is Rā, the creator of the names of his limbs, which came into being in the form of the gods in the train of Rā.

"I am he who is not driven back among the gods."

Who then is this? It is Tmu in his disk, or (as others say), It is Rā in his rising in the eastern horizon of heaven.

"I am Yesterday; I know Tomorrow."

Who then is this? Yesterday is Osiris, and Tomorrow is Rā, on the day when he shall destroy the enemies of Neb-er-tcher, and when he shall stablish as prince and ruler his son Horus, or (as others say), on the day when we commemorate the festival of the meeting of the dead Osiris with his father Rā, and when the battle of the gods was fought in which Osiris, lord of Amentet, was the leader.

What then is this? It is Amentet, that is to say the creation of the souls of the gods when Osiris was leader in Set-Amentet; or (as others say), Amentet is that

---

* E. A. Wallis Budge, *The Egyptian Book of the Dead* (New York: Dover, 1967), 280–82, 339.

In a papyrus associated with Chapter 17 of *The Book of the Dead*, the *benu* (phoenix), soul of Rā, stands beside the mummy of Ani. 10470/7. By permission of the British Museum.

which Rā hath given unto me; when any god cometh, he doth arise and doeth battle for it.

"I know the god who dwelleth therein."

Who then is this? It is Osiris, or (as others say), Rā is his name, even Rā, the self-created.

"I am the *bennu* bird which is in Annu, and I am the keeper of the volume of the book of things which are and of things which shall be."

Who then is this? It is Osiris, or (as others say), It is his dead body, or (as others say), It is his filth. The things which are are and the things which shall be are his dead body; or (as others say), They are eternity and everlastingness. Eternity is the day, and everlastingness is the night.

The Chapter of Changing into a Bennu

Saith Osiris, the scribe Ani, triumphant in peace: "I came into being from unformed matter, I created myself in the image of the god Khepera, and I grew in the form of plants. I am hidden in the likeness of the Tortoise. I am formed out of the atoms of all the gods. I am the yesterday of the four quarters of the world, and I am the seven uraei which came into existence in the East, the mighty one who illumineth the nations by his body. He is god in the likeness of Set; and Thoth dwelleth in the midst of them by judgment of the dweller in Sekhem and of the spirits of Annu. I sail among them, and I come; I am crowned, I am become a shining one, I am mighty, I am become holy among the gods. I am the god Khonsu who driveth back all that opposeth him.

HOMER (C. 8TH CENTURY B.C.)
THE ODYSSEY

At the beginning of the Western literary tradition of fabulous forms are the monstrous beings Homer's Odysseus meets on his homeward journey following the
Trojan War. The wandering hero enthralls the Phaeacian court of King Alcinous
with tales of the gigantic one-eyed Cyclops, the cannibalistic Laestrygonians, the
Sirens of the rocks, and the six-headed Scylla. In Book 12, instructions of the
witch Circe save Odysseus and his crew from destruction while he listens to the
song of the Sirens, and her advice (which he does not totally follow) guides him
through the perilous passage between devouring Scylla and swirling Charybdis.
They then sail on to the island of the sun-god Helios.

The ancient Greeks attributed to Homer the composition of both the *Odyssey*
and the *Iliad*. Scholars since have debated "the Homeric question" of authorship,
dates, and method of composition of the works, questioning the existence of a
"Homer" and whether the poems were stitched together from multiple shorter
works or were created by one or more poets. It is now generally accepted that the
two epics were composed around the eighth century B.C., that the *Iliad* is the
older of the two, that each is a single unified work, and that both were originally
oral compositions derived from a body of traditional material.

Neither Circe nor Odysseus describes the Sirens, who lure mariners to death
with the sweetness of their song. Elsewhere referred to as daughters of a Muse and
either Phorcys or the river god Achelous, they were usually portrayed in Greek
art as birds with the head or upper body of women. Preceding the voyage of
Odysseus, Jason's *Argo* had safely passed the Sirens' rock due to the even sweeter
singing of Orpheus. In some versions of their story, the Sirens—in despair after a
ship sails past them—throw themselves into the sea and become rocks. By the
time the creatures were described in medieval bestiaries and encyclopedias, their
bird parts had changed to fish tails, making them mermaids. In James Joyce's
Ulysses, the Sirens are Dublin barmaids.

Scylla was a beautiful nymph who aroused the anger of the gods. While she
was bathing, Circe sprinkled magic herbs into the water, transforming her into a
monster. Circe describes her to Odysseus as having twelve feet, six long necks,
and in each head three rows of teeth. Heracles killed her for devouring one of the
herd of Geryon's cattle, but her father Phorcys restored her to life. Scylla and
Charybdis have been variously interpreted, by ancient commentators up to modern seafaring authors who have attempted to duplicate the ten-year voyage of
Odysseus from Troy to Ithaca. Scylla is often identified with cephalopods and
Charybdis with a whirlpool in the Straits of Messina.

Notable multiheaded relatives of Scylla include dragons in Mesopotamian art,
the Greek Hydra, and the Beast of the Apocalypse in Revelation. "Between

Odysseus and the Sirens. An Attic Greek vase from Starnos, c. 490 B.C. Not described by Homer, the Sirens are here depicted as birds with the heads of women. E440. By permission of the British Museum.

Scylla and Charybdis" is a common phrase referring to a choice between two equally undesirable alternatives. As Circe described it to Odysseus, the passage between Scylla and Charybdis is an alternate route around the Wandering Rocks, through which Jason had sailed in search of the Golden Fleece.

For sirens, see Theobaldus, Bartholomaeus Anglicus, and Goethe.

The Sirens, Scylla, and Charybdis*

"Even as she spoke, the gold-throned morning came, and up the island the heavenly goddess went her way; I turned me toward my ship, and called my crew to

* *The Odyssey of Homer*, trans. George Herbert Palmer (Boston: Houghton, Mifflin, 1891), 189–92 (12.142–259).

come on board and loose the cables. Quickly they came, took places at the pins, and sitting in order smote the foaming water with their oars. And for our aid behind our dark-bowed ship came a fair wind to fill our sail, a welcome comrade, sent us by fair-haired Circe, the mighty goddess, human of speech. When we had done our work at the several ropes about the ship, we sat us down, while wind and helmsman kept her steady.

"Now to my men, with aching heart, I said: 'My friends, it is not right for only one or two to know the oracles which Circe told, that heavenly goddess. Therefore I speak, that, knowing all, we so may die, or fleeing death and doom, we may escape. She warns us first against the marvelous Sirens, and bids us flee their voice and flowery meadow. Only myself she bade to hear their song; but bind me with galling cords, to hold me firm, upright upon the mast-block,—round it let the rope be wound. And if I should entreat you, and bid you set me free, thereat with still more fetters bind me fast.'

"Thus I, relating all my tale, talked with my comrades. Meanwhile our stanch ship swiftly neared the Sirens' island; a fair wind swept her on. On a sudden the wind ceased; there came a breathless calm; Heaven hushed the waves. My comrades, rising, furled the sail, stowed it on board the hollow ship, then sitting at their oars whitened the water with the polished blades. But I with my sharp sword cut a great cake of wax into small bits, which I then kneaded in my sturdy hands. Soon the wax warmed, forced by the powerful pressure and by the rays of the exalted Sun, the lord of all. Then one by one I stopped the ears of all my crew; and on the deck they bound me hand and foot, upright upon the mast-block, round which they wound the rope; and sitting down they smote the foaming water with their oars. But when we were as far away as one can call and driving swiftly onward, our speeding ship, as it drew near, did not escape the Sirens, and thus they lifted up their penetrating voice:

"'Come hither, come, Odysseus, whom all praise, great glory of the Achaeans! Bring in your ship, and listen to our song. For none has ever passed us in a black-hulled ship till from our lips he heard ecstatic song, then went his way rejoicing and with larger knowledge. For we know all that on the plain of Troy Argives and Trojans suffered at the gods' behest; we know whatever happens on the bounteous earth.'

"So spoke they, sending forth their glorious song, and my heart longed to listen. Knitting my brows, I signed my men to set me free; but bending forward, on they rowed. And straightway Perimedes and Eurylochus arose and laid upon me still more cords and drew them tighter. Then, after passing by, when we could hear no more the Sirens' voice nor any singing, quickly my trusty crew removed the wax with which I stopped their ears, and set me free from bondage.

"Soon after we left the island, I observed a smoke, I saw high waves and heard a plunging sound. From the hands of my frightened men down fell the oars, and splashed against the current. There the ship stayed, for they worked the tapering oars no more. Along the ship I passed, inspiriting my men with cheering words, standing by each in turn:

" 'Friends, hitherto we have not been untried in danger. Here is no greater danger than when the Cyclops penned us with brutal might in the deep cave. Yet out of that, through energy of mine, through will and wisdom, we escaped. These dangers, too, I think some day we shall remember. Come then, and what I say let us all follow. You with your oars strike the deep breakers of the sea, while sitting at the pins, and see if Zeus will set us free from present death and let us go in safety. And, helmsman, these are my commands for you; lay them to heart, for you control the rudder of our hollow ship: keep the ship off that smoke and surf and hug the crags, or else, before you know it, she may veer off that way, and you will bring us into danger.'

"So I spoke, and my words they quickly heeded. But Scylla I did not name,— that hopeless horror,— for fear through fright my men might cease to row, and huddle all together in the hold. I disregarded too the hard behest of Circe, when she had said I must by no means arm. Putting on my glittering armor and taking in my hands my two long spears, I went upon the ship's fore-deck, for thence I looked for the first sight of Scylla of the rock, who brought my men disaster. Nowhere could I descry her; I tired my eyes with searching up and down the dusky cliff.

"So up the strait we sailed in sadness; for here lay Scylla, and there divine Charybdis fearfully sucked the salt sea-water down. Whenever she belched it forth, like a kettle in fierce flame all would foam swirling up, and overhead spray fell upon the tops of both the crags. But when she gulped the salt sea-water down, then all within seemed in a whirl; the rock around roared fearfully, and down below the bottom showed, dark with the sand. Pale terror seized my men; on her we looked and feared to die.

"And now it was that Scylla snatched from the hollow ship six of my comrades who were best in skill and strength. Turning my eyes toward my swift ship to seek my men, I saw their feet and hands already in the air as they were carried up. They screamed aloud and called my name for the last time, in agony of heart. As when a fisher, on a jutting rock, with long rod throws a bait to lure the little fishes, casting into the deep the horn of stall-fed ox; then, catching a fish, flings it ashore writhing; even so were these drawn writhing up the rocks. There at her door she ate them, loudly shrieking and stretching forth their hands in mortal pangs toward me. That was the saddest sight my eyes have ever seen, in all my toils, searching the ocean pathways.

"Now after we had passed the rocks of dire Charybdis and of Scylla, straight we drew near the pleasant island of the god. . . ."

HESIOD (C. 700 B.C.)
THEOGONY, THE PRECEPTS OF CHIRON

Pointing out parallels between the Babylonian *Enuma Elish* and Hesiod's *Theogony*, Walter Burkert, M. L. West, and other scholars hold that the Succession Myth of the genealogy of the gods came to Greece from the Near East. Unlike the Babylonian Tiamat's nameless brood of nightmare creatures, however, the earliest Greek monsters form part of a complex genealogy. These figures from Hesiod's epic cosmogony number among the distant mythical ancestors of fabulous animals.

The offspring of Sea and Earth, the Titans Ceto and Phorcys produced a host of unnatural beings, including the Gorgons, Medusa, Pegasus, the Dragon of the Hesperides, and the half-nymph, half-serpent Echidna, mother of Cerberus, the Hydra, the Chimera, the Sphinx, and the Nemean lion. Several of these figure prominently in adventures of the classical heroes Heracles, Perseus, and Bellerophon.

The *Theogony* opens with the poet's account of the Muses appearing to him while he tended his sheep on Mount Helicon and their teaching him to sing of "things that shall be and things that were aforetime." After invoking the Muses, Hesiod relates the origin and succession of the gods, from primordial beginnings through the revolt of the Titans and their overthrow by the Olympians.

Hesiod stands with Homer at the head of the Greek epic tradition and contrasting schools of heroic and didactic poetry. Of the two poets, Hesiod has been identified as a historical figure, now considered to be the author of both the *Theogony* and the pastoral *Works and Days*. The *Theogony* contains borrowings from Homer, notably the second, superfluous half of the description of the Chimera, repeated from the *Iliad* (6.213–15). These lines could be an interpolation, along with the possible later addition of the Ceto and Phorcys passage.

Many works originally attributed to Hesiod, such as *The Precepts of Chiron*, are of uncertain authorship. The proverbs the centaur Chiron teaches Achilles include an early Greek reference to the phoenix. In his *Myth of the Phoenix*, R. Van Den Broek offers a complex explanation of the riddle, proposing that the lifespan of the phoenix represents cycles of the transmigration of the soul.

See the earlier creation myth, *Enuma Elish*, and Ovid's tale of Perseus and Andromeda.

Creation and the Birth of Monsters *

Hail, children of Zeus! Grant lovely song and celebrate the holy race of the deathless gods who are for ever, those that were born of Earth and starry Heaven and gloomy Night and them that briny Sea did rear. . . .

---

* *Hesiod, The Homeric Hymns and Homerica*, trans. H. G. Evelyn-White (Cambridge: Harvard University Press, 1982), 85–89, 99–103, 75 (*Theogony*: 104-7, 116–28, 270-336).

Verily at the first Chaos came to be, but next wide-bosomed Earth, the ever-sure foundation of all the deathless ones who hold the peaks of snowy Olympus, and dim Tartarus in the depth of the wide-pathed Earth, and Eros (Love), fairest among the deathless gods, who unnerves the limbs and overcomes the mind and wise counsels of all gods and all men within them. From Chaos came forth Erebus and black Night; but of Night were born Aether and Day, whom she conceived and bare from union in love with Erebus. And Earth first bare starry Heaven, equal to herself, to cover her on every side, and to be an ever-sure abiding-place for the blessed gods. . . .

   . . . Ceto bare to Phorcys the fair-cheeked Graiae, sisters grey from their birth; and both deathless gods and men who walk on earth call them Graiae, Pemphredo well-clad, and saffron-robed Enyo, and the Gorgons who dwell beyond glorious Ocean in the frontier land towards Night where are the clear-voiced Hesperides, Sthenno and Euryale, and Medusa who suffered a woeful fate: she was mortal, but the two were undying and grew not old. With her lay the Dark-haired One in a soft meadow amid spring flowers. And when Perseus cut off her head, there sprang forth great Chrysaor and the horse Pegasus who is so called because he was born near the springs (*pegae*) of Ocean; and that other, because he held a golden blade (*aor*) in his hands. Now Pegasus flew away and left the earth, the mother of flocks, and came to the deathless gods: and he dwells in the house of Zeus and brings to wise Zeus the thunder and lightning. But Chrysaor was joined in love to Callirrhoë, the daughter of glorious Ocean, and begot three-headed Geryones. Him mighty Heracles slew in sea-girt Erythea by his shambling oxen on that day when he drove the wide-browed oxen to holy Tiryns, and had crossed the ford of Ocean and killed Orthus and Eurytion the herdsman in the dim stead out beyond glorious Ocean.

   And in a hollow cave she bare another monster, irresistible, in no wise like either to mortal men or to the undying gods, even the goddess fierce Echidna who is half a nymph with glancing eyes and fair cheeks, and half again a huge snake, great and awful, with speckled skin, eating raw flesh beneath the secret parts of the holy earth. And there she has a cave deep down under a hollow rock far from the deathless gods and mortal men. There, then, did the gods appoint her a glorious house to dwell in: and she keeps guard in Arima beneath the earth, grim Echidna, a nymph who dies not nor grows old all her days.

   Men say that Typhaon the terrible, outrageous and lawless, was joined in love to her, the maid with glancing eyes. So she conceived and brought forth fierce offspring: first she bare Orthus the hound of Geryones, and then again she bare a second, a monster not to be overcome and that may not be described, Cerberus who eats raw flesh, the brazen-voiced hound of Hades, fifty-headed, relentless and strong. And again she bore a third, the evil-minded Hydra of Lerna, whom the goddess, white-armed Hera nourished, being angry beyond measure with the mighty Heracles. And her Heracles, the son of Zeus, of the house of Amphitryon,

Bellerophon, astride Pegasus, attacking the Chimera. Fourth-century B.C. cup from Apulia, Italy. H 3253. By permission of the Museo Archeologico Nazionale, Naples.

together with warlike Iolaus, destroyed with the unpitying sword through the plans of Athene the spoil-driver. She was the mother of Chimaera who breathed raging fire, a creature fearful, great, swift-footed and strong, who had three heads, one of a grim-eyed lion, another of a goat, and another of a snake, a fierce dragon; in her forepart she was a lion; in her hinderpart, a dragon; and in her middle, a goat, breathing forth a fearful blast of blazing fire. Her did Pegasus and noble Bellerophon slay; but Echidna was subject in love to Orthus and brought forth the deadly Sphinx which destroyed the Cameans, and the Nemean lion, which Hera, the good wife of Zeus, brought up and made to haunt the hills of Nemea, a plague to men. There he preyed upon the tribes of her own people and had power over Tretus of Nemea and Apesas: yet the strength of stout Heracles overcame him.

And Ceto was joined in love to Phorcys and bare her youngest, the awful snake who guards the apples all of gold in the secret places of the dark earth at its great bounds. This is the offspring of Ceto and Phorcys.

The Life of a Phoenix

"A chattering crow lives out nine generations of aged men, but a stag's life is four times a crow's, and a raven's life makes three stags old, while the phoenix outlives nine ravens, but we, the rich-haired Nymphs, daughters of Zeus the aegis-holder, outlive ten phoenixes."

HYMN TO APOLLO
FROM THE HOMERIC HYMNS (C. 7TH CENTURY B.C.)

While *drakon* ("the sharp-sighted one") was the ancient Greeks' generic term for serpent, the Old World constrictor takes its name from Python (Pytho), the dragon Apollo slew on the slopes of Mt. Parnassus. The earliest known description of the battle, contained in *The Homeric Hymns*, is the *Hymn to Apollo*, which recounts the efforts of the son of Zeus and Leto to find a place to establish his sanctuary. The first site he selects is the home of the nymph Telphusa, but not wanting to share her glade with him, the nymph persuades him to consider Parnassus instead, where she knows a she-dragon lives, guarding a sacred spring. Apollo confronts Python, kills Telphusa for her trickery, and gathers priests for his sanctuary. In later versions of the myth, the monster is male, and the god is only a few days old when he attacks the beast.

Multifaceted Apollo, often portrayed playing the lyre, is the Greek god of light, the arts, and healing. Scholars have traced his mythological origins both to the Middle East and the North. Constructed at Delphi beginning about the seventh century B.C., the Sanctuary of Apollo served as the home of the Oracle for nearly a millennium. The god's battle with the monster was ritually reenacted in the amphitheater, and the stadium was used for the Pythian Games commemorating his victory. In the 1890s, the French School of Archeology moved the village of Delphi to excavate the Sanctuary ruins.

At first attributed to Homer, *The Homeric Hymns* is now regarded as a collection of compositions written by later rhapsodes and recited at religious festivals. The *Hymn to Apollo* is made up of two parts, sometimes printed as a single hymn, sometimes as two. The first, dealing with Apollo's birth on Delos, is considered to be much older than the Delphi section, the Delian and Pythian materials reflecting rival centers of Apollo worship. The earlier poem ends with the traditional reference to Homer: "He is a blind man, and dwells in rocky Chios: his lays are evermore supreme."

Both Western and Eastern dragons are commonly associated with water. Classical dragons are frequently guardians of springs.

See dragon lore in Sir James George Frazer and other dragon tales, especially in the *Enuma Elish*.

Apollo and Python*

How then shall I sing of you — though in all ways you are a worthy theme for song? Shall I sing of you as wooer and in the fields of love . . . ? Or shall I sing how at the first you went about the earth seeking a place of oracle for men, far-shooting Apollo? To Pieria you went down from Olympus and passed by sandy Lectus and Enienae and through the land of the Perrhaebi. . . .

Further yet you went, far-shooting Apollo, until you came to the town of the presumptuous Phlegyae who dwell on this earth in a lovely glade near the Cephisian lake, caring not for Zeus. And thence you went speeding swiftly to the mountain ridge, and came to Crisa beneath snowy Parnassus, a foothill turned towards the west: a cliff hangs over it from above, and a hollow, rugged glade runs under. There the lord Phoebus Apollo resolved to make his lovely temple, and thus he said:

"In this place I am minded to build a glorious temple to be an oracle for men, and here they will always bring perfect hecatombs, both they who dwell in rich Peloponnesus and the men of Europe and from all the wave-washed isles, coming to question me. And I will deliver to them all counsel that cannot fail, answering them in my rich temple."

When he had said this, Phoebus Apollo laid out all the foundations throughout, wide and very long; and upon these the sons of Erginus, Trophonius and Agamedes, dear to the deathless gods, laid a footing of stone. And the countless tribes of men built the whole temple of wrought stones, to be sung of for ever.

But near by was a sweet flowing spring, and there with his strong bow the lord, the son of Zeus, killed the bloated, great she-dragon, a fierce monster wont to do great mischief to men upon earth, to men themselves and to their thin-shanked sheep; for she was a very bloody plague. . . .

. . . Whosoever met the dragoness, the day of doom would sweep him away, until the lord Apollo, who deals death from afar, shot a strong arrow at her. Then she, rent with bitter pangs, lay drawing great gasps for breath and rolling about that place. An awful noise swelled up unspeakable as she writhed continually this way and that amid the wood: and so she left her life, breathing it forth in blood. Then Phoebus Apollo boasted over her:

* *Hesiod, The Homeric Hymns and the Homerica*, trans. Hugh G. Evelyn-White (Cambridge: Harvard University Press, 1982), 339–45, 349–51 (207–9, 214–18, 239–304, 356–74).

"Now rot here upon the soil that feeds man. You at least shall live no more to be a fell bane to men who eat the fruit of the all-nourishing earth, and who will bring hither perfect hecatombs. Against cruel death neither Typhoeus shall avail you nor ill-famed Chimera, but here shall the Earth and shining Hyperion make you rot."

Thus said Phoebus, exulting over her: and darkness covered her eyes. And the holy strength of Helios made her rot away there; wherefore the place is now called Pytho, and men call the lord Apollo by another name, Pythian; because on that spot the power of piercing Helios made the monster rot away.

Exotic Creatures

2

HERODOTUS (5TH CENTURY B.C.)
THE HISTORY

The earliest major prose source of the phoenix, the griffin, and other fabulous animals is *The History* of Herodotus, the virtual beginning of Western history writing and of European prose.

Herodotus, the man Cicero called "the Father of History," traveled extensively throughout the ancient world, from Egypt to Syria, Macedonia to Scythia, and collected what he saw, heard, and read to preserve "what men have done." The nine books of his *History* are named after the Muses. With the storyteller's voice and the historian's critical judgment, Herodotus weaves personal experience, eyewitness accounts, and tales of hearsay through his epic history of the wars between Greece and Persia. Within his wealth of material from the oral tradition are tales of exotic beasts, many associated with precious spices and gold.

Herodotus's famous account of the phoenix is the best-known early description of the immortal bird. While the tale is based on what is now one of the fragments from the *Periegesis* ("A Journey Round the World") by the Ionian historian Hecataeus of Miletus (6th–5th century B.C.), Herodotus is regarded as the major authoritative source of the Western fable.

In this early version, the Arabian bird appears in Egypt every 500 years, carrying its embalmed parent to the Temple of the Sun. Fire is not yet part of the death and rebirth cycle. Egyptian priests tell Herodotus

. . . it seems to be true that the extreme regions of the earth, which surround and shut up within themselves all other countries, produce the things which are the rarest, and which men reckon the most beautiful.

—Herodotus, *The History*

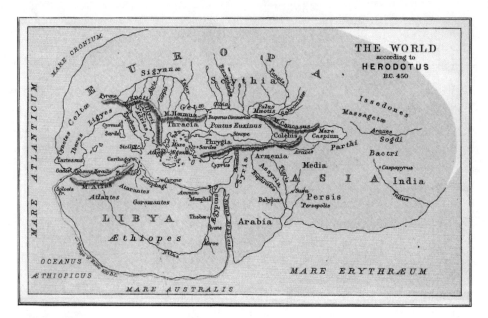

A map of the world based on the writings of Herodotus. From *Atlas of Ancient and Classical Geography* (London: J. M. Dent & Sons, 1942). Courtesy of J. M. Dent.

about the phoenix when he is in Heliopolis, shrine of the sacred *benu*, but the pictures he sees portray a colorful bird shaped like an eagle, not like the heron of the *benu* hieroglyph. Herodotus notes that he did not see an actual phoenix himself, and that he is skeptical of the story.

Herodotus later describes the winged serpents of Arabia as shaped like water snakes and having batlike wings. In one of his encyclopedic footnotes to his classic translation of the *History*, George Rawlinson identifies the creatures as locusts, insects from the East, which ibises could be expected to attack. As for the bones Herodotus thought were those of the winged serpents, Rawlinson cites French naturalist Georges Cuvier's explanation that the historian did not really know the source of the bones, except by hearsay.

The gold-guarding griffins of the remote North receive only brief mention in the *History*. While the beasts are merely named, not described, his references to them and the one-eyed Arimaspi (whom Herodotus regards as doubtful) are an essential authoritative source of traditional griffin lore, referred to by other writers and even debated by Sir Thomas Browne and Alexander Ross in the seventeenth century. Herodotus states that his own major source of that material was Aristeas of Proconnosus. Aristeas is reputed to be a seventh-century B.C. Greek traveler and author of the the *Arimaspia*, an epic no longer extant. Predating the writing of the *History*, Aeschylus had used the griffin/Arimaspian story earlier in the century. In *Prometheus Bound*, the punished god, chained in the mountains of Scythia, warns a visitor, Io: "Beware the sharp-beaked hounds of Zeus that bark not, the gryphons, and the one-eyed Arimaspian folk, mounted on horses, who dwell about the flood of Pluto's stream that flows with gold" (803–6). The griffin (Greek *gryps*, "hooked") had been a popular subject of Greek art since the seventh century B.C., and was the major fabulous creature depicted in Scythian goldwork.

Herodotus's animal tales of India and Arabia are similar in pattern to the griffin story, recounting how men try to acquire the gold of the giant ants and the spices of the cinnamon bird.

While Pomponius Mela and other classical writers later accepted the giant, gold-digging ants of Herodotus, others, such as Strabo, were skeptical. A nineteenth-century view was that the so-called "ants" were actually Tibetan miners. In the late twentieth-century, French ethnologist Michel Peissel discovered in the Himalayas tribal people who sift gold from earth dug up by marmots and learned that the Persian word for marmot is equivalent to "mountain ant."

The cinnamon bird, described by Aristotle and others, became the "cinomolgus" of the bestiaries.

For the phoenix, see especially the Egyptian *Book of the Dead*, Pliny, Tacitus, and Aelian. For the classical griffin, see especially Ctesias, Pliny, and Aelian.

The Sacred Phoenix of Egypt *

Egypt, though it borders upon Libya, is not a region abounding in wild animals. The animals that do exist in the country, whether domesticated or otherwise, are all regarded as sacred. . . .

They have also another sacred bird called the phoenix, which I myself have never seen, except in pictures. Indeed it is a great rarity, even in Egypt, only coming there (according to the accounts of the people of Heliopolis) once in five hundred years, when the old phoenix dies. Its size and appearance, if it is like the pictures, are as follows:—The plumage is partly red, partly golden, while the general make and size are almost exactly that of the eagle. They tell a story of what this bird does, which does not seem to me to be credible: that he comes all the way from Arabia, and brings the parent bird, all plastered over with myrrh, to the temple of the Sun, and there buries the body. In order to bring him, they say, he first forms a ball of myrrh as big as he finds that he can carry; then he hollows out the ball, and puts his parent inside, after which he covers over the opening with fresh myrrh, and the ball is then of exactly the same weight as at first; so he brings it to Egypt, plastered over as I have said, and deposits it in the temple of the Sun. Such is the story they tell of the doings of this bird.

* Herodotus, *The History of Herodotus*, trans. George Rawlinson (New York: D. Appleton, 1885), vol. 2, pp. 94, 105, 106–7, 407–10, 413–14, 417–18; vol. 3, p. 9 (2.65, 73, 75, 3.102, 105, 107, 111, 116, 4.13).

Winged Serpents of Arabia

I went once to a certain place in Arabia, almost exactly opposite the city of Buto, to make inquiries concerning the winged serpents. On my arrival I saw the back-bones and ribs of serpents in such numbers as it is impossible to describe: of the ribs there were a multitude of heaps, some great, some small, some middle-sized. The place where the bones lie is at the entrance of a narrow gorge between steep mountains, which there open upon a spacious plain communicating with the great plain of Egypt. The story goes, that with the spring the winged snakes come flying from Arabia towards Egypt, but are met in this gorge by the birds called ibises, who forbid their entrance and destroy them all. The Arabians assert, and the Egyptians also admit, that it is on account of the service thus rendered that the Egyptians hold the ibis in so much reverence.

Giant Ants of India

Besides these, there are Indians of another tribe, who border on the city of Caspatryus, and the country of Pactyïca; these people dwell northward of all the rest of the Indians, and follow nearly the same mode of life as the Bactrians. They are more warlike than any of the other tribes, and from them the men are sent forth who go to procure the gold. For it is in this part of India that the sandy desert lies. Here, in this desert, there live amid the sand great ants; in size somewhat less than dogs, but bigger than foxes. The Persian king has a number of them, which have been caught by the hunters in the land whereof we are speaking. These ants make their dwellings underground, and like the Greek ants, which they very much resemble in shape, throw up sand-heaps as they burrow. Now the sand which they throw up is full of gold. The Indians, when they go into the desert to collect this sand, take three camels and harness them together, a female in the middle and a male on either side, in a leading-rein. . . .

When the Indians reach the place where the gold is, they fill their bags with the sand, and ride away at their best speed: the ants, however, scenting them, as the Persians say, rush forth in pursuit. Now these animals are so swift, they declare, that there is nothing in the world like them; if it were not, therefore, that the Indians get a start while the ants are mustering, not a single gold-gatherer could escape. During the flight the male camels, which are not so fleet as the females, grow tired, and begin to drag, first one, and then the other; but the females recollect the young which they have left behind, and never give way or flag. Such, according to the Persians, is the manner in which the Indians get the greater part of their gold, some is dug out of the earth, but of this the supply is more scanty.

The Arabian Cinnamon Bird

Arabia is the last of inhabited lands towards the south, and it is the only country which produces frankincense, myrrh, cassia, cinnamon, and ladanum. The Arabians do not get any of these, except the myrrh, without trouble. . . .

Still more wonderful is the mode in which they collect the cinnamon. Where the wood grows, and what country produces it, they cannot tell — only some, following probability, relate that it comes from the country in which Bacchus was brought up. Great birds, they say, bring the sticks which we Greeks, taking the word from the Phoenicians, call cinnamon, and carry them up into the air to make their nests. These are fastened with a sort of mud to a sheer face of rock, where no foot of man is able to climb. So the Arabians, to get the cinnamon, use the following artifice. They cut all the oxen and asses and beasts of burthen that die in their land into large pieces, which they carry with them into those regions, and place near the nests: then they withdraw to a distance, and the old birds, swooping down, seize the pieces of meat and fly with them up to their nests; which, not being able to support the weight, break off and fall to the ground.

Fourth-century B.C. vase painting of gold-guarding griffins attacking one-eyed Arimaspians. GR 1856.10-1.19 (Vase E434). By permission of the British Museum.

Hereupon the Arabians return and collect the cinnamon, which is afterwards carried from Arabia into other countries.

The Gold-Guarding Griffins

The northern parts of Europe are very much richer in gold than any other region: but how it is procured I have no certain knowledge. The story runs, that the one-eyed Arimaspi purloin it from the griffins; but here too I am incredulous, and cannot persuade myself that there is a race of men born with one eye, who in all else resemble the rest of mankind. Nevertheless it seems to be true that the extreme regions of the earth, which surround and shut up within themselves all other countries, produce the things which are the rarest, and which men reckon the most beautiful.

Aristeas also, son of Caystrobius, a native of Proconnêsus, says in the course of his poem, that rapt in Bacchic fury, he went as far as the Issedones. Above them dwelt the Arimaspi, men with one eye; still further, the gold-guarding Griffins; and beyond these, the Hyperboreans, who extended to the sea. . . .

CTESIAS (LATE 5TH CENTURY B.C.)
INDICA

The first European book about India contains the earliest known descriptions of two well-known fabulous animals: the manticore and the unicorn. Although the *Indica* of Ctesias the Cnidian was, from the first, regarded as a highly colored account, these two passages have often been repeated or cited by other writers. The unicorn description in particular is an obligatory reference for anyone writing about the history of that creature.

Born in Cnidos, the Greek Ctesias (Ktesias) served for seventeen years as the physician of the Persian royal court, attending Darius II and Artexerxes Memnon. He compiled a history of Persia, the *Persica*, perhaps from official records, and without ever going to India wrote about that fabled land from tales he heard at court. All that survives of the books are fragments in the works of other writers and extracts compiled in the ninth century A.D. by Photius, Patriarch of Constantinople, in his *Bibliotheca* collection of classical prose.

Ctesias's man-eating *martikhora* (manticore) is a composite beast, described in the conventional traveler's-tale comparison of exotic parts with parts of animals with which the audience is likely to be familiar. Pausanias later identifies the beast as a tiger, but the man-faced creature with the spiked tail appears in medieval bestiaries and in natural histories as late as the eighteenth century. The best-known graphic depiction of the manticore is from Edward Topsell's *Historie of Foure-Footed Beastes*.

Ctesias relocates the "gold-guarding Griffins" of Herodotus from the remote North to the mountains of India, where they become four-footed birds, closer to the griffin's standard lion-eagle form.

The seminal two paragraphs of Ctesias's description of the wild ass of India establish integral parts of unicorn lore. Belief in the medicinal property of the beast's horn led to centuries of apothecary trade and, eventually, scholarly challenge. On the other hand, the characteristic of the animal's ferocity, akin to that of the biblical *reêm*, contributed to the medieval legend that the unicorn could be subdued only by a virgin. The author's description of the hunting of the beast prefigures a common motif in medieval art, notably represented in the series of Belgian tapestries known as "The Hunt of the Unicorn." In his *Lore of the Unicorn*, Odell Shepard proposes that the animal Ctesias describes is a composite of rhinoceros, wild ass, and antelope, while others have equated Ctesias's horse-like "wild ass" with the Indian rhinoceros.

Ctesias's *krokotta* (crocotta; kynolykos, cynolycus, "dog-wolf") is regarded as a variety of the hyena. Pliny adopted the beast as his crocotta, offspring of a wolf and dog.

"If Ctesias is to be believed" is typical of qualifications by later writers who then repeat his manticore and unicorn passages. The writer of "all perfect truth" has been called the first Greek fiction writer and his *Indica* compared to the tall-tale travels of Sir John Mandeville and Baron Munchausen. Defenders of Ctesias charge that Photius misrepresented his work by compiling only the passages on the marvels of India. The following selections from Ctesias were paraphrased by Photius.

For the manticore, see especially Aristotle, Pliny, Pausanias, Thomas Boreman, and Flaubert. For the unicorn, see especially Aristotle, Pliny, and Aelian.

The Martikhora *

He [ed., Ctesias] describes an animal called the *martikhora*, found in India. Its face is like a man's — it is about as big as a lion, and in colour red like cinnabar. It has three rows of teeth — ears like the human — eyes of a pale-blue like the human and a tail like that of the land scorpion, armed with a sting and more than a cubit long. It has besides stings on each side of its tail, and, like the scorpion, is armed

---

* *Ancient India as Described by Ktesias the Knidian*, ed. J. W. McCrindle (1882; rpt., Delhi, India: Manohar Reprints, 1973), 11–12, 16–17, 26–27, 32–33, 33–34 (7, 12, 25–26, 32, 33).

with an additional sting on the crown of its head, wherewith it stings any one who goes near it, the wound in all cases proving mortal. If attacked from a distance it defends itself both in front and in rear — in front with its tail, by uplifting it and darting out the stings, like shafts shot from a bow, and in rear by straightening it out. It can strike to the distance of a hundred feet, and no creature can survive the wound it inflicts save only the elephant. The stings are about a foot in length, and not thicker than the finest thread. The name *martikhora* means in Greek ἀνθρωποφάγος (i.e., man-eater), and it is so called because it carries off men and devours them, though it no doubt preys upon other animals as well. In fighting it uses not only its stings but also its claws. Fresh stings grow up to replace those shot away in fighting. These animals are numerous in India, and are killed by the natives who hunt them with elephants, from the backs of which they attack them with darts.

The Griffons of India

There is much silver in their part of the country, and the silver-mines though not deep are deeper than those in Baktria. Gold also is a product of India. It is not found in rivers and washed *from the sands* like the gold of the river Paktolos, but is found on those many high-towering mountains which are inhabited by the Griffons, a race of four-footed birds, about as large as wolves, having legs and claws like those of the lion, and covered all over the body with black feathers except only on the breast where they are red. On account of those birds the gold with which the mountains abound is difficult to be got.

The Wild Asses of India

Among the Indians, he proceeds, there are wild asses as large as horses, some being even larger. Their head is of a dark red colour, their eyes blue, and the rest of their body white. They have a horn on their forehead, a cubit in length (the filings of this horn, if given in a potion, are an antidote to poisonous drugs). This horn for about two palm-breadths upwards from the base is of the purest white, where it tapers to a sharp point of a flaming crimson, and, in the middle, is black. These horns are made into drinking cups, and such as drink from them are attacked neither by convulsions nor by the sacred disease (epilepsy). Nay, they are not even affected by poisons, if either before or after swallowing them they drink from these cups wine, water, or anything else. While other asses moreover, whether wild or tame, and indeed all other solid-hoofed animals have neither huckle-bones, nor gall in the liver, these *one-horned* asses have both. Their huckle-bone is the most beautiful of all I have ever seen, and is, in appearance and size, like that of the ox. It is as heavy as lead, and of the colour of cinnabar both on the surface, and all throughout. It is exceedingly fleet and strong, and no creature that pursues it, not even the horse, can overtake it.

On first starting it scampers off somewhat leisurely, but the longer it runs, it gallops faster and faster till the pace becomes most furious. These animals therefore can only be caught at one particular time — that is when they lead out their little foals to the pastures in which they roam. They are then hemmed in on all sides by a vast number of hunters mounted on horseback, and being unwilling to escape while leaving their young to perish, stand their ground and fight, and by butting with their horns and kicking and biting kill many horses and men. But they are in the end taken, pierced to death with arrows and spears, for to take them alive is in no way possible. Their flesh being bitter is unfit for food, and they are hunted merely for the sake of their horns and their huckle-bones.

The Krokottas

There is in Ethiopia an animal called properly the *Krokottas*, but vulgarly the *Kynolykos*. It is of prodigious strength, and is said to imitate the human voice, and by night to call out men by their names, and when they come forth at their call, to *fall upon them* and devour them. This animal has the courage of the lion, the speed of the horse, and the strength of the bull, and cannot be encountered successfully with weapons of steel.

All Perfect Truth

Ktêsias thus writing and romancing professes that his narrative is all perfect truth, and, to assure us of this, asseverates that he has recorded nothing but what he either saw with his own eyes, or learned from the testimony of credible eye-witnesses. He adds moreover that he has left unnoticed many things far more marvellous than any he has related, lest any one who had not a previous knowledge of the facts might look upon him as an arrant story-teller.

PLATO (427–347 B.C.)
PHAEDRUS

When the unicorn, manticore, and other marvelous beasts were in their literary infancy, being considered as possible new members of the animal kingdom, the aging monsters of mythology were beginning to lose their vitality.

Early in the *Phaedrus*, Plato's fictionalized figure of his teacher Socrates dis-
cusses the "truths" of myth and the demythologizing of accepted story. As he and
the young Phaedrus approach the shady river Ilissus in the heat of the day,
Socrates satirizes the "wise," who interpret myth as fables of the physical world. He
points out that the rationalizing of myth can ultimately lead to laborious, time-
consuming analysis of "inconceivable and impossible monstrosities" such as the
hybrid centaurs, gorgons, and chimeras. Socrates chooses, instead, to seek truth
through self-knowledge. Later in the dialogue, Socrates creates his own mythical
allegory of the soul's horse-drawn chariot as it rises from the material world of
appearances toward the intelligible world of eternal forms.

Included below in Plato's list of mythological monsters is the familiar-sounding
"chimeras dire." In this standard nineteenth-century translation, Benjamin
Jowett adds the adjective "dire," echoing Milton's "Gorgons and Hydras, and
Chimaeras dire" (*Paradise Lost*, 2.628).

The rationalizing of classical monsters and reduction of them to "the rules of
probability" are later repeated in challenges to the phoenix and other fabulous
animals.

For other classical rationalizations of mythological creatures, see Strabo and
Lucretius.

Inconceivable and Impossible Monstrosities *

Phaedr. I should like to know, Socrates, whether the place is not somewhere here
at which Boreas is said to have carried off Orithyia from the banks of the Ilissus.

Soc. Such is the tradition.

Phaedr. And is this the exact spot? The little stream is delightfully clear and
bright; I can fancy that there might be maidens playing near.

Soc. I believe that the spot is not exactly here, but about a quarter of a mile
lower down, where you cross to the temple of Agra, and there is, I think, some
sort of altar of Boreas at the place.

Phaedr. I don't recollect; but I wish that you would tell me whether you believe
this tale.

Soc. The wise are doubtful, and if, like them, I also doubted, there would be
nothing very strange in that. I might have a rational explanation that Orithyia
was playing with Pharmacia, when a northern gust carried her over the neighbouring rocks; and this being the manner of her death, she was said to have been
carried away by Boreas. There is a discrepancy, however, about the locality;
according to another version of the story she was taken from the Areopagus, and

---

* *The Dialogues of Plato*, trans. Benjamin Jowett (New York: Charles Scribner's Sons, 1887), vol.
1, pp. 585–86.

not from this place. Now I quite acknowledge that these explanations are very nice, but he is not to be envied who has to give them; much labour and ingenuity will be required of him; and when he has once begun, he must go on and rehabilitate centaurs and chimeras dire. Gorgons and winged steeds flow in apace, and numberless other inconceivable and impossible monstrosities and marvels of nature. And if he is skeptical about them, and would fain reduce them all to the rules of probability, this sort of crude philosophy will take up all his time. Now I have certainly not time for this; shall I tell you why? I must first know myself, as the Delphian inscription says; and I should be absurd indeed, if while I am still in ignorance of myself I were to be curious about that which is not my business. And therefore I bid farewell to all this; the common opinion is enough for me. For, as I was saying, I want to know not about this, but about myself. Am I indeed a wonder more complicated and swollen with passion than the serpent Typho, or a creature of a gentler and simpler sort, to whom Nature has given a diviner and lowlier destiny? . . .

ARISTOTLE (384–322 B.C.)
HISTORIA ANIMALIUM

The unicorn, manticore, and other animals with fabulous characteristics were assured of centuries of credibility by their inclusion in the *History of Animals*, one of Aristotle's several works of natural history that established him as the founder of what later developed into the science of zoology.

Between the earliest writings and the natural histories of the sixteenth century, Aristotle's zoological treatises stand virtually alone in their scientific intent and method. While other naturalists derived their material primarily from oral tradition and the accounts of other writers, Aristotle conducted a systematic investigation of animal life. He did use earlier authorities (notably Herodotus) and the reports of contemporaries — perhaps including those of exotic animals described by participants in the military expeditions of his former pupil, Alexander — but he relied as much as possible upon first-hand observation. Early in the *Historia*, he describes his approach:

> this is the natural method of procedure — to do this only after we have before us the ascertained facts about each item, for this will give us a clear picture of the subjects with which our exposition is to be concerned and the principles upon which it must be based. (491a.12–14)

Embryonic zoology, the *Historia* groups more than 500 animals according to their characteristics and parts, within broad categories of what Aristotle terms "blooded" and "bloodless." The pioneering book, while it was an achievement of classical science that was influential for centuries, does contain substantial misinformation, from "bloodless" animals to those creatures with fabulous characteristics, admitted through faulty observation or later by interpolation.

The Indian ass Aristotle describes is generally identified as the rhinoceros, while his one-horned oryx is usually explained as an animal that either had broken off one of its horns or had been seen in profile from a distance. Only a few pages later, he introduces the manticore with the qualification, "if we are to believe Ctesias," and elsewhere in the *Historia*, he writes that the author of *Indica* is "no very good authority, by the way." The florid manticore passage, virtually lifted from Ctesias, may well be an interpolation. Aristotle offers qualified acceptance of the salamander's imperviousness to fire; like the manticore description, this influential statement may be an interpolation. He also qualifies the account of the cinnamon bird. This bird is similar to the phoenix in that it builds its nest of spices in the tops of tall trees. Aristotle's account of the bird differs from that of Herodotus in terms of where the creature builds its nest and how the hunters acquire the precious spice.

Aristotle's zoological work towers above other ancient natural histories in scientific intent. In the early Middle Ages, he was superseded in academic regard by his teacher Plato and his *Historia* had far less influence upon medieval natural history than Pliny the Elder's compilation of the works of earlier authors. Following the fall of Rome, Aristotle's writings had survived through Boethius, and Avicenna and other Arabian writers, and were then revived in Latin translations and commentaries of Albertus Magnus, whose own Aristotelian book on animals stood apart from contemporary bestiaries and encyclopedias. Regarded in the thirteenth century as "master of all who know," Aristotle was a revered authority whose followers ironically ignored his scientific method, their slavish adherence to his works eventually leading to rationalistic challenge of Aristotelian dogma in the sixteenth and seventeenth centuries.

The Unicorn*

With regard to animals in general, some parts or organs are common to all, as has been said, and some are common only to particular genera; the parts, moreover, are identical with or different from one another on the lines already repeatedly laid down. . . .

Furthermore, of animals some are horned, and some are not so. The great majority of the horned animals are cloven-footed, as the ox, the stag, the goat;

---

* Aristotle, *Historia Animalium*, trans. D'Arcy Wentworth Thompson, vol. 4 of *The Works of Aristotle* (Oxford: Clarendon Press, 1910), 497b.5, 499b.15–20, 501a.5–10, 20–501b.1, 552b.15, 616a.5–10.

and a solid-hooved animal with a pair of horns has never yet been met with. But a few animals are known to be single-horned and single-hooved, as the Indian ass; and one, to wit the oryx, is single-horned and cloven-hooved.

Of all the solid-hooved animals the Indian ass alone has an astragalus or huckle-bone. . . .

The Martichoras

Again, in respect to the teeth, animals differ greatly both from one another and from man. All animals that are quadrupedal, blooded, and viviparous, are furnished with teeth; but, to begin with, some are double-toothed (or fully furnished with teeth in both jaws), and some are not. . . .

No animal of these genera is provided with double rows of teeth. There is, however, an animal of the sort, if we are to believe Ctesias. He assures us that the Indian wild beast called the "martichoras" has a triple row of teeth in both upper and lower jaw; that it is as big as a lion and equally hairy, and that its feet resemble those of the lion; that it resembles man in its face and ears; that its eyes are blue, and its colour vermilion; that its tail is like that of the land-scorpion; that it has a sting in the tail, and has the faculty of shooting off arrow-wise the spines that are attached to the tail; that the sound of its voice is a something between the sound of a pan-pipe and that of a trumpet; that it can run as swiftly as a deer, and that it is savage and a man-eater.

Man sheds his teeth, and so do other animals, as the horse, the mule, and the ass. . . .

The Salamander

The fact that certain animal structures exist which really cannot be burnt is evident from the salamander, which, so they say, puts the fire out by crawling through it.

The Cinnamon Bird

People who live where the bird comes from say that there exists a cinnamon bird which brings the cinnamon from some unknown localities, and builds its nest out of it; it builds on high trees on the slender top branches. They say that the inhabitants attach leaden weights to the tips of their arrows and therewith bring down the nests, and from the intertexture collect the cinnamon sticks.

LUCRETIUS (99–55 B.C.)
ON THE NATURE OF THINGS

In his epic-length philosophical poem, *De Rerum Natura*, the Roman Lucretius presents a mechanical universe, governed by the laws of nature rather than by the gods, whom he regards as capricious. Basing his science upon the atomistic theories of the Greek philosopher Epicurus (341–270 B.C.), Lucretius contends that because humans are mortal, the mind should be free of superstition. Classical monsters are here reduced to combinations of atoms, mere converging films of images.

For recent explanations of the creation of hybrid animals, see Peter Lum, Heinz Mode, and Lewis Thomas.

The Origin of Chimerical Creatures *

Let me now explain briefly *what it is that stimulates the imagination and where those images come from that enter the mind.*

My first point is this. There are a great many flimsy films from the surface of objects flying about in a great many ways in all directions. When these encounter one another in the air, they easily amalgamate, like gossamer or goldleaf. In comparison with those films that take possession of the eye and provoke sight, these are certainly of a much flimsier texture, since they penetrate through the chinks of the body and set in motion the delicate substance of the mind within and there provoke sensation. So it is that we see the composite shapes of Centaurs and Mermaids and dogs with as many heads as Cerberus, and phantoms of the dead whose bones lie in the embrace of the earth. The fact is that the films flying about everywhere are of all sorts: some are produced spontaneously in the air itself; others are derived from various objects and composed by the amalgamation of their shapes. The image of a Centaur, for instance, is certainly not formed from the life, since no living creature of this sort ever existed. But, as I have just explained, where surface films from a horse and a man accidentally come into contact, they may easily stick together on the spot, because of the delicacy and flimsiness of their texture. So also with other such chimerical creatures. Since, as I have shown above, these delicate films move with the utmost nimbleness and mobility, any one of them may easily set our mind in motion with a single touch; for the mind itself is delicate and marvellously mobile.

* Lucretius, *The Nature of the Universe*, trans. R.E. Latham (Baltimore, Md.: Penguin Classics, 1961), 152–53 (4.751–79).

JULIUS CAESAR (100–44 B.C.)
THE GALLIC WAR

"Caesar was of opinion that the Elk had but one horn," Edward Topsell wrote, citing a passage frequently quoted to lend authority to the existence of single-horned animals. As described in Julius Caesar's *De Bello Gallico* (51 B.C.), the unicorn stag is one of the beasts of the mysterious Hercynian Forest in the German mountains.

In Caesar's account of his campaigns in Gaul, each book covers a year of warfare.

For another Hercynian creature, see the ercinee of Solinus.

*The One-Horned Hercynian Stag**

The breadth of this Hercynian forest . . . extends a journey of nine days for an unburdened man. For it cannot be bounded otherwise, nor do they know measures of roads. . . . It is certain that many kinds of wild beasts are born in it, which are not seen in other places; from which those that greatly differ from the rest, and seem worthy to be handed down to memory, are these.

There is an ox in the shape of a stag, from the mid forehead of which, between the ears, a horn grows higher, and more straight than those horns which are known to us. From the top of this branches are spread out broadly like palm leaves. The appearance of the female and male is the same, the same form and size of the horns.

STRABO (C. 63 B.C.–A.D. 19)
THE GEOGRAPHY

Strabo's *Geography* is the earliest surviving treatise on the subject, an encyclopedic source of information on the historical geography of the ancient world. Early in his book, Strabo attempts to separate "truth" from Homeric "myth." As a Stoic who admired the *Iliad* and the *Odyssey* but believed religion was myth, he defends Homer as a geographer by allegorizing and rationalizing the epics.

---

* Julius Caesar, *Commentaries of Caesar on the Gallic War* (New York: David McKay, 1960), 343–44 (6.25–26).

Strabo discredits specific authors' accounts of the marvels of India, including tales of the monstrous races and gold-digging ants. In contrast to the obscure Deï-machus, Megasthenes (c. 350–290 B.C.) was well known for his *Indika*, the first full account of India from first-hand experience. Onesicritus and his superior, Nearchus, both wrote accounts of their voyage on Alexander's Indian expedition. Strabo later paraphrases Megasthenes's account of the fox-sized creatures that exhume precious metal while digging their mole-like burrows. Because the ant story was recounted by Herodotus, that noted historian's tale is indirectly impugned as well. A twentieth-century ethnologist has corroborated the early accounts, maintaining that the people living on a plateau above the Indus river still collect gold dust from the burrows of marmots, the actual "ants."

For the gold-digging ants, see especially Herodotus and Sir John Mandeville.

Fabrications of India*

. . . all who have written about India have proved themselves, for the most part, fabricators, but preëminently so Deïmachus; the next in order is Megasthenes; and then, Onesicritus, and Nearchus, and other such writers, who begin to speak the truth, though with faltering voice. I, too, had the privilege of noting this fact extensively when I was writing the "Deeds of Alexander." But especially do Deï-machus and Megasthenes deserve to be distrusted. For they are the persons who tell us about the "men that sleep in their ears," and the "men without mouths," and "men without noses"; and about "men with one eye," "men with long legs," "men with fingers turned backward"; and they revived, also, the Homeric story of the battle between the cranes and the "pygmies," who, they said, were three spans tall. These men also tell about the ants that mine gold and Pans with wedge-shaped heads; and about snakes that swallow oxen and stags, horns and all; and in these matters the one refutes the other, as is stated by Eratosthenes also. . . .

The Gold-Mining Ants of India

Nearchus says that the skins of gold-mining ants are like those of leopards. But Megasthenes speaks of these ants as follows: that among the Derdae, a large tribe of Indians living towards the east and in the mountains, there is a plateau approx-imately three thousand stadia in circuit, and that below it are gold mines, of which the miners are ants, animals that are no smaller than foxes, are surpass-

* Strabo, *The Geography of Strabo*, 8 vols., trans. Horace Leonard Jones. (Cambridge: Harvard University Press, 1969), vol. 1, p. 263; vol. 7, pp. 75–77 (2.1.9, 15.1.44).

ingly swift, and live on the prey they catch. They dig holes in winter and heap up the earth at the mouths of the holes, like moles; and the gold-dust requires but little smelting. The neighbouring peoples go after it on beasts of burden by stealth, for if they go openly the ants fight it out with them and pursue them when they flee, and then, having overtaken them, exterminate both them and their beasts; but to escape being seen by the ants, the people lay out pieces of flesh of wild beasts at different places, and when the ants are drawn away from around the holes, the people take up the gold-dust and, not knowing how to smelt it, dispose of it unwrought to traders at any price it will fetch.

OVID (43 B.C.–A.D. 17)
THE METAMORPHOSES

Ovid's "shifting story of the world," the most definitive and influential literary rendering of classical mythology, dramatizes the theme of transformation through the history of the gods, goddesses, and heroes, from the creation of the universe up to the poet's own time.

Like St. George after him, Perseus slays a monster to rescue a maiden. In Ovid's retelling of the Greek myth, Perseus has just killed the snake-haired Gorgon Medusa. As he flies toward home, still carrying her head, he sees a girl chained to a rock on the shore below. Queen Cassiopeia had offended a sea god, who sent Cetus to devour her lands. King Cepheus was told the only way to save the kingdom was to offer their daughter Andromeda to the sea beast. All the figures in the myth became constellations. Pliny reported that a skeleton of the monster was displayed in Rome.

Ovid's philosopher, Pythagoras (sixth century B.C.), voices the unifying mutability theme of the poem. After tracing the changes of animal forms, including the fabled formless mass licked into bruin shape, he describes the exceptional transformation of the phoenix, which is eternally reborn into its own likeness. Like the phoenix of Herodotus, this bird carries the remains of its parent to the City of the Sun every 500 years, but Ovid's immortal bird builds its nest of spices in a tall palm tree. At this stage of its own literary development, the phoenix fable does not yet detail the death and rebirth of the bird or include the element of fire.

Ovid was the leading poet of Rome when Augustus exiled him for life for what the poet insisted was an indiscretion but not a crime. He was revered by the English Renaissance poets.

See the St. George story in Jacobus de Voragine.

Perseus, Andromeda, and the Sea Beast *

. . . Perseus
Clipped wings to heels and buckled on the curved
Sword that he carried and as quickly leaped,
Sailing at ease full speed through cloudless air.
He traveled over countless multitudes
Until he saw Egyptian shore below him
Where Cepheus was king, where unjust Ammon
Had ordered Andromeda to be punished
Because the poor girl had a foolish mother
Who talked too much. . . .

. . .

Look out to sea! Swift as a diving, tossing,
Knife-sharp-nosed ship that cuts the waves, propelled
By sweat-soaked arms of galley slaves, the dragon
Sailed up while churning waters at its breast
Broke into spray, leeside and windward; plunging
It came as near to shore as a Balearic
Sling could send its shot. Perseus, leaping
From earth behind him, vaulted to mid-air;
The dragon saw his shadow on the sea
And plunged to tear at it. Then, as Jove's eagle,
When he has found a snake in a broad meadow
Turning its mottled body to the sun,
Falls on the unseeing creature from the air,
And as the bird, knowing the snake's forked tongue,
Grips its scaled neck and sinks his claws within it,
So Perseus dove upon the raging dragon,
Thrusting, hilt-deep, the sword into its shoulder.
Burning with its gaped wound, the dragon reared
Its bulk in air, then dived, veered like a boar
When it has been surrounded by quick hounds,
Loud with the kill. Perseus, dodging, swayed
Past snapping jaws on agile, dancing wings;
Then as the beast rolled its soft belly open,

* Ovid, *The Metamorphoses*, trans. Horace Gregory (1958; rpt. New York: New American Library, 1960), 131–33, 421, 425–26 (4.665–71, 706–38, 15.252–58, 391–407).

Or bared its neck, his crooked sword struck in:
At back grown tough with sea-wet barnacles,
At flanks, or at the thin and fishlike tail.
The beast began to vomit purple spew,
And Perseus' wings, damp with salt spray, grew heavy;
He saw a rock that pierced the shifting waters
As they stilled, now curtained by the riding
Of the waves, and leaped to safety on it.
With left hand grasping on a ledge of cliff
He struck his sword three times and then again
Into the dragon's bowels. Then all the shores,
Even the highest balconies of heaven,
From which the gods looked down on Perseus,
Rang with great cheers; Cepheus and his wife,
Cassiope, called to their hero as a gallant
Bridegroom who saved the glory of their house.

The Phoenix

"Nothing retains the shape of what it was,
And Nature, always making old things new,
Proves nothing dies within the universe,
But takes another being in new forms.
What is called birth is change from what we were,
And death the shape of being left behind.
Though all things melt or grow from here to there,
Yet the same balance of the world remains.

. . .

"How many creatures walking on this earth
Have their first being in another form?
Yet one exists that is itself forever,
Reborn in ageless likeness through the years.
It is that bird Assyrians call the Phoenix,
Nor does he eat the common seeds and grasses,
But drinks the juice of rare, sweet-burning herbs.
When he has done five hundred years of living
He winds his nest high up a swaying palm —
And delicate dainty claws prepare his bed
Of bark and spices, myrrh and cinnamon —

And dies while incense lifts his soul away.
Then from his breast — or so the legend runs —
A little Phoenix rises over him,
To live, they say, the next five hundred years.
When he is old enough in hardihood,
He lifts his crib (which is his father's tomb)
Midair above the tall palm wavering there
And journeys toward the city of the Sun,
Where in Sun's temple shines the Phoenix nest."

Pomponius Mela (fl. a.d. 44)
The Situation of the World

Griffins, giant ants, the phoenix, other wondrous birds, and the catoblepas all lived in remote areas of the world described by the first Latin geographer, Pomponius Mela.

His *De Chorographia* (also known as *De Situ Orbis*, c. a.d. 44) is comprised of three books presenting first the hemispheres and zones, then the Mediterranean world and progressing to the lesser known coasts of Europe, Asia, and Africa. Following the broad topographical conception of the Greek geographer Strabo, Mela's survey is a handbook for the general reader, filled with place names but containing few mathematical details. The fabulous creatures he places in Scythia, India, Arabia, and Ethiopia appear primarily in the final third of the work. Ending with a reference to islands to the west, Mela's book was one of many that reinforced belief in lands beyond the Straits of Gibraltar.

Of Tingentera, in Southern Spain, Mela wrote during the reign of Claudius, drawing heavily upon other writers. The griffins and one-eyed Arimaspi, winged serpents, giant ants, and the phoenix were all earlier described by Herodotus. *De Chorographia*, abounding in strange creatures and other marvels of nature, was an important source for Mela's younger contemporary, Pliny the Elder, and later for Solinus. Pliny, too, mentioned "sphinxes"—not the mythological feline–human composite of Egypt and Greece, but a kind of ape. Pliny termed Mela's Ethiopian horned "tragopomones" and horse-eared "pegasies" fabulous, but included the "Catoblepe" (catoblepas) in his own menagerie of wonder beasts. Edward Topsell, perhaps confusing the heavy-headed beast with Mela's reference to it living near the Gorgon Isles, called the catoblepas a Gorgon.

Mela's "Lycaon" is a wild wolf-like dog.

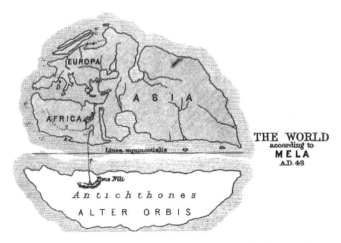

A map of the world based on the writings of Pomponius Mela. From *Atlas of Ancient and Classical Geography* (London: J. M. Dent & Sons, 1942). Courtesy of J. M. Dent.

The only English translation of Mela's Latin work is Arthur Golding's (1585). The following excerpts are this editor's modernized adaptation of Golding's translation.

Of Scythia *

The boundaries and location of Asia, extending to our Sea and the river Tanais, are such as I have shown before. Now to them that row back again down the same river into Maeotis, on the right hand is Europe, which was directly on the left side of them as they sailed up the stream. The river borders the mountain Riphey. The snow which falls continually makes the country inaccessible to travel. Beyond is a country of very rich soil, but it is uninhabitable because the Griffons (a cruel and unyielding kind of wild beast) jealously love the gold which lies above the ground and are very hostile to anyone who approaches it. The first men are Scythians, and of the Scythians, the first are the Arimaspians: which are reported to have but one eye apiece. From there up to Maeotis are the Issedones. . . .

* Pomponius Mela, *The worke of Pomponius Mela, the Cosmographer, concerning the Situation of the world*, trans. Arthur Golding (1585; Ann Arbor, Mich.: University Microfilms, 1958), Microfilm STC 177785, STCReel 436:3, pp. 35–36, 81–82, 87–88, 88–91.

Of India

India, a most famous country, is bordered not only by the East Ocean, but also the Southern, which we have called the Indishe Ocean, and on the West is bounded with the ridges of Mount Taurus. The country is so large that it takes a ship with full sails three score days and nights to pass around it.

. . . It is fruitful and inhabited by many kinds of men and beasts. There are ants as large as mastiffs which, like Griffons, are reported to keep gold dug out of the innermost parts of the earth, and to endanger the lives of anyone who dares to touch it.

Also, there are great serpents that overpower elephants by biting them and winding their tails about them. In some places, the soil is so fruitful that honey drips from leaves of trees, trees bear wool, and reeds split down the middle make boats able to carry two or even three men.

The Gulf of Arabia

The other gulf is enclosed by the Arabians. . . . There are many kinds of wild fowl, and many kinds of serpents. The most memorable of the serpents, little ones whose sting is immediate death, are reported to come from the mud of the frozen fens at a certain time of year and then fly in flocks toward Egypt, where they are encountered by another flock of birds called ibises, which fight with them and destroy them. Of birds, the most remarkable is the phoenix, which is always one of a kind. It is not conceived through mating, nor does it hatch, but when it has aged the full time of five hundred years, it broods upon a nest it has built of many spices, and there dies. Afterward growing again from its rotting flesh, it conceives itself and breeds itself again. When it is full fledged, it carries the bones of its old body wrapped in myrrh to Egypt, and there, in the city which they call by the name of the sun, it lays them upon a pyre of sweet-smelling Nardus and consecrates them with an honorable funeral. . . .

Of Ethiopia

There is a lake in which, if men wash themselves, their bodies become as crisp and shining as if they were anointed with oil. The same water is used for drinking; it is so sheer and so weak to bear up things that fall into it or are broken into it that it is not able to bear up the leaves that fall from the trees, so they sink down to the very bottom. There are also most cruel beasts, such as Lycaons spotted with all kind of colors, and sphinxes of such sort as we have read of. There are also wonderful birds, such as tragopomones which have horns, and pegasies which have ears like horses. But as men sail east along the coasts, they meet with nothing remarkable; all is waste, steep cliffs, and there are banks rather than shores. . . . Hereupon it is conjectured that the Nile being conceived in this spring, and carried forth a while through wayless places, and therefore unknown where he becomes himself again when he has proceeded into the East: but by being hidden so long, men think this fountain runs to some other place than to the Nile, and the Nile springs from some other head than from this fountain. Among them is bred a Catoblepe, a beast of no great size but with an oversized head always hanging downward to the ground. Even though he is able to do no harm at all by stinging or biting, to behold his eyes is immediate death. Nearby are the Gorgon Isles, sometimes (it is reported) the dwelling place of the Gorgon. The mainland itself ends at a promontory called Hesperionketas.

PLINY THE ELDER (A.D. 23/24–79)
NATURAL HISTORY

Pliny's monumental encyclopedia of human knowledge, encompassing all that was then known about the physical world and its inhabitants, is the major ancient treasure-house of fabulous animal lore.

Pliny states in his preface that he consulted 2000 volumes, and he lists nearly 500 authorities. His selections from histories, geographies, medical treatises, and other works were comprehensive but later regarded as indiscriminate and distorted by his love of the marvelous. Even so, the *Naturalis historia* was a standard authoritative work until it was discredited as science around the seventeenth century, and it remains an essential compendium of ancient learning. Of Pliny's many books, it is the only one to survive.

Along with Aristotle's writings, the zoological sections of the compiled *Natural History* (principally Books 8–11) were a standard source for the study of animals at least up through Edward Topsell's *Historie of Foure-Footed Beastes* (1607). Pliny echoes Aristotle repeatedly, but he believes in the infinite powers of nature and revels in describing fantastic creatures. Another of Pliny's important sources was Pomponius Mela. The *Natural History* was itself the central source for Solinus and was frequently cited in medieval bestiaries.

Following a catalog of the monstrous races, Pliny attributes the tale of the griffins and the one-eyed Arimaspi to Herodotus and to Herodotus's attested source, Aristeas of Proconnesus.

To the Greeks and Romans, the dragon was a large serpent. Pliny's description of the mutually fatal battle between Indian pythons and elephants (only a small section of Pliny's "dragon" writings) became the basis of dragon natural history for centuries thereafter.

Pliny's famous animals of Ethiopia passage presents a wildly colored menagerie of both actual and fabulous beasts. Among them, mentioned in Mela before him, are sphinxes (a variety of ape), horned and winged *pegasi*, and the heavy-headed catoblepas with the fatal look. From the *krokottas* (*kynolykos*, "dog-wolf") of Ctesias, Pliny derives his dog-wolf hyenas and his composite *leucrocota*, which, like Ctesias's creature, imitates the sound of the human voice. The ubiquitous manticore of Ctesias is also present. Pliny's yale, with the movable horns, became a bestiary and heraldic animal; his fierce unicorn added to the growing lore surrounding the beast, and his noxious basilisk became the major model for the legend. Pliny then moves on to the wolf and goes so far as to say that the story of the werewolf is false, "or else we must believe all the tales that the experience of so many centuries has taught us to be fabulous" (8.34).

His celebrated description of the phoenix presents Roman documentation of the bird. This multicolored Arabian phoenix, similar to that of Herodotus, is the size of an eagle. Like Ovid's bird, this one builds a nest of spices and dies in their fragrance, but here, the new phoenix grows from a maggot and its appearances at the City of the Sun coincide with the 540-year cycle of the astronomical Great Year. While the bird displayed in Rome was certainly a "fabrication," Pliny at first expresses uncertainty about the authenticity of the bird, saying "perhaps it is fabulous." He later satirizes doctors who prescribe medicines made from the bird's ashes and nest, "just as though the story were fact and not myth. It is to joke with mankind to point out remedies that return only after a thousand years" (29.9).

Pliny's Tritons and Nereids are legendary shapes of marine mammals. He openly rejects several birds, including the griffin and the cinnamon bird, but he relates the historical record of the sucking fish (a remora), the fabled echeneis that lives on through the medieval bestiaries.

Elsewhere, he extends traditional lore about the salamander, which he describes as a spotted, lizard-like creature that is "so chilly that it puts out fire by its contact, in the same way as ice does" (10.86).

Pliny died in the eruption of Vesuvius. As his nephew, Pliny "the Younger," recorded in a letter to his friend Tacitus, the naturalist first went to the scene to investigate the phenomenon and remained to help a friend. Philemon Holland's celebrated English translation of the *Natural History*, entitled *Historie of the World*, appeared in 1601.

For Pliny's influence upon medieval bestiaries, see especially Isidore of Seville and the "Latin Prose Bestiary."

The Griffins and the One-Eyed Arimaspi*

We have pointed out that some Scythian tribes, and in fact a good many, feed on human bodies — a statement that perhaps may seem incredible if we do not reflect that races of this portentous character have existed in the central region of the world, named Cyclopes and Laestrygones, and that quite recently the tribes of the parts beyond the Alps habitually practised human sacrifice, which is not far removed from eating human flesh. But also a tribe is reported next to these, towards the North, not far from the actual quarter whence the North Wind rises and the cave that bears its name, the place called the Earth's Door-bolt — the Arimaspi whom we have spoken of already, people remarkable for having one eye in the centre of the forehead. Many authorities, the most distinguished being Herodotus and Aristeas of Proconnesus, write that these people wage continual war around their mines with the griffins, a kind of wild beast with wings, as commonly reported, that digs gold out of mines, which the creatures guard and the Arimaspi try to take from them, both with remarkable covetousness.

Elephants and Dragons

Elephants are produced by Africa beyond the deserts of Sidra and by the country of the Moors; also by the land of Ethiopia and the Cave-dwellers, as has been said; but the biggest ones by India, as well as serpents that keep up a continual feud and warfare with them, the serpents also being of so large a size that they easily encircle the elephants in their coils and fetter them with a twisted knot. In this duel both combatants die together, and the vanquished elephant in falling crushes with its weight the snake coiled round it.

Wonder Animals of Ethiopia

Ethiopia produces lynxes in great numbers, and sphinxes with brown hair and a pair of udders on the breast, and many other monstrosities — winged horses armed with horns, called *pegasi*, hyenas like a cross between a dog and a wolf, that break everything with their teeth, swallow it at a gulp and masticate it in the belly; tailed monkeys with black heads, ass's hair and a voice unlike that of any

* Pliny, *Natural History*, 10 vols., trans. H. Rackham (Cambridge: Harvard University Press, 1983), vol. 2, p. 513; vol. 3, pp. 25–27, 53–59, 169–71, 293–95, 379–81, vol. 4, p. 63; vol. 8, pp. 465–67 (7.2; 8.11, 8.30–33, 9.4, 10.2, 10.70, 12.42, 32.1).

other species of ape; Indian oxen with one and with three horns; the *leucrocota*, swiftest of wild beasts, about the size of an ass, with a stag's haunches, a lion's neck, tail and breast, badger's head, cloven hoof, mouth opening right back to the ears, and ridges of bone in place of rows of teeth — this animal is reported to imitate the voices of human beings. Among the same people is also found the animal called the yale, the size of a hippopotamus, with an elephant's tail, of a black or tawny colour, with the jaws of a boar and movable horns more than a cubit in length which in a fight are erected alternately, and presented to the attack or sloped backward in turn as policy directs. But its fiercest animals are forest bulls, larger than the bulls of the field, surpassing all in speed, of a tawny colour, with blue eyes, hair turned backward, mouth gaping open to the ears, along with mobile horns; the hide has the hardness of flint, rejecting every wound. They hunt all wild animals, but themselves can only be caught in pits, and when caught always die game. Ctesias writes that in the same country is born the creature that he calls the *mantichora*, which has a triple row of teeth meeting like the teeth of a comb, the face and ears of a human being, grey eyes, a blood-red colour, a lion's body, inflicting stings with its tail in the manner of a scorpion, with a voice like the sound of a pan-pipe blended with a trumpet, of great speed, with a special appetite for human flesh. He says that in India there are also oxen with solid hoofs and one horn, and a wild animal named *axis*, with the hide of a fawn but with more spots and white ones, belonging to the ritual of Father Liber (the Orsacan Indians hunt monkeys that are a bright white all over the body). The fiercest animal is the unicorn, which in the rest of the body resembles a horse, but in the head a stag, in the feet an elephant, and in the tail a boar, and has a deep bellow, and a single black horn three feet long projecting from the middle of the forehead. They say it is impossible to capture this animal alive.

In Western Ethiopia there is a spring, the Nigris, which most people have supposed to be the source of the Nile, as they try to prove by the arguments that we have stated. In its neighbourhood there is an animal called the *catoblepas*, in other respects of moderate size and inactive with the rest of its limbs, only with a very heavy head which it carries with difficulty — it is always hanging down to the ground; otherwise it is deadly to the human race, as all who see its eyes expire immediately.

The basilisk serpent also has the same power. It is a native of the province of Cyrenaica, not more than 12 inches long, and adorned with a bright white marking on the head like a sort of diadem. It routs all snakes with its hiss, and does not move its body forward in manifold coils like the other snakes but advancing with its middle raised high. It kills bushes not only by its touch but also by its breath, scorches up grass and bursts rocks. Its effect on other animals is disastrous; it is believed that once one was killed with a spear by a man on horseback and the infection rising through the spear killed not only the rider but also the horse. Yet to a creature so marvellous as this — indeed kings have often wished to see a specimen when safely dead—the venom of weasels is fatal: so fixed is the decree of nature that nothing shall be without its match. They throw the basilisks into weasels' holes, which are easily known by the foulness of the ground, and the weasels kill them by their stench and die themselves at the same time, and nature's battle is accomplished.

Sea Monsters

An embassy from Lisbon sent for the purpose reported to the Emperor Tiberius that a Triton had been seen and heard playing on a shell in a certain cave, and that he had the well-known shape. The description of the Nereids also is not incorrect, except that their body is bristling with hair even in the parts where they have human shape; for a Nereid has been seen on the same coast, whose mournful song moreover when dying has been heard a long way off by the coast-dwellers; also the Governor of Gaul wrote to the late lamented Augustus that a large number of dead Nereids were to be seen on the shore. I have distinguished members of the Order of Knighthood as authorities for the statement that a man of the sea has been seen by them in the Gulf of Cadiz, with complete resemblance to a human being in every part of his body, and that he climbs on board ships during the hours of the night and the side of the vessel that he sits on is at once weighted down, and if he stays there longer actually goes below the water. During the rule of Tiberius, in an island off the coast of the province of Lyons the receding ocean tide left more than 300 monsters at the same time, of marvellous variety and size, and an equal number on the coast of Saintes, and among the rest elephants, and rams with only a white streak to resemble horns, and also many Nereids. Turranius has stated that a monster was cast ashore on the coast at Cadiz that had 24 feet of tail-end between its two fins, and also 120 teeth, the biggest 9 inches and the smallest 6 inches long. The skeleton of the monster to which Andromeda in the story was exposed was brought by Marcus Scaurus from the town of Jaffa in Judaea and shown at Rome among the rest of the marvels during his aedileship; it was 40 ft. long, the height of the ribs exceeding the elephants of India, and the spine being 1 ft. 6 inches thick.

The Phoenix

They say that Ethiopia and the Indies possess birds extremely variegated in colour and indescribable, and that Arabia has one that is famous before all others (though perhaps it is fabulous), the phoenix, the only one in the whole world and hardly ever seen. The story is that it is as large as an eagle, and has a gleam of gold round its neck and all the rest of it is purple, but the tail blue picked out with rose-coloured feathers and the throat picked out with tufts, and a feathered crest adorning its head. The first and the most detailed Roman account of it was given by Manilius, the eminent senator famed for his extreme and varied learning acquired without a teacher: he stated that nobody has ever existed that has seen one feeding, that in Arabia it is sacred to the Sun-god, that it lives 540 years, that when it is growing old it constructs a nest with sprigs of wild cinnamon and frankincense, fills it with scents and lies on it till it dies; that subsequently from its bones and marrow is born first a sort of maggot, and this grows into a chicken, and that this begins by paying due funeral rites to the former bird and carrying the whole nest down to the City of the Sun near Panchaia and depositing it upon an altar there. Manilius also states that the period of the Great Year coincides with the life of this bird, and that the same indications of the seasons and stars return again, and that this begins about noon on the day on which the sun enters the sign of the Ram, and that the year of this period had been 215, as reported by him, in the consulship of Publius Licinius and Gnaeus Cornelius. Cornelius Valerianus reports that a phoenix flew down into Egypt in the counsulship of Quintus Plautius and Sextus Papinius; it was even brought to Rome in the Censorship of the Emperor Claudius, A.U.C. 800 and displayed in the Comitium, a fact attested by the Records, although nobody would doubt that this phoenix was a fabrication.

Fabulous Birds

The pegasus bird with a horse's head and the griffin with ears and a terrible hooked beak — the former said to be found in Scythia and the latter in Ethiopia [from trans., Pliny seems to have these two reversed]—I judge to be fabulous; and for my own part I think the same about the bearded eagle attested by a number of people, a bird larger than an eagle, having curved horns on the temples, in colour a rusty red, except that its head is purple-red. Nor should the sirens obtain credit, although Dinon the father of the celebrated authority Clitarchus declares that they exist in India and that they charm people with their song and then when they are sunk in a heavy sleep tear them in pieces. Anybody who would believe that sort of thing would also assuredly not deny that snakes by licking the ears of the augur Melampus gave him the power to understand the language of birds, or the story handed down by Democritus, who mentions birds from a mixture of whose blood a snake is born, whoever eats which will understand the conversations of birds, and the things that he records about one crested lark in particular, as even without these stories life is involved in enormous uncertainty with respect to auguries. Homer mentions a kind of bird called the scops; many people speak of its comic dancing movements when it is watching for its prey, but I cannot easily grasp these in my mind, nor are the birds themselves now known. Consequently a discussion of admitted facts will be more profitable.

The Cinnamon Bird

In regard to cinnamomum and casia a fabulous story has been related by antiquity, and first of all by Herodotus, that they are obtained from birds' nests, and particularly from that of the phoenix, in the region where Father Liber was brought up, and that they are knocked down from inaccessible rocks and trees by the weight of the flesh brought there by the birds themselves, or by means of arrows loaded with lead; and similarly there is a tale of casia growing round marshes under the protection of a terrible kind of bats that guard it with their claws, and of winged serpents — these tales having been invented by the natives to raise the price of their commodities.

The Sucking Fish

The course of my subject has brought me to the greatest of Nature's works, and I am actually met by such an unsought and overwhelming proof of hidden power that inquiry should really be pursued no further, and nothing equal or similar can be found, Nature surpassing herself, and that in numberless ways. For what is more violent than sea, winds, whirlwinds, and storms? By what greater skill of man has Nature been aided in any part of herself than by sails and oars? Let there be added to these the indescribable force of tidal ebb and flow, the whole sea being turned into a river. All these, however, although acting in the same direction, are checked by a single specimen of the sucking fish, a very small fish. Gales may blow and storms may rage; this fish rules their fury, restrains their mighty strength, and brings vessels to a stop, a thing no cables can do, nor yet anchors or unmanageable weight that have been cast. It checks their attacks and tames the madness of the Universe with no toil of its own, not by resistance, or in any way except by adhesion. This little creature suffices in the face of all these forces to prevent vessels from moving. But armoured fleets bear aloft on their decks a rampart of towers, so that fighting may take place even at sea as from the wall of a fortress. How futile a creature is man, seeing that those rams, armed for striking with bronze and iron, can be checked and held fast by a little fish six inches long! It is said that at the battle of Actium the fish stopped the flagship of Antonius, who was hastening to go round and encourage his men, until he changed his ship for another one, and so the fleet of Caesar at once made a more violent attack. . . .

LUCAN (A.D. 39–65)
PHARSALIA

In classical myth, Chrysaor, the father of monsters, and the divine winged horse Pegasus spring from the blood of Medusa. In the *Pharsalia*, Lucan's historical epic of the Roman civil war, the fabulous two-headed amphisbaena and the basilisk are among the serpents also born from the blood after the hero Perseus carries the dripping head in his flight over the desert of Libya. Lucan enumerates the snakes and their deadly bites in a melodramatic account of the trek of defeated Cato's troops following Julius Caesar's victory over Pompey near the Thessalonian city of Pharsalus.

Many of the reptiles Lucan describes are later bestiary subjects, including the two-headed *amphisbaena* and the *iaculus* ("jaculus," from "javelin," so-called because of the reptile's aerial method of attack). The "dragons" here are constrictors, like Apollo's Python. Lucan gives a characteristically grisly twist to Pliny's story of the horseman who died from spearing a basilisk. The *salpuga* is a venomous ant.

The *Pharsalia* was unfinished when Lucan was implicated in a conspiracy against Nero and forced to commit suicide. He is said to have died reciting his own poetry.

Serpents of the Libyan Desert *

. . . Though that land is barren and those fields give increase to no good seed, yet they drank in poison from the gore of the dripping Medusa head—drank in from that savage blood a ghastly dew, which was made more potent by the heat and burnt into the crumbling sand.

In this land the blood, when it first stirred a head above the sand, sent up the asp whose swollen neck puts men to sleep; in no snake is more poison condensed; for more blood and a drop of clotted venom fell down here. Needing heat, the asp never of its own accord passes into cold regions, but traverses the desert as far as the Nile and no further. But we—shall we never be ashamed of gain?—import the bane of Africa to Italy and have made the asp an article of commerce. And there the huge *haemorrhois*, which will not suffer the blood of its victim to stay in the veins, opens out its scaly coils; there is the *cherysdros*, created to inhabit the Syrtis, half land and half sea; the *chelydrus*, whose track smokes as it glides along; the *cenchris*, which moves ever in a straight line—its belly is more thickly che-

* *Lucan*, trans. J. D. Duff (Cambridge: Harvard University Press, 1928), 557–61, 567 (9.696–736, 815–40).

quered and spotted than the Theban serpentine with its minute patterns; the *ammodytes*, of the same colour as the scorched sand and indistinguishable from it; the *crastes*, which wanders about as its spine makes it turn; the *scytale*, which alone can shed its skin while the rime is still scattered over the ground; the dried-up *dipsas*; the fell *amphisbaena*, that moves towards each of its two heads; the *natrix*, which pollutes waters, and the *iaculus*, that can fly; the *parias*, that is content to plough a track with its tail; the greedy *prester*, that opens wide its foaming mouth; the deadly *seps*, that destroys the bones with the body; and there the basilisk terrifies all the other snakes by the hissing it sends forth, and kills before it bites; it compels all the inferior serpents to keep their distance, and lords it over the empty desert. Dragons also, glittering with the sheen of gold, though worshipped in all other countries as harmless and divine, are made deadly by the heat of Africa: they draw in the air of heaven, birds and all; pursuing whole herds, they coil round mighty bulls and slay them with blows from their tail; nor is the elephant saved by his bulk — all things they consign to destruction, and need no poison to inflict death.

Amidst these plagues Cato travels on his waterless way with his hardy soldiers, witnessing the cruel fate of man after man, and strange forms of death accompanied by a trifling wound. . . .

. . . a serpent of the Nile froze the blood of hapless Laevus and stopped his heart. By no pain did he confess the wound, but suffered death by sudden unconsciousness, and went down by the way of sleep to join the ghosts of his comrades. The ripened poisons plucked by the wizards of Sais — poisons whose deadly stalks resemble the twigs of Arabia — do not infect the cup with so swift a death.

Behold! a fierce serpent, called by Africa *iaculus*, aimed and hurled itself at Paulus from a barren tree far off; piercing the head and passing through the temples, it escaped. Poison played no part there: death simultaneous with the wound snatched him away. Men discovered then how slow was the flight of the bullet from the sling, and how sluggish the whizz of the Scythian arrow through the air.

Ill-starred Murrus drove his spear through a basilisk, but that availed him nothing: the poison sped swiftly along the weapon and fastened on his hand. At once he bared his sword and cut it off with one stroke, right from the shoulder; and there he stood safe while his hand was destroyed, watching the semblance of the pitiful death that would have been his own. Who could suppose that the scorpion was fatal, or large enough to inflict speedy death? Yet heaven bears witness that the scorpion, threatening with its knotted tail and fierce with its sting erect, won the glory of defeating Orion. Who would fear to tread on the lair of the *salpuga*? Yet even to it the Stygian sisters gave power over their spinning.

So neither bright day nor black night brought rest to the wretched men: they could not trust the ground they lay on. . . .

TACITUS (C. A.D. 55–120)
THE ANNALS

In his chronicle of Roman emperors from Tiberius to Nero, Cornelius Tacitus sets the phoenix story in context of the period A.D. 32–37, during the reign of Tiberius. He analyzes the tale with a historian's objectivity, listing the bird's reported appearances, and pointing out that the interval between the last two sightings was less than the usual 500 years of the sun-bird's reputed life cycle. Other than the myrrh Herodotus mentions in his account, Tacitus provides few details of the bird's death and rebirth. He is, though, thought to be the first classical writer to refer to other birds joining the phoenix, a motif common in later texts. That single phrase of his, that the various phoenixes flew into the City of the Sun "with a multitude of companion birds marvelling at the novelty of the appearance," echoes down the centuries. While he is skeptical of the traditional phoenix tales, Tacitus believes the bird itself had sometimes been seen in Egypt.

Tacitus' other works include *Germania* and the *Histories*.

See especially the phoenix of Herodotus and Pliny. For other birds joining the phoenix in its flight, see Lactantius, Du Bartas, and Milton.

The Phoenix Appears in Egypt*

During the consulship of Paulus Fabius and Lucius Vitellius, the bird called the phoenix, after a long succession of ages, appeared in Egypt and furnished the most learned men of that country and of Greece with abundant matter for the discussion of the marvellous phenomenon. It is my wish to make known all on which they agree with several things, questionable enough indeed, but not too absurd to be noticed.

That it is a creature sacred to the sun, differing from all other birds in its beak and in the tints of its plumage, is held unanimously by those who have described its nature. As to the number of years it lives, there are various accounts. The general tradition says five hundred years. Some maintain that it is seen at intervals of fourteen hundred and sixty-one years, and that the former birds flew into the city called Heliopolis successively in the reigns of Sesostris, Amasis, and Ptolemy, the third king of the Macedonian dynasty, with a multitude of companion birds marvelling at the novelty of the appearance. But all antiquity is of course obscure. From Ptolemy to Tiberius was a period of less than five hundred years. Consequently some have supposed that this was a spurious phoenix, not from the

---

* Tacitus, *The Annals of Tacitus*, trans. Alfred John Church and William Jackson Brodribb (1900; rpt., Franklin Center, Pa.: Franklin Library, 1982), 185 (6.28).

regions of Arabia, and with none of the instincts which ancient tradition has attributed to the bird. For when the number of years is completed and death is near, the phoenix, it is said, builds a nest in the land of its birth and infuses into it a germ of life from which an offspring arises, whose first care, when fledged, is to bury its father. This is not rashly done, but taking up a load of myrrh and having tried its strength by a long flight, as soon as it is equal to the burden and to the journey, it carries its father's body, bears it to the Altar of the Sun, and leaves it to the flames. All this is full of doubt and legendary exaggeration. Still, there is no question that the bird is occasionally seen in Egypt.

Lucian (c. a.d. 125–190)
A True Story

The classical traveler's tale tradition from the adventures of Odysseus through the accounts of exotic peoples and places in the works of Herodotus and Ctesias culminates in the tallest tale of them all, Lucian of Samosata's *A True Story*. In the prologue to his exuberant Greek romance, the Syrian-born satirist promises his readers that his tales are all lies — unlike Ctesias, for one, who claimed as perfect truth what Lucian said "he had never seen himself nor heard from anyone else with a reputation for truthfulness" (1.3).

A storm in the western uncharted sea beyond the Straits of Gibraltar carries Lucian's ship to the moon, where Endymion is at war with Phaethon and his forces of the sun. Like other beings Lucian and his mariners encounter, the warriors of the sky are fantastic parodies of creatures described by travelers. A cavalry of gigantic winged ants and "dog-faced" men riding winged acorns are Lucian's versions of the fox-sized ants and dog-headed men of Herodotus. Lucian and his crew are later engorged by a 150-mile-long whale, one in the tradition of sea monsters that are mistaken for islands or that swallow seafarers. After visiting the Elysian Fields and the land of the dead, Lucian promises to recount other adventures in later books, what has been called Lucian's greatest lie of all.

A True Story, one of the earliest pieces of science fiction, influenced imaginary voyages for centuries after, including Cyrano de Bergerac's journey to the moon, the Baron Munchausen tales, François Rabelais's *Gargantua and Pantagruel*, and Jonathan Swift's *Gulliver's Travels*. Accredited with about eighty works, Lucian is also well known for his satiric dialogues.

For travelers' tales, see especially Homer, Herodotus, Ctesias, Philostratus, *The Arabian Nights*, *The Letter of Prester John*, and François Rabelais.

Nothing True to Tell*

. . . Well, on reading all these authors, I did not find much fault with them for their lying, as I saw that this was already a common practice even among men who profess philosophy. I did wonder, though, that they thought that they could write untruths and not get caught at it. Therefore, as I myself, thanks to my vanity, was eager to hand something down to posterity, that I might not be the only one excluded from the privileges of poetic licence, and as I had nothing true to tell, not having had any adventures of significance, I took to lying. But my lying is far more honest than theirs, for though I tell the truth in nothing else, I shall at least be truthful in saying that I am a liar. I think I can escape the censure of the world by my own admission that I am not telling a word of truth. Be it understood, then, that I am writing about things which I have neither seen nor had to do with nor learned from others — which, in fact, do not exist at all and, in the nature of things, cannot exist. Therefore my readers should on no account believe in them.

Once upon a time, setting out from the Pillars of Hercules and heading for the western ocean with a fair wind, I went a-voyaging . . .

Armies of the Moon and the Sun

That night we stopped there as his [Endymion's] guests, but at daybreak we arose and took our posts, for the scouts signalled that the enemy was near. The number of our army was a hundred thousand, apart from the porters, the engineers, the infantry and the foreign allies; of this total, eighty thousand were Vulture Dragoons and twenty thousand Grassplume-riders. The Grassplume is also a very large bird, which instead of plumage is all shaggy with grass and his wings very like lettuce-leaves. Next to these the Millet-shooters and the Garlic-fighters were posted. . . .

As to the enemy, on the left were the Ant Dragoons, with whom was Phaethon. They are very large beasts with wings, like the ants that we have, except in size: the largest one was two hundred feet long. They themselves fought, as well as their riders, and made especially good use of their feelers. They were said to number about fifty thousand. On their right were posted the Sky-mosquitoes, numbering also about fifty thousand, all archers riding on large mosquitoes. Next to them were the Sky-dancers, a sort of light infantry, formidable however, like all the rest, for they slung radishes at long range, and any man that they hit could not hold out a moment, but died, and his wound was malodorous. They were said to anoint their missiles with mallow poison. Beside them were

---

* A *True Story*, from *Lucian*, vol. 1, trans. A. M. Harmon (Cambridge: Harvard University Press, 1991), 251–53, 263–69 (1.4–5; 1.13, 1.16–17).

posted the Stalk-mushrooms, heavy infantry employed at close quarters, ten thousand in number. They had the name Stalk-mushrooms because they used mushrooms for shields and stalks of asparagus for spears. Near them stood the Puppycorns, who were sent him by the inhabitants of the Dog-star, five thousand dog-faced men who fight on the back of winged acorns. . . .

This, then, was the array with which Phaethon came on. Joining battle when the flags had been flown and the donkeys on both sides had brayed (for they had donkeys for trumpeters), they fought . . . .

PAUSANIAS (FL. C. A.D. 150)
DESCRIPTION OF GREECE

Pausanias's guide to Greece, still used as a handbook for archeologists and tourists, typically mixes descriptions of religious sites, monuments, and art with rationalized mythological background and folklore.

While he is regarded more highly for his antiquarian information than for his style and thought, the Greek traveler's ruminations on the marvelous touch upon the creation of fabulous animals. "Those who like to listen to the miraculous are themselves apt to add to the marvel," he wrote, "and so they ruin truth by mixing it with falsehood." On the other hand, he cautions that "everyone should be neither over-hasty in one's judgments, nor incredulous when considering rarities." Like Pliny before him, he rejects the werewolf as marvelous.

His first-hand description of the griffins on the helmet of Athena Parthenos typifies his first-hand descriptions that provide later generations with details of what has been lost. After Herodotus, this is one of many allusions to the lost *Arimaspia* of Aristeas. In describing the waters of the Stymphalus, he recounts a labor of Heracles, and the myth, in turn, leads to a kindred tale of fabulous Arabian birds. A headless sculpture at Tanagra evokes for him legends of the Triton and a personal experience of viewing a marine specimen of that name. He himself identifies as an actual animal the manticore described by Ctesias and paraphrased by Aristotle, Pliny, and others.

On Marvels and Truth*

. . . All through the ages, many events that have occurred in the past, and even some that occur to-day, have been generally discredited because of the lies built

---

* Pausanias, *Description of Greece*, 5 vols., trans. W. H. S. Jones (Cambridge: Harvard University Press, 1978), vol. 3, pp. 353–55; vol. 1, 123–25; vol. 4, pp. 5–7, 259–61, 261–63 (8.2.6, 1.24.4–7, 8.22.3–8, 9.21.1–2, 9.21.4–6).

up on a foundation of fact. It is said, for instance, that ever since the time of Lycaon a man has changed into a wolf at the sacrifice to Lycaean Zeus, but that the change is not for life; if, when he is a wolf, he abstains from human flesh, after nine years he becomes a man again, but if he tastes human flesh he remains a beast for ever. Similarly too it is said that Niobe on Mount Sipylus sheds tears in the season of summer. I have also heard that the griffins have spots like the leopard, and that the Tritons speak with human voice, though others say that they blow through a shell that has been bored. Those who like to listen to the miraculous are themselves apt to add to the marvel, and so they ruin truth by mixing it with falsehood.

Griffins on the Helmet of Athena Parthenos

. . . As you enter the temple that they name the Parthenon, all the sculptures you see on what is called the pediment refer to the birth of Athena, those on the rear pediment represent the contest for the land between Athena and Poseidon. The statue itself is made of ivory and gold. On the middle of her helmet is placed a likeness of the Sphinx . . . and on either side of the helmet are griffins in relief. These griffins, Aristeas of Proconnesus says in his poem, fight for the gold with Arimaspi beyond the Issedones. The gold which the griffins guard, he says, comes out of the earth; the Arimaspi are men all born with one eye; griffins are beasts like lions, but with the beak and wings of an eagle. I will say no more about the griffins. . . .

The Stymphalian Birds

In the Stymphalian territory is a spring, from which the emperor Hadrian brought water to Corinth. In winter the spring makes a small lake in Stymphalus, and the river Stymphalus issues from the lake; in summer there is no lake, but the river comes straight from the spring. This river descends into a chasm in the earth, and reappearing once more in Argolis it changes its name, and is called Erasinus instead of Stymphalus. There is a story current about the water of the Stymphalus, that at one time man-eating birds bred on it, which Heracles is said to have shot down. Peisander of Camira, however, says that Heracles did not kill the birds, but drove them away with the noise of rattles. The Arabian desert breeds among other wild creatures birds called Stymphalian, which are quite as savage against men as lions or leopards. These fly against those who come to hunt them, wounding and killing them with their beaks. All armour of bronze or iron that men wear is pierced by the birds; but if they weave a garment of thick cork, the beaks of the Stymphalian birds are caught in the cork garment, just as the

Heracles shoots the Stymphalian birds with a sling. Sixth-century B.C. Attic amphora. ABV 134.28. By permission of the British Museum.

wings of small birds stick in bird-lime. These birds are of the size of a crane, and are like the ibis, but their beaks are more powerful, and not crooked like that of the ibis. Whether the modern Arabian birds with the same name as the old Arcadian birds are also of the same breed, I do not know. But if there have been from all time Stymphalian birds, just as there have been hawks and eagles, I should call these birds of Arabian origin, and a section of them might have flown on some occasion to Arcadia and reached Stymphalus. Originally they would be called by the Arabians, not Stymphalian, but by another name. But the fame of Heracles, and the superiority of the Greek over the foreigner, has resulted in the birds of the Arabian desert being called Stymphalian even in modern times. In Stymphalus there is also an old sanctuary of Stymphalian Artemis, the image being of wood, for the most part gilded. Near the roof of the temple have been carved, among other things, the Stymphalian birds. Now it was difficult to discern clearly whether the carving was in wood or in gypsum, but such evidence as I had led me to conclude that it was not of gypsum but of wood. There are here also maidens of white marble, with the legs of birds, and they stand behind the temple.

The Triton

I saw another Triton among the curiosities in Rome, less in size than the one at Tanagra. The Tritons have the following appearance. On their heads they grow hair like that of marsh frogs not only in colour, but also in the impossibility of separating one hair from another. The rest of their body is rough with fine scales just as is the shark. Under their ears they have gills and a man's nose, but the mouth is broader and the teeth are those of a beast. Their eyes seem to me blue, and they have hands, fingers, and nails like the shells of the murex. Under the breast and belly is a tail like a dolphin's instead of feet.

The Martichoras of Ctesias

The beast described by Ctesias in his Indian history, which he says is called marti-choras by the Indians and man-eater by the Greeks, I am inclined to think is the tiger. But that it has three rows of teeth along each jaw and spikes at the tip of its tail with which it defends itself at close quarters, while it hurls them like an archer's arrows at more distant enemies; all this is, I think, a false story that the Indians pass on from one to another owing to their excessive dread of the beast. They were also deceived about its colour, and whenever the tiger showed itself in the light of the sun it appeared to be a homogeneous red, either because of its speed, or, if it were not running, because of its continual twists and turns, espe-cially when it was not seen at close quarters. And I think that if one were to tra-verse the most remote parts of Libya, India or Arabia, in search of such beasts as are found in Greece, some he would not discover at all, and others would have a different appearance. For man is not the only creature that has a different appear-ance in different climates and in different countries; the others too obey the same rule. For instance, the Libyan asps have a different colour as compared with the Egyptian, while in Ethiopia are bred asps quite as black as the men. So everyone should be neither over-hasty in one's judgments, nor incredulous when consider-ing rarities. For instance, though I have never seen winged snakes I believe that they exist, as I believe that a Phrygian brought to Ionia a scorpion with wings exactly like those of locusts.

AELIAN (C. A.D. 170–235)
ON ANIMALS

A popular and entertaining treasury of animal lore, *De Natura Animalium* joined the works of Aristotle and Pliny as a primary classical source of natural history. Aelian's book, like Pliny's *Natural History*, is a major classical repository of fabu-lous animals.

Claudius Aelianus, a friend of Philostratus, was a Roman rhetorician who wrote in Greek. He cites Greek but no Latin sources, and most of his excerpts from Herodotus and Aristotle, as well as others, were second-hand. While he refers to Aristotle frequently, *On Animals* is a random compendium of anecdotes, not a serious zoological study. The book's moralistic portrayal of animals made it an important source of material for the medieval bestiarists, and the work remains a valuable collection of writings no longer extant. The first printed edition of the book was a 1556 Latin translation prepared by the "father of modern zoology," Conrad Gesner.

The fantastic creatures Aelian describes have all appeared earlier in these pages. He specifically cites Ctesias, and all the other entries contain echoes of earlier writings, many of them previously collected by Pliny. Extensive scholarship has traced many of Aelian's multiple sources, but it is not always certain what Aelian took from others — or from whom in particular — and what he invented. He himself said he had never traveled beyond the Italian peninsula nor had ever been on a ship.

To avoid "tedium rising from monotony," Aelian imposes no order upon his material. Fantastic beasts are scattered throughout the work, and different characteristics of even a single animal sometimes appear in different places. Besides the creatures presented below, the echeneis, the "Ants of India that guard the gold," and the cinnamon bird appear in Aelian's book.

In the tradition of Pliny and Lucan, Aelian's basilisk is lethal, but here the beast's poison travels up a walking stick, not up the spear of a horseman or foot soldier. With qualification, Aelian bases his manticore upon the man-faced beast of Ctesias. Aelian's traditional gold-guarding griffins, like Ctesias's, are black with red chests, but have white wings. Unlike Egyptian priests, Aelian's phoenix knows when its 500-year cycle is complete because it is a child of nature. Although Aelian contrasts the amphisbaena with the mythical monsters of antiquity, the creature he describes is actually a fantastic relative of the multi-headed Hydra and Chimera. He expands upon Ctesias's purple-headed wild ass of India, but does not recognize that the *cartazonus* he describes is actually a rhinoceros, an animal he and his readers could have seen at the Roman Circus.

The Basilisk*

The Basilisk measures but a span, yet at the sight of it the longest snake not after an interval but on the instant, at the mere impact of its breath, shrivels. And if a man has a stick in his hand and the Basilisk bites it, the owner of the rod dies.

*   *

*   Aelian, *On Animals*, 3 vols., trans. A. F. Scholfield (Cambridge: Harvard University Press, 1972), vol. 1, pp. 93, 193–95, 233–37, 241–43; vol. 2, 79–81, 243–45; vol. 3, 289–91 (2.5, 2.30, 4.21, 4.27, 6.58, 9.23, 16.20, 4.52).

The Lion dreads a Cock, and the Basilisk too, they say, goes in fear of the same bird: at the sight of one it shudders, and at the sound of its crowing it is seized with convulsions and dies. This is why travellers in Libya, which is a nurse of such monsters, in fear of the aforesaid Basilisk take with them a Cock as companion and partner of their journey to protect themselves from so terrible an infliction.

The Martichoras

There is in India a wild beast, powerful, daring, as big as the largest lion, of a red colour like cinnabar, shaggy like a dog, and in the language of India it is called *Martichoras*. Its face however is not that of a wild beast but of a man, and it has three rows of teeth set in its upper jaw and three in the lower; these are exceedingly sharp and larger than the fangs of a hound. Its ears also resemble a man's, except that they are larger and shaggy; its eyes are blue-grey and they too are like a man's, but its feet and claws, you must know, are those of a lion. To the end of its tail is attached the sting of a scorpion, and this might be over a cubit in length; and the tail has stings at intervals on either side. But the tip of the tail gives a fatal sting to anyone who encounters it, and death is immediate. If one pursues the beast it lets fly its stings, like arrows, sideways, and it can shoot a great distance; and when it discharges its stings straight ahead it bends its tail back; if however it shoots in a backward direction, as the Sacae do, then it stretches its tail to its full extent. Any creature that the missile hits it kills; the elephant alone it does not kill. These stings which it shoots are a foot long and thickness of a bulrush. Now Ctesias asserts (and he says that the Indians confirm his words) that in the places where those stings have been let fly others spring up, so that this evil produces a crop. And according to the same writer the Mantichore for choice devours human beings; indeed it will slaughter a great number; and it lies in wait not for a single man but would set upon two or even three men, and alone overcomes even that number. All other animals it defeats: the lion alone it can never bring down. That this creature takes special delight in gorging human flesh its very name testifies, for in the Greek language it means *man-eater*, and its name is derived from its activities. Like the stag it is extremely swift.

Now the Indians hunt the young of these animals while they are still without stings in their tails, which they then crush with a stone to prevent them from growing stings. The sound of their voice is as near as possible that of a trumpet.

Ctesias declares that he has actually seen this animal in Persia (it had been brought from India as a present to the Persian King)— if Ctesias is to be regarded as a sufficient authority on such matters. At any rate after hearing of the peculiarities of this animal, one must pay heed to the historian of Cnidos.

The Gryphons of India

I have heard that the Indian animal the Gryphon is a quadruped like a lion; that it has claws of enormous strength and that they resemble those of a lion. Men commonly report that it is winged and that the feathers along its back are black, and those on its front are red, while the actual wings are neither but are white. And Ctesias records that its neck is variegated with feathers of a dark blue; that it has a beak like an eagle's, and a head too, just as artists portray it in pictures and sculpture. Its eyes, he says, are like fire. It builds its lair among the mountains, and although it is not possible to capture the full-grown animal, they do take the young ones. And the people of Bactria, who are neighbours of the Indians, say that the Gryphons guard the gold in those parts; that they dig it up and build their nests with it, and that the Indians carry off any that falls from them. The Indians however deny that they guard the aforesaid gold, for the Gryphons have no need of it (and if that is what they say, then I at any rate think that they speak the truth), but that they themselves come to collect the gold, while the Gryphons fearing for their young ones fight with the invaders. They engage too with other beasts and overcome them without difficulty, but they will not face the lion or the elephant. Accordingly the natives, dreading the strength of these animals, do not set out in quest of the gold by day, but arrive by night, for at that season they are less likely to be detected. Now the region where the Gryphons live and where the gold is mined is a dreary wilderness. And the seekers after the aforesaid substance arrive, a thousand or two strong, armed and bringing spades and sacks; and watching for a moonless night they begin to dig. Now if they contrive to elude the Gryphons they reap a double advantage, for they not only escape with their lives but they also take home their freight, and when those who have acquired a special skill in the smelting of gold have refined it, they possess immense wealth to requite them for the dangers described above. If however they are caught in the act, they are lost. And they return home, I am told, after an interval of three or four years.

The Phoenix

The Phoenix knows how to reckon five hundred years without the aid of arithmetic, for it is a pupil of all-wise Nature, so that it has no need of fingers or anything else to aid it in the understanding of numbers. The purpose of this knowledge and the need for it are matters of common report. But hardly a soul among the Egyptians knows when the five-hundred-year period is completed; only a very few know, and they belong to the priestly order. But in fact the priests have difficulty in agreeing on these points, and banter one another and maintain that it is not now but at some date later than when it was due that the divine bird will arrive. Meantime while they are vainly squabbling, the bird miraculously guesses the period by signs and appears. And the priests are obliged to give way and confess that they devote their time "to putting the sun to rest" with their talk; but they do not know as much as birds.

The Amphisbaena

Poets and the compilers of ancient legends, among whom is Hecataeus the chronicler, may sing of the Hydra of Lerna, one of the Labours of Heracles; and Homer may sing of the Chimaera with its three heads, the monster of Lycia kept by Amisodarus the Lycian king for the destruction of many, of varied nature, and absolutely invincible. Now these seem to have been relegated to the region of myths. The Amphisbaena however is a snake with two heads, one at the top and one in the direction of the tail. When it advances, as need for a forward move-ment impels it, it leaves one end behind to serve as tail, while the other it uses as a head. Then again if it wants to move backwards, it uses the two heads in exactly the opposite manner from what it did before.

Unicorns

[THE CARTAZONUS]

In certain regions of India (I mean in the very heart of the country) they say that there are impassable mountains full of wild life, and that they contain just as many animals as our own country produces, only wild. . . .

And in these same regions there is said to exist a one-horned beast which they call *Cartazonus*. It is the size of a full-grown horse, has the mane of a horse, red-dish hair, and is very swift of foot. Its feet are, like those of the elephant, not articulated and it has the tail of a pig. Between its eyebrows it has a horn growing out; it is not smooth but has spirals of quite natural growth, and is black in colour. This horn is also said to be exceedingly sharp. And I am told that the creature has the most discordant and powerful voice of all animals. When other animals approach, it does not object but is gentle; with its own kind however it is inclined to be quarrelsome. And they say that not only do the males instinctively butt and fight one another, but that they display the same temper towards the females, and carry their contentiousness to such a length that it ends only in the death of their defeated rival. The fact is that strength resides in every part of the animal's body, and the power of its horn is invincible. It likes lonely grazing-ground where it roams in solitude, but at the mating season, when it associates with the female, it becomes gentle and the two even graze side by side. Later when the season has

passed and the female is pregnant, the male Cartazonus of India reverts to its savage and solitary state. They say that the foals when quite young are taken to the
King of the Prasii and exhibit their strength one against another in public shows,
but nobody remembers a full-grown animal having been captured.

[Tʜᴇ Wɪʟᴅ Assᴇs ᴏғ Iɴᴅɪᴀ]

I have learned that in India are born Wild Asses as big as horses. All their body is
white except for the head, which approaches purple, while their eyes give off a
dark blue colour. They have a horn on their forehead as much as a cubit and a
half long; the lower part of the horn is white, the upper part is crimson, while the
middle is jet-black. From these variegated horns, I am told, the Indians drink, but
not all, only the most eminent Indians, and round them at intervals they lay rings
of gold, as though they were decorating the beautiful arm of a statue with
bracelets. And they say that a man who has drunk from this horn knows not, and
is free from, incurable diseases; he will never be seized with convulsions nor with
the sacred sickness as it is called, nor be destroyed by poisons. Moreover if he has
previously drunk some deadly stuff, he vomits it up and is restored to health.

Pʜɪʟᴏsᴛʀᴀᴛᴜs (ᴄ. ᴀ.ᴅ. 170–245)
Tʜᴇ Lɪғᴇ ᴏғ Aᴘᴏʟʟᴏɴɪᴜs ᴏғ Tʏᴀɴᴀ

As recorded by Flavius Philostratus, "The Athenian," marvels abound in the
Indian journey of the wandering prophet Apollonius—from jars of rain and wind
to sands of bronze. The travelers feast with the sages and discuss the magical
beasts of India with Iarchus, the head Brahman.

Along with Aelian, Philostratus was a member of the literary circle of Empress
Julia Domna. He wrote that she presented him with the memoirs of Apollonius,
composed by a disciple named Damis, and requested that he write a life of the
first-century mystic to counterbalance the rumors that Apollonius was a charla-
tan. Using multiple sources and first-hand research of cult sites, Philostratus set
down the travels, acts, and sayings of a figure that some said rivaled Jesus Christ.
Scholars have questioned the authenticity of Damis, suggesting that he might
have been a figure Philostratus invented as a mouthpiece for himself.

The Indian manticore of Ctesias appears again, as a tall tale which Apollonius
rejects. The Indian griffins are traditional creatures in that they guard gold, are
sacred to the sun, and pull the solar chariot, but their webbed feet are unconven-
tional wings, and they are unable to best the tiger. Like the bird of Herodotus, this

phoenix resembles an eagle, builds its nest of spices, and visits Egypt every 500 years, but it nests at the source of the Nile, flies about India, and dies singing, like the fabled swan. Elsewhere in his book, Philostratus elaborately describes a "dragon hunt" for earth-shaking serpents whose heads contain gems of mystical power.

Philostratus's account of India was among the many targets of Christian attack of the book. "For here," wrote the ecclesiastical historian Eusebius of Caesarea (c. 260 – 340), "we shall have to admit that the tales of Thule, and any other miraculous legends ever invented by any story-tellers, turn out to be by comparison with these quite reliable and perfectly true" (*The Treatise of Eusebius*, 16).

The Mythological Animals of India*

And inasmuch as the following conversation also has been recorded by Damis as having been held upon this occasion with regard to the mythological animals and fountains and men met with in India, I must not leave it out, for there is much to be gained by neither believing nor yet disbelieving everything.

[THE MARTICHORAS]

Accordingly Apollonius asked the question, whether there was there an animal called the man-eater (*martichoras*); and Iarchas replied: "And what have you heard about the make of this animal? For it is probable that there is some account given of its shape." "There are," replied Apollonius, "tall stories current which I cannot believe; for they say that the creature has four feet, and that his head resembles that of a man, but that in size it is comparable to a lion; while the tail of this animal puts out hairs a cubit long and sharp as thorns, which it shoots like arrows at those who hunt it." And he further asked about the golden water which they say bubbles up from a spring, and about the men who live underground and the pigmies also and the shadow-footed men; and Iarchas answered his questions thus: "What have I to tell you about animals or plants or fountains which you have seen yourself on coming here? For by this time you are as competent to describe these to other people as I am; but I never yet heard in this country of an animal that shoots arrows or of springs of golden water."

[GRIFFINS]

As to the gold which the griffins dig up, there are rocks which are spotted with drops of gold as with sparks, which this creature can quarry because of the

* Philostratus, *The Life of Apollonius of Tyana; The Epistles of Apollonius and the Treatise of Eusebius*, 2 vols., trans. F. C. Conybeare (Cambridge: Harvard University Press, 1960), vol. 1, pp. 327–29, 333–35 (3.45, 3.48, 3.49–50).

strength of its beak. "For these animals do exist in India," he said, "and are held in veneration as being sacred to the Sun; and the Indian artists, when they represent the Sun, yoke four of them abreast to draw the imaged car; and in size and strength they resemble lions, but having this advantage over them that they have wings, they will attack them, and they get the better of elephants and of dragons. But they have no great power of flying, not more than have birds of short flight; for they are not winged as is proper with birds, but the palms of their feet are webbed with red membranes, such that they are able to expand them, and make a flight and fight in the air; and the tiger alone is beyond their powers of attack, because in swiftness it is akin to the winds."

[The Phoenix]

"And the phoenix," he said, "is the bird which visits Egypt every five hundred years, but the rest of that time it flies about in India; and it is unique in that it is an emanation of sunlight and shines with gold, in size and appearance like an eagle; and it sits upon the nest which is made by it at the springs of the Nile out of spices. The story of the Egyptians about it, that it comes to Egypt, is testified to by the Indians also, but the latter add this touch to the story, that the phoenix which is being consumed in its nest sings funeral strains for itself. And this is also done by the swans according to the account of those who have the wit to hear them."

In such conversations with the sages Apollonius spent the four months which he passed there, and he acquired all sorts of lore both profane and mysterious.

Solinus (c. a.d. 200)
Collection of Remarkable Facts

Much of the fabulous lore in the bestiaries and on medieval maps is derived from a single small compendium of ancient marvels, Gaius Julius Solinus's geography, *Collectanea Rerum Memorabilium* ("Collection of Remarkable Facts," later known as *Polyhistor*). One of the most honored and frequently cited European works for about 1400 years, the phenomenal *Collectanea* has been translated into English only once and is now regarded as a badly written, badly compiled collection. Few books have enjoyed such a remarkable history.

Most of the Roman grammarian's book is a compilation of tales from Pliny's *Natural History,* leading detractors to call him "Pliny's ape." Solinus also borrowed heavily from the first Roman geographer, Pomponius Mela. Because Pliny was himself a compiler, who also used Mela as a source, Solinus's descriptions of fabulous animals are filled with echoes of earlier writers. If nothing else, the *Collectanea* is a rich summation of classical writings on the marvelous. Albertus Magnus, for one, accused Solinus of being "guilty of many untruths."

Following are modernized excerpts from Arthur Golding's 1587 translation from the Latin. Golding also translated the geography of a Solinus source, Pomponius Mela. In both books, the griffins live in the snowbound area of Mount Riphey; the "Catoblepe" (catoblepas) and the gold-digging ants are also in Mela. (In both of Golding's translations, the ants are as big as mastiffs.) Golding's "cockatrice" is a later name for the basilisk, even though the creature described is the deadly classical serpent, not the later serpent–cock hybrid. The luminous ercinee is included in bestiaries.

The early hybrid name for the giraffe, "Camelopardalis," has been retained in its scientific genus name. The "eale" is Pliny's yale. The phoenix, cynnamolgus, manticore, unicorn, and other fabulous creatures found earlier in Pliny's *Natural History* appear elsewhere in the *Collectanea*.

The Arimaspes *

The Arimaspes, which are situated about Gesglithron, are a people that have but one eye. Beyond them and the Mountain Riphey is a country continually covered with snow, called Pteropheron. For the incessant falling of the hoarfrost and snow makes it look like feathers. A damned part of the world is it, and drowned by nature itself in the cloud of endless darkness, and utterly shut up in extreme cold as in a prison, even under the very North Pole. Only of all lands it knows no distinction of times, neither receives it anything else of the air than everlasting winter. In the Asiatik Scythia are rich lands, but notwithstanding uninhabitable.

For whereas they abound in gold and precious stones, the Gryffons possess all, a most fierce kind of fowl, and cruel beyond all cruelty, whose outrageousness stops all comers, so that hardly and seldom arrive any there. For as soon as they see them they tear them in pieces, as creatures made of purpose to punish the rashness of covetous folk.

The Arimaspes fight with them to get away their precious stones. . . .

The Ercinee

The Forest of Hertzwald breeds birds whose feathers shine and give light in the dark, though the night be ever so close and cloudy. And therefore men of that

* Solinus, *The Excellent and Pleasant Worke of Julius Solinus Polyhistor*, trans. Arthur Golding (1587; Gainesville, Fla.: Scholars' Facsimiles & Reprints, 1955).

country do most of their outgoings by night so that they may use the birds for a help to direct their journey by. Casting the birds before them in the open paths, they keep their way by the shining of those feathers.

The Amphisbene

The Amphisbene rises with two heads, whereof one is in his accustomed place and the other where his tail should be. Whereupon it comes to pass that with both heads forward at once, he creeps in a circle.

The Cockatrice

On the left hand of Cyrene is Affrick, on the right side Egypt, on the foreside the rough and harborless sea, on the back part divers barbarous nations, and a wilderness not to be come unto, uninhabited and forlorn, which breeds the Cockatrice, such a singular mischief as is not in all the whole world beside. It is a serpent almost half a foot long, white, with, as it were, a little miter, proportioned in lines on his head. He is given to the utter destruction not only of man and beast, or whatsoever has life, but even of the earth itself, which he afflicts and burns up wheresoever he has his deadly den. . . . The citizens of Pergamus gave a full sestertium for the carcass of a Cockatrice, and hung it up in a net of gold in the Temple of Apollo, which was notable for the great workmanship, so that neither spiders should spin there, nor birds fly in there.

Draconce

. . . There is cut out of the Dragon's brains a stone called Draconce, but it is not a stone unless it be taken from them while they are alive. For if the Serpent die before, the hardness vanishes away with his life. The kings of the East wear these although they are so hard that no man can devise to imprint or engrave anything in it: and whatsoever is beautiful in it is not made by man's hand, because no other color should strain the pure natural whiteness. An author named Sothacus says that he has seen this jewel and declares by what means it is come by. Men of excellent courage and audacity search out the holes where the serpents lie. Then watching until they come forth to feed, and passing by them with as much speed as they can, they cast them herbs to provoke sleep. So when they be fast asleep, they cut the stones out of their heads, and getting the booty of their heady enterprise, enjoy the reward of their rashness.

Wild Beasts of Aethiope

The places which the Aethiopes possess are full of wild beasts, whereof one is the Nabis which we call a Camelopardalis. It is necked like a horse, footed like an Ox, headed like a Camel, and of a bright bay colour powdered with white spots. This beast was shown first in Rome at the games that Caesar the Dictator made in the Lists. Almost about the same time also were brought from thence monsters called Celphies, whose hind feet from the ankle up to the top of the calf were like a man's leg, and likewise his forefeet resembled a man's hand. Notwithstanding, these were never seen by the Romans but once. Before the shows of Cneus Pompeius, the Romans had never seen the Rhinoceros openly. This beast is of a pale russet colour: in his nose is a horn that bows upward. He makes it sharp, pointed like a knife, by whetting it upon stones. He fights with it against the Elephants, being almost as long as they, but somewhat shorter legged, and with this his natural weapon he pushes at their bellies, as the only part which he knows may be pierced with striking. By the River Nigris breeds the Catoblepe, a little sluggish beast with a great heavy jaw, and a venomous sight. For they that happen to come in his sight die. There be Ants as big as a Mastiff, that have talons like Lions. With these they scrape up sands of gold, which they keep so that no man may fetch it away. If any man tries, they pursue him to death.

The Eale of Inde

There is an Eale, otherwise like a Horse, tailed like an Elephant, of colour black, chapped like a Boar, armed with horns more than a cubit long, pliable to whatever use he chooses to put them. For they are not stiff, but turn as need shall require in fighting. He puts out the one when he fights, and rolls up the other.

LACTANTIUS (C. A.D. 260–340)
PHOENIX

One of the most complete and influential accounts of the phoenix, the *Carmen de ave phoenice* is a synthesis of classical lore with themes commonly interpreted as Christian. The poem is also distinctive in that it varies the classical pattern of the tale by describing the bird's rebirth through fire.

Lactantius was born in Africa, converted to Christianity in middle age, and was a tutor of the eldest son of Constantine. An early Christian Latin author, he was highly regarded for his religious prose and called the Christian Cicero. While the *Phoenix* is generally attributed to him, its authorship is disputed. Some of his defenders have contended that he composed the predominantly classical poem prior to his conversion. In any case, the work was a major source of Claudian's pagan *Phoenix* and was the basis of the religious Old English *Phoenix*.

Like the traditional phoenix, the sun-bird of Lactantius periodically builds its nest of spices in a tall tree in a remote land, dies, is reborn, and carries its ashes in a ball of myrrh to the Egyptian City of the Sun. In Lactantius's poem, though, the bird flies from its paradisiacal home in "the grove of the Sun" to far-off Syria to build its nest of death and rebirth. Also, flame enters the tale, an element that soon after becomes central to the standard phoenix story; in this version, the body of the dead bird bursts into flame. As in accounts following Tacitus, other birds join it in homage of its rebirth, in this case accompanying it on its return flight from Egypt. Lactantius embroiders the story with classical mythology, etymologies, and lush descriptions of the earthly paradise, the flaming nest of spices, and the plumage of the bird. This phoenix is female ("or male she is — which you will") and lives 1000 years.

The poet describes the bird's daily ritual, her song and habits, her death and immolation, and rebirth. With overtones that Christian authors interpreted as allegorical, she "builds herself a cradle or sepulchre . . . for she dies to live and yet begets herself." She "commends her soul" and is "a bird of happy lot and happy end to whom God's own will has granted birth from herself." She gains "eternal life by the boon of death."

A prose translation of the influential poem is excerpted below.

For Christian association of the phoenix with resurrection, see St. Clement, St. Ambrose, the Latin *Physiologus*, and the Old English *Phoenix*.

Phoenix*

There is a far-off land, blest amid the first streaks of dawn, where standeth open the mightiest portal of the everlasting sky, yet not beside the rising of the summer or the winter Sun, but where he sheds daylight from the heavens in spring. There a plain spreads out its open levels; no knoll swells there, no hollow valley gapes, yet that region o'ertops by twice six ells our mountains whose ridges are reckoned high. Here is the grove of the Sun, a woodland planted with many a tree and green with the honours of eternal foliage. . . .

In this grove, in these woods, dwells the peerless bird, the Phoenix, peerless, since she lives renewed by her own death. An acolyte worthy of record, she yields

* Lactantius, *Phoenix*, from *Minor Latin Poets*, trans. J. Wight Duff and Arnold M. Duff (Cambridge: Harvard University Press, 1961), 651–65.

obedience and homage to Phoebus: such the duty that parent Nature assigned to her for observance. Soon as saffron Aurora reddens at her rising, soon as she routs the stars with rosy light, thrice and again that bird plunges her body into the kindly waves, thrice and again sips water from the living flood. Soaring she settles on the topmost height of a lofty tree which alone commands the whole of the grove, and turning towards the fresh rising of Phoebus at his birth, awaits the emergence of his radiant beam. And when the sun has struck the threshold of the gleaming portal and the light shaft of his first radiance has flashed out, she begins to pour forth notes of hallowed minstrelsy and to summon the new day in a marvellous key which neither tune of nightingale nor musical pipe could rival in Cirrhean modes; nay, let not the dying swan be thought capable of imitating it, nor yet the tuneful strings of Cyllenean lyre.

After Phoebus has given his steeds the rein into the open heavens and in ever onward course brought forth his full round orb, then that bird with thrice repeated beat of the wing yields her applause, and after three obeisances to the fire-bearing prince holds her peace. She it is also who marks off the swift hours by day and night in sounds which may not be described, priestess of the grove and awe-inspiring ministrant of the woods, the only confidant of thy mysteries, Phoebus. When she has already fulfilled a thousand years of life and long lapse of time has made it burdensome to her, she flees from her sweet and wonted nest in the grove, so that in the closing span she may restore her bygone existence, and when in passion for re-birth she has left her sacred haunts, then she seeks this world where Death holds sovereignty. Despite her length of years she directs her swift flight into Syria, to which she herself of old gave the name of "Phoenice," and seeks through desert wilds the care-free groves, here where the sequestered woodland lurks among the glades. Then she chooses a palm-tree towering with airy crest which bears its Greek name "Phoenix" from the bird: against it no hurtful living creatures could steal forth, or slippery serpent, or any bird of prey. Then Aeolus imprisons the winds in overarching grottoes, lest their blast harass the bright-gleaming air, or the cloud-wrack from the South banish the sunrays throughout the empty tracts of heaven and do harm to the bird. Thereafter she builds herself a cradle or sepulchre — which you will — for she dies to live and yet begets herself. She gathers for it from the rich forest juicy scented herbs such as the Assyrian gathers or the wealthy Arabian, such as either the Pygmaean races or India culls or the Sabaean land produces in its soft bosom. Here she heaps together cinnamon and effluence of the aromatic shrub that sends its breath afar and balsam with its blended leaf. Nor is there lacking a slip of mild casia or fragrant acanthus or the rich dropping tears of frankincense. Thereto she adds the tender ears of downy spikenard, joining as its ally the potency of thy myrrh, Panachaea. Forthwith in the nest she has furnished she sets her body that awaits its change — withered limbs on a life-giving couch: thereafter with her beak she casts the scents on her limbs, around them and above, being appointed to die in her own funeral. Then she commends her soul amid the varied fragrances without a fear for the trustworthiness of a deposit so great. Meanwhile her body, by birth-giving death destroyed, is aglow, the very heat producing flame and catching fire from the ethereal light afar: it blazes and when burned dissolves into ashes. These ashes she welds together, as if they were concentrated by moisture in a mass, possessing in the result what takes the place of seed. Therefore, 'tis said, rises a living creature first of all without limbs, but this worm is said to have a milky colour: when suddenly at the appointed hour it has grown enormously, gathering into what looks like a round egg, from it she is remoulded in such shape as she had before, bursting her shell and springing to life a Phoenix: 'tis even so that larvae in the country fastened by their threads to stones are wont to change into a butterfly. Hers is no food familiar in this world of ours: 'tis no one's charge to feed the bird as yet unfledged: she sips ambrosial dews of heavenly nectar fallen in a fine shower from the star-bearing sky. Such is her culling, such her sustenance, encompassed by fragrant spices until she bring her appearance to maturity. But when she begins to bloom in the spring-time of her youth, she flits forth already bent on a return to her ancestral abodes. Yet ere she goes, she takes all that remains of what was her own body — bones or ashes and the shell that was hers — and stores it in balsam oil, myrrh, and frankincense set free, rounding it into ball-shape with loving beak. Bearing this in her talons she speeds to the City of the Sun, and perching on the altar sets it in the hallowed temple. Marvellous is her appearance and the show she makes to the onlooker: such comeliness has the bird, so ample a glory. To begin with, her colour is like the colour which beneath the sunshine of the sky ripe pomegranates cover under their rind; like the colour in the petals of the wild poppy when Flora displays her garb at the blush of dawn. In such a dress gleam her shoulders and comely breast: even so glitter head and neck and surface of the back, while the tail spreads out variegated with a metallic yellow, amid whose spots reddens a purple blend. The wing-feathers are picked out by a contrasted sheen, as 'tis the heaven-sent rainbow's way to illuminate the clouds. The beak is of a fine white with a dash of emerald green, glittering jewel-like in its clear horn as it opens. You would take for twin sapphires those great eyes from between which shoots a bright flame. All over the head is fitted a crown of rays, in lofty likeness to the glory of the Sun-god's head. Scales cover the legs, which are variegated with a metallic yellow, but the tint which colours the claws is a wonderful rose. To the eye it has a blended semblance between the peacock's appearance and the rich-hued bird from Phasis. Its size the winged thing that springs from the Arabs' lands is scarce able to match, whether wild animal it be or bird. Yet 'tis not slow like large-sized birds which are of sluggish movement by reason of their heavy weight, but 'tis light and swift, filled with a royal grace: such is its bearing ever to the eyes of men. Egypt draws nigh to greet the marvel of so great a sight and the crowd joyfully hails the peerless bird. Straightway they grave its form on hallowed marble and with a fresh title mark both the event and the day. Every breed of fowl unites in the assemblage: no bird has thoughts of prey nor yet of fear. Attended by a chorus of winged creatures, she flits through the high air, and the band escorts her, gladdened by their pious task. But when the company has reached the breezes of ether unalloyed, it presently returns: she then ensconces herself in her true haunts. Ah, bird of happy lot and happy end to whom God's own will has granted birth from herself! Female or male she is, which you will—whether neither or both, a happy bird, she regards not any unions of love: to her, death is love; and her sole pleasure lies in death: to win her birth, it is her appetite first to die. Herself she is her own offspring, her own sire and her own heir, herself her own nurse, her own nurseling evermore—herself indeed, yet not the same; because she is both herself and not herself, gaining eternal life by the boon of death.

CLAUDIAN (C. A.D. 370–404)
THE PHOENIX, LETTER TO SERENA

At the end of the classical period of their literary history, both the griffin and the phoenix are among Claudian's animals bearing wedding gifts to Orpheus and Eurydice, and Phoebus Apollo himself ignites the phoenix in "heavenly flame" to assure the bird's immortal cycle.

A Greek-speaking Alexandrian who wrote in Latin, Claudian is regarded as the last important poet of the classical tradition. In the court of the Western emperor Honorius during the final years of barbarian invasions from the north, he wrote a variety of political and military verses, including panegryrics on Honorius and his minister, the Roman general Stilicho, whom Honorius later executed. Stilicho's wife, Serena, arranged Claudian's marriage to one of her protégées.

The passages below come from Claudian's shorter poems: *The Phoenix* and *Letter to Serena*. His retelling of the phoenix fable is heavily indebted to Lactantius's account. Saba was an Arabian town well-known for its spices. The wedding feast of Orpheus, who charmed all nature with his lyre, opens a verse letter to Claudian's patroness. Some consider this work to be the poet's last, written on the occasion of his own marriage, shortly before his death.

The Phoenix*

. . . Now the Phoenix's bright eye grows dim and the pupil becomes palsied by the frost of years, like the moon when she is shrouded in clouds and her horn begins

---

* Claudian, *The Phoenix* and *Letter to Serena*, from *Claudian*, 2 vols, trans. Maurice Platnauer (Cambridge: Harvard University Press, 1922), vol. 2, pp. 227–29, 257.

to vanish in the mist. Now his wings, wont to cleave the clouds of heaven, can scarce raise them from the earth. Then, realizing that his span of life is at an end and in preparation for a renewal of his splendour, he gathers dry herbs from the sun-warmed hills, and making an interwoven heap of the branches of the precious tree of Saba he builds that pyre which shall be at once his tomb and his cradle.

On this he takes his seat and as he grows weaker greets the Sun with his sweet voice; offering up prayers and supplications he begs that those fires will give him renewal of strength. Phoebus, on seeing him afar, checks his reins and staying his course consoles his loving child with these words: "Thou who art about to leave thy years behind upon yon pyre, who, by this pretence of death, art destined to rediscover life; thou whose decease means but the renewal of existence and who by self-destruction regainest thy lost youth, receive back thy life, quit the body that must die, and by a change of form come forth more beauteous than ever."

So speaks he, and shaking his head casts one of his golden hairs and smites willing Phoenix with its life-giving effulgence. Now, to ensure his rebirth, he suffers himself to be burned and in his eagerness to be born again meets death with joy. Stricken with the heavenly flame the fragrant pile catches fire and burns the aged body. The moon in amaze checks her milk-white heifers and heaven halts his revolving spheres, while the pyre conceives the new life; Nature takes care that the deathless bird perish not, and calls upon the sun, mindful of his promise, to restore its immortal glory to the world.

Straightway the life spirit surges through his scattered limbs; the renovated blood floods his veins. The ashes show signs of life; they begin to move though there is none to move them, and feathers clothe the mass of cinders. He who was but now the sire comes forth from the pyre the son and successor; between life and life lay but that brief space wherein the pyre burned. . . .

The Marriage of Orpheus

At the first kindling of Orpheus' marriage-torch when festive Hymen filled the countryside of Thrace the beasts and gay-plumaged birds strove among themselves what best gifts they could bring their poet. Mindful of the cave whose sounding rocks had offered a wondrous theatre for his tuneful lyre, the lynxes brought him crystal from the summits of Caucasus; griffins golden nuggets from regions of the north; doves wreaths of roses and other flowers which they had flown to gather from Venus' meadow; the swan bore from the stream of its native Padus amber broken from the boughs of the famed sisters; while the cranes, after their war with the pygmies, recrossed the Nile and gathered in their mouths the precious pearls of the Red Sea. There came, too, immortal Phoenix from the distant East, bearing rare spices in his curvèd talons. No bird nor beast was there but brought to that marriage-feast tribute so richly deserved by Orpheus' lyre. . . .

HORAPOLLO (4TH CENTURY A.D.?)
THE HIEROGLYPHICS

The only treatise on Egyptian hieroglyphics thought to have survived from antiquity was perhaps produced around the fourth century A.D. by an Egyptian from Nilopolis, one "Horapollon" or "Horus Apollo." Erik Iversen, in his *Myth of Egypt and Its Hieroglyphs*, relates that while neither the *Hieroglyphica* nor its author was directly referred to by other classical writers, an Italian traveler claimed to have discovered a manuscript of the work on a Greek island in 1419. After the book was printed in 1505, it appeared in thirty editions over the next century, becoming for the Renaissance the standard authority on the subject. In the early nineteenth century, Jean François Champollion, the decipherer of the Rosetta Stone, confirmed that the book contained several accurate symbols. Some Egyptologists since have argued that the book's distorted allegorizing impeded the study of hieroglyphics for centuries.

Regardless of its authorship and date of composition, the *Hieroglyphica's* animal lore parallels the *Physiologus* in its moralistic treatment of animals. In Horapollo's book, the filial affection of storks, the self-castration of the hunted beaver, and the poison of the basilisk all look ahead to lore in the medieval bestiaries.

Horapollo's book contains contradictory portrayals of the basilisk, first as the serpent of eternity and second as the deadly beast. His phoenix, associated with the sun, traditionally carries its dead parent to Heliopolis every 500 years, but its death and rebirth differ from the standard fable, and this solar phoenix causes the life-giving and eternal Nile to rise and overflow.

See the phoenix in the Egyptian *Book of the Dead* and Herodotus.

The Hieroglyphic Basilisk and Phoenix*

ETERNITY

When they wish to symbolize Eternity, they draw the sun and the moon, because they are eternal elements. But when they wish to represent Eternity differently, they draw a serpent with its tail concealed by the rest of its body. This the Egyptians call *Ourain*, but the Greeks a *Basilisk*. They make this of gold and put it on the heads of the gods. It symbolizes Eternity because, of the three kinds of serpents, this alone is immortal, the others being mortal. Should it blow upon any other animal, even without biting it, its victim dies. Wherefore, since it seems to have power over life and death, they put it on the heads of the gods.

---

* Horapollo, *The Hieroglyphics of Horapollo*, trans. George Boas (New York: Pantheon Books, 1950), 57, 98, 75, 75, 96–97 (1, 61, 34, 35, 57).

A MAN REVILED BY DENUNCIATION AND GROWN SICK OF IT

When they wish to indicate a man who has been reviled and denounced and has fallen sick because of it, they draw a basilisk. For by his breath the basilisk kills those who approach him.

THE SOUL DELAYING HERE A LONG TIME

When they wish to depict the soul delaying here a long time, or a flood, they draw the phoenix. The soul, since of all things in the universe, this beast is the longest-lived. And a flood, since the phoenix is the symbol of the sun, than which nothing in the universe is greater. For the sun is above all things and looks down upon all things. And therefore it is named *polus*.

THE RETURN OF THE LONG-ABSENT TRAVELLER

To indicate a traveller returned from a long journey, again do they draw a phoenix. For this bird in Egypt, when the time of its death is about to overtake it, is 500 years old. After its debt is paid, if it does as fate decrees in Egypt, its funeral rites are conducted in accordance with the mysteries. And whatever the Egyptians do in the case of the other sacred animals, the same do they feel obliged to do for the phoenix. For it is said by the Egyptians beyond all other birds to cherish the sun, wherefore the Nile overflows for them because of the warmth of this god. . . .

A LONG-ENDURING RESTORATION

When they wish to indicate a long-enduring restoration, they draw the phoenix. For when this bird is born, there is a renewal of things. And it is born in this way. When the phoenix is about to die, it casts itself upon the ground and is crushed. And from the ichor pouring out of the wound, another is born. And this one immediately sprouts wings and flies off with its sire to Heliopolis in Egypt and once there, at the rising of the sun, the sire dies. And with the death of the sire, the young one returns to its own country. And the Egyptian priests bury the dead phoenix.

Part

Beasts
of God

11

The Sixth Day of Creation, a late eleventh-century or early twelfth-century Italian ivory plaque of God creating the animals. Among the creatures are a cockatrice and a griffin. By permission of The Cloisters, Metropolitan Museum of Art, New York. Gift of J. Pierpont Morgan, 1917.

As the classical world declines, animals of the imagination enter expanding Christianity from other ancient sources. Translated from Hebrew texts into Greek in the third and second centuries B.C., the Septuagint contains words later rendered as "phoenix," "dragon," "unicorn," and "basilisk." The Church Fathers, basing religious teachings on holy scripture, make the phoenix a sign of resurrection and the unicorn an embodiment of the divine and earthly natures of Christ. Animal tales from Near Eastern, European, and Asian traditions are collected in the *Physiologus*, perhaps in Egypt in the second century A.D., and later allegorized by Christian writers into lessons on good and evil, God and Satan. The *Physiologus*, in turn, evolves over centuries into the bestiary and is translated into languages from Arabic to Icelandic. Actual and imaginary animals alike then spread from bestiaries into encyclopedias, and bestiary art influences cathedral sculpture and other Christian iconography.

During the centuries-long development of the *Physiologus* and the medieval bestiaries, animals of the imagination figure in many other kinds of stories: in epics, chronicles, saints' lives, monks' tales, and romances. Most of these are from Northern Europe, and most are copied, adapted, or composed by ecclesiastics. Beowulf and St. George meet the dragon in mortal combat. St. Columba confronts the monster of Loch Ness, and Alexander the Great devises a stratagem to rid a city wall of the basilisk. In Scandinavian mythology, the god Thor fishes for the cosmic Midgard Serpent. Often portrayed as evil during the Middle Ages, the griffin assumes a totally different role in Dante's *Divine Comedy*, in which it pulls the chariot of the Church and ascends to Paradise.

Prefiguring the Age of Exploration, medieval travelers of the twelfth to the fourteenth centuries venture into lands no Europeans had ever seen. Mixed with the tales of actual travelers such as Benjamin of Tudela, Marco Polo, and Ibn Battuta are the legendary voyage of St. Brendan and the influential hoaxes of *The Letter of Prester John* and the *Travels* of Sir John Mandeville. Among the exotic animals from the fabled Western Isles to the China Seas are creatures of the imagination.

Scripture and Apochrypha 3

THE BIBLE

The presence of fantastic creatures in various translations of the sacred writings of Judaism and Christianity forms an essential part of the animals' histories. Mention of several of them in various translations of the Bible — the supreme written authority for the Middle Ages — validated their existence and helped establish their symbolic roles in medieval literature and art.

The scriptural phoenix, unicorn, basilisk, and dragon, as well as others, were all cited in allegorical commentaries of the Church Fathers and in the *Physiologus*. Canonical authority gave credence to the animals' natural history right up through Edward Topsell's 1607 edition of his *Historie of Foure-Footed Beastes* and became a central issue in the seventeenth-century debate over their existence. Also in the Bible are animals of a more mythical character, including Behemoth and Leviathan and the apocalyptic beasts of Revelation.

The Hebrew texts of the Old Testament were first translated into Greek in the third and second centuries B.C. According to legend, the name of the work, the Septuagint, derived from its composition by a group of seventy-two Jewish scholars. St. Jerome's Vulgate, the Bible of the Western Church, was a commissioned Latin translation from Old Testament Hebrew and New Testament Greek, completed by a group of Christian translators around A.D. 404. The most influential English translation, revised since, is the 1611 Authorized King James Version,

> Ask now the beasts, and they shall teach thee.
>
> —Job 12.7

95

Fabulous creatures with actual animals in a twelfth-century marble arch, perhaps from the former French church of St. Cosmus. *Left to right*: a manticore, pelican, cockatrice, siren, griffin, amphisbaena or dragon, centaur, and lion. By permission of The Cloisters, Metropolitan Museum of Art, New York, Kennedy Fund.

"translated out of the original tongues." All or part of the Bible now exists in more than a thousand languages.

Biblical animals reflect the complex evolution of the texts over millennia. A single animal may have different names in different translations, and a single name may be used for several different animals. Some original names have not been positively identified. Some animals denoted by European translators were probably not known to biblical writers.

A fabulous animal in one translation may be an actual animal in another. The King James Version contains fantastic beasts that do not always appear in corresponding passages in other — especially later — translations, namely the unicorn, dragon, and the cockatrice (basilisk). These animals were still generally accepted in the natural history of the early seventeenth century, when the Authorized Version was produced. Since the discrediting of such creatures later in the century, biblical translators have tended to select the names of actual animals over those of their imaginary counterparts. Nineteenth-century natural history writers were particularly intent upon matching biblical beasts with living animals.

The Hebrew *reêm* became the Greek *monoceros*, the Latin *unicornus*, and the King James *unicorn*. The King James "unicorn" is, in some other versions, "wild ox." The biblical "dragon" is sometimes a large serpent or sea monster; the "dragons" in Job's powerful lament, "I am a brother to dragons" (Job 30:29), is apparently a mistranslation of the Hebrew *tan*, elsewhere translated as "jackal" or "wolf." The "cockatrice" is elsewhere rendered "viper." Isaiah's fiery flying serpent (Is. 14:29) has been interpreted as a darter, a long-billed snakebird with a metaphorically burning bite.

The King James Bible does not contain the phoenix, but the immortal bird does appear in Catholic versions. "I would say, in my nest I shall die and like the Phoenix extend my days" (Job 29:18) is, in King James, "I shall die in my nest, and I shall multiply my days as the sand." Other versions also use "sand," sometimes with a note: "or phoenix." For the Douai Bible translation of "Phoenix" in "The just man will flourish like a Phoenix" (Ps. 92:12), the King James, and others, use "palm-tree."

The griffin of the Bible is the griffon vulture, not the fabulous beast.

Behemoth and Leviathan—usually identified, respectively, with either the hippopotamus or elephant, and the crocodile or the whale—have mythic grandeur in the heightened language of the climactic chapters of Job. In Jewish mythology, Behemoth embodies the powers of the land and Leviathan the powers of the sea, while Islamic tradition holds that Behemoth is the foundation of the world. In the Leviathan passage, "neesings" is an archaic form of "sneeze." Apocalyptic vision shapes the composite locusts and the "great red dragon" of the Revelation of St. John the Divine. The locusts, with faces of men and the tails of scorpions, are reminiscent of the scorpion-men born of Babylonian Tiamat.

Following is a representative sampling of biblical references to fantastic and mythical creatures. All the entries are from the Authorized King James Version. All the passages excepting those on the beasts of Revelation are from the Old Testament, many from the book of Job and the prophets. Verse numbers have been dropped from the body of the text.

For direct citings of scriptural authority to validate the actuality or the religious symbolism of particular animals, see especially the Church Fathers, the medieval bestiaries, and Edward Topsell. For debate over biblical authority, see Sir Thomas Browne and Alexander Ross. For the discrediting of most fabulous beasts in the Bible, see J. G. Wood. Also, see D. H. Lawrence's apocalyptic dragon, Gustav Flaubert's fictionalization of the vision of St. Anthony, and Julian Barnes's novelistic treatment of fabulous beasts on Noah's ark.

The Cockatrice

The wolf also shall dwell with the lamb, and the leopard shall lie down with the kid; and the calf and the young lion and the fatling together; and a little child shall lead them. And the cow and the bear shall feed; their young ones shall lie down together: and the lion shall eat straw like the ox. And the sucking child shall play on the hole of the asp, and the weaned child shall put his hand on the cockatrice' den. They shall not hurt nor destroy in all my holy mountain: for the earth shall be full of the knowledge of the Lord, as the waters cover the sea.

Isaiah 11:6–9

Rejoice not thou, whole Palestina, because the rod of him that smote thee is broken: for out of the serpent's root shall come forth a cockatrice, and his fruit shall be a fiery flying serpent.

Isaiah 14:29

None calleth for justice, nor any pleadeth for truth: they trust in vanity, and speak lies; they conceive mischief, and bring forth iniquity. They hatch cockatrice' eggs, and weave the spider's web: he that eateth of their eggs dieth, and that which is crushed breaketh out into a viper.

Isaiah 59:4–5

For, behold, I will send serpents, cockatrices, among you, which will not be charmed, and they shall bite you, saith the Lord.

Jeremiah 8:17

The Dragon

And I went out by night by the gate of the valley, even before the dragon well, and to the dung port, and viewed the walls of Jerusalem, which were broken down, and the gates thereof were consumed with fire.

Nehemiah 2:13

I am a brother to dragons, and a companion to owls.

Job 30:29

Praise the Lord from the earth, ye dragons, and all deeps. . . .

Psalms 148:7

The beasts of the field shall honour me, the dragons and the owls: because I give waters in the wilderness, and rivers in the desert, to give drink to my people, my chosen.

Isaiah 43:20

And I will make Jerusalem heaps, and a den of dragons; and I will make the cities of Judah desolate, without an inhabitant.

Jeremiah 9:11

The Unicorn

God brought them out of Egypt; he hath as it were the strength of an unicorn.

Numbers 23:22

[PROPHECY OF MOSES]

And for the precious things of the earth and fulness thereof, and for the good will of him that dwelt in the bush: let the blessing come upon the head of Joseph, and upon the top of the head of him that was separated from his brethren. His glory is like the firstling of his bullock, and his horns are like the horns of unicorns: with them he shall push the people together to the ends of the earth. . . .

Deuteronomy 33:16–17

[THE LORD SPEAKING TO JOB OUT OF THE WHIRLWIND]

Will the unicorn be willing to serve thee, or abide by thy crib? Canst thou bind the unicorn with his band in the furrow? or will he harrow the valleys after thee? Wilt thou trust him, because his strength is great? or wilt thou leave thy labour to him? Wilt thou believe him, that he will bring home thy seed, and gather it into thy barn?

Job 39:9–12

The voice of the Lord breaketh the cedars; yea, the Lord breaketh the cedars of Lebanon. He maketh them also to skip like a calf; Lebanon and Sirion like a young unicorn.

Psalms 29:5–6

For, lo, thine enemies, O Lord, for, lo, thine enemies shall perish; all the workers of iniquity shall be scattered. But my horn shalt thou exalt like the horn of an unicorn: I shall be anointed with fresh oil.

Psalms 92:9–10

And the unicorns shall come down with them, and the bullocks with the bulls; and their land shall be soaked with blood, and their dust made fat with fatness.

Isaiah 34:5–7

Behemoth and Leviathan

[THE LORD SPEAKING TO JOB OUT OF THE WHIRLWIND]

Behold now behemoth, which I made with thee; he eateth grass as an ox. Lo now, his strength is in his loins, and his force is in the navel of his belly. He moveth his tail like a cedar: the sinews of his stones are wrapped together. His bones are as strong pieces of brass; his bones are like bars of iron. He is the chief of the ways of God: he that made him can make his sword to approach unto him. Surely the mountains bring him forth food, where all the beasts of the field play. He lieth under the shady trees, in the covert of the reed, and fens. The shady trees cover him with their shadow; the willows of the brook compass him about. Behold, he drinketh up a river, and hasteth not: he trusteth that he can draw up Jordan into his mouth. He taketh it with his eyes: his nose pierceth through snares.

Canst thou draw out leviathan with an hook? or his tongue with a cord which thou lettest down? Canst thou put an hook into his nose? or bore his jaw through with a thorn? . . . Who can open the doors of his face? his teeth are terrible round about. His scales are his pride, shut up together as with a close seal. One is so near to another, that no air can come between them. They are joined one to another, they stick together, that they cannot be sundered. By his neesings a light doth shine, and his eyes are like the eyelids of the morning. Out of his mouth go burning lamps, and sparks of fire leap out. Out of his nostrils goeth smoke, as out of a seething pot or cauldron. His breath kindleth coals, and a flame goeth out of his mouth. . . . He maketh the deep to boil like a pot: he maketh the sea like a pot of ointment. He maketh a path to shine after him; one would think the deep to be hoary. Upon earth there is not his like, who is made without fear. He beholdeth all high things: he is a king over all the children of pride.

Job 40:15–24; 41:1–2, 14–21, 31–34

Beasts of the Apocalypse

And the fifth angel sounded, and I saw a star fall from heaven unto the earth: and to him was given the key of the bottomless pit. And he opened the bottomless pit: and there arose a smoke out of the pit, as the smoke of a great furnace; and the sun and the air were darkened by reason of the smoke of the pit. And there came out of the smoke locusts upon the earth: and unto them was given power, as the scorpions of the earth have power. . . . And the shapes of the locusts were like unto horses prepared unto battle; and on their heads were as it were crowns like gold, and their faces were as the faces of men. And they had hair as the hair of women, and their teeth were as the teeth of lions. And they had breastplates, as it were breastplates of iron; and the sound of their wings was as the sound of chariots of many horses running to battle. And they had tails like unto scorpions, and there were stings in their tails: and their power was to hurt men five months.

Revelation 9:1–3, 7–10

And there appeared another wonder in heaven; and behold a great red dragon, having seven heads and ten horns, and seven crowns upon his heads. . . . And

The War in Heaven. St. Michael and his angels cast out the great dragon, Satan, and his angels. Early fourteenth century, Normandy, France, from the Cloisters Apocalypse. Fol. 20v. By permission of Metropolitan Museum of Art, New York, The Cloisters Collection, 1968.

there was war in heaven: Michael and his angels fought against the dragon; and the dragon fought and the angels, and prevailed not; neither was their place found any more in heaven. And the great dragon was cast out, that old serpent, called the Devil, and Satan, which deceiveth the whole world: he was cast out into the earth, and his angels were cast out with him.

Revelation 12:3, 7–10

THE GREEK APOCALYPSE OF BARUCH
(2ND CENTURY A.D.?)

In the Judaic *Greek Apocalypse of Baruch*, an archangel appears to Baruch as he weeps over the destruction of Jerusalem and tells him, "Come, and I will show thee the mysteries of God." The angel guides the prophet past dog-like men with the feet of stags, past the Dragon of Hades and Adam's tree in the Earthly Paradise and on up through the heavens. At the third heaven, the phoenix of oriental tradition accompanies the chariot of the sun through the day, absorbing the sun's heat with its own body to protect sinful mankind.

Like the Egyptian *benu* and the fabled classical bird, Baruch's phoenix is a sunbird. Similar to its European counterpart at different stages of development, this phoenix has wings of fire; renewed at dawn, it stretches its wings with the rising sun. Also, cinnamon and a worm figure in both classical writings and Baruch's account of the bird. While the European bird continually dies and is reborn at an interval of centuries, the Jewish bird passes through a daily cycle of renewal and exhaustion. Baruch's gigantic bird, whose wings cover the sun, has characteristics in common with the Jewish *ziz*, the Persian *simurg*, the Arabian *anka* and *rukh*, and other oriental "wonder birds."

The Greek Apocalypse of Baruch (3 Baruch) is one of several religious books attributed to the friend and secretary of the prophet Jeremiah (seventh century B.C.), beginning with the apocryphal *Book of Baruch*. Other apocalyptic versions include a Syriac text and the Slavonic condensation of the *Greek Apocalypse*. Mentioned by the third-century A.D. Church Father Origen, the incomplete *Greek Apocalypse* (it ends in the fifth of presumably seven heavens) was virtually unknown to the West until it was edited and published by M. R. James in 1897. Italics and brackets have been omitted from the excerpt below.

For other apocalyptic beasts, see Revelation and Gustav Flaubert. For oriental "wonder birds," see Sir Henry Yule.

The Phoenix of the Third Heaven*

And he took me and led me where the sun goes forth; and he showed me a chariot and four, under which burnt a fire, and in the chariot was sitting a man, wearing a crown of fire, and the chariot was drawn by forty angels. And behold a bird circling before the sun, and about nine cubits away. And I said to the angel, What is this bird? And he said to me, This is the guardian of the earth. And I said, Lord, how is he the guardian of the earth? Teach me. And the angel said to me, This bird flies alongside of the sun, and expanding his wings receives its fiery rays. For if he were not receiving them, the human race would not be preserved, nor any other living creature. But God appointed this bird thereto. And he expanded his wings, and I saw on his right wing very large letters, as large as the space of a threshing-floor, the size of about four thousand modii; and the letters were of

* *The Greek Apocalypse of Baruch*, from *Pseudepigrapha*, vol. 2 of *The Apocrypha and Pseudepigrapha of the Old Testament*, ed. R. H. Charles (Oxford: Clarendon Press, 1913), 536–38.

gold. And the angel said to me, Read them. And I read, and they ran thus: Neither earth nor heaven bring me forth, but wings of fire bring me forth. And I said, Lord, what is this bird, and what is his name? And the angel said to me, His name is called Phoenix. (And I said), And what does he eat? And he said to me, The manna of heaven and the dew of earth. And I said, Does the bird excrete? And he said to me, He excretes a worm, and the excrement of the worm is cinnamon, which kings and princes use. But wait and thou shalt see the glory of God. And while he was conversing with me, there was as a thunder-clap, and the place was shaken on which we were standing. And I asked the angel, My Lord, what is this sound? And the angel said to me, Even now the angels are opening the three hundred and sixty-five gates of heaven, and the light is being separated from the darkness. And a voice came which said, Light-giver, give to the world radiance. And when I heard the noise of the bird, I said, Lord, what is this noise? And he said, This is the bird who awakens from slumber the cocks upon earth. For as men do through the mouth, so also does the cock signify to those in the world, in his own speech. For the sun is made ready by the angels, and the cock crows.

And I said, And where does the sun begin its labours, after the cock crows? And the angel said to me, Listen, Baruch: All things whatsoever I showed thee are in the first and second heaven, and in the third heaven the sun passes through and gives light to the world. But wait, and thou shalt see the glory of God. And while I was conversing with him, I saw the bird, and he appeared in front, and grew less and less, and at length returned to his full size. And behind him I saw the shining sun, and the angels which draw it, and a crown upon its head, the sight of which we were not able to gaze upon, and behold. And as soon as the sun shone, the Phoenix also stretched out his wings. But I, when I beheld such great glory, was brought low with great fear, and I fled and hid in the wings of the angel. And the angel said to me, Fear not, Baruch, but wait and thou shalt also see the setting.

And he took me and led me towards the west; and when the time of the setting came, I saw again the bird coming before it, and as soon as he came I saw the angels, and they lifted the crown from its head. But the bird stood exhausted and with wings contracted. And beholding these things, I said, Lord, wherefore did they lift the crown from the head of the sun, and wherefore is the bird so exhausted? And the angel said to me, The crown of the sun, when it has run through the day — four angels take it, and bear it up to heaven, and renew it, because it and its rays have been defiled upon earth; moreover it is so renewed each day. And I Baruch said, Lord, and wherefore are its beams defiled upon earth? And the angel said to me, Because it beholds the lawlessness and unrighteousness of men, namely fornications, adulteries, thefts, extortions, idolatries, drunkenness, murders, strife, jealousies, evil-speakings, murmurings, whisperings, divinations, and such like, which are not well-pleasing to God. On account of these things is it defiled, and therefore is it renewed. But thou askest concerning the bird, how it is exhausted. Because by restraining the rays of the sun through the fire and burning heat of the whole day, it is exhausted thereby. For, as we said before, unless his wings were screening the rays of the sun, no living creature would be preserved.

And they having retired, the night also fell, and at the same time came the chariot of the moon, along with the stars. . . .

Allegories of the Fathers

St. Clement (1st century a.d.)
Epistle to the Corinthians

A letter by St. Clement of Rome to the church of Corinth is one of the earliest writings to interpret the phoenix as a Christian symbol of the resurrection of the flesh. St. Clement I (the first of fourteen popes bearing the name) is generally regarded as the third successor of Peter as Bishop of Rome. The lengthy, authoritative letter rebuking lay Corinthians for recklessly ejecting clergy was unsigned, but it was attributed to him without question. A rare reproof of one Christian community by another, the letter (c. a.d. 96) reiterated the beliefs of the early Church and stressed obedience to God and His earthly representatives.

By superimposing the Christian tradition upon the concurrent classical story, the *Epistle to the Corinthians* is a critical document in the literary history of the fabled bird. Clement composed his letter five centuries after Herodotus introduced the bird to the West, shortly after Pliny's account, and centuries before classical summing up of the tale and the addition of the element of fire in the poems of Lactantius and Claudian. While Clement's phoenix is a reiteration of traditional lore from authors skeptical about the bird, Clement states directly that, "There is a bird which is called the phoenix," accepting the "strange phenomenon" from the East as natural history. He then asks rhetorically if it is little wonder that God bestows resurrection on

What can be more express and more significant for our subject; or to what other thing can such a phenomenon bear witness?

—Tertullian
On the Resurrection of the Flesh

believers, "considering that He demonstrates the greatness of His promise by means even of a bird?"

The letter, publicly read in Corinth throughout the century following its composition, was revered by the early Church, perhaps even integrated into the liturgy of the Eucharist. The Christian allegorization of the phoenix flourished for a millennium in the writings of the Church Fathers, the bestiaries, and in religious art.

Chapter headings and verse numbers have been omitted.

See the classical phoenix of Herodotus, Ovid, and Pliny, and the Christian phoenix of St. Ambrose and the Latin *Physiologus*.

The Phoenix a Sign of Resurrection*

Let us consider, beloved, how the Lord is continually revealing to us the resurrection that is to be. Of this He has constituted the Lord Jesus Christ the first-fruits, by raising Him from the dead. Let us look, beloved, at the resurrection in regard to the seasons. Day and night demonstrate a resurrection: the night sleeps and the day arises; the day departs and night returns. Let us take the crops, to see how and in what manner the planting takes place. "The sower sent forth" and cast each of the seeds into the ground, and they, falling on the ground dry and bare, decay. Then from their decay the greatness of the Lord's providence raises them up, and from one seed many grow up and bring forth fruit.

Let us look at the strange phenomenon which takes place in the East, that is, in the regions near Arabia. There is a bird which is called the phoenix. This bird, the only one of its species, lives five hundred years. As the time of its dissolution in death approaches, it makes a nest of incense and myrrh and other spices, into which it enters when its time is completed, and dies. Now, as its flesh decays a worm is born, which is nourished by the moisture of the dead bird and grows wings. Then, growing strong, it picks up that nest, in which are the bones of its predecessor, and carries them from the country of Arabia as far as Egypt, to the city called Heliopolis. And in the daylight, in the sight of all, flying to the altar of the Sun, it places them there and so sets out on its return. Then the priests look up the records of the years, and they find that it has come at the end of the five-hundredth year.

Do we think it something great and marvellous, then, if the Creator of the universe shall bring about a resurrection of those who served Him in holiness, in the confidence of a good faith, considering that He demonstrates the greatness of His

*   *The Letter of St. Clement of Rome to the Corinthians*, trans. by Francis X. Glimm, from *The Apostolic Fathers* volume of *The Fathers of the Church* series (New York: Christian Heritage, 1948), 29–31 (chapters 24–27).

promise by means even of a bird? For He says somewhere: "And Thou shalt raise me up, and I will praise Thee," and "I lay down and slept; I rose up for Thou art with me." And again, Job says: "And Thou shalt raise up this flesh of mine which has endured all these things."

With this hope, then, let our souls be bound to Him who is faithful in His promises and just in His judgments. . . .

St. Basil (c. a.d. 330–79)
Exegetic Homilies

Variously translated from the Hebrew *reêm* as "monoceros," "wild ox," and "buffalo," the unicorn of Scripture became one of the most important symbolic animals in early and medieval Christianity. The dual natures of Christ and the unicorn are explicated in a sermon of St. Basil the Great, a fourth-century bishop of Caesarea. In the homily, Christ is both the sacrificial Lamb of God and the fierce Son of unicorns, while the unicorn represents both baseness and divine glory and power. Most of the biblical references to the unicorn — and most of them are from the Psalms — are cited in the sermon.

Born in Caesarea of a wealthy Christian family, St. Basil was a major organizer of monasticism in the Eastern Church. Both his brothers were bishops, and his sister, Macrina, established her own monastic community. One of his best-known writings defends the role of pagan literature in Christian education. The Greek *Physiologus* was sometimes attributed to him.

See the unicorn in the Bible, the Greek *Physiologus*, and J. G. Wood.

The Son of Unicorns *

Remember the calf in Exodus, which they fashioned through idolatry, which Moses beat to powder and gave to the people to drink. In a manner similar to that calf, He will utterly destroy all Libanus and the practice of idolatry prevailing in it. "And as the beloved son of unicorns." The only-begotten Son, He who gives His life for the world whenever He offers Himself as a sacrifice and oblation to God for our sins, is called both Lamb of God and a Sheep. "Behold," it is said, "the lamb of God." And again: "He was led like a sheep to slaughter." But, when

---

* St. Basil, *Exegetic Homilies*, trans. Sister Agnes Clare Way, vol. 46 of *The Fathers of the Church* (Washington, D.C.: Catholic University of America, 1963), 204–5.

Madonna and unicorn, depicting association of the unicorn with Christ. By permission of
The Pierpont Morgan Library, New York.

it is necessary to take vengeance and to overthrow the power attacking the race of men, a certain wild and savage force, then He will be called the Son of unicorns. For, as we have learned in Job, the unicorn is a creature, irresistible in might and unsubjected to man. "For, thou canst not bind him with a thong," he says, "nor will he stay at thy crib." There is also much said in that part of the prophecy about the animal acting like a free man and not submitting to men. It has been observed that the Scripture has used the comparison of the unicorn in both ways, at one time in praise, at another in censure. "Deliver," he says, "my soul from the sword . . . and my lowness from the horns of the unicorns." He said these words complaining of the warlike people who in the time of passion rose up in rebellion against him. Again, he says, "My horn shall be exalted like that of the unicorn." It seems that on account of the promptness of the animal in repelling attacks it is frequently found representing the baser things, and because of its high horn and freedom it is assigned to represent the better. On the whole, since it is possible to find the "horn" used by Scripture in many places instead of "glory," as the saying: "He will exalt the horn of his people," and "His horn shall be exalted in glory," or also, since the "horn" is frequently used instead of "power," as the saying: "My protector and the horn of my salvation," Christ is the power of God; therefore, He is called the Unicorn on the ground that He has one horn, that is, one common power with the Father.

St. Ambrose (c. a.d. 339–97)
Hexameron

Son of a prefect, educated in Rome, and popularly elected Bishop of Milan even prior to his baptism, St. Ambrose is credited with introducing Eastern Church thought into the Latin Church. In his writings interlaced with scripture are Christian interpretations of the phoenix.

St. Ambrose's series of sermons on the six days of creation (a.d. 386–88) contains many echoes of St. Basil's treatment of the same subject less than twenty years before. "The oarage of his wings" is from Virgil, another important source of the Ambrose *Hexameron*. The phoenix, by Ambrose's time an established symbol of Christian resurrection, was among the animals created on the fifth day. Unlike St. Clement, St. Ambrose qualifies the story. No fire is mentioned in the tale, even though the homily was composed after the *Phoenix* of Lactantius, in which fire is an important element in the bird's cycle of death and rebirth. Description of the creature followed by a *significatio* is structurally similar to entries in *Physiologus* and the bestiaries. St. Ambrose's instructive moral is an elaborate allegory equating the phoenix nest with a casket, the casket with human faith, and even martyred St. Paul with the phoenix.

The *Hexameron* contains a description of the partridge that parallels a passage from a Latin *Physiologus*, early evidence of the existence of that collection, and the Ambrose sermons were an important source of the later bestiaries. Ambrose was one of several Church Fathers credited with producing the *Physiologus*.

See the Christian phoenix in the Bible, St. Clement, and the Latin *Physiologus*. For other hexamerons containing fabulous animals, see not only St. Basil but also Du Bartas and John Swan.

The Phoenix and the Resurrection*

These matters [ed., transformations of the silkworm and chameleon] have been mentioned in order that you may be aroused by the force of such examples as these to a belief in the change which will be ours at the Resurrection. We refer to that change which the Apostle clearly indicates when he says: "We shall all indeed rise, but we shall not all be changed." And further on he says: "And the dead shall rise incorruptible and we shall be changed. For this corruptible body must put on incorruption and this mortal body must put on immortality." Many, interpreting the nature and appearance of that transformation which they have not attained, are not without giving it an incongruous explanation, based on an anticipation which they do not merit.

In the regions of Arabia there is reported to be a bird called the phoenix. This bird is said to reach the ripe old age of 500 years. When the phoenix realizes that he is coming to the end of his life, he builds himself a casket of incense, myrrh, and other aromatic plants, into which he enters and dies when his time has come. From the moisture proceeding from his flesh he comes to life again. In the course of time this bird puts on "the oarage of his wings" until he is restored to his primitive form and appearance. By the very act of his resurrection the phoenix furnishes us a lesson by setting before us the very emblems of our own resurrection without the aid of precedent or of reason. We accept the fact that birds exist for the sake of man. The contrary is not true: that man exists for the sake of birds. We have here an example of the loving care which the Author and Creator of the birds has for His own saints. These He does not allow to perish, just as He does not permit in the case of one sole bird when He willed that the phoenix should rise again, born of his own seed. Who, then, announces to him the day of his death, so that he makes for himself a casket, fills it with goodly aromas, and then enters it to die there where pleasant perfumes succeed in crowding out the foul odor of death?

* St. Ambrose, *The Six Days of Creation,* from *Saint Ambrose; Hexameron, Paradise, and Cain and Abel,* trans. John J. Savage, vol. 42 of *The Fathers of the Church* (New York: Fathers of the Church, 1961), 219–20.

You, too, man, should avail yourself of a casket: "strip off the old man with his deeds and put on the new." Your casket, your sheath, is Christ who protects and conceals you in the day of evil. Do you wish to be convinced that it is a casket of protection? "In my quiver he hath hidden me," Scripture declares. The casket, then, is your faith. Fill it with the goodly aroma of your virtues, that is, of chastity, compassion, and justice, and immerse yourself wholly in the inmost mysteries of faith, which are fragrant with the sweet odors of your significant deeds. May your exit from this life find you clothed with that faith, so that "your bones may be made fat" and "be like a watered garden," thus coming to life and flourishing. Be aware, therefore, of the day of your death, as the Apostle Paul realized when he said: "I have fought the good fight, I have finished the course, I have kept the faith. There is laid up for me a crown of justice." Like the good phoenix, he entered his casket, filling it with the sweet aroma of martyrdom.

POPE GREGORY I (c. a.d. 540–604)
MORALS ON THE BOOK OF JOB

The deadly classical basilisk becomes a symbol of Satan in medieval art and theological writings. In his textbook of biblical commentary and moral teachings, Pope Gregory the Great equates the basilisk, Leviathan, and the Beast of the Apocalypse with "the head of the sons of perdition." Isaiah is a major scriptural source for his explications on the basilisk, while the monster's poisonous breath derives from the classical tradition represented by Pliny. Gregory also cites verses from Job describing the mythical Leviathan.

Prior to becoming pope, Gregory began writing his influential *Morals on the Book of Job* (*Moralia*) while serving as papal ambassador to the court of Constantinople. Gregorian chants are traditionally attributed to his development of the liturgy.

See the Bible. For Leviathan, also see Milton. For the basilisk, see Heinrich Kramer and James Sprenger, and the biblical "cockatrice" of J. G. Wood.

Leviathan a Basilisk*

Out of his nostrils goeth smoke.
For the sight of the eyes is pained by smoke. Smoke is therefore said to go out of his nostrils; because by the craft of his miracles a darkening doubt is generated for

---

* Pope Gregory, *Morals on the Book of Job* (London, 1844), vol. 31, pp. 612–13.

an instant even in the heart of the Elect. A smoke goes out of the mouth of Leviathan, because, on account of his lying wonders, a mist of alarm confuses the eyes even of good minds. For when his terrible signs have been seen, then do gloomy thoughts crowd together in the hearts of the Elect. . . .

As of a heated and boiling pot.
For at that time every soul is as a boiling pot, sustaining the assaults of its thoughts, like the foam of boiling waters, which both the fire of zeal puts in motion, and temporal oppression, after the manner of a pot, keeps confined within. Whence John also, when relating the wonders of this beast, added, *So that he maketh fire come down from heaven.* For fire to come down from heaven, is for flames of zeal to pour forth from the heavenly souls of the Elect. But because this Leviathan is called in another place not merely a serpent, but also a basilisk, because he rules over unclean spirits, or reprobate men, as Isaiah says, *Out of the serpent's root shall come forth a basilisk,* we must attentively observe how a basilisk destroys, that by the doings of the basilisk, his malice may be more plainly made known to us. For a basilisk does not destroy with its bite, but consumes with its breath. It often also infects the air with its breath, and withers with the mere blast of its nostrils whatever it has touched, even when placed at a distance.

We are hence, then, compelled to consider, because smoke is said to proceed from his nostrils, even before he appears openly, what he is daily working in the hearts of men by the smoke of his pestilent breath. For because, as we said also above, the sight of the eyes is weakened by smoke, smoke is rightly said to proceed from the nostrils of him, by whose hurtful inspirations an evil thought arises in the hearts of men, by which the keenness of the mind is blunted, so that the inward light is not seen. . . .

A Fabulous Bestiary 5

astern Mediterranean animal lore from folk tradition—given written form in the Egyptian *Book of the Dead*, the Septuagint, and the works of classical writers, notably Herodotus, Pliny the Elder, and Aelian—flourished throughout the Middle Ages in the *Physiologus* and its expanded later version, the bestiary. The phoenix and unicorn numbered among the fabulous creatures in the most ancient version of this collection of moralized animal tales, and other fantastic beasts joined them as the book grew over the span of a thousand years, becoming one of the most widely disseminated and most popular books of medieval times.

"Physiologus" is usually translated as "the naturalist," probably referring at first to the author and eventually to the book itself. Although the author, location, and date of the original compilation are obscure, specialists generally agree that the collected descriptions of nearly fifty animals, trees, and minerals were composed in Greek in or near Alexandria, perhaps as early as the second century A.D. Material in the collection derived primarily from the heterogeneous body of Egyptian, Indian, Hebrew, Greek, and Roman folklore. Among the animals from the book's supposed area of origin are the Egyptian crocodile, hydrus, ibis, ichneumon, and the phoenix, animals also included in the *Hieroglyphica* of Horapollo (perhaps fourth century).

Animal entries in the book typically begin with a quotation from the Bible, followed by "Physiologus says," then a legend of the creature, an allegorical religious interpretation in the exegetical manner of the Church Fathers, and the closing, "Physiologus speaks well (or 'wisely') of the . . . ." The structure

The creatures of this sensible world signify the invisible things of God.

—St. Bonaventure

Griffin. Typical of bestiaries, the beast is depicted as predatory. Harley MS 4751, folio 7v. By permission of the British Library.

and content of *Physiologus* entries suggest that a Christian writer or writers added biblical references and interpretive *significatios* to ancient folkloric material to teach Christian lessons to the lay faithful. Different traditions held that Solomon or Aristotle composed the animal legends and that Basil allegorized them. Ambrose, John Chrysostom, Epiphanius, and Jerome were also among the many churchmen thought to have used *Physiologus* material and credited with composition of the work.

While the original composition no longer exists, the Greek *Physiologus* is extant in several versions. By the fifth century, it had been translated into Arabic, Armenian, Ethiopian, and Syriac in the Near East, and into Latin in the West. In A.D. 496, Pope Gelasius I purportedly placed the Latin *Physiologus* on the Church Index. The oldest extant Latin translations are from the eighth to the tenth centuries, earlier papal condemnation notwithstanding.

By the twelfth century, the *Physiologus* had been expanded and transformed into a new kind of book of nature. The "bestiary" incorporated the etymological approach and animal lore of the encyclopedist Isidore of Seville (c. 560–636), and beasts both actual and fantastic—many from the works of Pliny, Solinus, and Aelian—multiplied in number, swelling the size of the collection. The fabulous leucrota, manticore, yale, cinomolgus, basilisk, and amphisbaena joined a host of domestic animals, birds, fish, reptiles, and worms not in the *Physiologus*. Some bestiaries contained three times the number of *Physiologus* entries. Unclassified in the *Physiologus*, animals were ordered in sections based upon Isidore's categories of beasts, birds, reptiles and fishes, beginning with the lion in its ancient position as king of all the beasts. Even introductions to the sections were added, and typically, the bestiaries were also enlarged by the addition of paintings illustrating the text. While the *Physiologus* was rarely illustrated, the bestiaries tended to be lavishly illuminated, creating animal models for other forms of Christian art.

It is estimated that 90 percent of the animal entries in the *Physiologus* and bestiaries are based upon actual animals. Most of the standard versions of both genres contain the phoenix and unicorn (monoceros), the classic siren and onocentaur (usually in a single entry), and the Hydra. The caladrius, the aspidochelone (whale), salamander, echeneis (remora), and serra (sawfish, swordfish, flying fish) are all actual animals with particularly fantastic characteristics.

As their popularity grew in spite of isolated objections, the bestiaries were translated into the vernacular: Anglo-Saxon, German, Icelandic, and the Romance languages.

A common fixture in monasteries and a source of sermons and textbooks, bestiaries—although never canonized—were effective for centuries as a vehicle for spreading Christian teachings to a broad audience. Bestiary stories were rarely of literary quality, but were appealing and easily understood.

Some commentators—notably T. H. White—have regarded *Physiologus* and the bestiaries as serious works of medieval natural history; most view them as didactic pseudoscience that approaches nature as a metaphor of religious truth, not as a subject to be studied for its own sake. The bestiarists do not distinguish between actual and fabulous animals. Within the allegories, the animals themselves—regardless of whether they are actual or fantastic—are less important than what they represent. The collections typify the metaphorical approach to nature, dominant between the zoological studies of Aristotle and the natural histories of the sixteenth century.

During the centuries of the bestiaries' widespread circulation, related works were produced, including Old English religious writings, St. Bernard's famous condemnation of "contradictory forms," and Hildegard of Bingen's natural history works. While bestiaries were enjoying considerable popularity in the thirteenth century, Richard de Fournival innovatively juxtaposed the bestiary and courtly love traditions, creating a new secular genre, the "Bestiary of Love." Also during that century, the encyclopedic works of Alexander Neckham, Vincent of Beauvais, Bartholomaeus Anglicus, and others included bestiary lore, generally presenting animals more as objects of natural history than as theological lessons. In his natural history, Albertus Magnus was skeptical of several bestiary creatures and rejected many tales as fabulous.

The importance of the bestiaries declined along with the epoch of the Middle Ages, but the influence of bestiaries on animal studies is evident as late as Edward Topsell's moralistic natural history. Their animal lore has taken secular symbolic form in heraldry from the Middle Ages to the present day. Modern scholarship discovered *Physiologus* and the bestiaries in the late nineteenth century, and interest in the subject has increased ever since, resulting in a vast and vital body of research.

The following reproductions from illuminated bestiaries are from different manuscripts than the entries they accompany.

The Greek *Physiologus*
(2nd–5th centuries a.d.)

The prototype of the medieval bestiary, the *Physiologus*, is generally thought to have been compiled near Alexandria in the second century a.d. Among the standard forty-eight or forty-nine stories in the collection are entries on the fabulous phoenix, ant-lion, unicorn, the mythical siren and onocentaur, and the legendary caladrius, salamander, and sawfish (serra). The hydrippus (sea horse) and griffin are included in other Eastern versions.

The ant-lion (Greek, *mirmecoleon*; Latin, *formicoleon*) was a creation of mistaken etymology, developing from a Greek word meaning "a lion among ants" into a monstrous composite. The "ant lion" is an insect of the family *Myrmeleontidae*. The medieval legend of the unicorn captured by a virgin appears in both the Greek and later Latin texts of the *Physiologus*; the Greek version below identifies Christ with the unicorn, the Virgin Mary with the virgin of the tale, and includes the legend of the purifying horn. The Hydrippus (hippocampus) is not included in the standard Latin translations; in this tale, the creature is a Moses figure followed by other fish the way birds attended the Phoenix. From a Syrian text, the Eastern griffin as sun-bird has much in common with the phoenix in *The Greek Apocalypse of Baruch*. A bird from the East, not from the mountains of the far North, this griffin is associated with the Godhead, while later bestiaries portray it in its Western monster form.

See also the Church Fathers, the Latin *Physiologus*, and the bestiaries.

The Ant-Lion*

Eliphas the king of Theman said: "The Ant-Lion perished for lack of food" (*Job* 4, 11).

---

* *Physiologus*, trans. James Carlill, from *The Epic of the Beast*, ed. William Rose (London: George Routledge, 1900) 189, 199–200, 206, 231.

Physiologus says that he has the countenance of a Lion and the hinder parts of an ant. His father is a flesh-eater but his mother is a plant-eater. When now they beget the Ant-Lion they beget him with two attributes: he cannot eat flesh, for that is contrary to the nature of his mother; and he cannot get nourishment from plants, for that is against the nature of his father: so he perishes because there is no food for him.

So, likewise, has every man a double spirit contrary in all its ways. Man cannot go two ways nor speak double in prayer. It is not well to say Yes and No. Let your Yea be Yea and your Nay Nay: "For woe be to the sinner that goeth two ways" (*Sirach*, 2, 12).

The Unicorn

"Thou hast exalted my horn," said the Psalmist, "like the horn of the Unicorn" (*Ps.* 92, 11).

Physiologus relates of the Unicorn that it has the following attribute. It is a small beast like a goat; but it is very wary and the hunter cannot approach it because it possesses great cunning. It has a horn in the middle of its head. Let us

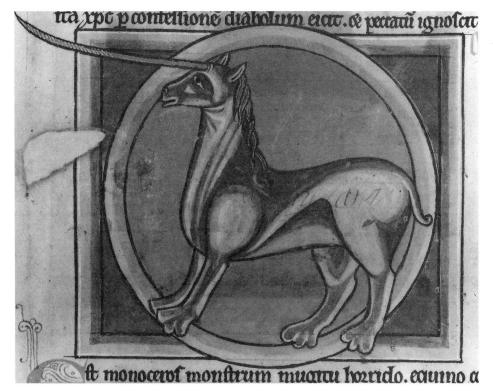

Unicorn. Miniature from a twelfth-century *Physiologus* manuscript. Harley 4751, f. 15, 50418. By permission of the British Library.

now relate how it is caught. They send to it a pure virgin all robed. And the Unicorn springs into the lap of the maiden, and she subdues him, and he follows her; and so she leads him to the King's palace.

By this we see that the Unicorn is the image of our Saviour, the horn of salvation raised for us in the house of our father David. The heavenly powers could not of themselves accomplish the work, but he had to become flesh and to dwell in the body of the true virgin Mary.

There is a further attribute of the Unicorn. In the places where he dwells there is a great lake, and to this lake all beasts resort to drink. But before they assemble themselves comes the snake, and casts her poison on the water. And the beasts when they observe the poison dare not drink, but stand aside and wait for the Unicorn. He comes and goes straight into the lake, and marks the sign of the Cross with his horn; and thereupon the poison becomes harmless, and all those beasts drink.

The Hydrippus or Sea-Horse

There is also a beast called the Hydrippus. The front part of his body resembles a horse, but from the haunch backwards he has the shape of a fish. He swims in the sea, and is the leader of all fishes. But in the Eastern parts of the earth there is a gold-coloured fish whose body is all bright and burnished, and it never leaves its home. When the fish of the sea have met together and gathered themselves into flocks, they go in search of the Hydrippus; and, when they have found him, he turns himself towards the East, and they all follow him, all the fish both from the North and from the South; and they draw near to the golden fish, the Hydrippus leading them. And, when the Hydrippus and all the fish are arrived, they greet the golden fish as their King, and then they return back again each to his own region, And as they go the male fish swim in front and the female after, so that they may receive the spawn which is cast away by the males.

The Hydrippus signifies Moses, the first of the prophets. The sea signifies the world, and the fishes signify the way of righteousness. They turn first to the prophets by whom they are conducted to the Holy Ghost. Those who follow not the Hydrippus, but wander away, fall into the nets of the fishers, who signify the prophets of Baal and the counsels of destruction. But those who listen to prophesying and obey it fall not into the nets.

Well indeed spake Physiologus of the Hydrippus.

The Gryphon

The Gryphon is the largest bird of all the birds of heaven. It lives in the far East in an inlet of the ocean-stream. And, when the sun rises over the water-depths and lights the world with its beams, the Gryphon spreads out its wings and receives the rays of the sun. And another rises with it, and the two fly together towards the sunset, as it is written: "Spread thy wings, dispenser of light; give the world light."

In like manner stand the two Gryphons for the Godhead, that is for the Archangel Michael and the Holy Mother of God, and they receive thy spirit, so that it may not be said: "I know you not."

Well now spake Physiologus concerning the Gryphon.

THE LATIN *PHYSIOLOGUS*
(4TH–11TH CENTURIES A.D.)

The ancient collection of allegorized animal lore known as the Greek *Physiologus* may have begun to appear in Latin texts around the time of St. Jerome's Vulgate translation of the Bible (completed about A.D. 404). Jerome himself was one of the Church Fathers traditionally credited with authorship of the book. St. Ambrose is thought to have used a passage from the Latin *Physiologus* in his *Hexameron* (A.D. 386–388) and was named as the heretical author when the work was assigned to the Index in A.D. 496. Despite the condemnation, the *Physiologus* and the bestiaries derived from it formed a major part of the Christian literature of Europe throughout the Middle Ages.

Along with the unicorn, the phoenix is a major fantastic creature in the several Latin texts from versions of the Greek *Physiologus*. Like St. Clement, the bestiarist states matter-of-factly that there *is* a bird called the phoenix living in Arabia, but fire is an element in this version of the tale, while it was not in the homilies of St. Clement and St. Basil.

Here, after the bird burns on the pyre in Heliopolis, the priests note the creature's rebirth over a period of three days. Sir John Mandeville repeats these details of death and regeneration in his fourteenth-century *Travels*.

The work from which the following entry is reprinted, Michael J. Curley's *Physiologus*, is the first English translation of a complete Latin *Physiologus*.

On the Phoenix *

The Savior said in the Gospel, "I have the power to lay down my life, and I have the power to take it again." And the Jews were angered by his words. There is a

---

* *Physiologus*, trans. Michael J. Curley (Austin: University of Texas Press, 1979), 13–14.

The phoenix gathers twigs for its funeral nest and then dies in fire to be born again. Royal Bestiary 12 CXIX, folio 49v. By permission of the British Library.

species of bird in the land of India which is called the phoenix, which enters the wood of Lebanon after five hundred years and bathes his two wings in the fragrance. He then signals to the priest of Heliopolis (that is, the city named Heliopolis) during the new month, that is, Adar, which in Greek is called Farmuti or Phamenoth. When the priest has been signaled, he goes in to the altar and heaps it with brushwood. Then the bird enters Heliopolis laden with fragrance and mounts the altar, where he ignites the fire and burns himself up. The next day then the priest examines the altar and finds a worm in the ashes. On the second day, however, he finds a tiny birdling. On the third day he finds a huge eagle which taking flight greets the priest and goes off to his former abode.

If this species of bird has the power to kill himself in such a manner as to raise himself up, how foolish are those men who grow angry at the words of the Savior, "I have the power to lay down my life, and I have the power to take it again." The phoenix represents the person of the Savior since, descending from the heavens, he left his two wings full of good odors (that is, his best words) so that we, holding forth the labors of our hand, might return the pleasant spiritual odor to him in good works. Physiologus, therefore, speaks well of the phoenix.

Isidore of Seville (c. 560–636)
Etymologies

The *Etymologies* of St. Isidore, Bishop of Seville, helped redirect the development of the *Physiologus* into what became the bestiaries of the later Middle Ages. A compilation of the writings of ancient authors and the Church Fathers, Isidore's encyclopedia of secular "science" was a major reference book until the early Renaissance. Beginning in about the eleventh century, bestiarists expanded the Latin *Physiologus* with flora and fauna from his zoology, arranged creatures according to his classification, and used his etymologies to explain their names.

Isidore's entries contain traditional folkloric material, but without Christian allegory. He diverges from the medieval metaphorical approach to nature by presenting both actual and fabulous creatures as individual members of the animal kingdom, not as moral emblems. The griffin is classified among "beasts of prey."

The passages below contain details that parallel Pliny's descriptions of the respective creatures.

A chapter preceding Isidore's section on animals catalogs the monstrous races of Pliny, Solinus, and others, including the dog-headed Cynocephali, one-eyed Cyclopes, headless Blemmyes, large-eared Panotti, one-legged Sciopodes, and horned and goat-footed satyrs. "Other fabulous monstrosities of the human race are said to exist," he concludes, "but they do not; they are imaginary."

The Griffin*

The Gryphes are so called because they are winged quadrupeds. This kind of wild beast is found in the Hyperborean Mts. In every part of their body they are lions, and in wings and head are like eagles, and they are fierce enemies of horses. Moreover they tear men to pieces.

Draco

The dragon (*draco*) is the largest of all serpents and of all living things upon earth. This the Greeks call ὁράκοντα. And it was taken into the Latin so that it was called *Draco*. And frequently being dragged from caves it rushes into the air, and the air is thrown into commotion on account of it. And it is crested, has a small face and narrow blow-holes through which it draws its breath and thrusts

* *An Encyclopedist of the Dark Ages: Isidore of Seville*, trans. Ernest Brehaut (1912; rpt., New York: Burt Franklin Reprints, 1972), 225–29.

The common dragon and elephant motif, as described by Isidore, from Pliny. From the twelfth-century "Royal Bestiary." By permission of the British Library.

out its tongue. And it has its strength not in its teeth but in its tail, and it is dangerous for its stroke, rather than for its jaws.

It is harmless in the way of poison, but poison is not necessary for it to cause death, because it kills whatever it has entangled in its folds. And from it the elephant is not safe because of its size. For it lies in wait near the paths by which elephants usually go, and entangles the elephant's legs in its folds, and kills it by strangling. It grows in Ethiopia and in India, in the very burning of perennial heat.

The Salamander

The Salamander is so called because it is strong against fire; and amid all poisons its power is the greatest. For other [poisonous animals] strike individuals; this slays very many at the same time; for if it crawls up a tree, it infects all the fruit with poison and slays those who eat it; nay, even if it falls in a well, the power of the poison slays those who drink it. It fights against fires, and alone among living things, extinguishes them. For it lives in the midst of flames without pain and without being consumed, and not only is it not burned, but it puts the fire out.

The Echeneis

Echeneis, a small fish, half-a-foot long, took its name because it holds a ship back by clinging to it. Though the winds rush and the gusts rage it is seen nevertheless that the ship stands still as if rooted in the sea, and does not move, not because the fish holds it back but merely because it clings to it.

THEOBALDUS (C. 11TH CENTURY)
PHYSIOLOGUS

Regarded as the most popular collection of the *Physiologus*, the metrical version by Theobaldus was widely used as a school text. The identity, dates, and nationality of Theobaldus are obscure. Among the thirteen animals in his book — along with the whale sailors mistake for an island — are the classical sirens and onocentaurs. These two creatures are often combined in a single *Physiologus* or bestiary entry to illustrate duplicity. In later bestiaries, "syrens" are winged white snakes.

  See the Greek and Latin *Physiologus*. For sirens, see Homer, Bartholomaeus Anglicus, and Goethe.

The Sirens *

Sirens are monsters of the sea, resounding with loud voices and moulding their songs with many measures; sailors very often approach them without caution; and they cause sleep through the overpowering sweetness of their voices and produce sometimes shipwreck and sometimes peril of death. Those who have escaped them have reported them to be like this: from the navel up they are like a most beautiful maiden and — what makes them monsters — from there downwards they are birds.

---

* *Theobaldi "Physiologus,"* trans. P. T. Eden (Leiden, Netherlands: E. J. Brill, 1972), 61–63.

The Onocentaurs

Onocentaurs likewise have a double nature: in them there is an ass combined with a man's body. Very many men are thus two-faced in their behaviour, saying one thing to you, the next moment doing another; what they say in public does not accord with what they do in private. In just the same way there are many who talk about virtue and indulge their vices; how dazzlingly attractive these men find the stage.

THE OLD ENGLISH *PHOENIX*, FROM
THE EXETER BOOK (C. 10TH CENTURY)

Like homilies of the Church Fathers and the *Physiologus*, the Old English version of the phoenix story transforms pagan materials into a Christian allegory of resurrection. The first half of the 677-line poem is based on the work attributed to Lactantius (c. A.D. 260–340); the second half is an elaborate explication of the phoenix story in terms of Christian teachings.

The poet renders traditional materials in characteristically Anglo-Saxon imagery, describing spices as "bright treasure" and the sun-bird's nest as "the brave warrior's hall." At the same time, following the oriental opulence of Lactantius's decriptions, the lyrical first half of the poem is far more descriptive and richly colored than other Anglo-Saxon poetry.

Near the end of the Christian allegory, before describing the terrors of Judgment Day and the resurrection of the faithful, the poet cites the authority of Job (29.18 and 19.25–6) for using the death and rebirth of the phoenix as "a token of glory."

Transcribed around the year 1000, the unsigned poem from the Anglo-Saxon *Exeter Book* is of disputed authorship but is traditionally attributed to Cynewulf. Also in *The Exeter Book* are poems on the panther, whale, and partridge, which comprise the Old English *Physiologus*.

Below are excerpts from both halves of the phoenix poem.

The Phoenix*

When the wind lies still, the weather is fair,
The bright gem of heaven shines holy,

---

*   Translated for this volume by Raymond P. Tripp, Jr., from *The Exeter Book*, ed. G. P. Krapp and E. V. K. Dobbie (New York: Columbia University Press, 1936), lines 180–240, 545–75.

A phoenix in flames. From the twelfth-century "Royal Bestiary." By permission of the British Library.

The sky is clear, the waters' strength
Stands still, and every storm is
Put to sleep under the sky, and from the south shines
The warm weather-candle, making sweet light for men,
Then in the branches he begins to build,
A nest to prepare. He has a great need
That he may be able to turn old age quickly
Through the fire of knowledge back into life,
To feel young life. Then from far and near
The sweetest he collects and gathers
Of delightful herbs and of forest blossoms
To his dwelling place, each noble fragrance
Of the delightful herbs which the World-King,
The Father of each creation, made upon earth
To have every kind of essence,
Sweet under the sky. There he himself bears
Into the tree bright treasures;
There the wild bird builds a house,
Bright and delightful, and there lodges
Himself in that upper room, and surrounds

In that leafy shade his body and feathers
On every side with holy fragrances
And the noblest blossoms of earth.
He sits eager to fly away. When the sky-gem
In summer time, the hottest sun,
Shines over shadows, and follows its course,
Lights up the world, then his house
Becomes heated through the bright sky.
The herbs grow warm, his pleasant dwelling steams
With sweet odors, then burns in flames
Through the grasp of fire the bird and nest.
     The pyre is ignited. Then flame covers
The gory house, fiercely seizes,
Yellow fire feeds and burns the Phoenix,
Many many years old. Then the fire takes
The passing body, life has gone its way,
The fated hoard of life, then flesh and bone
The funeral fire sets on fire. But to him comes
After a period of time life anew,
After the embers he once more begins
After the fury of flame to come together,
Stuck into a ball. Then clean is
The brightest of nests, consumed by the fire
The brave warrior's hall; the body is cooled,
The bone-vessel broken, and the burning subsides.
Then out of the pyre in the likeness of an apple
In the ashes is one more to be seen,
From which grows a worm, wondrously fair,
Just as if he from an egg was hatched forth,
Shining out of the shell. Then in the shade he grows,
So that at first he is like an eagle's chick,
A fair young bird; then further yet
He thrives in joys, so that he is in shape like
A mature eagle, and after that
Dressed in feathers, such as he in the beginning was,
Bright blooming. . . .
     Let no man among the race of men
Think that I make verse and write songs
From lying words. Listen to the wisdom
Of Job's stories. With a bold heart
Fired by the breath of spirit, he spoke,
Bathed in wonder, he sang these words:

"I do not grumble secretly in my heart
That I, a man, shall die in my nest,
Bone tired, and then hobble sad away
On a long journey, covered with clay,
Worried by my life, in the arms of dirt,
If after my death, by God's gift,
Like the Phoenix bird after rising
In new life, I can claim as my own
Happiness with God, where dear friends
Praise the Beloved. Never will I see
Even to eternity the end of that life,
Its lights and joys. Though my body must
Turn into mould in its hall of earth,
To the delight of worms, the God of hosts
After the hour of death will free my soul
And call it to wonder. Never will my hope
Crack in my heart, for in the King of Angels
I have a firm pledge of endless joy."
　　Thus old and sage a man in far off days
Chanted with knowing mind, God's spokesman,
About his rising up into unending life,
That we more readily might understand
The token of glory that the shining bird
By his burning shows. . . .

St. Bernard (1090–1153)
Apologia

Bestiarists commonly used the composite technique of travelers in describing their subjects, comparing parts of an exotic beast to those of a well-known animal. These figurative hybrids were depicted literally in bestiary art, religious sculpture, and later in heraldry. One who objected to the profusion of mixed forms in religious art was St. Bernard, founder of the abbey of Clairvaux, reformer leader of the strict Cistercian order. Later, by the power of his preaching in France and Germany on behalf of Pope Eudenius III, he helped launch the Second Crusade (1147–1149).

In an 1125 letter to William, abbot of Saint Thiery, Bernard vigorously attacked "contradictory" forms as distracting and ostentatiously expensive images that violate nature. While he does not name figures such as sirens, centaurs, and the Hydra, Bernard describes monstrous forms evocative of well-known fantastic creatures. He treats the depiction of beasts as deformed images, not as religious allegories.

Later, immersed in church politics, Bernard referred to himself as a hybrid monster: "I have become a sort of modern chimera, neither a cleric nor a layman." His letter, known as the *Apologia*, has been regarded as a central document for the study of medieval art.

Contradictory Forms*

... in the cloisters, before the eyes of the brothers while they read—what is that ridiculous monstrosity doing, an amazing kind of deformed beauty and yet a beautiful deformity? What are the filthy apes doing there? The fierce lions? The monstrous centaurs? The creature part man and part beast? The striped tigers? The fighting soldiers? The hunters blowing their horns? You see many bodies under one head, and conversely many heads on one body. On one side the tail of a serpent is seen on a quadruped, on the other side the head of a quadruped is on the body of a fish. Over there an animal has a horse for the front half and a goat for the back; here a creature which is horned in front is equine behind. In short, everywhere so plentiful and astonishing a variety of contradictory forms is seen that one would rather read in the marble than in books, and spend the whole day wondering at every single one of them than in meditating on the law of God. Good God! If one is not ashamed of the absurdity, why is one not at least troubled at the expense?

HILDEGARD OF BINGEN (1098–1179)
THE BOOK OF LIFE'S MERITS

The first woman to write substantially about the unicorn, Odell Shepard maintains in his *Lore of the Unicorn*, was the twelfth-century abbess, mystic, artist, poet, scientist, composer, and author, Hildegard of Bingen. Within her prolific writings, the unicorn varies from a medicinal source to a visionary symbol of Christ.

* "Apologia 29," from Conrad Rudolph, *The "Things of Greater Importance": Bernard of Clairvaux's Apologia and the Medieval Attitude Toward Art* (Philadelphia: University of Pennsylvania Press, 1990), 11–12.

At one point, she explains that the creature acquired its medicinal properties by eating herbs of the Earthly Paradise. While she was apparently not aware of the legendary powers of alicorn, she proclaimed that a salve made from unicorn liver and egg yolks cured leprosy and that a belt and shoes made from unicorn hide protected the wearer from disease. In her version of unicorn capture, a naturalist catches a unicorn by surprise while it is sitting and watching a group of young women. Hildegard points out that the unicorn is drawn to high-born women, not to those of peasant stock.

Elsewhere, she identifies the unicorn with Christ and the virgin with the Virgin Mary: "For he himself rested as a unicorn in the lap of the Virgin and later as a goat climbed up the mountain of virtues and miracles through which he altogether overcame the Devil and crushed his power (*Opera*, p. 87)." *Physiologus* unicorn entries develop similar religious parallels, equating the unicorn's resting in the lap of the virgin with the Annunciation.

The divine unicorn also figures prominently in the following excerpt from one of Hildegard's visionary writings, a highly-colored mystical allegory in which the unicorn Christ purges and purifies the world. The biblical unicorn is fierce, and in *Physiologus* lore, the unicorn purifies poisonous water with the power of its horn.

Generally known as St. Hildegard although she was never canonized, the founder of Rupertsberg Abbey dictated and illustrated her visions and produced several theological and scientific works. Also, she corresponded with popes, emperors, kings, and clergy, including St. Bernard of Clairvaux. Virtually ignored for centuries, Hildegard's writings were reexamined by nineteenth-century ecclesiastical scholars, and recognition of her multifaceted achievement as a medieval woman has spread in the late twentieth-century.

See the Bible, Greek *Physiologus*, and St. Basil.

The Mystical Unicorn*

CONCERNING THE MAN WHO MOVED HIMSELF WITH THE FOUR CORNERS OF THE EARTH

Then I saw a man moving his whole self with the four corners of the earth. And behold at his left thigh, licking his knees, appeared a unicorn, who said:

WORDS OF THE UNICORN

"What has been made will be destroyed and what has not been made will be built. Sin will be weighed in every man and good from just works will be brought

---

* Translated for this volume by Mary Margolies DeForest from *Liber vitae meritorum*, in *Sancta Hildegardis Opera*, ed. Joannes Baptista Pitra (Monte Cassino, 1882), 222–23.

to perfection in him and he will return into another life because of his good reputation."

And I was considering whether other faults, which I had seen before, would
appear here, and nothing like them was shown to me.

CONCERNING THE POWER OF GOD IN THE END OF THE WORLD

And again I heard a voice from the sky, saying to me: "Most powerful God, whose
power is over all people, will show His power at the end of the world, when He
will change himself into another miracle."

GOD WILL SHAKE THE ENDS OF THE EARTH

For as you see, that the man moving his whole self with the four quarters of the
earth means that God, showing his power at the end of the world with the virtues
of the skies, will shake all the ends of the earth in such a way that every soul will
prepare itself for judgment.

CHRIST THE JUDGE WILL EXAMINE EVERYTHING

Consequently, also at the left thigh a unicorn appears, since He who resisted the
Devil in sacred humanity, and who laid him low with the sword of chastity is certainly the Son of God, who will come in human shape; who licks his knees, that is
receiving judicial power from God the Father, cries out that the whole world must be
purged with fire and must be called back into a different way and also the perversity
of men must be weighed by his judgment, and the sanctity in good and upright deeds
in man must be led to perfection, and so the souls of the just will then cross over to
the blessedness of eternal life with the greatest glory and the greatest joy.

THAT ALL SINS WILL BE PURGED IN THE WORLD

For when God has perfected the virtues of his strength in man, He will raise his
strength in the clouds, and will remove the ash by which the elements are
clouded; and He will do this with such great terror that all things that are on earth
will be moved and all things stained with the sins of men will be purged. Then too
God will destroy Aquilo [the North Wind] and all the strength of Aquilo and He
will cast down the Devil in his victorious arms and he will strip him of his spoils.

ABOUT THE NEW SKY AND NEW EARTH

Then red sky and pure earth will appear, because they have been purged along
with other elements; since now they bear some barrier in the clouding over of the

celestial things, but then they shall blaze in newness. Then too, man, who emerges blessed, purged in the same elements, will be like the golden circle of the wheel, and then blazing in spirit and flesh, and every barrier of occult secrets will lie open. Thus blessed men will cleave to God, and He will give them full joy.

A Latin Prose Bestiary (12th century)

The collection of allegorized animal tales that first emerged in the form of the ancient *Physiologus* evolved into the bestiaries, which reached their greatest popularity in the twelfth and thirteenth centuries.

The older material in the bestiaries was still likely to open and close with the "Physiologus says" and "Physiologus therefore speaks well of" formulas, and the animal lore to be allegorized through Scripture and end with a Christian lesson derived from the tale. Newer material from Isidore, Pliny, Lucan, Aelian, Solinus, and others doubled and even tripled the size of the original collection. Descriptions of these additional animals usually begin with an explanation of the creature's name and contain no biblical frame or moral.

Among the new bestiary animals are several fabulous beasts based upon creatures described by ancient authors. Pliny's leucrocota ("Leucrota"), the imagined offspring of a hyena and an antelope, takes on different composite forms in the bestiaries. Pliny is considered the first to mention the yale, and he established the standard lore of the basilisk. Pliny's details could have reached the bestiaries through Solinus. Also here are Ctesias's manticore ("Manticora"), Aristotle's cinnamon bird ("Cinomolgus") and Lucan's two-headed amphisbaena ("Amphisvena").

The modern reader is most familiar with the bestiaries through T. H. White's *Book of Beasts*, his translation of a twelfth-century bestiary in the Cambridge University Library (II.4.26). White is a major proponent of the serious natural history intent of the medieval bestiarists. *The Book of Beasts* is the first full version of a Latin prose bestiary to be translated into English; also, no complete Latin prose bestiary had ever before been printed, even in Latin. The illustrations accompanying selections below — modern renderings of the original art — are also reproduced from White's book.

See T. H. White's diagrams of bestiary sources and influence in Part IV of this volume.

Leucrota*

A beast gets born in India called the LEUCROTA, and it exceeds in velocity all the wild animals there are. It has the size of a donkey, the haunches of a stag, the breast and shins of a lion, the head of a horse, a cloven hoof, and a mouth opening as far as its ears. Instead of teeth, there is one continuous bone: but this is only as to shape, for in voice it comes near to the sounds of people talking.

Manticora

A beast is born in the Indies called a MANTICORA. It has a threefold row of teeth meeting alternately: the face of a man, with gleaming, blood-red eyes: a lion's body: a tail like the sting of a scorpion, and a shrill voice which is so sibilant that it resembles the notes of flutes. It hankers after human flesh most ravenously. It is so strong in the foot, so powerful with its leaps, that not the most extensive space nor the most lofty obstacle can contain it.

The Yale

There is a beast called a YALE, which is as big as a horse, has the tail of an elephant, its colour black and with the jowls of a boar. It carries outlandishly long horns which are adjusted to move at will. They are not fixed, but are moved as the needs of battle dictate, and, when it fights, it points one of them forward and folds the other one back, so that, if it hurts the tip of this one with any blow, the sharpness of the other one can take its place.

* *The Book of Beasts: Being a Translation from a Latin Bestiary of the Twelfth Century*, trans. and ed. T. H. White (1954; rpt., New York: Dover Publications, 1984), 48–49, 51–52, 54–55, 130, 168–69, 177.

The Cinomolgus

Another Arabian bird, the CINOMOLGUS, is called this because he builds his nests in the very highest trees, making them out of Cinnamon. Since people are not able to climb to such a height, owing to the altitude and fragility of the branches, they try to hit the nests with weighted missiles, and so to bring down the cinnamon. The nests sell for very high prices, because merchants prize these cinnamon fruits more than most.

The Basilisk

The BASILISK is translated in Greek and Latin as *"Regulus"* (a prince) because it is the king of serpents — so much so, that people who see it run for their lives, because it can kill them merely by its smell. Even if it looks at a man, it destroys him. At the mere sight of a Basilisk, any bird which is flying past cannot get across unhurt, but, although it may be far from the creature's mouth, it gets frizzled up and is devoured.

Nevertheless, Basilisks are conquered by weasels. Men put these into the lairs in which they lie hid, and thus, on seeing the weasel, the Basilisk runs away. The weasel follows and kills it. God never makes anything without a remedy. Finally, a Basilisk is striped length-wise with white marks six inches in size.

The Basilisk, moreover, like the scorpion, also frequents desert places, and before people can get to the rivers it gives them hydrophobia and sends them mad. Its hiss is the same as that of the Regulus, for it can kill with its noise and burn people up, as it were, before it bites them.

The Amphivena

This is called an AMPHIVENA because it has two heads. One head is in the right place and the other is in its tail. With one head holding the other, it can bowl along in either

direction like a hoop. This is the only snake which stands the cold well, and it is
the first to come out of hibernation. Lucan writes of it:

> "Rising on twin-born heads comes dangerous
>   Amphisbaena
> And her eyes shine like lamps."

PHILIPPE DE THAUN (12TH CENTURY)
THE BESTIARY

Popularity of the bestiary spread with its vernacular translations. The earliest
French bestiary (c. 1125) is the metrical version of Philippe de Thaun, dedicated
to Alisa, second wife of Henry I. Based on the Latin *Physiologus* and incorporating
material from Isidore of Seville and the ancient authors, Philippe's bestiary is a
collection of thirty-eight chapters on birds, beasts, and stones. The scriptural
citations of the *Physiologus* are all but dropped from the entries, but religious
lessons receive full allegorical treatment. Philippe ends one of the *significatios*
with what is actually an explanation of the bestiary approach to nature: "We
ought to worship God, and thank him very much, when he made everything for
people to take example; there is nothing in this world which does not give example, if one knew how to ask, inquire, and prove it."

Philippe's elaborate allegory of the serra (sawfish, swordfish, flying fish)
departs from the *Physiologus* in that his beast is a lion, bird and fish composite
known as the Lion of the Sea. He interprets the beast as Satan, not as what
other bestiarists describe as the faithful who tire of doing good works and sink
into sin.

Philippe's Cetus bears the same name as the sea beast in the Perseus and
Andromeda myth; it is based on the standard *Physiologus* whale (also "Aspidochelone" and "Jasconius"), that is so large that mariners believe it to be an island
and so sweet of breath that unsuspecting fish swim into its mouth. Derived from
an actual creature but fabulous in size, the island beast figures in one of the most
widespread tales of the sea.

The phoenix, caladrius, and other fabulous and legendary creatures of the
Physiologus are also included in Philippe's bestiary.

For the island beast, see *The Voyage of St. Brendan*, Olaus Magnus, and
Milton.

The Serra*

Serra is a beast of the sea; it has wings to fly, and it has the head of a lion, and the tail of a fish. When it sees ships on the deep sea, it rises aloft. It does the ship great injury, as it goes before the ship and holds off the wind so that it has none, nor can the ship all that time run on at all. When the beast does that, it has its wings extended. When it cannot move in the air, it lets the ship go, then it plunges into the sea to devour the fish. The ship goes floating away, which she was injuring; and that we show in the form which we take.

Serra in this life signifies the Devil; and the sea, that is the world; the ship, the people who are in it; and we understand holy inspiration by the wind. When serra surprizes the ship, then it withdraws from it the wind. So the Devil takes from people holy inspiration; when they hear sermon and preaching, they will not listen to it, but will interrupt it. The Devil does it to them; he withdraws the Holy Spirit from them. Therefore said the Lord God to his people in truth: "They who are of God hear the desired speech."

There is hardly a mortal man who does not think well and ill. When he is in evil thoughts, then serra has seized upon him; when man returns to good, serra cannot injure him. When he (the Devil) cannot tempt the holy man, nor turn him to evil, then he plunges into the sea to devour the fish; that is, he puts himself in the world; he takes and confounds men — whom he finds in evil, in criminal sin, — as serra does the fish. Here ends the discourse.

Cetus

Cetus is a very great beast; it lives always in the sea; it takes the sand of the sea, spreads it on its back, raises itself up in the sea, and will be in tranquility. The seafarer sees it, thinks that it is an island, goes to arrive there to prepare his meal. The whale feels the fire and the ship and the people, then he will plunge if he can, and will drown them.

The cetus is the Devil, and the sea is the world; and the sands are the riches of the world; and the soul, the steersman; the body, the ship which he ought to keep; and the fire is love, because man loves his gold, his gold and his silver; when the devil perceives that, and he shall be the more sure, then he will drown him.

And this says the writing, cetus has such a nature, that when he wants to eat, he begins to gape, and the gaping of his mouth sends forth a smell, so sweet and

---

* *The Bestiary*, from *Popular Treatises on Science*, ed. Thomas Wright (London, 1841), 103–4, 108.

A popular bestiary motif of sailors mistaking a giant fish for an island. Harley MS 4751, fol. 69. By permission of the British Library.

so good that the little fish, who will like the smell, will enter into his mouth, and then he will kill them, thus he will swallow them; and similarly the Devil will strangle the people, who shall love him so much that they will enter into his mouth. This saith the Bestiary, a book of science.

PIERRE DE BEAUVAIS (13TH CENTURY)
THE BESTIARY

The *Bestiary* of Pierre de Beauvais is a French prose translation of the Latin *Physiologus*. Little is known of the author other than that he was from Picardy and is credited with several didactic works in verse and prose. His *Bestiary* is extant in both a long and a short version.

Pierre's legendary "charadrius" (caladrius), a bird that knows whether a sick person will live or die, faithfully follows the standard *Physiologus* chapter. Many birds, from the seagull to the white wagtail, have been proposed as the prototype of this creature. The selection below is from Guy R. Mermier's translation of the shorter version of Pierre's *Bestiary*, the first English translation of the work.

For a secular, courtly love interpretation of the caladrius, see Richard de Fournival. For a "scientific" approach to the caladrius, see Albertus Magnus.

*The Charadrius**

There is a bird called *caladre* (charadrius). It is mentioned in the Deuteronomy (Deut. 14:18), one of the five books of Moïse, that one should never eat of its flesh. Physiologus says that this bird is totally white, and that there is not a trace of black in this bird. The thigh of the charadrius is used to cure the redness of the eyes of those people who are losing their eyesight. This bird is to be found in royal households. If anyone is ill, the charadrius will tell whether the patient will die or live. If the sick person is to die, the charadrius turns its eyes away, and it is thus known that this person is going to die. However if the illness is not fatal, the charadrius will look at the patient straight into his eyes and will thus absorb the illness. Then the bird will fly up toward the sun in order to burn off all of the illness of the sick person.

This charadrius is the symbol of our Lord Jesus Christ who is all white and who has no trace of black in him (cf. Eph. 5:27). As he says himself in the Gospel: "The prince of this world came to me and he found nothing bad in me" (John 14:30). The one who committed no sin and in the mouth of whom no guile was found (I Peter 2:22) came down from Heaven to the sick Jewish people and he turned his face away from them because they were unbelievers, and instead, he turned his face toward us, Gentiles, and he removed all our sickness (Matt. 8:17), and he absorbed all our sins (Is. 53:4) when he was raised on the holy cross. And when he ascended to Heaven, he took our miserable flesh and he gave us gifts

* A *Medieval Book of Beasts; Pierre de Beauvais' Bestiary*, trans. Guy R. Mermier (Lewiston, N.Y.: Edwin Mellon Press, 1992), 27–28.

(Ps. 68:18; Eph. 4:8). To those who did not believe in him, he said: "To all those who received him, he gave the power to become children of God" (John 1:12), to those indeed who believe in his name.

RICHARD DE FOURNIVAL (1201–1260)
THE BESTIARY OF LOVE AND RESPONSE

During the period of the medieval bestiary's greatest popularity, Richard de Fournival, a cleric, violently juxtaposed the established Christian genre with secular courtly love literature, producing a unique bestiary form that intentionally violates both traditions. The two parts of the title itself suggest de Fournival's revolutionary combination of Christian morality with erotic love, and animals with the distant platonic beloved. His use of the Aristotelian senses further jars the platonic love convention of the troubadours. The work is in prose, and he begins his ironic bestiary with the cock rather than the traditional lion.

Master Richard is the courtly lover, seeking the favor of his "fair, sweetest beloved." She is the caladrius who turns away from him, a dying man. He is a unicorn set up for slaughter by the hunter, Love. The *Response* by an anonymous woman to whom he has sent his bestiary of love accompanies several of the extant manuscripts of the book. Spirited and intellectual, she subtly resists his courtship animal by animal. She ends her *Response* with: "In my view, when a person does not wish to do a thing, there are multiple refusals. Let that suffice for good understanding." The translator, Jeanette Beer, points out that similarities between the works of de Fournival and Pierre de Beauvais suggest that the prose French bestiary might have been one of the sources of *Le Bestiaire d'amour*.

Master Richard's pleas and the Lady's responses, from separate sections of the book, are here juxtaposed.

See the caladrius in Pierre de Beauvais and Albertus Magnus.

The Lady as Caladrius*

[MASTER RICHARD]

. . . When this bird is brought into the presence of a sick person, if the caladrius will look that person full in the face, that is a sign that he will recover. But if the

---

* *Master Richard's Bestiary of Love and Response*, trans. Jeanette Beer (Berkeley: University of California Press, 1986), 10, 46–47, 14–15, 47.

caladrius turns aside and refuses to look at him, the sick person is judged doomed to die.

And so it seems to me, fair, sweetest love, that since you are distressed I ever pleaded with you, and since you would readily have enjoyed my acquaintance and kept company with me provided that I said nothing of my sickness, you never wanted to look at me, a sick man, full in the face. Consequently, I must be given up for dead. For by this you have thrown me into the sort of distress that accompanies utter despair without hope of mercy. That is death by love. For as in death there is no recovery, so there is no hope of love's joy when there is no expectation of mercy. . . .

[THE LADY'S RESPONSE]

. . . I must be on my guard much more than if I had the wisdom of The Caladrius of which I have heard you tell.

For it is of such a nature that it knows when a sick man must get well or die, so that I have understood from you that when the bird is brought before a person who is lying sick in bed, it will turn its face away if he must die, but wondrously it looks him straight in the face if he will live. Wherefore I say that if I were as wise as the caladrius, I should not be wary of this act of giving birth, whatever the nature of the conception.

The Lover as Unicorn

[MASTER RICHARD]

Thus I say that if I was captured through hearing and through sight, it was not surprising if I lost my good sense and my memory in the process. For hearing and sight are the two doors of memory, as was said earlier, and they are two of man's noblest senses. For man has five senses: sight, hearing, smell, taste, and touch, as was said earlier.

I was captured also by smell, like the Unicorn which falls asleep at the sweet smell of maidenhood. For such is its nature that no beast is so cruel to capture. It has a horn in the middle of its forehead which can penetrate all armor, so that no one dares to attack or ambush it except a young virgin. For when the unicorn senses a virgin by her smell, it kneels in front of her and gently humbles itself as if to be of service. Consequently, the clever hunters who know its nature place a maiden in its path, and it falls asleep in her lap. And then when it is asleep the hunters, who have not the courage to pursue it while awake, come out and kill it.

That is just how Love avenged itself on me. For I had been the haughtiest young man of my generation toward Love, and I thought I had never seen a woman that I would want for my own, a woman I would love as passionately as I

The Unicorn in Captivity, perhaps representing the captured lover. The seventh and final panel of the famous *Hunt of the Unicorn* series of tapestries, c. 1500. By permission of Metropolitan Museum of Art, New York, The Cloisters Collection, Gift of John D. Rockefeller, Jr., 1937.

had been told one loved. Then Love, who is a clever hunter, put a maiden in my path and I fell asleep at her sweetness and I died the sort of death that is appropriate to Love, namely despair without expectation of mercy. . . .

[THE LADY'S RESPONSE]

By God, here is sovereign medicine, and such a beast well deserves to be loved. For I know of a truth that there is no beast to be feared like the soft word that comes deceiving. And I truly believe that against that soft word one can have little protection, any more than one can against The Unicorn. By my faith, I fear that unicorn very much. For I know well that there is nothing so wounding as fair speech for, to tell the truth, nothing can pierce a hard heart like a soft and well-placed word.

BARTHOLOMAEUS ANGLICUS (EARLY 13TH CENTURY)
ON THE PROPERTIES OF THINGS

Physiologus and the bestiaries were among the ancient and medieval sources of the most popular of the thirteenth-century encyclopedias compiled by clerics. Bartholomew the Englishman's *De Proprietatibus Rerum*, prepared for "plain people," was translated into English by John Trevisa in 1398 and was printed in numerous languages and editions throughout Europe in the fifteenth and sixteenth centuries.

The natural history section of the collection contains traditional lore of several fabulous animals, including the basilisk, catoblepas, griffin, manticore, and phoenix. Renaissance poets Guillaume de Salluste du Bartas and Robert Chester were heavily indebted to Bartholomew's animal lore. The mermaid entry below is Robert Steele's adaptation of the Trevisa translation. The mermaid and the siren were largely interchangeable in medieval bestiaries.

For the siren, see Homer, Theobaldus, and Goethe; for the mermaid, see Pliny's Nereids, John Guillim, and Samuel Purchas.

The Mermaid*

The mermaid is a sea beast wonderly shapen, and draweth shipmen to peril by sweetness of song. The Gloss on Is. xiii. saith that sirens are serpents with crests. And some men say, that they are fishes of the sea in likeness of women. Some men feign that there are three Sirens some-deal maidens, and some-deal fowls with claws and wings, and one of them singeth with voice, and another with a pipe, and the third with an harp, and they please so shipmen, with likeness of song, that they draw them to peril and to shipbreach, but the sooth is, that they were strong hores, that drew men that passed by them to poverty and to mischief. And Physiologus saith it is a beast of the sea, wonderly shapen as a maid from the navel upward and a fish from the navel downward, and this wonderful beast is glad and merry in tempest, and sad and heavy in fair weather. With sweetness of song this beast maketh shipmen to sleep, and when she seeth that they are asleep, she goeth into the ship, and ravisheth which she may take with her, and bringeth him into a dry place, and maketh him first lie by her, and if he will not or may not, then she slayeth him and eateth his flesh. Of such wonderful beasts it is written in the great Alexander's story.

---

* *Mediaeval Lore from Bartholomew Anglicus*, ed. Robert Steele (1893; rpt., New York: Cooper Square, 1966), 166–67.

ALBERTUS MAGNUS (C. 1200–1280)
DE ANIMALIBUS

During the flourishing of allegorical animal lore in the bestiaries of the thirteenth century, Albert of Cologne produced a work that challenged the medieval approach to nature. His systematic natural history, appended to his translation and commentary of Aristotle's animal studies, treats animals as part of the natural world, not as symbols or moral lessons. Albert's study is regarded as the most important zoological work between Pliny's first-century *Natural History* and the sixteenth-century *Historia Animalium* of Conrad Gesner. It is an invaluable compilation and discussion of ancient and medieval animal lore.

Books 22–26 of *De Animalibus* contain about 500 species, arranged alphabetically within categories of movement: walking, flying, swimming, and crawling. While Albert does not cite scripture or the *Physiologus*, many of his sources are sources of the bestiaries, and he includes virtually all the bestiary creatures in his study. Unlike the bestiarists, though, he uses personal observation and critical judgment to evaluate popular fable and traditional authority.

Restricted by the knowledge of his age, Albert does, of course, repeat some received information — from Aristotle, Pliny, the Arabian scholar Avicenna, and others — but he does not automatically accept authority. He attempts to separate fact and fable in Pliny. He writes that Solinus "is guilty of many untruths" and that Solinus and an obscure author, Jorach, "are much given to falsification." Albert often prefaces his descriptions with "some say," "some authors allege," "according to folk tales," "the story goes," and similar qualifications. He attempts to be empirical in his descriptions, even of uncertain animals, and whenever possible he supplies explanations from the natural sciences, as in his optical analysis of the basilisk's gaze and the asbestos material called "salamander's wool."

Albert's translations and commentaries of all Aristotle's works into Latin did much to introduce Aristotelian science to European learning. Theologian, scientist, philosopher, teacher, alchemist, mentor of Thomas Aquinas, Albert was regarded as *doctor universalis* for encompassing the knowledge of his age. The bestiaries eventually declined in importance, but much of the animal lore Albert questioned or refuted lived on into the 1600s. Albert's challenges to popular beliefs look ahead to Sir Thomas Browne's 1646 *Pseudodoxia Epidemica* ("Vulgar Errors"). Albert was centuries ahead of his time.

For the tree goose (barnacle goose), see later in this volume the Old English Riddle and Giraldus Cambrensis, accounts of the bird composed prior to Albertus; see also the sixteenth-century eyewitness description of John Gerard. For other treatments of what Albertus calls "salamander's wool," see *The Letter of Prester John* and Marco Polo.

Tree Geese*

BARLIATES, which are known colloquially as "boumgans" or tree geese, are mistakenly described by some writers as birds which arise from trees and derive their vitality from the sap that courses within the bark of tree trunks and branches. Furthermore, these writers claim the geese are sometimes generated from pieces of rotten wood floating in the sea, especially fragments of silver-fir. They base this claim on the proposition that no one has ever seen these birds mating or laying eggs. But this is absolutely absurd because I myself and many of my colleagues have observed these birds copulating, laying eggs and feeding their young.

The Caladrius

CALADRIUS or CALADRION is a bird which some say is completely white and lives in the country of Persia, though even here it is rarely encountered since it has so many natural enemies. Many kings have demanded this bird for augury because Alexander, the King of kings, is said to have discovered its unique aptness for predicting the future. When brought into the presence of a sick person, the bird is reputed to give prognostic signs that indicate the severity of the disease and point the way to a cure. After being set before the patient, if the bird turns its face and eyes toward the victim, it signifies he should be cured. Supposedly, the noxious humor associated with the disease is leaving the patient's body and evaporating; the bird turns toward the evanescent vapor, transfixed by the possibility of being infected; then it flies away, dispelling the infectious vapors into the open air. On the other hand, if the bird is placed in front of the ill person and averts its face and eyes, this means the individual will die, because the noxious matter is trapped in the patient's body and there is no odor of escaping vapors to catch the bird's attention. Be that as it may, augury by the use of birds does not fall within the scope of our present inquiry.

The meat of this bird's inner thigh is beneficial for eye disorders.

Caristae

CARISTAE, according to Solinus and Jorach, are birds which can fly through the flames without harm, burning neither their body nor their feathers. However, these philosophers are much given to falsification and I suspect this to be one of their deceits.

* *Albert the Great: Man and the Beasts; de animalibus (Books 22-26)*, trans. James J. Scanlan, M.D. (Binghamton, N.Y.: Medieval and Renaissance Texts and Studies, 1987), 210, 210–11, 212–13, 288–89, 290, 393, 396–98, 409–10.

The Phoenix

FENIX, according to some authors who devoted more attention to mystical themes than to the natural sciences, is supposed to be an Arabian bird found in parts of the East. Those authors claim the bird is unisexual, lacking a male spouse and having no commingling of the sexes. They further allege that the phoenix, after coming into the world, lives a solitary life spanning three hundred and forty years.

The story goes . . . [the familiar lore is omitted here].

These authors report an event which ostensibly occurred one time in the Egyptian city of Heliopolis where a native priest was the witness. A phoenix gathered branches from aromatic spice trees, built a structure from these sacrificial woods, set itself afire and, by the mode of reincarnation mentioned above, reappeared first as a worm, then turned into a bird and flew away. But as Plato says: "We ought not disparage those things reported to have been written in the books of the sacred temples."

The Griffin

GRIFES according to folk tales are said to be birds, but their credibility as real animals is not based on the experience of philosophers nor the evidence of natural science. The tales relate how the foreparts of these birds — i.e. their head, beak, wings and forefeet — resemble an eagle, though on a much larger scale. The posterior portion of the animal, including the tail and rear legs, looks like a lion. The forefeet have long aquiline talons, while the rear feet have short but massive leonine claws which they use as cups for drinking; thus, griffins are said to have both long and short claws. They are supposed to live in the mountains of the extreme North, are especially inimical to horses and men, and are so strong they can carry off a horse and its rider. Their mountain aeries are claimed to be laden with gold and gems, particularly emeralds. The stories also tell that griffins deposit agates in their nests because of the agate's special beneficial properties.

The Amphisbaena

AMFYSIBENA (Worm lizard) is a serpent which Avicenna and the Arabs call "anksymen." Solinus, who is guilty of many untruths, makes the false assertion that this serpent has two heads. Now, no animal by nature has two heads; Solinus was deceived because this serpent has the ability to jump in two directions, forward and backward; this happens because of the mobility of its ribs in either direction; further, its two ends are equal in size, as well as being of the same thickness as the center of its body.

It is a small serpent which the Greeks call "amphim" because of the weakness of both ends. Its bite produces excruciating pain which creeps through the entire body of its victim in a short time. . . .

The Basilisk

BASYLYSCUS is the snake which in Latin translation is called "regulus," but has the same sound in Greek, "basiliscus."

. . . it kills by its gaze, for everyone on whom its fixed stare falls dies as a result. Pliny and some other writers maintain that the basilisk strikes a man dead with its gaze only if it spies the man first; contrariwise, I do not think this is true, because it has no basis in reason. Neither Avicenna nor Semerion, both of whom are natural philosophers who speak from experience, tell this story. Nor is the reason it kills by its gaze, as some allege, because rays emitted from its eyes destroy those upon whom they fall. The opinion of natural scientists is that rays do not emerge from the eyes; rather, the cause of the corrupting influence is the visual energy which is diffused over very long distances because of the subtlety of its substantial nature; herein lies its ability to destroy and kill everything. . . .

They claim that wherever the ashes of a basilisk have been scattered, no spiders weave their webs nor do other venomous creatures appear; hence, the ancients strewed basilisk's ashes in their temples.

Hermes asserts that silver melted in the ashes of a basilisk takes on the splendor, weight and density of gold.

Some authors allege that there is a certain type of basilisk which can fly, but I have not been able to confirm this in the texts of the most reputable philosophers.

Furthermore, some writers claim that basilisks are generated from the egg of a rooster; this is patently false, if not downright impossible.

When Hermes teaches that the basilisk develops in glass, he is not referring to the true basilisk but to a certain alchemical elixir by which metals are converted from one form to another.

The Salamander

SALAMANDRAS is a serpent in the sense that it bears some similarity to a snake. What the Greeks call "salamander," we now call "stellio." The ancient writers entertained a wide variety of notions about this animal. Some, including Pliny and Solinus, say the salamander is the same as the chameleon, i.e. the "earth lion." In actuality it is an oviparous quadruped which has the shape of a lizard but a face composed from the face of a pig and an ape. Pliny states that it has long, straight hindlegs attached to its belly, an elongated flexible tail that tapers to a thin end, claws that hook in a delicate arch, a roughened body and skin like a crocodile.

Some claim the salamander has a kind of wool that resists combustion in fire because the flames cannot enter its pores. However, what has been presented to me as purported "salamander's wool" has turned out on close examination not even to be of animal origin. Some claim this fleecy substance is the down of a certain plant, but I have not been able to corroborate this from personal experience. As a matter of fact, I have judged it to be iron floss. By way of explanation, wherever large masses of iron are smelted, the molten metal sometimes forms bubbles which burst and release a blast of fiery vapor. If this smoke is trapped on a piece of cloth, or even by hand, or if it adheres by itself to the roof of the smelting furnace, there accumulates a layer of brown or sometimes whitish substance that looks like wool. This iron floss, and any article made from it, will not burn in fire; but itinerant peddlers call it "salamander's wool."

Following the lead of the philosopher Jorach, many writers say this animal is able to live in fire, but this is completely false. . . .

Storied Menagerie

St. Adamnan (c. 628–704)
The Life of St. Columba

In the seventh-century biography of St. Columba, Adamnan (Adomnan), ninth abbot of the monastery of Iona, relates what is generally credited with being the earliest account of the celebrated Loch Ness Monster. In the tradition of Marduk, Apollo, Perseus, Beowulf, and St. George, the holy man encounters a monstrous creature, but, no dragon-slayer, he controls the beast.

The historical Columba (c. A.D. 521–597) sailed from Ireland with twelve Church brothers to the Inner Hebrides island of Iona in about 563. He founded there the monastery and scriptorium that became a major outpost of the Church and Western learning through centuries of barbarism. Using the monastery as a missionary headquarters, Columba journeyed throughout Scotland, converting the pagan Picts. It was on one such excursion to the Highlands that he was said to have quelled the monster of the River Ness. The Lugne mocu-Min (MacMin) of the tale has been identified with a historical prior. Manuscripts and the relics of St. Columba were eventually moved to Ireland after Viking raids in the ninth century. One tradition holds that the illuminated *Book of Kells* was produced on Iona.

The Loch Ness water beast did not resurface until the twentieth century, when several Loch Ness sightings of a saurian form were recorded, establishing the legend of the celebrated creature affectionately known as "Nessie."

> He saw . . . a dreadful dragon come flying from the West that did enlumine the whole country with the flashing of his eyes.
>
> —Geoffrey of Monmouth
> *Histories of the Kings of Britain*

St. Columba and the Ness Monster*

CONCERNING A CERTAIN WATER BEAST DRIVEN AWAY BY THE POWER
OF THE BLESSED MAN'S PRAYER

. . . at another time, when the blessed man was for a number of days in the
province of the Picts, he had to cross the river Ness. When he reached its bank,
he saw a poor fellow being buried by other inhabitants; and the buriers said that,
while swimming not long before, he had been seized and most savagely bitten by
a water beast. Some men, going to his rescue in a wooden boat, though too late,
had put out hooks and caught hold of his wretched corpse. When the blessed
man heard this, he ordered notwithstanding that one of his companions should
swim out and bring back to him, by sailing, a boat that stood on the opposite
bank. Hearing this order of the holy and memorable man, Lugne mocu-Min
obeyed without delay, and putting off his clothes, excepting his tunic, plunged
into the water. But the monster, whose appetite had earlier been not so much
sated as whetted for prey, lurked in the depth of the river. Feeling the water
above disturbed by Lugne's swimming, it suddenly swam up to the surface, and
with gaping mouth and with great roaring rushed towards the man swimming
the middle of the stream. While all that were there, barbarians and even the
brothers, were struck down with extreme terror, the blessed man, who was
watching, raised his holy hand and drew the saving sign of the cross in the
empty air; and then, invoking the name of God, he commanded the savage
beast, and said: "You will go no further. Do not touch the man; turn backward
speedily." Then, hearing this command of the saint, the beast, as if pulled back
with ropes, fled terrified in swift retreat; although it had before approached so
close to Lugne as he swam that there was no more than the length of one short
pole between man and beast.

Then, seeing that the beast had withdrawn and that their fellow-soldier Lugne
had returned to them unharmed and safe, in the boat, the brothers with great
amazement glorified God in the blessed man. And also the pagan barbarians who
were there at the time, impelled by the magnitude of this miracle that they themselves had seen, magnified the God of the Christians.

---

* _Adomnan's Life of Columba_, trans. Alan Orr Anderson and Marjorie Ogilvie Anderson (London:
Thomas Nelson, 1961), 387–89.

BEOWULF (C. 8TH CENTURY)

The familiar monster-slayer material of myth and folk tale achieves epic stature in a poem that stands at the beginnings of English literature. In *Beowulf*, an anonymous Anglo-Saxon poet generally regarded as Christian weaves actual Scandinavian places, figures, and events from heroic tradition through accounts of the hero's battles with three monsters.

The longer of the poems's two distinct parts concerns the youthful exploits of the Geat prince Beowulf. Coming to the aid of King Hrothgar of Denmark, he defeats the gigantic Grendel and the demon's mother, two folkloric monsters that the Christian poet calls the descendants of Cain. After returning to his native Sweden, Beowulf becomes king and reigns wisely for fifty years before a dragon terrorizes his kingdom and destroys the royal hall itself.

Teutonic dragon lore, looking ahead to Beowulf's final battle, is introduced after the death of Grendel. A minstrel praising Beowulf compares him to the hero Sigemund, who single-handedly killed a hoard guardian and sailed home with its treasure. In the later *Volsung Saga* and *Niebelungenlied*, Sigemund's son, Sigurd (Siegfried), slays the dragon Fafnir. The *Beowulf* poet introduces the dragon in a long passage describing the hoard it has guarded for 300 years and its nightly vengeance on the kingdom for the theft of a golden flagon. Unlike Sigemund, Beowulf is aided by a kinsman in his dragon fight, and the battle is fatal for both hero and beast. The poem ends with the treasure being buried along with Beowulf's ashes in a barrow overlooking the sea. Following is the conclusion of the battle, when Wiglaf joins Beowulf in the fight. A "byrnie" is a mail shirt.

The single manuscript of *Beowulf* to survive, now in the British Museum, is thought to have been copied by two scribes around the year 1000. It was damaged in a library fire in 1731; two copies of it were made later in the century.

For other dragon battles, see the *Enuma Elish*, the *Hymn to Apollo*, Jacobus de Voragine, Edmund Spenser, and J. R. R. Tolkien.

The Fight with the Dragon*

> . . . This was the first time
> For young Wiglaf, that he should join
> The rush of war with his dear lord. His mind
> Did not melt, nor his legacy of strength
> Go weak in the fight, as the worm found out,

---

* *Beowulf: An Edition and Literary Translation, in Progress,* trans. Raymond P. Tripp, Jr. (Denver, Colo.: Society for New Language Study, 1990), 69, 70–71 (2625–30, 2661–710]

Interlaced dragons from the seventh-century *Book of Durrow*. By permission of Trinity College, Dublin.

After they had come together. . . .
    He waded through the reek with keen-headed
Help for his lord, with golden words and few.
"Dear Beowulf, live up to all you have done,
As in your youth you said you would never
As long as you had life let right fame
Fall away. Now, long famous for your deeds,
Pure prince, you must with all your might
Serve your worthy life well. I will help!"
    At these words, the worm came angrily on
For a second time, a foul gust of hate,
Worm-infested fire, most loathsome of men,
To fall upon his foes. Waves of fire burned
Shield to rim. A scorching byrnie could not
Yield much help for the young spear-warrior,
But the youth under his kinsman's cover
Went strong in arm, when his own board was
Reduced to flaming dust. Then the captain
King's mind took fame in hand, struck so hard
With his blade of war, that between his hand
And that hateful head shattered Naegling stood,
Went weak in the fight, Beowulf's own sword,
Old-etched in gray! Its edges of iron
Were not fated to be enough to help
The man in battle; his hand was too strong.
That man, I heard, with his swing overtaxed
Every wound-hard weapon he had carried
Into battle, not a wight better for it.
    Then for a third time was that stealthy brute,
That fire-fierce dragon, reminded of old feuds.
He rushed that hero when he got a chance,
Aggressively grim, went hot for the neck
With his bitter teeth. Beowulf throbbed red,
The life-blood of his soul rippled in gore.
    Then I heard at his great prince's need
That this upright earl showed such arm-work,
Such craft and keenness, as he was born to.
He never heeded the head, but burned his hand
Where he helped out with his family strength,
Striking this spiteful ghost with such spite
Low down, clever in arms, that his pretty sword
Plunged through fat plated flesh, and fire began

At last to cool. The king was master still
Of arm and will and bared the bitter sharp
Dagger he bore on his smoldering byrnie.
The Weders' chief wrote the worm off across
The middle, felled his foe. Strong arms let life
Leak out. They had served him up together,
Two kinsmen pledged as should man and knife be,
Thanes at need! But that was the sinking king's
Last moment of winning work in this world. . . .

THE ANGLO-SAXON CHRONICLE (9TH CENTURY)

In the earliest English chronicle, fiery flying "dragons" are among the celestial signs of the Viking ravaging of Lindisfarne monastery. Albertus Magnus later wrote, "I find it impossible to believe the anecdotes about dragons that fly through the air, breathing forth incandescent flames, unless they refer to certain vapors called 'dragons.'" *The Oxford English Dictionary* defines this usage as "a shooting star with a luminous train."

The Anglo-Saxon Chronicle was first compiled about 890 during the reign of Alfred and continued up to 1154. It is the earliest extensive prose work in English. The attack on Iona's sister monastery was the first of centuries of Norse raids. Siga is thought to have been a bishop.

For dragon portents, see Geoffrey of Monmouth.

A Portent of Dragons *

793. This year began with ominous signs over Northumbria, and these utterly panicked the people. Huge streaks of flame rushed across the full length of the sky, and flaming dragons as well were seen flying through the air, bringing fierce hunger with them. And not long after that, on 8 June of this same year, ravaging heathens ruthlessly levelled God's Church in Lindisfarne with shameless robbing and butchering of men. And Siga died on 22 February.

---

* *The Anglo-Saxon Chronicle*, translated for this volume by Raymond P. Tripp, Jr., from *Two of the Saxon Chronicles*, ed. Charles Plummer (Oxford: Clarendon Press, 1897).

OLD ENGLISH RIDDLE
FROM *THE EXETER BOOK* (C. 10TH CENTURY)

Among the nearly 100 riddles in the Old English *Exeter Book* is one of the earliest treatments of the fabled barnacle goose, considered the earliest account in English. Not known in classical times, the tale of a goose hatched either from barnacles or from the fruit of trees is medieval lore from northern European countries. The story was spread by the eyewitness account of Giraldus Cambrensis in the twelfth century. Following Cambrensis, the bird was included in bestiaries, and despite a papal edict and debunking by Albertus Magnus, the tale lived on in learned controversy up to the eighteenth century.

The anonymous riddles from *The Exeter Book*, influenced by Latin renditions of the genre, personify subjects from everyday life, such as wind, mead, an anchor, a drinking horn, a book worm, and a jay's spring song. According to the standard G. P. Krapp and E. V. K. Dobbie numbering of the *Exeter Book* riddles, the barnacle goose is no. 10.

For more on the barnacle goose, see Giraldus Cambrensis, Albertus Magnus, John Gerard, and William Jones.

*The Barnacle Goose**

My nib was in a narrowness, and I, under the water,
the water under flowing, was cradled deep
in the ocean currents. I awoke in the water of life,
covered by waves above,
my body secure on a travelling beam.
I was truly alive when I rose from the embraces
of the sea and the ship. I was clothed
in black and white when the air lifted me,
living, above into the wind from the wave
and bore me far across the seal-baths.
Say what I am called.

* Translated for this volume by Gregory K. Jember from *The Exeter Book*, ed. G. P. Krapp and E. V. K. Dobbie (New York: Columbia University Press, 1936).

Geoffrey of Monmouth (c. 1100–1155)
Histories of the Kings of Britain

Dragon omens presage momentous events in the chronicle that established the figure of King Arthur in European literature. In Geoffrey of Monmouth's *Historia Regum Britanniae* (c. 1136), the beasts of prophecy and dream represent the Britons and Saxons, and Arthur himself.

A body of legend had already begun to grow around the name of "Arthur" when Geoffrey, an Oxford cleric, produced in Latin his history of Britain — from "Brute, the first King of the Britons, onward to Cadwallader." A considerable portion of the book — derived from traditional story and the chronicles of Gildas (sixth century) and Nennius (ninth century) — is devoted to the embellished story of Arthur. Recounting the birth, conquests, and mortal wounding of the warrior king, the *Historia* is the most complete presentation of Arthurian matter up to its time. The book achieved enormous popularity in Norman England and on the Continent, leading to the widespread medieval development of Arthurian legend. Geoffrey claimed to have translated his chronicle from "a certain most ancient book in the British language," given him by Walter, Archdeacon of Oxford, but his attribution is now generally considered a fabrication to validate material that is largely fictional. His legendary matter served as a source for Chaucer, Shakespeare, and others.

Nearly midway through the history, the young Merlin is chosen as a sacrifice to powers that continually destroy the foundations of King Vortigern's fortress. Merlin saves himself by envisioning the meaning of the battling red and white dragons of the earth, prophesying the future of the Britons. After precipitating the birth of Arthur, Merlin leaves the tale. Yet another dragon portent occurs later in the chronicle, after Arthur rejects Roman demands for tribute and determines to conquer the Imperial City. While the Kings of the Orient are on the march toward Britain, Arthur and his knights set sail for the Continent. During the voyage, Arthur dreams of a deadly struggle to come, enacted by a dragon and a bear.

Dragons in many forms are integral to Arthurian material. Arthur's father is Uther Pendragon ("Pendragon" meaning literally, "head of the dragon"). According to Geoffrey, Arthur wore a golden helmet "graven with the semblance of a dragon." After the Romans left Britain, the Roman–Briton warlords adopted their dragon emblems, which eventually became the Red Dragon of Wales, the heraldic form of the Briton beast in Merlin's prophecy.

For dragon portents, see *The Anglo-Saxon Chronicle*.

Merlin prophesies before King Vortigern above the cistern containing the fighting red and white dragons. MS6, fol. 43v. By permission of the Lambeth Palace Library, London.

Prophecies of Merlin *

Accordingly, while Vortigern, King of the Britons, was yet seated upon the bank of the pool that had been drained, forth issued the two dragons, whereof the one was white and the other red. And when the one had drawn anigh unto the other, they grappled together in baleful combat and breathed forth fire as they panted. But presently the white dragon did prevail, and drave the red dragon unto the

---

* Geoffrey of Monmouth, *Histories of the Kings of Britain*, trans. Sebastian Evans (New York: Everyman's Library, E. P. Dutton, 1920), 117–18, 178–79.

verge of the lake. But he, grieving to be thus driven forth, fell fiercely again upon the white one, and forced him to draw back. And whilst that they were fighting on this wise, the King bade Ambrosius Merlin declare what this battle of the dragons did portend. Thereupon he straightway burst into tears, and drawing in the breath of prophecy, spake, saying:

"Woe unto the Red Dragon, for his extermination draweth nigh; and his caverns shall be occupied of the White Dragon that betokeneth the Saxons whom thou hast invited hither. But the Red signifieth the race of Britain that shall be oppressed of the White. Therefore shall the mountains and the valleys thereof be made level plain and the streams of the valleys shall flow with blood. The rites of religion shall be done away and the ruin of the churches be made manifest. At the last, she that is oppressed shall prevail and resist the cruelty of them that come from without. For the Boar of Cornwall shall bring succour and shall trample their necks beneath his feet. The islands of the Ocean shall be subdued unto his power, and the forests of Gaul shall he possess. The house of Romulus shall dread the fierceness of his prowess and doubtful shall be his end. Renowned shall he be in the mouth of the peoples, and his deeds shall be as meat unto them that tell thereof. Six of his descendants shall follow his sceptre, but after them shall rise up the German Worm. The Wolf of the sea shall exalt him, unto whom the woods of Africa shall bear company. Again shall religion be done away, and the Sees of the Primates shall be transmuted. The dignity of London shall adorn Dorobernia and men shall resort unto the seventh shepherd of York in the realm of Armorica. Menevia shall be robed in the pall of the City of Legions and a preacher of Ireland shall be stricken dumb on account of an infant in the womb. It shall rain a shower of blood, and a baleful famine shall prey upon mortal men. When these things befal, then shall the Red one grieve, yet when he hath undergone his travail shall he wax strong. Then shall the calamity of the White be hastened and that which is builded in his little garden shall be overthrown. . . ."

Arthur's Dream

All needful ordinance made, they started on their expedition Britainwards at the beginning of the Kalends of August. When Arthur learned that they were upon the march, he made over the charge of defending Britain unto his nephew Mordred and his Queen Guenevere, he himself with his army making for Hamo's Port, where he embarked with a fair breeze of wind. And whilst that he was thronged about with his numberless ships, and was cleaving the deep with a prosperous course and much rejoicing, a passing deep sleep as about the middle of the night did overtake him, and in his sleep he saw in dream a certain bear flying in the air, at the growling whereof all the shores did tremble. He saw, moreover, a dreadful dragon come flying from the West that did enlumine the whole country with the flashing of his eyes. And when the one did meet the other there was a marvellous fight betwixt them, and presently the dragon leaping again and again upon the bear, did scorch him up with his fiery breath and cast down his shrivelled carcass to the earth. And thereby awakened, Arthur did relate his dream unto them that stood by, who expounded the same unto him saying that the dragon did betoken himself, but the bear some giant with whom he should encounter; that the fight did foretoken a battle that should be betwixt them, and that the dragon's victory should be his own. Natheless, Arthur did conjecture otherwise thereof, weening that such vision as had befallen him was more like to have to do with himself and the Emperor. At last, when the night had finished her course and the dawn waxed red, they came to in the haven of Barfleur, and pitching their tents thereby, did await the coming of the Kings of the islands and the Dukes of the neighbour provinces.

SNORRI STURLUSON (1179–1241)
THE PROSE EDDA

Among the dragons in medieval literature is a primeval mythological form of the cosmic serpent: the Midgard Serpent (Jörmungandr, Midgard's Worm) of Scandinavian mythology. Spawned by the god Loki and the giantess Angrboda and hurled from celestial Asgard by Odin, the monster grew in the ocean until — like the ancient symbol of the serpent of eternity — it encircled the earth with its tail in its mouth.

In the company of the Babylonian Marduk and a host of other dragon-slayers is the Teutonic Thor, who encounters the monster three times. The first meeting between the two was in the hall of the giant Útgarda-Loki, when the giant challenged the god with three tests: emptying a horn of mead, lifting a cat, and wrestling an old woman. After the god failed all three tests and the hall disappeared, it was revealed that the giant's magic mead was the ocean, the cat the Midgard Serpent, and the crone Old Age. Thor vengefully seeks out the monster on a fishing trip with the giant Hymir, and long after, during Ragnarøk (the Twilight of the Gods), the war god of the Aesir slays the beast, only to die himself from the serpent's venomous breath.

All three of the tales are recounted in Snorri Sturluson's *Prose Edda* (c. 1220), a handbook for poets derived from traditional lays of the gods, many of which are collected in *The Poetic Edda* (*Elder Edda*). The two Icelandic *Eddas* are the major literary sources of Scandinavian mythology. Snorri's book is comprised of an author's prologue, an epitome of pagan myth, and sections on the subjects and diction of skaldic verse. The myths are related in dialogue form in "The Tricking of Gylfi," in which Gylfi (Gangleri), the King of the Swedes, asks about the gods in order to discover their power. Hárr is one of the disguises of Odin.

The fishing episode, below, immediately follows the tale of Thor in the hall of Útgarda-Loki. Himinbrjotr, Hymir's ox, has been translated as "Heaven-bellowing" and "Heavenspringer." As told in this version, the robust story has a comic, tall-tale quality, with naturalistic details. Thor's catching the serpent was often depicted in Scandinavian art.

Thor and the Midgard Serpent*

Then said Gangleri: "Very mighty is Útgarda-Loki, and he deals much in wiles and in magic; and his might may be seen in that he had such henchmen as have great prowess. Now did Thor ever take vengeance for this?" Hárr answered: "It is not unknown, though one be not a scholar, that Thor took redress for this journey of which the tale has but now been told; and he did not tarry at home long before he made ready for his journey so hastily that he had with him no chariot and no he-goats and no retinue. He went out over Midgard in the guise of a young lad, and came one evening at twilight to a certain giant's, who was called Hymir. Thor abode as guest there overnight; but at dawn Hymir arose and clothed himself and made ready to row to sea a-fishing. Then Thor sprang up and was speedily ready, and asked Hymir to let him row to sea with him. But Hymir said that Thor would be of little help to him, being so small and a youth, 'And thou wilt freeze, if I stay so long and so far out as I am wont.' But Thor said that he would be able to row far out from land, for the reason that it was not certain whether he would be the first to ask to row back. Thor became so enraged at the giant that he was forthwith ready to let his hammer crash against him; but he forced himself to forbear, since he purposed to try his strength in another quarter. He asked Hymir what they should have for bait, but Hymir bade him get bait for himself. Then Thor turned away thither where he saw a certain herd of oxen, which Hymir owned; he took the largest ox, called Himinbrjotr and cut off its head and went therewith to the sea. By that time Hymir had shoved out the boat.

"Thor went aboard the skiff and sat down in the stern-seat, took two oars and rowed; and it seemed to Hymir that swift progress came of his rowing. Hymir rowed forward in the bow, and the rowing proceeded rapidly; then Hymir said that they had arrived at those fishing-banks where he was wont to anchor and angle for flat-fish. But Thor said that he desired to row much farther, and they took a sharp pull; then Hymir said that they had come so far that it was perilous

* Snorri Sturluson, *The Prose Edda*, trans. Arthur Gilchrist Brodeur (New York: American–Scandinavian Foundation, 1960), 68–70.

The Midgard Serpent prepares to swallow Thor's oxhead bait. Seventeenth-century Icelandic manuscript. Left, a depiction of Valhalla, home of the gods. *Snora Edda*, AM 738 4to. Courtesy of Stofun Arna Magnussonar, Reykjavik, Iceland; photograph by the Arnamagn Institute, Copenhagen.

to abide out farther because of the Midgard Serpent. Thor replied that they would row a while yet, and so he did; but Hymir was then sore afraid. Now as soon as Thor had laid by the oars, he made ready a very strong fishing-line, and the hook was no less large and strong. Then Thor put the ox-head on the hook and cast it overboard, and the hook went to the bottom; and it is telling thee the truth to say that then Thor beguiled the Midgard Serpent no less than Útgarda-Loki had mocked Thor, at the time when he lifted up the Serpent in his hand.

"The Midgard Serpent snapped at the ox-head, and the hook caught in its jaw; but when the Serpent was aware of this, it dashed away so fiercely that both Thor's fists crashed against the gunwale. Then Thor was angered, and took upon him his divine strength, braced his feet so strongly that he plunged through the ship with both feet, and dashed his feet against the bottom; then he drew the Serpent up to the gunwale. And it may be said that no one has seen very fearful sights who might not see that: how Thor flashed fiery glances at the Serpent, and the Serpent in turn stared up toward him from below and blew venom. Then, it is said, the giant Hymir grew pale, became yellow, and was sore afraid, when he saw the Serpent, and how the sea rushed out and in through the boat. In the very moment when Thor clutched his hammer and raised it on high, then the giant fumbled for his fish-knife and hacked off Thor's line at the gunwale, and the Serpent sank down into the sea. Thor hurled his hammer after it; and men say that he struck off its head against the bottom; but I think it were true to tell thee that the Midgard Serpent yet lives and lies in the encompassing sea. But Thor swung his fish and brought it against Hymir's ear, so that he plunged overboard, and Thor saw the soles of his feet. And Thor waded to land."

JACOBUS DE VORAGINE (1228/9–1298)
THE GOLDEN LEGEND

In his book of saints' lives, Jacobus de Voragine recounts a common medieval tale of a young knight on a charger rescuing a maiden from a dragon. This particular hero was St. George, whose deeds earned for him the status of patron saint of England and for the red cross on his armor its place in heraldry and on the Union Jack. His killing of the monster, a symbolic triumph of good over evil, became a favorite subject of both medieval and Renaissance artists, rivaling depiction of the Archangel Michael's expelling the Devil from heaven.

Although virtually nothing is known about his life, St. George is generally considered to be a historical martyr of the Near East whose legend was introduced to Europe by returning Crusaders. The dragon story was a late addition to the tales of his torture and martyrdom, popularized through Jacobus's *Legenda Sanctorum* ("Legends of the Saints"). George's tomb, at Lydda, in Palestine, is only miles away from the legendary site of Perseus's battle with the sea dragon; close parallels between the St. George story and that of Perseus and Andromeda suggest that the saint's tale may be indebted to the Greco–Roman myth. St. George becomes the Red Cross Knight in Edmund Spenser's *Faerie Queene*.

Other well-known dragon stories in Jacobus's book involve St. Margaret, the patron saint of childbirth. Refusing marriage with the governor of Antioch, Margaret is tortured and imprisoned, and in her cell appears a dragon, which she subdues with the sign of the cross. In another version of the tale — which Jacobus terms apochryphal — the dragon swallows her, only to be burst open by the power of the cross. The maiden emerges alive, but is later beheaded. The book also contains the lives of the Church Fathers represented in Chapter 4 of this anthology.

The archbishop of Genoa's collection of moral lessons based on folklore of the saints was translated throughout Europe. So revered that it came to be known as *The Golden Legend*, the book was immensely popular up to the Reformation. The work was one of the first books printed in English, produced by William Caxton in 1483. The entry below is the Caxton translation, from his chapter, "Of the Lyf of Saynt George Martyr." In the unaltered fifteenth-century prose, spelling and punctuation are inconsistent.

Saynt George and the Dragon*

Saynt George was a knyght and borne in capadose. On a tyme he came in to the prouynce of Lybye to a cyte whyche is sayd Sylene. And by this cyte was a stagne or a ponde lyke a see, wherein was a dragon whyche enuenymed alle the contre. And on a tyme the peple were assemblid for to slee hym, & whan they sawe hym they fledde. And when he came nyghe the cytee he venymed the peple wyth his breeth, and therfore the peple of the cytee gaue to hym euery day two sheep for to fede hym, by cause he shold doo no harme to the peple, and whan the sheep fayled there was taken a man and a sheep.

Thenne was an ordenaunce made in the towne that there shold be taken the chyldren and yonge peple of them of the towne by lotte, and eueryche as it fyl, were he gentil or poure, shold be delyuerd whan the lotte fyl on hym or hyr. So it happed that many of them of the towne were thenne delyuerd, in soo moche that the lotte fyl vpon the kynges doughter, wherof the kyng was sory and sayd vnto the peple.

For the loue of the goddes take golde and syluer and all that I haue, & lete me haue my doughter.

* William Caxton, trans., *The Golden Legend of Master William Caxton*, vol. 1 of the Kelmscott Edition (London: Hammersmith, 1892), 454–55.

St. George and the dragon. From the *Belles Heures de Jean, Duc de Berry*. Fol. 167r.
French, c. 1410–16. By permission of Metropolitan Museum of Art, New York, The
Cloisters Collection, 1954.

They sayd, how syr, ye haue made and ordeyned the lawe and our chyldren
been now deed, and ye wold doo the contrarye. Your doughter shal be gyuen or
ellys we shal brenne you and your hows.

When the kyng saw he myght nomore doo he began to wepe, and sayd to his
doughter, now shal I neuer see thyn espousayls. Thenne retorned he to the peple
and demaunded viii dayes respyte, and they graunted hit to hym. And whan the
viii dayes were passed they came to hym and sayd, thou seest that the cyte peris-
sheth.

Thenne dyd the kyng doo araye his doughter lyke as she shold be wedded, and
enbraced hyr, kyssed hir and gaue hir his benedyccion, and after ledde hyr to the
place where the dragon was.

Whan she was there, saynt george passed by, & whan he sawe the lady he
demaunded the lady what she made there, & she sayd, goo ye your waye fayre
yonge man that ye perysshe not also.

Thenne sayd he, telle to me what haue ye, & why ye wepe, and doubte ye of
no thynge. When she sawe that he wold knowe she sayd to hym how she was
delyuerd to the dragon. Thenne sayd saynt george, Fayre doughter, doubte ye no
thynge herof, for I shall helpe the in the name of Jhesu Cryste. She said, for goddes sake good knyght goo your waye and abyde not wyth me, for ye may not
delyuer me. Thus as they spake to gyder the dragon apperyd, and came rennyng to

them, and saynt George was vpon his hors, and drewe out his swerde and gar-nysshed hym wyth the signe of the crosse, & rode hardely ageynst the dragon which came toward hym, and smote hym with his spere and hurte hym sore, and threwe hym to the grounde. And after sayd to the mayde, delyuer to me your gyrdel & bynde hit about the necke of the dragon, and be not aferde. Whan she had doon soo the dragon folowed hyr as it had been a meke beest and debonayr. Thenne she ledde hym in to the cyte, and the peple fledde by mountayns and valeyes, and sayd, alas, alas, we shall be alle deed.

Thenne saynt George sayd to them, ne doubte ye no thynge, wythout more, byleue ye in god Jhesu cryste, & doo you to be baptysed and I shal slee the dragon.

Thenne the kyng was baptysed & al his peple, and saynt george slewe the dragon and smote of his heed, and commaunded that he shold be throwen in the feldes, and they took iiii cartes wyth oxen that drewe hym out of the cyte.

Thenne were there wel fyftene thousand men baptised, without wymmen and chyldren, and the kyng dyd doo make a chirche there of our lady and of saynt George, in the whiche yet sourdeth a founteyn of lyuyng water whiche heleth seek peple that drynke therof.

After this the kyng offred to Saint george as moche money as there myght be nombred, but he refused alle and commaunded that it should be gyuen to poure peple for goddes sake, and enioyned the kynge iiii thynges, that is, that he shold haue charge of the chyrches, & that he shold honoure the preestes, and here theyr seruyce dylygently, and that he shold haue pyte on the poure peple, and after kyssed the kyng and departed.

GESTA ROMANORUM (13TH CENTURY)

Gesta Romanorum ("The Deeds of the Romans") was one of the Middle Age's most popular compilations of tales, used by clerics to both instruct and entertain illiterate audiences. Inappropriately titled, the Latin collection is a mixture of classical, oriental, and European folklore and legend, complete with moralistic *significatio*. Through transcription, the loosely structured book developed into different versions and appeared in many printed editions. Its wealth of heterogeneous tales made it a standard source book for later writers.

The *Gesta Romanorum* tale in which Alexander the Great kills a basilisk draws on the tradition established by Pliny that the basilisk kills not only with its noxious breath but with its look. Turning a deadly gaze back on itself by means of a shield or mirror is a common folkloric motif. Alexander was the subject of a popular cycle of medieval romances contemporaneous with the *Gesta Romanorum*.

For Alexander, see also *The Romance of Alexander*.

King Alexander and the Basilisk*

Alexander the Great was lord of the whole world. He once collected a large army, and besieged a certain city, around which many knights and others were killed without any visible wound. Much surprised at this, he called together his philosophers, and said, "My masters, how is this? My soldiers die, and there is no apparent wound!" "No wonder," replied they; "on the walls of a city is a basilisk, whose look infects your soldiers, and they die of the pestilence it creates." "And what remedy is there for this?" said the king.

"Place a mirror in an elevated situation between the army and the wall where the basilisk is; and no sooner shall he behold it, than his own look, reflected in the mirror, will return upon himself, and kill him." And so it was done.

APPLICATION

My beloved, look into the glass of *reflection*, and, by remembrance of human frailty, destroy the vices which time elicits.

—— 🦁 ——

DANTE ALIGHIERI (1265–1321)
THE DIVINE COMEDY

In a mystical climax of the supreme poetic synthesis of medieval Christianity, the focal figure is a griffin, its lion-eagle parts associated with the earthly and divine natures of Christ. Presented as a monster in much art and literature of the Middle Ages, the creature is a triumphant religious image in Dante's *Divine Comedy*.

The griffin appears at a major turning point of the *Commedia*, at the end of the second stage of the soul's allegorical journey from Hell to Paradise. On the summit of the Mountain of Purgatory, the Earthly Paradise, Dante and his classical guide, Virgil, witness a heavenly pageant led by the seven spirits of God and followed by twenty-four elders representing the books of the Old Testament and the Four Beasts of the Gospels. Climaxing the procession, itself joined by dancing Virtues and more elders, is the Sacred Griffon, pulling the Chariot of the Church. Virgil departs when Dante's ideal love, Beatrice, appears as the agent of purification and as the poet's guide through Paradise. In a beatific vision, Dante sees the

* *Gesta Romanorum*, trans. Charles Swan, revised by Wynnard Hooper (1876; rpt., New York: Dover, 1959), 244–45.

griffin's dual nature reflected in her eyes. The procession moves into a wood and stops at a withered tree, the Garden of Eden's Tree of Knowledge, which is also the source of the Holy Rood. When the griffin ties the pole of the chariot to the tree, the barren branches burst into full leaf. The members of the Heavenly Pageant sing a hymn beyond human understanding, overwhelming Dante. While he sleeps, the griffin leads the attending company to Paradise.

The Sacred Griffon is traditionally interpreted as a symbolic representation of Christ, the red and white lion parts signifying His human nature, the golden bird parts His divine nature. Seven centuries earlier, Isidore of Seville had suggested similar correspondences in his *Etymologies*, declaring, "Christ is a lion because he reigns and has great strength; and an eagle because, after the Resurrection, he ascended to heaven." Alexander's Griffin Flight, widespread in medieval literature and art, may have been a source of Dante's sacred beast.

The following excerpts are from Cantos 29, 31, and 32 of the *Purgatorio*.

The Sacred Griffon *

> When I had chosen on the river's edge
> Such station, that the distance of the stream
> Alone did separate me; there I stayed
> My steps for clearer prospect, and beheld
> The flames go onward, leaving, as they went,
> The air behind them painted as with trail
> Of liveliest pencils; so distinct were marked
> All those seven listed colours, whence the sun
> Maketh his bow, and Cynthia her zone.
> These streaming gonfalons did flow beyond
> My vision; and ten paces, as I guess,
> Parted the outermost. Beneath a sky
> So beautiful, came four and twenty elders,
> By two and two, with flower-de-luces crown'd.
> All sang one song: "Blessed be thou among
> The daughters of Adam! and thy loveliness
> Blessed forever!" After that the flowers,
> And the fresh herblets, on the opposite brink,
> Were free from that elected race; as light
> In heaven doth second light, came after them
> Four animals, each crown'd with verdurous leaf.

* Dante Alighieri, *The Divine Comedy of Dante*, trans. Henry F. Cary (New York: Thomas Y. Crowell, 1897), 301–3, 310, 312–14 (29.69–92, 102–16, 147–50, 31.113–27, 32.33–62, 80–89).

Dante's sacred griffin pulling the chariot of the Church. Sixteenth-century Italian wood-cut. By permission of the Houghton Library, Harvard University.

> With six wings each was plumed; the plumage full
> Of eyes; and the eyes of Argus would be such,
> Were they endued with life. . . .
>   The space, surrounded by the four, enclosed
> A car triumphal: on two wheels it came,
> Drawn at a Griffon's neck; and he above
> Stretch'd either wing uplifted, 'tween the midst
> And the three listed hues, on each side, three;
> So that the wings did cleave or injure none;
> And out of sight they rose. The members, far
> As he was bird, were golden; white the rest,

With vermeil intervein'd. So beautiful
A car, in Rome, ne'er graced Augustus' pomp,
Or Africanus'; e'en the sun's itself
Were poor to this; that chariot of the sun,
Erroneous, which in blazing ruin fell
At Tellus' prayer devout, by the just doom
Mysterious of all-seeing Jove. . . .
　　　Whenas the car was o'er against me, straight
Was heard a thundering, at whose voice it seemed
The chosen multitude were stayed; for there,
With the first ensigns, made they solemn halt.

·　·　·

And then they led me to the Griffon's breast,
Where, turned toward us, Beatrice stood.
"Spare not thy vision. We have stationed thee
Before the emeralds, whence love, erewhile,
Hath drawn his weapons on thee." As they spake,
A thousand fervent wishes riveted
Mine eyes upon her beaming eyes, that stood,
Still fixed toward the Griffon, motionless.
As the sun strikes a mirror, even thus
Within those orbs the twofold being shone;
For ever varying, in one figure now
Reflected, now in other. Reader! muse
How wondrous in my sight it seemed, to mark
A thing, albeit stedfast in itself,
Yet in its imaged semblance mutable.

·　·　·

. . . Onward had we moved, as far,
Perchance, as arrow at three several flights
Full winged had sped, when from her station down
Descended Beatrice. With one voice
All murmur'd "Adam"; circling next a plant
Despoiled of flowers and leaf, on every bough.
Its tresses, spreading more as more they rose,
Were such, as 'midst their forest wilds, for height,
The Indians might have gazed at. "Blessed thou,
Griffon! whose beak hath never plucked that tree

Pleasant to taste: for hence the appetite
Was warped to evil." Round the stately trunk
Thus shouted forth the rest, to whom returned
The animal twice-gendered: "Yea! for so
The generation of the just are saved."
And turning to the chariot-pole, to foot
He drew it of the widowed branch, and bound
There, left unto the stock whereon it grew.
     As when large floods of radiance from above
Stream, with that radiance mingled, which ascends
Next after setting of the scaly sign,
Our plants then bourgeon, and each wears anew
His wonted colours, ere the sun have yoked
Beneath another star his flamy steeds;
Thus putting forth a hue more faint than rose,
And deeper than the violet, was renew'd
The plant, erewhile in all its branches bare.
Unearthly was the hymn, which then arose.
I understood it not, nor to the end
Endured the harmony. . . .
         . . . thus to myself
Returning, over me beheld I stand
The piteous one, who, cross the stream, had brought
My steps. "And where," all doubting, I exclaimed,
"Is Beatrice?"—"See her," she replied,
"Beneath the fresh leaf, seated on its root.
Behold the associate choir, that circles her.
The others, with a melody more sweet
And more profound, journeying to higher realms,
Upon the Griffon tend. . . ."

Travelers' Tales

THE ROMANCE OF ALEXANDER

From the historical military campaigns of Alexander the Great (356–323 B.C.) grew one of the most popular bodies of travel and romance literature of the Middle Ages. Alexander's expeditions through Persia, Egypt, and India, encompassing the known world, formed the basis of the adventures and wonder tales collected in multiple versions of the Alexander legend. Figuring among the later accounts is a menagerie of fantastic beasts and the world conqueror's "Celestial Journey."

The original Alexander story, the Greek Pseudo-Callisthenes, may have been produced in Alexandria in the second century A.D. A mixture of historical and legendary material, the Pseudo-Callisthenes spread both East and West, introduced in Europe through a third-century Latin translation. Following a tenth-century Latin version, the Alexander material developed into popular romances of the twelfth and thirteenth centuries. Accounts of the marvels of India, in the tradition of Ctesias and Apollonius of Tyana, were incorporated into the romance from the spurious *Letter on India to Aristotle*, addressed to Alexander's former tutor. The letter heavily influenced fictional travel literature, including *The Letter of Prester John*, and the *Travels* of Sir John Mandeville.

In the first of the excerpts below, phantasmagorical beasts described in the letter to Aristotle invade Alexander's camp. Some of the monsters are hybrids, some extraordinary in size, such as the single-horned

There are in our country elephants and other animals called dromedaries and also white horses and wild bulls of seven horns, white bears, and the strangest lions of red, green, black, and blue color.

—*The Letter of Prester John*

169

Odontotyrannos (Greek, "tooth-king," which some have identified with the crocodile). The "scorpion-tails" suggest Ctesias's description of the manticore.

Alexander's flight, with its heavily Christian action and moral, is here told by Alexander himself in a letter to his mother, Olympias. In this particular entry, the birds are not specifically identified as griffins, but Alexander's heavenly ascent in a seat or chariot attached to griffins was a favorite subject of medieval artists, who portrayed it in tapestries, mosaics, sculpture, and illuminated manuscripts. The ascent tale follows shortly after Alexander's account of his descent into the sea in a glass jar.

In art and lore, griffins also pull the chariots of Cretan goddesses, Zeus, Apollo, Nemesis, and, in Dante's *Divine Comedy*, the Church. The serpent Alexander sees encircling the earth, like Oceanus of the Greeks, takes the form of the Midgard Serpent in Teutonic mythology.

The following excerpts are from Richard Stoneman's translation, the first full translation of different versions of the Greek Alexander romance into English.

For Alexander, see the *Gesta Romanorum*.

The Beasts of India*

"I ordered the men to pitch camp, to prepare the beds and to light fires. About the third hour of the night, when the moon was high, the beasts that lived in the wood came out to drink from the lake. There were scorpions 18 inches long, sand-burrowers, both white and red. We were very frightened. Some of the men were killed, and there was tremendous groaning and wailing. Then four-footed beasts began to come out to drink. Among them were lions bigger than bulls — their teeth alone were 2 feet long — lynxes, panthers, tigers, scorpion-tails, elephants, ox-rams, bull-stags, men with six hands, strap-footed men, dog-partridges and other kinds of wild animals. Our alarm grew greater. We drove some of them off with our weapons. We set fire to the woods. The serpents ran into the fire. Some we stamped on and killed with our swords, but most were burnt; and this lasted until the sixth hour of the night, when the moon set. Shaken by fear and terrible dread, we stood wondering at their varied forms. And suddenly a wild animal came that was larger than any elephant, called the Odontotyrannos; and it wanted to attack us. I ran back and forth and beseeched my brave companions to make fires and protect themselves lest they meet a horrible death. The beast in its eagerness to hurt the men ran and fell into the flames. From there it charged into the army, killing twenty-six men at once. But some of our other brave men struck down and slew this one-horned beast. Thirteen hundred men were hardly

* *The Greek Alexander Romance*, trans. Richard Stoneman (London: Penguin Books, 1991), 183–84, 123.

able to drag him away. When the moon went down night foxes leapt out of the sand, some 8, and some 12 feet long; and crocodiles emerged from the wood and killed the baggage-carriers. There were bats larger than pigeons, and they had teeth. Night crows were perching by the lake; we hunted them down and cooked a large dinner. The creatures never attacked humans nor did they dare to approach the fire. When it was day, all these animals went away. Then I ordered that the local guides, of whom we had fifty and who had led us to those evil places, be tortured and taken and thrown into the river. Then we collected our things, and moved on 12 miles."

Alexander's Celestial Journey

"Then I began to ask myself again if this place was really the end of the world, where the sky touched the earth. I wanted to discover the truth, and so I gave orders to capture two of the birds that lived there. They were very large white

Alexander prepares for his Griffin Flight. From the Bodley manuscript. By permission of the Houghton Library, Harvard University.

birds, very strong but tame; they did not fly away when they saw us. Some of the soldiers climbed on to their backs, hung on tightly, and flew off. The birds fed on carrion, with the result that a great many of them came to our camp, attracted by the dead horses. I captured two of them and ordered them to be given no food for three days. On the third day I had something like a yoke constructed from wood, and had this tied to their throats. Then I had an ox-skin made into a large bag, fixed it to the yoke, and climbed in, holding two spears, each about 10 feet long and with a horse's liver fixed to the point. At once the birds soared up to seize the livers, and I rose up with them into the air, until I thought I must be close to the sky. I shivered all over because of the extreme coldness of the air, caused by the beating of the birds' wings.

"Soon a flying creature in the form of a man approached me and said, 'O Alexander, you have not yet secured the whole earth, and are you now exploring the heavens? Return to earth as fast as possible, or you will become food for these birds.' He went on, 'Look down on the earth, Alexander!' I looked down, somewhat afraid, and behold, I saw a great snake curled up, and in the middle of the snake a tiny circle like a threshing-floor. Then my companion said to me, 'Point your spear at the threshing-floor, for that is the world. The snake is the sea that surrounds the world.'

"Thus admonished by Providence above, I returned to earth, landing about seven days' journey from my army. I was now frozen and half-dead with exhaustion. Where I landed, I found one of the satraps who was under my command; borrowing 300 horsemen from him, I returned to my camp. Now I have decided to make no more attempts at the impossible. Farewell."

THE VOYAGE OF ST. BRENDAN
(9TH CENTURY)

Independent of Mediterranean seafaring, and earlier than Viking expansion, Irish monks sailed hide *curraghs* to islands in the North Atlantic, venturing at least as far west as Iceland. The most renowned of these ecclesiastical sailors was St. Brendan (Brandon, c. 484–578), founder and abbot of Clonfert, in Galway. He is thought to have traveled extensively, from Ireland to the Scottish islands and perhaps to Wales. By the ninth century, he became the legendary hero of the *Navigatio Sancti Brendani Abbatis*, a Latin account of his seven-year voyage to the Promised Land of the Saints. Among the adventures of the saint and his crew of monks in their skin craft are fabulous encounters with the largest "monster" of the ocean and a voracious griffin.

The Voyage of St. Brendan is filled with details of monastic practices, and even though sailing distances between islands are typically measured here in biblical terms of forty days, the epic tale contains enough description of seafaring and references to landfalls to suggest that it was informed by accounts of actual North Atlantic voyages. Translated into the vernacular throughout Europe, the *Voyage* is extant in more than a hundred manuscripts. The Brendan legend influenced Irish seafaring tales known as *Imrama*.

The Earthly Paradise Brendan found became known as St. Brendan's Island, which for the next 900 years was variously located on maps and navigational charts from Madeira to the West Indies. Some scholars believed St. Brendan had reached North America, and in the 1970s the English scholar-sailor Tim Severin proved the possibility of such a voyage by sailing a craft of tanned skins from Ireland to Newfoundland.

In the excerpts below, "Jasconius" is a Latin derivation of the Irish word for "fish." The Easter landing on the beast occurs between the monks' visits to the Island of Sheep and the Paradise of Birds and is repeated later in the tale. Sailors mistaking a whale for an island is a common folk motif. The bird that pursues the griffin had earlier dropped bunches of grapes to the hungry crew.

Jasconius*

When they approached the other island, the boat began to ground before they could reach its landing-place. Saint Brendan ordered the brothers to disembark from the boat into the sea, which they did. They held the boat on both sides with ropes until they came to the landing-place. The island was stony and without grass. There were a few pieces of driftwood on it, but no sand on its shore. While the brothers spent the night outside in prayers and vigils, the man of God remained sitting inside in the boat. For he knew the kind of island it was, but he did not want to tell them, lest they be terrified.

When morning came he ordered each of the priests to sing his Mass, which they did. While Saint Brendan was himself singing his Mass in the boat, the brothers began to carry the raw meat out of the boat to preserve it with salt, and also the flesh which they had brought from the other island. When they had done this they put a pot over a fire. When, however, they were plying the fire with wood and the pot began to boil, the island began to be in motion like a wave. The brothers rushed to the boat, crying out for protection to the holy father. He drew each one of them into the boat by his hand. Having left everything they had had on the island behind, they began to sail. Then the island

* *The Voyage of St. Brendan: Journey to the Promised Land*, trans. John J. O'Meara (Atlantic Highlands, N.J.: Humanities Press, 1976), 18–19, 48.

St. Brendan and his monks celebrate mass on the back of the giant whale, Jasconius. St. Brendan's island, the Promised Land of the Saints, is located to the north. *Novi Orbis Indiae Occidentalis*, a 1621 map by Honorius Philoponus. G.7237. By permission of the British Library.

moved out to sea. The lighted fire could be seen over two miles away. Saint Brendan told the brothers what it really was, saying:

"Brothers, are you surprised at what this island has done?"

They said:

"We are very surprised and indeed terror-stricken."

He said to them:

"My sons, do not be afraid. God revealed to me during the night in a vision the secret of this affair. Where we were was not an island, but a fish — the foremost of all that swim in the ocean. He is always trying to bring his tail to meet his head, but he cannot because of his length. His name is Jasconius."

The Gryphon

When they had gone on board, the boat's sail was hoisted to steer where the wind directed. After they had sailed, the bird called the Gryphon appeared to them, flying from far away towards them. When his brothers saw it they started saying to the holy father:

"That beast has come to devour us."

The man of God said to them:

"Do not be afraid. God is our helper. He will defend us on this occasion too."

The bird stretched her talons to seize the servants of God. Just then, suddenly, the bird which on the earlier occasion brought them the branch with the fruits, flew swiftly up to the Gryphon, which immediately made to devour her. But this bird defended herself until she overcame and tore out the eyes of the Gryphon. The Gryphon then flew high up into the sky so that the brothers could scarcely see her. But her killer pursued her until she killed her. For the Gryphon's body fell into the sea near the boat before the eyes of the brothers. The other bird returned to her own place.

THE ARABIAN NIGHTS

At least 600 years before *The Arabian Nights* was first published in the West in the early eighteenth century, traditional tales collected in it were spread throughout Europe by travelers and Crusaders returning from the East. Among those were fantastic stories incorporated into the adventures of Sindbad, the quintessential fictional traveler whose seven voyages have been called "the Arabian *Odyssey*." His second voyage includes the most famous account of the roc (rukh, ruc), a fabulous oriental bird not previously known to the West through classical tradition, bestiaries, or encyclopedias.

As Sindbad himself indicates, the legend of the "Rukh" was already widespread by the time he encountered the bird. Roc lore is found in medieval Arabian writings from scientific works to books of marvels. Marco Polo was told the roc lived in Madagascar, and Ibn Battuta learned of the bird from superstitious sailors in the China Seas. Identified with the condor and other large birds, the roc is one of many gigantic oriental birds. A bird carrying a human is a common motif in myth and folklore, from Zeus as an eagle transporting Ganymede to Olympus, to Garuda bearing the Indian god Vishnu. Even Geoffrey Chaucer, in *The House of Fame*, is carried off by Jupiter's loquacious eagle, the two discussing philosophy during their flight through the firmament.

Sindbad's second voyage — as are all his others — is resonant with traditional lore. His aerial adventure with the roc is reminiscent of the Griffin Flight of Alexander, and the bird's seizing a serpent from the Valley of Diamonds is thought to derive from Garuda's battles with the Nagas. Later, like Odysseus escaping from the Cyclops' cave under a ram, Sindbad attaches himself to a diamond-studded slab of meat to be carried off by another gigantic bird. Also during the second voyage, a roc snatches up a *karkadan* (Persian unicorn) with an elephant impaled upon its horn. On Sindbad's fifth voyage, parent rocs avenge the eating of their young by dropping boulders on the departing ship — like the Cyclops attempting to destroy the ship of Odysseus. Elsewhere in the Sindbad voyages is reference to an Indian Ocean bird that came from seashells (the oriental version of the Western barnacle goose) and the familiar tale of sailors anchoring on a sea beast, thinking it is solid land. The roc also appears in several other tales in *The Arabian Nights*.

The Arabian Nights (*The Arabian Nights' Entertainments* and *The Thousand and One Nights*) is a vast frame collection of Moslem folklore, structured by the tales Scheherazade (Shahrazad) tells her royal husband, each night leaving a story unfinished in order to delay her execution. Derived from oral tradition, developed over time, the stories are thought to have been written down by the fifteenth century. Antoine Gallard (1646–1715) introduced the material to Europe in his French translation of one of the Arabic versions, the first of many translations that established the book as an integral part of Western literature.

In Sir Richard Burton's major nineteenth-century translation of the total work — from which the following entry is taken — is an important note on the "Rukh" and "the fable world-wide of the *Wundervogel*" ("wonder birds").

For more on the roc, see especially Sir Henry Yule.

Sindbad and the Roc*

And Shahrazad perceived the dawn of day and ceased saying her permitted say. When it was the 543rd night, she said,

It hath reached me, O auspicious King, that when Sindbad the Seaman's guests were all gathered together he thus bespake them:—I was living a most enjoyable life until one day my mind became possessed with the thought of travelling about the world of men and seeing their cities and islands; and a longing seized me to traffic and to make money by trade. Upon this resolve I took a great store of cash and, buying goods and gear fit for travel, bound them up in bales. Then I went down to the river bank, where I found a noble ship and brand-new about to sail, equipped with sails of fine cloth and well manned and provided; so I took passage in her, with a number of other merchants, and after embarking our goods we weighed anchor the same day. Right fair was our voyage and we sailed from place to place and from isle to isle; and whenever we anchored we met a

---

* Richard F. Burton, ed. and trans., *The Book of the Thousand Nights and a Night* (1881; rpt., New York: Heritage Press, 1962), 2024–27.

A giant roc-like bird rescues a shipwrecked sailor. A thirteenth-century Persian miniature from Al-Qazwini's *Wonders of Creation*. British Library Or. MS 12220, fol. 72v. By permission of the British Library.

crowd of merchants and notables and customers, and we took to buying and selling and bartering. At last Destiny brought us to an island, fair and verdant, in trees abundant, with yellow-ripe fruits luxuriant, and flowers fragrant and birds warbling soft descant; and streams crystalline and radiant; but no sign of man showed to the descrier, no, not a blower of the fire. The captain made fast with us to this island, and the merchants and sailors landed and walked about, enjoying the shade of the trees and the song of the birds, that chanted the praises of the One, the Victorious, and marvelling at the works of the Omnipotent King. I landed with the rest; and, sitting down by a spring of sweet water that welled up among the trees, took out some vivers I had with me and ate of that which Allah Almighty had allotted unto me. And so sweet was the zephyr and so fragrant were the flowers, that presently I waxed drowsy and, lying down in that place, was soon drowned in sleep. When I awoke, I found myself alone, for the ship had sailed and left me behind, nor had one of the merchants or sailors bethought himself of me. I searched the island right and left, but found neither man nor

Jinn, whereat I was beyond measure troubled and my gall was like to burst for stress of chagrin and anguish and concern, because I was left quite alone, without aught of worldly gear or meat or drink, weary and heartbroken. . . . I was indeed even as one mad and Jinn-struck and presently I rose and walked about the island, right and left and whither, unable for trouble to sit or tarry in any one place. Then I climbed a tall tree and looked in all directions, but saw nothing save sky and sea and trees and birds and isles and sands. However, after a while my eager glances fell upon some great white thing, afar off in the interior of the island; so I came down from the tree and made for that which I had seen; and behold, it was a huge white dome rising high in air and of vast compass. I walked all around it, but found no door thereto, nor could I muster strength or nimbleness by reason of its exceeding smoothness and slipperiness. So I marked the spot where I stood and went round about the dome to measure its circumference which I found fifty good paces. And as I stood, casting about how to gain an entrance, the day being near its fall and the sun being near the horizon, behold, the sun was suddenly hidden from me and the air became dull and dark. Methought a cloud had come over the sun, but it was the season of summer; so I marvelled at this and lifting my head looked steadfastly at the sky, when I saw that the cloud was none other than an enormous bird, of gigantic girth and inordinately wide of wing which, as it flew through the air, veiled the sun and hid it from the island. At this sight my wonder redoubled and I remembered a story,—

And Shahrazad perceived the dawn of day and ceased to say her permitted say. When it was the 544th night, she said,

It hath reached me, O auspicious King, that Sindbad the Seaman continued in these words:—My wonder redoubled and I remembered a story I had heard aforetime of pilgrims and travellers, how in a certain island dwelleth a huge bird, called the "Rukh" which feedeth its young on elephants; and I was certified that the dome which caught my sights was none other than a Rukh's egg. As I looked and wondered at the marvellous works of the Almighty, the bird alighted on the dome and brooded over it with its wings covering it and its legs stretched out behind it on the ground, and in this posture it fell asleep, glory be to Him who sleepeth not! When I saw this, I arose and, unwinding my turband from my head, doubled it and twisted it into a rope, with which I girt my middle and bound my waist fast to the legs of the Rukh, saying in myself, "Peradventure, this bird may carry me to a land of cities and inhabitants, and that will be better than abiding in this desert island." I passed the night watching and fearing to sleep, lest the bird should fly away with me unawares; and, as soon as the dawn broke and morn shone, the Rukh rose off its egg and spreading its wings with a great cry flew up into the air, dragging me with it; nor ceased it to soar and to tower till I thought it had reached the limit of the firmament; after which it descended, earthwards, little by little, till it lighted on the top of a high hill. As soon as I found myself on the hard ground, I made haste to unbind myself, quaking for fear of the bird, though it took no heed of me nor even felt me; and, loosing my turband from its feet, I made off with my best speed. Presently, I saw it catch up in its huge claws something from the earth and rise with it high in air, and observing it narrowly I saw it to be a serpent big of bulk and gigantic of girth, wherewith it flew away clean out of sight. . . .

THE LETTER OF PRESTER JOHN
(12TH–14TH CENTURIES)

During the Crusades of the twelfth century, a letter describing the marvels of a distant kingdom began circulating throughout Europe. "Prester John," Christian emperor of all the Indias, invited the Byzantine emperor Manuel to visit his vast domain, be exalted in his household, and share all that he possessed. His kingdom stretched from Babylon to lands where the sun rose, across seventy-two provinces whose kings paid him tribute. "In our territories," he said, "are found elephants, dromedaries, and camels, and almost every kind of beast that is under heaven." A river from Paradise flowed with precious gems through lands that knew neither poverty nor strife, and in his palace of ebony, ivory, and crystal, 3000 subjects ate daily at a table made of emerald.

The letter, thought to be originally in Latin, was an anonymous fiction, its author more likely to have been a Western monk than an Eastern emperor. While the compilation of traditional lore was unabashedly exaggerated and fanciful, seemingly not intended to be taken literally, it established the already growing legend of an oriental king who would aid the Crusaders in their struggle against the infidels. Several years after the letter became known, Pope Alexander III purportedly wrote to Prester John a letter dated September 22, 1177, and sent his physician, Philip, abroad to deliver it. The emissary never returned from his mission. Over the following centuries, Prester John's fabled empire shifted from Asia to Africa, appeared on maps, and was sought out by travelers.

New versions and translations of the letter added marvels to marvels, forming an encyclopedic collection of medieval folklore. By the time of the following translation from the French, the birds and beasts only mentioned in the original letter had become a host of fabulous creatures from classical and oriental tradition. The griffins of Prester John are not classical guardians of gold but are Eastern "wonder birds" that carry off oxen and horses, and like the birds in Alexander's Celestial Journey, can transport humans. The Eastern "Yllerion" (Allerion, Ilerion), with feathers as sharp as those of the Stymphalian birds, are phoenix-like in that there is a limited number of them in the world at any one

time. The phoenix's cycle of death by fire and rebirth from ashes is the standard
fable known in the West, but the bird's flight to the sun is associated with a different oriental tradition, as embodied in *The Greek Apocalypse of Baruch.* Unlike
Marco Polo, who maintains that "salamander" was a substance, not an animal,
Prester John tells of worms that spin flame-resistent cloth; both Prester John and
Marco Polo write that such material is cleansed by fire. The apocalyptic winged
and many-headed dragon performs a traditional treasure-guarding role. Mentioned elsewhere in the letter are the monstrous races, including dog-headed,
horned, and one-eyed men. Like Ctesias, Prester John maintains that all he
writes is true.

Of all the animal lore in the manuscript, perhaps the most notable is the story
of the lion and the unicorn. The letter may hold the distinction of being the written source of the tale, which does not appear in classical writings or the bestiaries.
Edmund Spenser retells it in *The Faerie Queene,* and the Grimm Brothers' Brave
Little Tailor captures a unicorn by tricking it into embedding its horn in a tree.
King James VI (crowned 1603) established the English lion and the Scottish unicorn as supporters of the heraldic arms of Great Britain. Battles between a lion
and a beast that was single-horned in profile were depicted in Babylonian and
Assyrian bas-reliefs, and the two animals have been called mythical solar and
lunar symbols.

Borrowings from the Alexander romance and the Sindbad voyages have been
identified in the letter, and the work heavily influenced another spurious book of
marvels, Sir John Mandeville's *Travels.*

The Beasts of Prester John *

Prester John, by the Grace of God most powerful king over all Christian kings,
greetings to the Emperor of Rome and the King of France, our friends. We wish
you to learn about us, our position, the government of our land, and our people
and beasts. And since you say that our Greeks, or men of Grecian race, do not
pray to God the way you do in your country, we let you know that we worship and
believe in Father, Son, and the Holy Ghost, three persons in one Deity and one
true God only. We attest and inform you by our letter, sealed with our seal, of the
condition and character of our land and men. . . .

Our land is divided into four parts, for there are so many Indias. In Great India
lies the body of the Apostle Saint Thomas for whom our Lord has wrought more
miracles than for the [other] saints who are in heaven. And this India is toward

* Vsevolod Slessarev, *Prester John: The Letter and the Legend* (Minneapolis: University of Minnesota Press, 1959), 67–79.

the East, for it is near the deserted Babylon and also near the tower called Babel. In another province toward the North there is a great abundance of bread, wine, meat, and everything necessary for the human body.

There are in our country elephants and other animals called dromedaries and also white horses and wild bulls of seven horns, white bears, and the strangest lions of red, green, black, and blue color. We have also wild asses with two little horns, wild hares as big as sheep, and swift horses with two little horns who gallop faster than any other animal. You should also know that we have birds called griffins who can easily carry an ox or a horse into their nest to feed their young. We have still another kind of birds who rule over all other fowl in the world. They are of fiery color, their wings are as sharp as razors, and they are called Ylle-rion. In the whole world there are but two of them. They live for sixty years, at the end of which they fly away to plunge into the sea. But first they hatch two or three eggs for forty days till the young ones come out. Then the old pair, father and mother, take off and go to drown themselves in the sea, as it was said before. And all the birds who meet them escort them till they are drowned. And when this has happened, the companions return and they go to the fledglings and feed them till they grow up and can fly and provide for themselves. Likewise, you should know that we have other birds called tigers who are so strong and bold that they lift and kill with ease an armored man together with his horse. . . .

There are in our land also unicorns who have in front a single horn of which there are three kinds: green, black, and white. Sometimes they kill lions. But a lion kills them in a very subtle way. When a unicorn is tired it lies down by a tree. The lion goes then behind it and when the unicorn wants to strike him with his horn, it dashes into the tree with such a force that it cannot free itself. Then the lion kills it. . . .

You should also know that in our country there is a bird called phoenix which is the most beautiful in the world. In the whole universe there is but one such bird. It lives for a hundred years and then it rises toward the sky so close to the sun that its wings catch fire. Then it descends into its nest and burns itself; and yet out of the ashes there grows a worm which at the end of a hundred days becomes again as beautiful a bird as it was ever before. . . .

Let it be known to you that the Sandy Sea originates in our country and that it has a swift surf and produces frightful waves. Nobody can cross it, no matter how one tries, except us, for we let ourselves be carried by the griffins, as Alexander did when he was about to conquer the enchanted castle. Not far from this sea there flows a river in which one finds many precious stones and herbs that are good for many medicines. . . .

In another region of our land there is a mountain on which nobody can dwell because of its great heat. Certain worms who cannot live save in fire sustain themselves there. Near this mountain we keep constantly forty thousand men who maintain a great fire. And when these worms sense the heat of the fire and come out of the earth, they enter the flames and spin there a thread similar to the one made by the silkworms. Out of this thread we make garments for us and our ladies and we wear them at the great holidays of the year. Whenever we wish to wash them, we put them into fire whence they come clean and fresh. . . .

There grows in our country also the tree of life from which the holy oil is coming. This tree is completely dry and a serpent is guarding and watching it day and night, all the year round, except on Saint John's day, when it is fast asleep, and this is the time when we approach it. During the whole year it yields but three pounds which gather drop by drop. When we have come close to the holy oil, we take it and go back cautiously for fear that the serpent may pursue us. This tree is only a day's journey from the earthly paradise. When the serpent awakens, it becomes angry and hisses so loudly that it can be heard a day's march away. It is three times as big as a horse and it has nine heads and a pair of wings. And after we have crossed the sea, it turns around, while we proceed and take the holy oil to the Patriarch of St. Thomas and he consecrates it and anoints us Christians with it. The rest we send to the Patriarch of Jerusalem, and he in turn sends it to the Pope of Rome who blesses it and adds to it olive oil and sends it to all Christians beyond the sea. . . .

Know that all the scribes on earth could not report or describe the riches of our palace and our chapel. Everything we have written to you is as true as there is God, and for nothing in the world would we lie, since God and St. Thomas would confound us and deprive us of our title.

If you desire from us something that we can fulfill, do not hesitate to ask, for we shall do it gladly. We beg you to keep in mind the holy pilgrimage, and may it take place soon, and may you be brave and of great courage, and pray, do not forget to put to death those treacherous Templars and pagans and, please, send us an answer with the envoy who brought the presents. We entreat the King of France to greet from us all loyal Christians beyond the sea and to send us some valiant knight of noblest French blood. We pray to our Lord to keep you in the grace of the Holy Spirit. Amen.

Written in our holy palace in the year five hundred and seven since our birth.

Here end the sundry tales of men, beasts, and birds

in

the land of Prester John

MANY A NEW AND ENTERTAINING STORY ABOUT
THE BEASTS IN PRESTER JOHN'S LAND

BENJAMIN OF TUDELA (FL. 1159–1173)
ITINERARY

One of the earliest medieval travelers, Rabbi Benjamin of Tudela, Spain, journeyed across Europe to the western borders of China, and through the Near East and Egypt to make contact with far-flung Jewish communities. Translator Martin Nathan Adler notes that Benjamin ventured farther to the East than any known Westerner before him, and that, in his detailed account of people and places, he may have been the first European to mention China (Zin). Among his observations is a story he heard of how sailors devised a plan to survive the stormy China Sea of Nikpa by being snatched up by griffins. The story is a variant of a number of Eastern tales of humans being carried off by gigantic birds and appears again in medieval romances, including *Huon of Burdeux*.

For more on rapacious griffins, see Sir John Bourchier and Sir Henry Yule. For a child being carried off by a "Garuda" bird, see Antonio Pigafetta.

*Griffins of the China Seas**

Thence to cross over to the land of Zin is a voyage of forty days. Zin is in the uttermost East, and some say that there is the Sea of Nikpa, where the star Orion predominates and stormy winds prevail. At times the helmsman cannot govern his ship, as a fierce wind drives her into this Sea of Nikpa, where she cannot move from her place; and the crew have to remain where they are till their stores of food are exhausted and then they die. In this way many a ship has been lost, but men eventually discovered a device by which to escape from this evil place. The crew provide themselves with hides of oxen. And when this evil wind blows which drives them into the Sea of Nikpa, they wrap themselves up in the skins, which they make waterproof, and, armed with knives, plunge into the sea. A great bird called the griffin spies them out, and in the belief that the sailor is an animal, the griffin seizes hold of him, brings him to dry land, and puts him down on a mountain or in a hollow in order to devour him. The man then quickly thrusts at the bird with a knife and slays him. Then the man issues forth from the skin and walks till he comes to an inhabited place. And in this manner many a man escapes.

---

* *The Itinerary of Benjamin of Tudela*, trans. Marcus Nathan Adler (1907; rpt., New York: Philipp Feldhiem, n.d.), 66.

Giraldus Cambrensis (c. 1146–1223)
Topography of Ireland

The best-known and perhaps earliest extensive written report of the fabulous birth of the actual "barnacle" goose is that of Gerald of Wales in his *Topographia Hibernia*. This account, written in Latin by a Welsh ecclesiastic who traveled through Ireland, gave eyewitness credence to the tradition that a certain species of goose was born from barnacles. The belief—while debated—persisted in learned books for another six centuries.

The tale was part of Northern European folklore at least as early as an Anglo-Saxon riddle, transcribed around the tenth century, whose details presupposed common knowledge. A kindred legend held that certain kinds of geese grew from trees, like fruit. The Church took the story seriously. Cambrensis refers to bishops and others eating the bird on fast days because it was not born of flesh, and in 1212 Pope Innocent III prohibited the practice. Writing less than a hundred years after Cambrensis, Albertus Magnus declared that tales of geese being born from either barnacles or trees were "absolutely absurd," because he and his friends observed the copulation of such birds and the hatching of their eggs. Albertus's rejection notwithstanding, barnacle and tree goose lore grew through other first-hand accounts, was cautiously sanctioned by Conrad Gesner in his *Historia Animalium* in 1555, and appeared in natural histories up to the late eighteenth century. The "barnacles" that were thought to be embryos of geese were later identified as members of the crab family.

Cambrensis explains the phenomenal generation of the barnacle goose in terms of the powers of nature and God.

For a later eyewitness account of the barnacle goose, see John Gerard.

Of Barnacles, Which Grow from Fir Timber, and Their Nature*

There are . . . here many birds called barnacles, which nature produces in a wonderful manner, out of her ordinary course. They resemble the marsh-geese, but are smaller. Being at first gummy excrescences from pine-beams floating on the waters, and then enclosed in shells to secure their free growth, they hang by their beaks, like seaweeds attached to the timber. Being in process of time well covered with feathers, they either fall into the water or take their flight in the free air, their nourishment and growth being supplied, while they are bred in this very unaccountable and curious manner, from the juices of the wood in the sea-water.

* *The Historical Works of Giraldus Cambrensis*, trans. Thomas Forester, rev. and ed. Thomas Wright (London: George Bell, 1892), 36–37.

I have often seen with my own eyes more than a thousand minute embryos of birds of this species on the seashore, hanging from one piece of timber, covered with shells, and already formed. No eggs are laid by these birds after copulation, as is the case with birds in general; the hen never sits on eggs in order to hatch them; in no corner of the world are they seen either to pair, or build nests. Hence, in some parts of Ireland, bishops and men of religion make no scruple of eating these birds on fasting days, as not being flesh, because they are not born of flesh. But these men are curiously drawn into error. For, if any one had eaten part of the thigh of our first parent, which was really flesh, although not born of flesh, I should think him not guiltless of having eaten flesh. . . . The first creature was begotten of clay; this last is engendered of wood. The one, proceeding from the God of nature for once only, was a stupendous miracle; the other, though not less admirable, is less to be wondered at, because imitative nature often performs it. But human nature is so constituted, that it holds nothing to be precious and admirable but what is uncommon and of rare occurrence. The rising and setting of the sun, than which there is nothing in the world more beautiful, nothing more fit to excite our wonder, we pass by without any admiration, because they are daily presented to our eyes; while an eclipse of the sun fills the whole world with astonishment, because it rarely occurs. The procreation of bees from the honeycomb, by some mysterious inspiration of the breath of life, appears to be a fact of the same kind.

Tree geese (barnacles) from a thirteenth-century bestiary, produced only decades after Giraldus Cambrensis described them. Harley MS 4751, fol. 36. By permission of the British Library.

MARCO POLO (C. 1254–1324)
TRAVELS

The account of the first traveler to cross the entire continent of Asia, name the countries, and describe their inhabitants and natural history changed world maps and helped generate the Age of Exploration. Marco Polo's *Travels* covered his twenty-five years of travel with his merchant father and uncle and their service in the court of Kublai Khan (1271–1295). The book revealed the Far East to the West. Within its revision of the Western perception of the world were challenges to Western images of animals later considered fabulous.

In a Genoan prison in 1298, perhaps with the help of notes, Marco dictated his Asian experience to Rustichello, a hack romancer. Despite traces of professional storytelling and romanticizing, *Description of the World*, as it was first called, is, overall, a detailed, matter-of-fact account by a reliable observer.

Like Aristotle and Albertus Magnus, the Venetian traveler attempts to regard animals as animals, not as symbols or fantastic creations, and he treats actual exotic beasts as wonders in themselves. In describing the salamander, the unicorn, and the griffin, Marco is careful to distinguish them from the creatures of fable.

The association of the actual salamander with fire is at least as old as Aristotle, and a second tradition — described in *The Letter of Prester John*—held that asbestos was a product of the animal. Like Albertus Magnus before him, Marco called the belief that it was a creature that lived in fire "fabulous nonsense," but he claimed that the salamander was a substance (asbestos), not an animal at all.

The unicorn is "altogether different from what we fancied," Marco Polo said, an "ugly beast" that lives in mud. The Western confusion of the actual rhinoceros with the fabulous unicorn began with Ctesias (late fifth century B.C.). Marco's description of the Asian rhinoceros in the jungles of Sumatra employs the standard composite method of early travelers.

He called a Madagascar bird "Gryphon," but said the creature is "entirely different from what our stories and pictures make it." Marco himself did not actually visit Madagascar, but relating a tale he was told, he replaces Western griffin lore with the Eastern story of the "Ruc" (roc, rukh), a bird so large that it carries off elephants. In the nineteenth century, discoveries of the bones and fossilized eggs of the *Aepyornis maximus* were found on Madagascar, suggesting this sixteen-foot-tall ostrich-like bird could have been the model for the fabulous roc. One of its eggs, in the British Museum, measures 9 x 13 inches. The "Ruc" feather he describes (perhaps an interpolation) has been variously explained as palm leaves and bamboo shoots.

Marco Polo's book altered the cartographic shape of the world. The Catalan Atlas of 1375 depicts the caravan of the Polo family crossing a continent newly delineated by Marco Polo's account. As Rudolf Wittkower points out in his *Alle-*

gory and the Migration of Symbols, though, Marco's revised images of the unicorn and the griffin were graphically distorted to conform to the public's expectations. Only decades after the Catalan map, eagle–lion griffins, spiral-horned unicorns, and winged dragons illustrate Marco's travels in the *Livre de Merveilles* (1403). The illustrator's dragons are traditional images based on what Wittkower calls Marco's own distorted hearsay description of the Chinese crocodile (a beast that Marco says has only two legs).

Elsewhere in the *Travels* are dog-faced and tailed men and a Mongol chieftan Marco identifies as Prester John.

Journeys of the Polos are manifested in fifteenth-century maps, and a Latin edition of the *Travels* in the Biblioteca Columbia at Seville contains copious marginalia believed written by Christopher Columbus.

For more on Marco Polo's "Ruc," see Sir Henry Yule. For more on the roc, see *The Arabian Nights*.

The Salamander of Chingintalas *

Chingintalas is also a province at the verge of the Desert, and lying between north-west and north. It has an extent of sixteen days' journey, and belongs to the Great Kaan, and contains numerous towns and villages. There are three different races of people in it — Idolaters, Saracens, and some Nestorian Christians. At the northern extremity of this province there is a mountain in which are excellent veins of steel and ondanique. And you must know that in the same mountain there is a vein of the substance from which Salamander is made. For the real truth is that the Salamander is no beast, as they allege in our part of the world, but is a substance found in the earth; and I will tell you about it.

Everybody must be aware that it can be no animal's nature to live in fire, seeing that every animal is composed of all the four elements. Now I, Marco Polo, had a Turkish acquaintance of the name of Zurficar, and he was a very clever fellow. And this Turk related to Messer Marco Polo how he had lived three years in that region on behalf of the Great Kaan, in order to procure those Salamanders for him. He said that the way they got them was by digging in that mountain till they found a certain vein. The substance of this vein was then taken and crushed, and when so treated it divides as it were into fibres of wool, which they set forth to dry. When dry, these fibres were pounded in a great copper mortar, and then washed, so as to remove all the earth and to leave only the fibres like fibres of wool. These were then spun, and made into napkins. When first made these nap-

---

* *The Travels of Marco Polo; The Complete Yule–Cordier Edition*, ed. Sir Henry Yule and Henri Cordier, 2 vols. (1903; rpt., New York: Dover, 1993); vol. 1, pp. 212–13; vol. 2, pp. 76–77, 285, 411–13.

kins are not very white, but by putting them into the fire for a while they come out as white as snow. And so again whenever they become dirty they are bleached by being put in the fire.

Now this, and nought else, is the truth about the Salamander, and the people of the country all say the same. Any other account of the matter is fabulous nonsense. And I may add that they have at Rome a napkin of this stuff, which the Great Kaan sent to the Pope to make a wrapper for the Holy Sudarium of Jesus Christ.

The Great Serpents of Carajan

In this province are found snakes and great serpents of such vast size as to strike fear into those who see them, and so hideous that the very account of them must excite the wonder of those to hear it. I will tell you how long and big they are.

You may be assured that some of them are ten paces in length; some are more and some less. And in bulk they are equal to a great cask, for the bigger ones are about ten palms in girth. They have two forelegs near the head, but for foot nothing but a claw like the claw of a hawk or that of a lion. The head is very big, and the eyes are bigger than a great loaf of bread. The mouth is large enough to swallow a man whole, and is garnished with great pointed teeth. And in short they are so fierce-looking and so hideously ugly, that every man and beast must stand

The dragons of Carajan, artistic exaggeration of Marco Polo's description of crocodiles. From the *Livre des Merveilles*. MS fr. 2810, fol. 55v. By permission of the Bibliothèque Nationale, Paris.

in fear and trembling of them. There are also smaller ones, such as of eight paces long, and of five, and of one pace only.

The Unicorns of Basma

When you quit the kingdom of Ferlec you enter upon that of Basma. This also is an independent kingdom, and the people have a language of their own; but they are just like beasts without laws or religion. They call themselves subjects of the

Unicorn with elephants, an artistic version of Marco Polo's account of the Indian rhinoceros. From the *Livre des Merveilles*. MS. fr. 2810, fol. 85. By permission of the Bibliothèque Nationale, Paris.

Great Kaan, but they pay him no tribute; indeed they are so far away that his men could not go thither. Still all these Islanders declare themselves to be his subjects, and sometimes they send him curiosities as presents. There are wild elephants in the country, and numerous unicorns, which are very nearly as big. They have hair like that of a buffalo, feet like those of an elephant, and a horn in the middle of the forehead, which is black and very thick. They do no mischief, however, with the horn, but with the tongue alone; but this is covered all over with long and strong prickles and when savage with any one they crush him under their knees and then rasp him with their tongue. The head resembles that of a wild boar, and they carry it ever bent towards the ground. They delight much to abide in mire and mud. 'Tis a passing ugly beast to look upon, and is not in the least like that which our stories tell of as being caught in the lap of a virgin; in fact, 'tis altogether different from what we fancied. There are also monkeys here in great numbers and of sundry kinds; and goshawks as black as crows. These are very large birds and capital for fowling.

Islands of the Gryphon Birds

You must know that this Island lies so far south that ships cannot go further south or visit other Islands in that direction, except this one, and that other of which we have to tell you, called Zanghibar. This is because the sea-current runs so

The artist has added a griffin to Marco Polo's account of the Madagascar roc. From the fifteenth-century *Livre des Merveilles*. MS fr. 2810, folio 88. By permission of the Bibliothèque Nationale, Paris.

strong towards the south that the ships which should attempt it never would get back again. Indeed, the ships of Maabar which visit this Island of Madeigascar, and that other of Zanghibar, arrive thither with marvellous speed, for great as the distance is they accomplish it in 20 days, whilst the return voyage takes them more than 3 months. This I say is because of the strong current running south, which continues with such singular force and in the same direction at all seasons.

'Tis said that in those other Islands to the south, which the ships are unable to visit because this strong current prevents their return, is found the bird *Gryphon*, which appears there at certain seasons. The description given of it is however entirely different from what our stories and pictures make it. For persons who had been there and had seen it told Messer Marco Polo that it was for all the world like an eagle, but one indeed of enormous size; so big in fact that its wings covered an extent of 30 paces, and its quills were 12 paces long, and thick in proportion. And it is so strong that it will seize an elephant in its talons and carry him high into the air, and drop him so that he is smashed to pieces; having so killed him the bird gryphon swoops down on him and eats him at leisure. The people of those isles call the bird *Ruc*, and it has no other name. So I wot not if this be the real gryphon, or if there be another manner of bird as great. But this I can tell you for certain, that they are no half lion and half bird as our stories do relate; but enormous as they be they are fashioned just like an eagle.

The Great Kaan sent to those parts to enquire about these curious matters, and the story was told by those who went thither. He also sent to procure the release of an envoy of his who had been despatched thither, and had been detained; so both those envoys had many wonderful things to tell the Great Kaan about those strange islands, and about the birds I have mentioned. They brought (as I heard) to the Great Kaan a feather of the said Ruc, which was stated to measure 90 spans, whilst the quill part was two palms in circumference, a marvellous object! The Great Kaan was delighted with it, and gave great presents to those who brought it. They also brought two boars' tusks, which weighed more than 14 lbs. a-piece; and you may gather how big the boar must have been that had teeth like that! They related indeed that there were some of those boars as big as a great buffalo. There are also numbers of giraffes and wild asses; and in fact a marvellous number of wild beasts of strong aspect.

ODORIC OF PORDENONE (C. 1286–1331)
THE JOURNAL OF FRIAR ODORIC

One of the early Franciscan travelers around the time of Marco Polo, Odoric journeyed for fourteen years through India, Malaysia, China, and Tibet and was the first known European to visit Lhasa. While at the court of the Emperor in Peking, he heard the tale of lamb-like animals born from gourds, which reminded him of "bernacles," European tree geese. Upon his return to Italy the year before his death, Odoric dictated an account of his travels.

Odoric's description of the animal plant is incorporated uncredited into the *Travels* of Sir John Mandeville. The Vegetable Lamb of Tartary (also "barometz") is identified with a golden, lamb-shaped Chinese plant.

For the barnacle goose, see especially Giraldus Cambrensis and John Gerard.

The Vegetable Lamb and Other Miraculous Things *

Four great feasts in a year doeth the Emperor Can celebrate: namely, the feast of his birth, the feast of his circumcision, the feast of his coronation, and the feast of his marriage. And unto these feasts he inviteth all his barons, his stage-players, and all such as are of his kindred. . . . Then come the women musicians and sing sweetly before the Emperor, which music was more delightful unto me. After them come in the lions and do their obeisance unto the great Can. Then the jugglers cause golden cups full of wine to fly up and down in the air, and to apply themselves unto men's mouths that they may drink of them. These and many other strange things I saw in the court of the great Can, which no man would believe unless he had seen them with his own eyes, and therefore I omit to speak of them. I was informed also by certain credible persons, of another miraculous thing, namely that in a certain kingdom of the said Can, wherein stand the mountains called Kapsei (the kingdom's name is Kalor) there grow great gourds or pompions, which being ripe, do open at the tops, and within them is found a little beast like unto a young lamb, even as I myself have heard reported, that there stand certain trees upon the shore of the Irish Sea, bearing fruit like unto a gourd, which, at a certain time of the year do fall into the water, and become birds called bernacles, and this is most true.

IBN BATTUTA (1304–1377)
TRAVELS

A year after the death of Marco Polo, Abu Abdullah Mohammed (later known as Ibn Battuta) set out on a pilgrimage to Mecca that led to nearly thirty years of

---

* *The Journal of Friar Odoric*, from *The Travels of Sir John Mandeville* (1900; rpt., New York: Dover, 1964), 352–54.

travel covering 75,000 miles across Africa and Asia (1325-1354). The greatest Arabian traveler of the Middle Ages, the Berber from Tangier accumulated wives, children, and retinue while logging three times the total miles of Marco Polo. He saw more of the world than anyone had ever recorded up to his time, and he might have traveled farther than anyone prior to the nineteenth century.

His dictated travel account, *A Donation to Those Interested in the Curiosities of the Cities and Marvels of the Ways*, records his journeys from West Africa to the China Seas, Central Asia, and India to East Africa. At the beginning and near the end of his book, gigantic birds of oriental folklore play an important narrative role. One night near Alexandria, during his first pilgrimage to Mecca, Battuta dreams that a giant bird carries him towards "the Holy House" and then far beyond to the East, presaging the years of travel to come. Twenty years later, after escaping a revolt in Khanbaliq (Peking), he relates with all the elements of classic narrative a voyage into "a sea which we did not know" and an encounter with what his superstitious crew believes to be the "Rukh" (roc). What they first thought was a suspended island Sir Henry Yule has since interpreted as a mirage. Scholars have questioned whether Ibn Battuta actually traveled as far north in Eastern China as the city of Peking.

Filled with details of Moslem life and a variety of adventures, Ibn Battuta's account was far less geographically accurate and influential than Marco Polo's *Travels*. The book circulated in Moslem countries primarily in summaries and was virtually unknown in Europe until the nineteenth century.

Bracketed words or phrases are those of the translator.

For the roc, see also *The Arabian Nights*.

The Bird of Dream*

That night, while I was sleeping on the roof of the cell, I dreamed that I was on the wing of a great bird which was flying with me towards Mecca, then to Yemen, then eastwards, and thereafter going towards the south, then flying far eastwards, and finally landing in a dark and green country, where it left me. I was astonished at this dream and said to myself "If the shaykh can interpret my dream for me, he is all that they say he is." Next morning, after all the other visitors had gone, he called me and when I had related my dream interpreted it to me saying: "You will make the pilgrimage [to Mecca] and visit [the Tomb of] the Prophet, and you will travel through Yemen, 'Iráq, the country of the Turks, and India. You will stay there for a long time and meet there my brother Dilshád the Indian, who will rescue you from a danger into which you will fall." Then he gave me a travelling-

---

* *Ibn Battúta; Travels in Asia and Africa, 1325–1354*, trans. H. A. R. Gibb (New York: Augustus M. Kelley, 1969), 48–50, 301–2.

provision of small cakes and money, and I bade him farewell and departed. Never since parting from him have I met on my journeys aught but good fortune, and his blessings have stood me in good stead.

The Sighting of a Rukh

When the revolt broke out and flames of disorder were kindled, Shaykh Burhán ad-Dín and others advised me to return to [Southern] China before the disturbances became chronic. They presented themselves with me to the representatives of Sultan Fírúz, who sent three of his suite to escort me and wrote orders for my treatment as a guest [on the journey]. We travelled down the river to Khansá and thence to Qanjafú and Zytún, and on reaching the last I found the junks ready to sail for India. Amongst them was a junk belonging to al-Maklik az-Záhir, the ruler of Jáwa [Sumatra], the crew of which were Muslims. His agent knew me and was delighted at my arrival. We sailed with fair winds for ten days, but as we approached the land of Tawálisí, the wind changed, the sky darkened, and it rained heavily. We passed ten days without seeing the sun, and then entered a sea which we did not know. The crew of the junk became alarmed and wished to return to China, but that was out of the question. We passed forty-two days not knowing in what sea we were.

On the forty-third day there was visible to us at early dawn a mountain, projecting from the sea at a distance of about twenty miles from us, and the wind was carrying us straight towards it. The sailors were puzzled and said "We are nowhere near land, and there is no record of a mountain in the sea. If the wind drives us on it we are lost." So all on board began to humble themselves and concentrate their thoughts on God, and renew their repentance. We implored God in prayer and sought the mediation of his prophet [Muhammad]—on whom be the Blessing and Peace of God; the merchants vowed to distribute large sums in alms, and I wrote down their vows for them in a register with my own hand. The wind calmed a little, and later on when the sun rose we saw that the mountain had risen into the air, and that daylight was visible between it and the sea. We were amazed at this, and I saw the crew weeping, and taking farewell of one another. So I said "What is the matter with you?" They replied "What we thought was a mountain is the Rukh, and if it sees us it will make an end of us." We were at that moment less than ten miles away from it. Just then God of His mercy sent us a favourable wind, which turned us in another direction, so that we did not see it and could not learn its true shape.

Two months after this we reached Jáwa and landed at [the town of] Sumutra. . . .

SIR JOHN MANDEVILLE (14TH CENTURY)
TRAVELS

One of the most renowned travel books ever written is a pivotal work in the history of fabulous animals. Used by mapmakers and explorers as a description of the world, Sir John Mandeville's *Travels* (c. 1356) is actually a skillful fictionalization of material from multiple classical and medieval sources. Like fantastic animals themselves, the book was first accepted as fact, eventually rejected as fiction, and finally regarded as an enduring creation of the imagination.

"Sir John Mandeville" writes in his prologue that he was born in St. Albans, England, and after thirty-four years of travel "through many diverse lands, and many provinces and kingdoms and isles," returned home an old and weary man and recorded his journeys. (In different versions of the manuscript, the author's dates are 1322–1356 or 1332–1366.) Actual authorship of the book is still uncertain. Jean d'Outremeuse, a compiler in Liège, France, supposedly claimed that a dying physician, Jean de Bourgognes, revealed that he himself had written the *Travels* under a pseudonym. An inscription on a Liège tomb is thought to have linked Jean de Bourgognes with John Mandeville, but the entire issue remains tangled in scholarly controversy. What is certain is the centuries-long popularity and influence of the book. About 300 manuscripts of the *Travels* survive, far outnumbering the seventy of Marco Polo's work, and explorers and cartographers from Columbus to Gerard Mercator accepted the narrative as authoritative. For a time, "Mandeville" was even called "the Father of English Prose." Even after Sir John came to represent the archetypal lying traveler, the book remained popular as an entertainment. Attempting to offer fiction as believable fact, the *Travels* can be said to represent the beginning of the modern travel-fiction genre.

Mandeville's narrative begins as a guidebook to the Holy Land for European pilgrims and continues as an account of the author's travels in the far places of the world, through Persia and the Indies of Prester John to Cathay. Although a few details in the book indicate that the author actually might have traveled outside of Europe, most of his material has been traced to a variety of sources, including Herodotus, Pliny, Solinus, the Alexander Romances, *The Letter of Prester John*, and the journal of Friar Odoric. Much of the classical material may have come from the encyclopedia of Vincent of Beauvais.

While his sources are many, Mandeville artfully transforms them through the unifying voice of the narrator. The author's phoenix passage echoes the rebirth details in the phoenix entry in the Latin *Physiologus*, and its opulent description of the bird's plumage is akin to that of Lactantius and the Old English *Phoenix*. Mandeville synthesizes traditions from Herodotus through the Church Fathers, telescoping the Egyptian sun-bird's development into a Christian symbol. Elaborating upon Friar Odoric's description of the vegetable lamb and his reference to tree geese, Mandeville personalizes the material, declaring, "Of that fruit I have eaten," and — typically — he humanely addresses the differences between cultures, suggesting that each regards the other's marvels as impossibilities.

Later in the same chapter, Mandeville describes the land of Bacharia (Bactria), where cotton plants "bear wool," and centaurian "hippotaynes" eat men ("when they may take them"). His depiction of the griffin is one of the most famous in all fabulous-beast literature. These griffins are not the classical gold-guarding creatures, but are gigantic relatives of the fabulous Eastern birds described in *The Letter of Prester John* as birds that "can easily carry an ox or a horse into their nest to feed their young." Like the horn of the unicorn, a cup made from a gryphon's claw was thought to detect poison. Legend held that the claw could be acquired only by a holy man who received it in payment for curing an ill griffin. Mandeville compares the griffin talon to the horns of other animals, and, indeed, a griffin claw referred to in an early eighteenth-century version of the *Travels* is an ibex horn, now in the British Museum. Mandeville's horse-carrying beast conforms to the tradition of the griffin being a mortal enemy of the horse.

Mandeville places the gold-digging ants of Herodotus in the land of Prester John. Elsewhere in the *Travels*, the fictional author presents the monstrous races of Ctesias, Pliny, and others.

The excerpts below, in modernized spelling but archaic diction, are from the 1725 Cotton Manuscript, one of the three major English versions of the *Travels*.

For fiction satirizing exaggerated travelers' tales, see Lucian and Rabelais.

The Phoenix in Heliopolis*

In Egypt is the city of Heliopolis, that is to say, the city of the Sun. In that city there is a temple, made round after the shape of the Temple of Jerusalem. The priests of that temple have all their writings, under the date of the fowl that is clept phoenix; and there is none but one in all the world. And he cometh to burn himself upon the altar of that temple at the end of five hundred year; for so long he liveth. And at the five hundred years' end, the priests array their altar honestly, and put thereupon spices and sulphur vif and other things that will burn lightly; and then the bird phoenix cometh and burneth himself to ashes. And the first day next after, men find in the ashes a worm; and the second day next after, men find a bird quick and perfect; and the third day next after, he flieth his way. And so there is no more birds of that kind in all the world, but it alone, and truly

* *The Travels of Sir John Mandeville* (1900; rpt. New York: Dover, 1964), 32–33, 174, 177, 198–99.

that is a great miracle of God. And men may well liken that bird unto God, because that there ne is no God but one; and also, that our Lord arose from death to life the third day. This bird men see often-time fly in those countries; and he is not mickle more than an eagle. And he hath a crest of feathers upon his head more great than the peacock hath; and his neck is yellow after colour of an oriel that is a stone well shining; and his beak is coloured blue as ind; and his wings be of purple colour, and his tail is barred overthwart with green and yellow and red. And he is a full fair bird to look upon, against the sun, for he shineth full gloriously and nobly.

Woodcuts from Anton Sorg's 1481 edition of Mandeville. From *The Travels of Sir John Mandeville* (rpt., New York: Dover, 1964). Courtesy of Dover Publications.

The Vegetable Lamb of Tartary

Now shall I say you, suingly, of countries and isles that be beyond the countries that I have spoken of.

Wherefore I say you, in passing by the land of Cathay toward the high Ind and toward Bacharia, men pass by a kingdom that men clepe Caldilhe, that is a full fair country.

And there groweth a manner of fruit, as though it were gourds. And when they be ripe, men cut them atwo, and men find within a little beast, in flesh, in bone, and blood, as though it were a little lamb without wool. And men eat both the fruit and the beast. And that is a great marvel. Of that fruit I have eaten, although it were wonderful, but that I know well that God is marvellous in his works. And, natheles, I told them of as great a marvel to them, that is amongst us, and that was of the

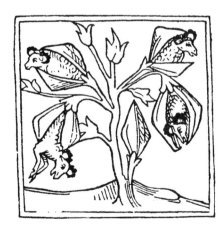

Bernakes. For I told them that in our country were trees that bear a fruit that become birds flying, and those that fell in the water live, and they that fall on the

earth die anon, they be right good to man's meat. And hereof had they as great
marvel, that some of them trowed it were an impossible thing to be.

The Beasts of Bacharia

From that land go men toward the land of Bacharia, where be full evil folk and
full cruel. In that land be trees that bear wool, as though it were of sheep, whereof
men make clothes and all things that may be made of wool.

In that country be many hippotaynes that dwell sometime in the water and
sometime on the land. And they be half man and half horse, as I have said before.

And they eat men when they may take
them.

And there be rivers of water that be
full bitter, three sithes more than is the
water of the sea.

In that country be many griffins,
more plenty than in any other country.
Some men say that they have the body
upward as an eagle and beneath as a
lion; and truly they say sooth, that they
be of that shape. But one griffin hath
the body more great and is more strong
than eight lions, of such lions as be on
this half, and more great and strong than an hundred eagles such as we have
amongst us. For one griffin there will bear, flying to his nest, a great horse, if he
may find him at the point, or two oxen yoked together as they go at the plough.
For he hath his talons so long and so large and great upon his feet, as though they
were horns of great oxen or of bugles or of kine, so that men make cups of them to
drink of. And of their ribs and the pens of their wings, men make bows, full
strong, to shoot with arrows and quarrels.

From thence go men by many journeys though the land of Prester John, the
great Emperor of Ind. And men clepe his realm the Isle of Pentexoire.

The Hills of Gold That Pismires Keep

Toward the east part of Prester John's land is an isle good and great, that men
clepe Taprobane, that is full noble and full fructuous. . . .

In the isle . . . of this Taprobane be great hills of gold, that pismires keep full
diligently. And they fine the pured gold, and cast away the un-pured. And these

pismires be great as hounds, so that no man dare come to those hills, for the pismires would assail them and devour them anon. So that no man may get of that gold, but by great sleight. And therefore when it is great heat, the pismires rest them in the earth, from prime of the day into noon. And then the folk of the country take camels, dromedaries, and horses and other beasts, and go thither, and charge them in all haste that they may; and after that, they flee away in all haste that the beasts may go, or the pismires come out of the earth. . . .

Part

Strange
and
Dubious
Creatures

III

Edward Topsell's unicorn, from Konrad Gesner, *Curious Woodcuts of Fanciful and Real Beasts* (New York: Dover, 1971). Courtesy of Dover Publications.

The revival of learning through the invention of printing and the expansion of knowledge through voyages of exploration help shift Western attention from the kingdom of God to human achievement and the natural world. Before the didactic bestiaries' decline in popularity, both actual and fantastic bestiary animals have already been incorporated into the predominantly secular art and science of heraldry. The griffin, dragon, and other of nature's "monsters" are ensconced in coats of arms and handbooks of heraldry even as these animals of the imagination appear in multiple literary genres in printed books. Some are in new editions of classical and medieval works; others in contemporary travel books, alchemical writings, literary epics, novels, Shakespearean drama, and even in some natural histories, notably Edward Topsell's.

Doubts about the creatures rise in an increasingly rationalistic age and climax with Sir Thomas Browne's challenge of the credibility of traditional authorities, to whom such animals owed their literary existence. In spite of Alexander Ross's impassioned defense of tradition, such animals are, after millennia, discredited as fabulous.

Heraldic Monsters

8

During the flourishing of the bestiaries in the twelfth and thirteenth centuries, yet another medieval depiction of animals developed. Creatures from the bestiaries and cathedral art joined other designs in heraldry. Deeply indebted to religious iconography, heraldry evolved secularly while the bestiaries declined in favor, and by the time certain animals were rejected as fabulous, images of those creatures had already become established on coats of arms of the most respected families and institutions of Europe. The griffin, dragon, unicorn, and other fabulous beasts have to this day remained an integral part of heraldry, a graphic sanctuary that has helped protect them from cultural extinction.

Shields had been decorated since ancient times, and animals such as the imperial Roman eagle had represented empires, but armory, a branch of heraldry, symbolized the lineage of individuals. The same object or animal depicted on a knight's shield was repeated on his surcoat, helmet crest, banner, and ornamental horse "trapping." While no single country is generally credited with originating the art and science of heraldry, French terms became the most widely used in *blazon*, the technical verbal description of a coat of arms.

Deriving in great part from the bestiaries, animal charges consisted of both actual and fabulous beasts. Early heraldic artists, like the bestiarists, accepted the griffin, dragon, and other fantastic hybrids as actual beasts, no less believable than the mule offspring of an ass and a horse. In heraldry, such creatures, considered freaks of nature, were generically termed "mon-

. . . there remains some other sorts of exorbitant Creatures, differing from others, either in Essence, or Quality. . . .

—Randle Holme
The Academy of Armory

Dragon

Wyvern

Cockatrice

Heraldic fabulous beasts from James Fairbairn, *Heraldic Crests*, ed. A.C. Fox-Davies (rpt., New York: Dover, 1993). Courtesy of Dover Publications.

sters." In creating them, heraldic artists graphically mirrored the composite technique of ancient and medieval travelers' descriptions of animals.

Two of the most widely depicted actual animals in early heraldry were the eagle (both single- and double-headed), symbol of imperial power, and the lion, representing royal sovereignty. Perhaps the first fantastic beast to enter the heraldic menagerie was a combination of those two, the eagle-lion griffin, which was emblazoned on the seal of Richard de Revers, Earl of Exeter, in 1167. The heraldic head of the griffin differs from that of the eagle only by the depiction of pointed ears. It is said that the standard heraldic griffin, with wings, is female, whereas the rare figure of a griffin with spikes rather than wings spreading from its shoulders is male. On coats of arms and crests and as a supporter, the griffin is presented in several positions, but most commonly *segreant*, the equivalent of *rampant* (rearing up). A rare heraldic variation of the griffin is the opinicus, with the head and wings of an eagle, the body of a lion, and the tail of a camel. One proposed explanation of the origin of the heraldic griffin is that it resulted from the process of *dimidiation*, the *impaling* (juxtaposition) of two vertically halved coats of arms, representing both the husband's and the wife's sides of the family. Such a speculation, inventive as it is, does not, though, take into account that the griffin had been a popular subject in art since ancient times.

Before the dragon's entry into armory, the Romans had used it on a badge. The dragon was an emblem associated in legend with Uther Pendragon and Arthur, and it appeared on shields and banners of King Harold's warriors in the Bayeux Tapestry's portrayal of the Battle of Hastings. The heraldic four-legged dragon has scales on its back, ribbed bat wings, the stomach of a crocodile, eagle talons, and a serpentine tail. The earlier wyvern is a two-legged version of the dragon, and the cockatrice is similar except for its cock's head. A supporter in the coat of arms of Henry VIII and other Tudor kings, the red dragon was changed to gold by Queen Elizabeth I. The red dragon is the official badge of Wales.

Earlier heraldic writers did not include the unicorn in the "monster" category, even though the unicorn of armory is a mixed beast with the head, mane and body of a horse, the legs and hooves of a deer, the tail of a heraldic lion, a beard, and a long spiraled horn. It appears with the lion as a supporter of the royal arms of both Scotland and England.

Although many heraldic figures bear wings, there are only a few fabulous birds in armory. One of those is the phoenix, which is represented on crests as a *demi* (half) eagle on a nest of flames. A phoenix with the motto, "Her death itself will make her live," was associated with the martyred Joan of Arc, and the immortal bird was on a badge of Elizabeth I. Another heraldic creature depicted in fire is the salamander.

Hybrid animals multiplied in English heraldry during Tudor times. Even figures based upon actual animals, such as the heraldic "tyger," panther, and antelope, assumed new creative forms. The yale, described by Pliny and included in bestiaries as an animal with movable horns, entered heraldry in the fifteenth

Griffin

Unicorn

Phoenix

Lion of the sea

Hippocampus

century. The "enfield" had the head of a fox, tail and hind legs of a wolf, body of a lion, chest of a grayhound, and taloned forefeet. The rare "bagwyn" had an antelope head with long horns curving backward over a horse body. And then there were the literal combinations based on the notion that all land animals had their counterparts in the sea: sea-lions, sea-wolves, sea-dogs, sea-cows, the sea-horse (hippocampus), and numerous others, some with wings as well as tails of fish or serpents.

Like the development of fabulous creatures themselves, heraldic evolution all but stopped during the late seventeenth and eighteenth centuries, but resumed in the nineteenth century with charges from the Industrial Revolution and new combinations of animals. Meanwhile, the earlier creatures remained intact, established in heraldic tradition.

JOHN GUILLIM (1565–1621)
A DISPLAY OF HERALDRY

John Guillim's authoritative record of contemporary coats of arms is, as well, a rich collection of early seventeenth-century natural history. Along with actual bestiary animals, creatures later regarded as fabulous began entering heraldry during the early development of that art and science of hereditary symbols. In Guillim's *Display of Heraldrie* (1611), the griffin, dragon, and other hybrids are classified as "monsters." Not named among the original animals in the Garden of Eden, these grotesque beasts were thought to have been generated after Adam's fall. Among that group is the "reremouse" (bat), a mixture of bird and beast, the only bird to bear live young. At the end of his chapter on existing monsters, Guillim lists several "double-shaped" animals. Earlier, Guillim placed the unicorn with the stag and camel. "Monster" was retained in heraldic terminology even after hybrid creatures were discredited as fabulous.

After Guillim's death, editors continued to expand his book for the next hundred years. The following facsimile pages are from the fifth edition (1664). Modern authority A. C. Fox-Davies acknowledges that Guillim was regarded by many as "the high priest of English armory."

Italics in the prefatory excerpt below are retained from the original to be consistent with the facsimile pages that follow.

Terminology Note: A record of the coats of arms of hereditary lines, *A Display of Heraldry* contains specialized heraldic terminology, particularly in the verbal description (*blazon*) that introduces each entry. The heraldic *tinctures* are the metals *argent* (silver) and *or* (gold) and the colors *azure* (blue), *gules* (red), *purpure* (purple), *sable* (black), and *vert* (green). Hooves having a different tincture from the body are *unguled*. Animals with claws and talons a different tincture than the body are *armed*, and those with legs a different color are *membered*. Those with a different colored crest are *crested*, and those with wattles of a different color are *jolloped*. Hair and crown of different tincture than the body are *crined* and *crowned*. On a *counterchanged* shield, the tinctures on one half are reversed on the other half.

The major stances of animal *charges* (symbols) referred to in the entries below are: *passant* (walking) and *counter-passant* (two charges walking opposite directions), *rampant* (rearing up), *sejant* (sitting), and *segreant* (griffin rampant stance). Animal charges have wings *displayed* (outspread) and tails *nowed* (knotted). They have heads *erased* (cut off with a ragged edge) or *couped* (cut off so they do not touch the edge of the shield); mermaids have hair *flotant*. *Flowerdeluce* is the *fleur-de-lis*, the emblem of the kings of France.

The *field* is the shield's surface on which the arms are blazoned (drawn). *Chief* is the upper third division of the shield. *Ordinaries* (geometric charges) include the *par bend* (the upper right diagonal half of the shield), the *pale* (vertical band down the middle third of the shield), and the *chevron* (inverted V). A *bordure* is a border around the outer edge of the shield.

The Monsters of Heraldry *

Another sort there is of *exorbitant Animals*, much more prodigious then all the former: such are those *Creatures formed*, or rather *deformed* with the confused shapes of *Creatures* of different kinds and qualities. These (according to some *Authors*) are called in Latine *Monstra, à Monstrando*, for fore-shewing some strange events. These *Monsters* (saith Saint *Augustine*) cannot be reckoned amongst those good *Creatures* that God created before the transgression of *Adam*: for those did God (when he took the survey of them) pronounce to be *valde bona*, for they had in them neither accesse nor defect, but were the perfect workmanship of Gods creation. And of them *Zanchius* saith, that *Eorum deformitas habet usus; cum & Deo serviant, ad gloriam ipsius illustrandam, & electis ad salutem promovendam.* If *Man* had not transgressed the Law of the Maker, this dreadfull deformity (in likelihood) had not happened in the procreation of *Animals*, which some *Philosophers* do call *Peccata Naturae*, Errors in Nature, *Quoniam natura impeditur in horum generatione, ne possit quale velit producere animal*. Some examples of this kind here ensue.

---

* John Guillim, A *Display of Heraldry*, 5th ed. (1664; Ann Arbor, Mich.: University Microfilms, 1982), Wing G2220, Wing Reel 1358:28, pp. 257–58.

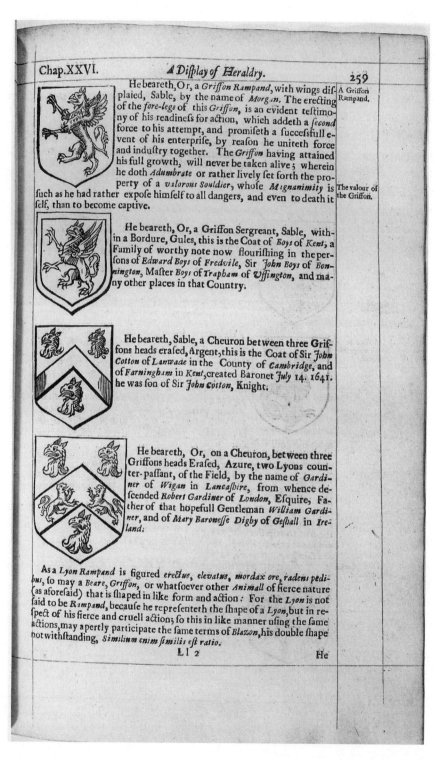

A Griffon Rampand.

He beareth, Or, a *Griffon Rampand*, with wings difplaied, Sable, by the name of *Morgan*. The erecting of the *fore-legs* of this *Griffon*, is an evident teftimony of his readinefs for action, which addeth a *fecond* force to his attempt, and promifeth a fuccefsfull event of his enterprife, by reafon he uniteth force and induftry together. The *Griffon* having attained his full growth, will never be taken alive; wherein he doth *Adumbrate* or rather lively fet forth the property of a *valorous Souldier*, whofe *Magnanimity* is fuch as he had rather expofe himfelf to all dangers, and even to death it felf, than to become captive.

The valour of the Griffon.

He beareth, Or, a Griffon Sergreant, Sable, within a Bordure, Gules, this is the Coat of *Boys* of *Kent*, a Family of worthy note now flourifhing in the perfons of *Edward Boys* of *Fredvile*, Sir *John Boys* of *Bonnington*, Mafter *Boys* of *Trapham* of *Uffington*, and many other places in that Country.

He beareth, Sable, a Cheuron between three Griffons heads erafed, Argent, this is the Coat of Sir *John Cotton* of *Lanwade* in the County of *Cambridge*, and of *Farningham* in *Kent*, created Baronet *July* 14. 1641. he was fon of Sir *John Cotton*, Knight.

He beareth, Or, on a Cheuron, between three Griffons heads Erafed, Azure, two Lyons counter-paffant, of the Field, by the name of *Gardiner* of *Wigan* in *Lancafhire*, from whence defcended *Robert Gardiner* of *London*, Efquire, Father of that hopefull Gentleman *William Gardiner*, and of *Mary Baroneffe Digby* of *Gefhall* in *Ireland*.

As a *Lyon Rampand* is figured *erectus, elevatus, mordax ore, radens pedibus*, fo may a *Beare, Griffon*, or whatfoever other *Animall* of fierce nature (as aforefaid) that is fhaped in like form and action: For the *Lyon* is not faid to be *Rampand*, becaufe he reprefenteth the fhape of a *Lyon*, but in refpect of his fierce and cruell action; fo this in like manner ufing the fame actions, may apertly participate the fame terms of *Blazon*, his double fhape notwithftanding, *Similium enim fimilis eft ratio.*

L l 2								He

Monstrous creatures. Facsimile pages from John Guillim's *Display of Heraldry* (London, 1664). Syn.4.66.6. By permission of the Syndics of Cambridge University Library.

He beareth, *per bend, Or,* and *Gules,* three *Griffons heads* erased, counterchanged on a Chief, *Argent,* a *Flowerdeluce* between two *Roses* of the second, by the name of *Rycroft* or *Roycroft,* who from *Abivill* in *Normandy,* planted themselves in *Lancashire,* from whence are derived the severall Stems in *Shropshire, Cheshire, Devonshire,* and *London;* and is borne by *Josiah Rycroft* of *London,* Merchant.

He beareth, Azure, three Dragons heads erased, Or, a chief, Argent, by the name of *Cutler,* this Coat is borne by *John Cutler* of *London,* Esquire.

A Wiverne, his wings displaied.

He beareth, Argent, a *Wiverne,* his wings displaied, and *Taile Nowed,* Gules, by the the name of *Drakes.* This word *Nowed,* is as much to say in *Latine* as *Nodatus.* This *Taile* is said to be *Nowed,* because it is intricately knotted with divers infoldings, after the manner of a *Frette :* Like as a *Griffon* doth participate of a *Fowle* and a *Beast,* as aforesaid : so doth the *Wiverne* partake of a *Fowle* in the *Wings* and *Legs,* and with a *Snake, Adder,* or such other *Serpents* (as are not of *Gressible* kind, but *Glide* along upon their *Belly*) and doth resemble a *Serpent* in the *Taile.*

The *Poets* do feign that *Dragons* do keep, or (according to our *English* phrase) sit abroad upon *Riches* and *Treasures,* which are therefore committed to their charge, because of their admirable sharpnesse of sight, and for that they are supposed (of all other living things) to be the most valiant. *Adag. col.* 515. Whereof *Ovid. Metamorph.* 7.

Pervigilem superest herbis sopire Draconem. The *Dragons* are naturally so *hot,* that they cannot be cooled by drinking of *water,* but still gape for the Aire to refresh them, as appeareth, *Jeremiah* 14. 6. *And the wild Asses did stand in the high places, they snuffed up the wind like Dragons; their eyes did faile because there was no grasse.*

A Cockatrice displaied.

He beareth, Sable, a *Cockatrice displaied,* Argent, crested, membred, and jollopped, Gules, by the name of *Buggine.* The *Cockatrice* is called in Latine *Regulus,* for that he seemeth to be a little King amongst *Serpents,* not in regard of his quantity, but in respect of the infection of his *pestiferous* and *poysonsull* aspect, wherewith he poisoneth the Aire. Not unlike those devillish *Witches,* that do work the destruction of silly
Infants

Infants, as alſo of the Cattell of ſuch their neighbours, whoſe proſperous eſtate is to them a moſt greivous eye-ſore. Of ſuch Virgil in his Bucolicks makes mention, ſaying,

Neſcio quis teneros oculus mihi faſcinat Agnos.
I know not what wicked eye hath bewitched my tender Lambs.

He beareth, Argent, a Reremouſe diſplaied, Sable, by the name of Bakſter. The Ægyptians (ſaith Pie-rius) uſed to ſignifie by the Reremouſe, a man that having ſmall means and weak power, either of No-bility, or of Fortune, or yet ſtored with pregnancy of wit, hath neverthelesſe ſtepped up ſo ſuddenly, that he might ſeem not ſo much to be ſupported by the earth, as by a ſudden flight to be exalted a-bove the ſame. Sometimes you ſhall find this bird borne in the form of ſome Ordinary; for ſo ſhall you ſee them borne diſplayed in Pale, three of them one above another. As in the Enſignes of the Kingdome of India, ſorted amongſt the Coat-Armours of the innumerous multitude of the great aſſembly holden at the Councell of Conſtance, Anno Dom. 1414. This little creature doth par-take both with beaſt and bird, in ſuch nearneſſe of reſemblance to either of them, as that it may (with reaſon) be doubted, of whether kind he is. By occaſion whereof he taketh advantage in the battell between beaſts and birds (mentioned in the Fables of Æſop) to flutter aloft above them to behold the event of that dangerous fight, with a reſolution to incline to the ſtronger part. Of all Birds (according to Pliny) this alone bringeth forth young alive, and none but ſhe hath wings made of panicles or thin skins. So is ſhe the onely bird that ſuckleth her young with her paps, and giveth them milke.

He beareth, Azure, an Harpey with her wings diſ-cloſed, her Haire flotant, Or, Armed of the ſame. This Coat ſtandeth in Huntington Church. Of this kind of bird (or rather Monſter) Virgil writeth in this man-ner;

Triſtius haud illis monſtrum, nec ſævior ulla
Peſtis & ira deum, Stygiis ſeſe extulit undis,
Virginei volucrum vultus, fœdiſſima vultus
Ingluvies, unceq; manus & pallida ſemper
Ora fame.——

Of monſters all, moſt monſtrous this; no greater wrath
God ſends 'mongſt men; it comes from depth of pitchy Hell:
And Virgins face, but wombe-like gulſe unſatiate hath,
Her hands are griping clawes, her colour pale and fell.

The

The Harpey diſplaied.

The *Field*, Azure, an *Harpey* diſplayed, *Crined, Crowned,* and *Armed,* Or. Theſe are the *Armes* of the noble *City* of *Norenberga*, which according to ſome Authors, is ſcituate in the very *Center* of the vaſt and ſpacious Country of *Germany*. The *Harpey* (ſaith *Upton*) ſhould be given to ſuch perſons as have committed man-ſlaughter, to the end that by the often view of their *Enſigns* they might be moved to bewaile the foulneſs of their offence.

A Mermaid.

He beareth, Argent, a *Mermaid*, Gules, *Crined* Or, holding a *Mirror* in her right hand, and a *Combe* in her left, by the name of *Ellis*.

To theſe muſt be added, *Montegres, Satyres, Monk-fiſhes*. As alſo *Lyons-dragons, Lyons-poiſons*, and whatſoever other double-ſhaped *Animall* of any two or more of the particular kinds before handled.

A Renaissance Miscellany

WILLIAM CAXTON (C. 1422–1491)
THE MIRROUR OF THE WORLD

During the Age of Exploration, traditional fabulous-animal lore circulated in the new medium of printed books. Portuguese voyages were already under way when William Caxton, the first English printer, produced his *Mirrour of the World* (1481), the first illustrated book printed in England and one of the earliest encyclopedias in English. In a period of only ten weeks, Caxton translated into English the French *Image du Monde*, which was itself a 1245 translation from a Latin compilation of authorities. Caxton writes in his preface that books preserve the past in "perpetual memorye and remembraunce" and that this book in particular "ought to be visyted, redde & knowen, by cause it treateth of the world and of the wondreful dyuision therof." Among the book's marvels of India and other lands are animal descriptions derived from classical travelers' tales and combined with later traditions.

> And yet may Africa have a Prerogative in Rarities, and some seeming Incredibilities be true.
>
> —Samuel Purchas
> *Hakluytus Posthumus*

Caxton's gold-guarding griffins are so strong they can carry off a horse and its rider. The man-faced, scorpion-tailed manticore has the eyes of a goat instead of a man, and the voice of a serpent. Elsewhere in Caxton's book are the unicorn, basilisk, and phoenix. Only Caxton's barnacle goose (below), from Giraldus Cambrensis, is originally a nonclassical creature.

Caxton gave the English-speaking world its first printed editions of Chaucer's *Canterbury Tales*, Mal-

Hippogriff

Mermaid

Phoenix

Printer's colophons from Henry Lewis Johnson, *Decorative Ornaments and Alphabets of the Renaissance* (rpt., New York, Dover, 1991). Courtesy of Dover Publications.

lory's *Morte d'Arthur*, and Jacobus de Voragine's *Golden Legend*. His original spelling and punctuation have been retained in the *Mirrour of the World* excerpts below.

For Caxton, see also his translation of Jacobus de Voragine.

Dragons and Gryffons *

In Ynde is an yle named Probane, where ben founded ten cytees and plente of other townes, where as euery yere ben two somers & two wynters; and ben so attemprid that there is alway verdure, and vpon the trees ben contynuelly flowres, leeuis and fruyt. And it is moche plenteuous of gold and syluer, and moche fertyle of other thynges.

There be the grete montaynes of gold and of precyous stones and of other richesses plente. But noman dar approche it for the dragons and for the gryffons wylde whiche haue bodyes of lyouns fleyng, which easily bere a man away armed and syttyng vpon his hors, when he may sease hym with his clawes and vngles.

Ther ben yet plente of other places so delectable, so swete and so spyrytuel that, yf a man were therin, he shold saye that it were a very paradys.

Manticora

Another maner of bestes there is in Ynde that ben callyd manticora; and

* *Caxton's Mirrour of the World*, ed. Oliver H. Prior (London: Early English Text Society, 1913), 70, 73, 98.

hath visage of a man, & thre huge grete teeth in his throte. He hath eyen lyke a ghoot and body of a lyon, tayll of a Scorpyon and voys of a serpente, in suche wyse that by his swete songe he draweth to hym the peple and deuoureth them. And is more delyuerer to goo than is fowle to flee.

Barnacles

We haue in thise parties many thinges that they of Asye and of Affryke haue none. There is toward Irlonde on the one syde a maner of byrdes that flee, and they growen on trees and on olde shipp sides by the bylles. And whan they be nygh rype, they that falle in the water lyue, and the other not; they ben callyd barnacles.

LUDOVICO DE VARTHEMA (FL. 1503–1508)
ITINERARIO

Of the many "sightings" of unicorns reported from the Renaissance on, the best known is that of the Italian traveler Ludovico de Varthema (Barthema, Vartomannus, Lewis Vartoman, etc.). In the record of his travels from East Africa to Malaysia, Varthema describes two single-horned creatures at the Temple of Mecca. He reports that the older of the pair of animals that the King of Ethiopia presented as gifts to the Sultan of Mecca had a horn three *bracci* in length and the younger four *palmi*. (*Bracci* and *palmi* are forearm and hand measurements.) Both animals had cloven forefeet and back feet covered with hair.

Odell Shepard notes in his *Lore of the Unicorn* that while Varthema does not actually say he saw the creatures, the exactness of the description suggests he was an eyewitness. The passage was often cited and sometimes questioned by Renaissance naturalists. One believer, Shepard quotes, was Samuel Purchas (1625): "The only report that I have found in any credible Author of Unicornes: neither in 120 yeares which have passed since have I found one Relation to second it." In the nineteenth century, Sir Richard Burton wrote in his *Personal Narrative of a Pilgrimage to Al-Madinah & Meccah* that Varthema's unicorns might "possibly have been African antelopes, which a *lusus naturae* had deprived of their second horn. But the suspicion of fable remains." Editor George Percy Badger concluded a lengthy 1863 footnote on unicorn "sightings" by saying he was inclined "to rely on the credibility of Varthema, and to believe that he saw at Meccah two ordinary specimens of the famous unicorn, an animal which further research in the unexplored parts of Central Africa, or among the mountains of Thibet, may yet bring to light." Twentieth-century "unicornization" by Dr. W. Franklin Dove and Ringling Brothers and Barnum & Bailey has demonstrated what is now regarded as an ancient African and Nepalese practice of artificially joining the horn buds of young animals to produce herd leaders. This discovery is a possible vindication of reports of many early travelers, including Varthema.

Varthema also describes unicorns he saw in the city of Zeila, animals with single horns pointing backward rather than forward. By Vartema's time, the kingdom of the legendary Prester John had shifted from India to Ethiopia. *Zerzalino* is sesame and *brazzo* an arm's-length.

Varthema is considered the second non-Muslim to visit the Holy City, following Pedro de Covilhao, and the first European to write an authentic account of it.

For earlier unicorns, see Ctesias, Pliny, and Aelian. For accounts of unicorn sightings, see W. Winwood Reade.

Unicorns in the Temple of Mecca *

THE CHAPTER CONCERNING THE UNICORNS IN THE TEMPLE OF MECCA,
NOT VERY COMMON IN OTHER PLACES.

In another part of the said temple is an enclosed place in which there are two live unicorns, and these are shown as very remarkable objects, which they certainly are. I will tell you how they are made. The elder is formed like a colt of thirty months old, and he has a horn in the forehead, which horn is about three *braccia* in length. The other unicorn is like a colt of one year old, and he has a horn of about four *palmi* long. The colour of the said animal resembles that of a dark bay horse, and his head resembles that of a stag; his neck is not very long, and he has some thin and short hair which hangs on one side; his legs are slender and lean like those of a goat; the foot is a little cloven in the fore part, and long and goatlike, and there are some hairs on the hind part of the said legs. Truly this monster must be a very fierce and solitary animal. These two animals were presented to the Sultan of Mecca as the finest things that could be found in the world at the present day, and as the richest treasure ever sent by a king of Ethiopia, that is, by a Moorish king. He made this present in order to secure an alliance with the said Sultan of Mecca.

* *The Travels of Ludovico de Varthema in Egypt, Arabia Deserta and Arabia Felix, in Persia, India, and Ethiopia, A.D. 1503 to 1508*, trans. John Winter Jones, ed. George Percy Badger (London: Hakluyt Society, 1863), 46–49, 86–88.

The Unicorns of Zeila

THE CHAPTER CONCERNING ZEILA, A CITY OF ETHIOPIA, AND OF THE
ABUNDANCE OF IT, AND CONCERNING SOME ANIMALS OF THE SAID CITY,
SUCH AS SHEEP AND COWS.

The beforenamed city of Zeila is a place of immense traffic, especially in gold and elephants' teeth. Here also are sold a very great number of slaves, which are those people of Prester John whom the Moors take in battle, and from this place they are carried into Persia, Arabia Felix, and to Mecca, Cairo, and into India. In this city people live extremely well, and justice is excellently administered. Much grain grows here and much animal food, oil in great quantity, made not from olives but from *zerzalino*, honey and wax in great abundance. Here is found a kind of sheep, the tail of which weighs fifteen or sixteen pounds, and with the head and neck quite black, but the whole of the rest of the body white. There are also some other sheep, which have tails a *brazzo* long and twisted like vines, and they have the dewlap like that of a bull, which almost touches the ground. Also in this place I found a certain kind of cows, which had horns like a stag and were wild, which had been presented to the Sultan of the said city. I also saw there other cows, which had a single horn in the forehead, which horn is a *palmo* and a half in length, and turns more towards the back of the cow than forwards. The colour of these is red, that of the former is black. The place has poor walls and a bad port, nevertheless it is situated on level ground and the mainland. The king of the Zeila is a Moor, and has many soldiers, both foot and horse. The people are warlike. Their dress consists of a shirt. They are olive-coloured. They go badly armed, and are all Mohammedans.

ANTONIO PIGAFETTA (C. 1490–1535)
MAGELLAN'S VOYAGE

Within one of the major documents of the voyages of exploration is perhaps the earliest European description of the fabled bird of paradise as well as the familiar tale of a gigantic Eastern bird so strong it can carry off a buffalo or elephant.

Antonio Pigafetta's journal is the only complete record of the first circumnavigation of the world. Ferdinand Magellan's commission by King Charles I of Spain to reach the East Indies by sailing west began with 270 men in five ships in 1519; after mutiny, desertion, starvation, and Magellan's murder by natives in the Philippines, only the *Victoria*, carrying eighteen men and the captain, returned to Spain in 1522. From his daily journal, Antonio Pigafetta prepared his chronicle of the three-year expedition, complete with cartographic sketches. Magellan's own log having been lost, most of the details of the disastrous but historic voyage would never have been known had it not been for Pigafetta's record.

Pigafetta relates that the *Victoria* sailed from the Moluccas with a full cargo of cloves and two brilliantly plumed dead birds, a gift from the King of Bachian to the King of Spain. The spices from the Indies paid for the voyage and incited others to sail to the rich East Indies. The birds of paradise, in spite of Pigafetta's mention of their legs, introduced to Europe the Indonesian legend of beautiful legless birds that came from paradise, fed on dew, and never touched earth. Even though Aristotle had declared there could be no footless bird, Linnaeus classified the birds as *Paradisea apoda*, "without feet." The fable was perpetuated in natural histories up to the nineteenth century. The birds, marketed to Europe by Dutch traders, were simply dried skins prepared by natives of the East Indies. Varieties of the birds were variously known as *manucodiata* (the birds of God), *passares de sol* (birds of the sun), and *avis paradeus* (paradise bird).

The tale of the "Garuda" bird that Pigafetta heard from Moorish sailors derives from the body of fables of people carried by great birds, best known in Europe through Sindbad the Sailor's encounters with the roc. In the mythology of India, Garuda is the vehicle of the god Vishnu. Translator Lord Stanley writes that "Garuda" is Sanskrit and Malay for "griffin." Rudolf Wittkower, in *Allegory and the Migration of Symbols*, points out that in a sixteenth-century engraving celebrating Magellan's discovery of a passage to the East, the Dutch artist Johannes Stradanus depicts Pigafetta's gigantic Garuda flying above the ocean, an elephant in its talons (see illustration).

For the bird of paradise, see Guillaume de Salluste du Bartas, Ambroise Paré, and Henry Davenport Northrup. For "relatives" of the Garuda bird, see the roc and griffin in Chapter 7, the griffins in Sir John Bourchier, and the roc in Sir Henry Yule.

Birds of Paradise*

This day, the King of Bachian, with the consent of the King of Tadore, came on shore, preceded by four men holding up daggers in their hands, to make alliance with us: he said, in the presence of the King of Tadore and of all his suite, that he would always be ready for the service of the King of Spain, that he would keep in his name the cloves left in his island by the Portuguese, until another Spanish squadron arrived there, and he would not give them up without his consent. He

* *The First Voyage Round the World*, trans. and ed. Lord Stanley of Alderley (London: Hakluyt Society, 1874), 143, 154–55.

A gigantic roc-like bird carries off an elephant—*upper left corner* of Johannes Stradanus's sixteenth-century engraving, *Magellan's Discovery of the Straits*. Derived from Antonio Pigafetta's tale of the "Garuda" bird in the Eastern ocean. Courtesy of the Warburg Institute, University of London.

sent through us to the King of Spain a present of a slave and two bahars of cloves. He would have wished to have sent ten bahars, but our ships were so heavily laden, that we could not receive any more.

He also gave us for the King of Spain two most beautiful dead birds. These birds are as large as thrushes; they have small heads, long beaks, legs slender like a writing pen, and a span in length; they have no wings, but instead of them long feathers of different colours, like plumes: their tail is like that of the thrush. All the feathers, except those of the wings, are of a dark colour; they never fly, except when the wind blows. They told us that these birds come from the terrestrial Paradise, and they call them "bolon dinata" that is divine birds.

Tale of the Garuda Bird

They also related to us that beyond Java Major, towards the north in the Gulf of China, which the ancients named Sinus Magnus, there is an enormous tree named Campanganghi, in which dwell certain birds named Garuda, so large that they take with their claws, and carry away flying, a buffalo, and even an elephant, to the place of the tree, which place is named Puzathaer. The fruit of this tree is called Buapanganghi, and is larger than a water melon. The Moors of Burné, whom we had with us in the ships, told us they had seen two of these birds, which had been sent to their king from the kingdom of Siam. No junk, or other vessel, can approach this tree within three or four leagues, on account of the great whirlpools which the water makes there. They related to us, moreover, how in a wonderful manner what is related of this tree became known, for a junk, having been carried there by the whirlpools, was broken up, and all the seamen perished, except a child who attached himself to a plank and was miraculously borne near the tree, upon which he mounted. There he placed himself under the wing of one of these birds, which was asleep, without its perceiving him, and next day the bird having taken flight carried him with it, and having seen a buffalo on the land, descended to take it; the child took advantage of the opportunity to come out from under its wing, and remained on the ground. In this manner the story of these birds and of the tree became known, and it was understood that those fruits which are frequently found in the sea came from that place.

Heinrich Kramer (c. 1430–1505) and James Sprenger (c. 1436–1496)
Malleus Maleficarum

The "Witches' Hammer" (c. 1486), by two Dominican inquisitors, was regarded for centuries as the ultimate authority on the detection and punishment of witches. A handbook for judges, the encyclopedic work on satanism was composed in response to Pope Innocent VIII's 1484 Papal Bull on the alarming spread of witchcraft in northern Germany. One of the many crimes of witchcraft detailed in the work is the sometimes fatal bewitching of the evil eye. The authors support their accusations with traditional basilisk lore beginning with Pliny, who — like they — also referred to the mesmerizing gaze of the wolf. Like others, they question why any man able to kill a basilisk does not, himself, die from the monster's poison. Two centuries before Kramer and Sprenger, Albertus Magnus rejected the belief that eyes emitted noxious rays. The citing of authorities from Arabian philosophers to the Bible contributes to the disarmingly rational tone of the inquisitors' argument.

Basilisk from Johann Stabius's sixteenth-century *De Labyrintho*. From Richard Huber's *Treasury of Fantastic and Mythological Creatures* (New York: Dover, 1981). Courtesy of Dover Publications.

Basilisks and the Power of the Eye*

. . . there may be a certain fascination cast by the eyes over another person, and this may be harmful and bad.

And it is of this fascination that Avicenna and Al-Gazali have spoken; S. Thomas too thus mentions this fascination, Part I, question 117. For he says the mind of a man may be changed by the influence of another mind. And that influence which is exerted over another often proceeds from the eyes, for in the eyes a certain subtle influence may be concentrated. For the eyes direct their glance upon a certain object without taking notice of other things, and although the vision be perfectly clear, yet at the sight of some impurity, such as, for example, a woman during her monthly periods, the eyes will as it were contract a certain impurity. This is what Aristotle says in his work *On Sleep and Waking*, and thus if

* Heinrich Kramer and James Sprenger, *The Malleus Maleficarum*, trans. Montague Summers (1928; rpt., New York: Dover, 1971), 17–18.

anybody's spirit be inflamed with malice or rage, as is often the case with old women, then their disturbed spirit looks through their eyes, for their countenances are most evil and harmful, and often terrify young children of tender years, who are extremely impressionable. And it may be that this is often natural, permitted by God; on the other hand, it may be that these evil looks are often inspired by the malice of the devil, with whom old witches have made some secret contract. . . .

All this is borne out by the commentators upon the Psalm, *Qui timent te unidebunt me*. There is a great power in the eyes, and this appears even in natural things. For if a wolf see a man first, the man is struck dumb. Moreover, if a basilisk see a man first its look is fatal; but if he see it first he may be able to kill it; and the reason why the basilisk is able to kill a man by its gaze is because when it sees him, owing to its anger a certain terrible poison is set in motion throughout its body, and this it can dart from its eyes, thus infecting the atmosphere with deadly venom. And thus the man breathes in the air which it has infected and is stupefied and dies. But when the beast is first seen by the man, in a case when the man wishes to kill the basilisk, he furnishes himself with mirrors, and the beast seeing itself in the mirrors darts out poison towards its reflection, but the poison recoils and the animal dies. It does not seem plain, however, why the man who thus kills the basilisk should not die too, and we can only conclude that this is on account of some reason not clearly understood.

So far we have set down our opinions absolutely without prejudice and refraining from any hasty or rash judgement, not deviating from the teachings and writings of the Saints. We conclude, therefore, that the Catholic truth is thus, that to bring about these evils which form the subject of discussion, witches and the devil always work together, and that in so far as these matters are concerned one can do nothing without the aid and assistance of the other.

LEONARDO DA VINCI (1452–1519)
THE NOTEBOOKS

Leonardo's notebooks, composed over decades, encompass the vast range of his scientific and esthetic interests, from a child in the womb to the mechanics of flight. Filled with independent speculation on a wide variety of subjects, the notebooks are an embodiment of the Renaissance spirit of inquiry.

The notebook entry, "How to Make an Imaginary Animal Appear Natural," reflects Leonardo's break with the past. When commissioned to depict the head of a monster, the young artist is said to have modeled his composite subject on a collection of strange actual creatures, including hedgehogs and lizards. The process, as described in the notebooks, is a reversal of the standard travelers' tale technique of portraying an actual but exotic beast in terms of animals familiar to the audience.

More dependent on authorities than most of the notebook entries, "A Bestiary" is derived from medieval bestiaries, and contains classical lore, but the allegories are secular rather than religious. The section contains nearly a hundred brief descriptions of both actual and fabulous animals. Leonardo may have prepared the collection for students he was tutoring in Latin.

How to Make an Imaginary Animal Appear Natural*

You know that you cannot make any animal without it having its limbs such that each bears resemblance to that of some one of the other animals. If therefore you wish to make one of your imaginary animals appear natural — let us suppose it to be a dragon — take for its head that of a mastiff or setter, for its eyes those of a cat, for its ears those of a porcupine, for its nose that of a greyhound, with the eyebrows of a lion, the temples of an old cock and the neck of a water-tortoise.

A Bestiary

CRUELTY

The basilisk is so exceedingly cruel that when it cannot kill animals with the venom of its gaze it turns towards the herbs and plants, and looking fixedly upon them makes them wither up.

BLANDISHMENTS

The siren sings so sweetly as to lull the mariners to sleep, and then she climbs upon the ships and kills the sleeping mariners.

CONSTANCY

For constancy the phoenix serves as a type; for understanding by nature its renewal it is steadfast to endure the burning flames which consume it, and then it is reborn anew.

* *The Notebooks of Leonardo da Vinci*, ed. Edward MacCurdy (1939; rpt., New York: George Braziller, 1958), 890–91, 1076, 1078–79.

A lady with a unicorn. Sketch by Leonardo da Vinci. By permission of the Ashmolean Library, Oxford, England.

INTEMPERANCE

The unicorn through its lack of temperance, and because it does not know how to control itself for the delight that it has for young maidens, forgets its ferocity and wildness; and laying aside all fear it goes up to the seated maiden and goes to sleep in her lap, and in this way the hunters take it.

PARACELSUS (c. 1490–1541)
THE TREASURE OF THE ALCHEMISTS,
OF ANIMALS BORN FROM SODOMY

Son of a physician and named after the Greek philosopher Theophrastus, Aureolus Philippus Theophrastus Bombast, of Hohenheim, called himself Paracelsus. The "para" in his name perhaps meant surpassing the Roman encyclopedist Aulus Cornelius Celsus, whose *De medicina* (1478) was one of the first and most popular medical books printed in the Renaissance. Scorning the Greek and Arabian medical authorities then esteemed, Paracelsus combined alchemy, astrology, and philosophy in devising chemical treatment for disease. His work has been both attacked as charlatanism and credited with being the forerunner of modern pharmacology. Among his occult writings are a description of the alchemical phoenix and an explanation of the generation of hybrid monsters.

The pseudoscience of alchemy originated in Alexandria in the first centuries A.D., developed in China and the Middle East, and flourished in Europe from the twelfth to the seventeenth centuries. An early form of chemistry, alchemy was primarily concerned with transmuting base metals into gold with the aid of the "philosopher's stone," which "healed" impure ("sick") metals. Alchemists believed that the four Aristotelian elements of earth, air, water, and fire accounted for all matter, that mercury and sulphur derived from them, and that it was possible to transmute any substance into any other. Gold, they thought, grew from prime matter like plant and animal life, and developed toward perfection like the human soul. They believed that the natural evolution of base metals into gold could be accelerated by a four-step process, each stage having its corresponding color: prime matter (black), mercury (white), sulphur (red), and gold. Through this process, the base metal is "killed" and "revived" into a purified form. The heated metal blackens and disintegrates into ash, and the new, congealed metal rises phoenixlike from the ashes.

The phoenix is the alchemical sign for sulfur and corresponds to the color red, emblematic of the rebirth of the prime metal turned to ashes by fire. The passage on the generation of traditional marine hybrids and other monsters is a detailed, figurative explanation of the Renaissance beliefs — expressed in heraldry — that sea animals corresponded to land animals and that monstrous creatures were actual freaks of nature.

Other than the phoenix, the salamander, the dragon, and the unicorn are also symbols of the alchemical process.

For alchemy, see Carl Jung. For the birth of monsters, see the *Enuma Elish*, Hesiod, and Lucretius.

The Alchemical Phoenix*

This work, the Tincture of the Alchemist, need not be one of nine months; but quickly, and without any delay, you may go on by the Spaygric Art of the Alchemists, and, in the space of forty days, you can fix this alchemical substance, exalt it, putrefy it, ferment it, coagulate it into a stone, and produce the Alchemical Phoenix. But it should be noted well that the Sulphur of Cinnabar becomes

---

* *The Hermetical and Alchemical Writings of Aureolus Philippus Theophrastus Bombast, of Hohenheim, called Paracelsus the Great*, ed. Arthur Edward Waite (London, 1894); from *The Treasure of the Alchemists*, 40; from *De Animalibus natis ex Sodomia*, 123–24n.

the Flying Eagle, whose wings fly away without wind, and carry the body of the phoenix to the nest of the parent, where it is nourished by the element of fire, and the young ones dig out its eyes: from whence there emerges a whiteness, divided in its sphere, into a sphere and life out of its own heart, by the balsam of its inward parts, according to the property of the cabalists.

The Birth of Hybrid Monsters

. . . There are many monsters in the sea which are not products of the original creation, but are born from the sperm of fishes of unlike species coming together contrary to the genuine order of Nature. Thus monsters are sometimes found in the sea exhibiting the form of man, which yet have not been generated *ex sodomia* from men, but arise by the conjunction of diverse fishes. . . . Even among men monsters are sometimes found that remind us partly of a human being, and partly of an animal. This is a repellent subject, but requires to be fully explained, that the first birth may be correctly understood. The same also takes place in the sea. There is, for example, the syren, of which the upper parts are those of a woman and the lower those of a fish. This does not form part of the original creation, but is a hybrid offspring from the union of two fishes of the same kind, but of different forms. Other marine animals are also found, which, without corresponding exactly to man, yet resemble him more than any other animal. However, like the rest of the brutes, they lack mind or soul. They have the same relations to man as the ape, and are nothing but the apes of the sea. As often as they unite, marine monsters of this kind are produced. Another such monstrous generation is the monachus or monk-like fish. But there are many genera of fishes, and many modes of generation, which do not always result from the sperm familiar or customary to them, but happen in various other ways. For example, certain monsters are drowned in the sea, and are devoured by the fishes. Now, if a sperm, constituted in exaltation, were to perish by immersion, and having been consumed by a fish, were again exalted within it, a certain operation would undoubtedly follow from the nature of the fish and the sperm, whence it may be gathered that the majority of marine animals which recall the human form are in this manner produced. Yet, having the nature of a fish, they live in the waters and rejoice therein. The marine dog, the marine spider, and the marine man are of this class. If they are generated in any other way, it must be set down to sodomia. But there may be a third cause, namely, when spermatica of this kind acquire digestion, and by reason of this conjunction a birth takes place. . . . Monsters are likewise generated in the air, from the droppings of the stars from above. For a sperm falls from the stars. The winds also in their courses bring many strange things from other regions to which they are indigenous. The sperm of spiders, toads, and other creatures floating in the air are resolved, and hence other living things are produced. In this way grasshoppers and other monsters are begotten, their generation being of one only and not of two. Such births are more venomous and impure than are other worms. Therefore, houses ought to be scrupulously cleaned, or else so constructed as not to favour the accumulation of much filth. For the air is efficacious against seeds dispersed in this manner. The earth is, however, the most fruitful matrix of monstrous growths. There the animals of both land and sea congregate. The basilisk is generated from the sperm of a toad and a cock. The sperm of the cock uniting with that of the hen produces an egg. But if the cock emit the sperm without the hen doing likewise, the egg will be imperfect, and something will be generated unnaturally. There is another kind of basilisk, produced by the union, *sodomitice*, of a cock and a toad. After the same manner, lizards unite with geckoes, and the copulation produces a peculiar worm, partaking of the nature of each, and known as a dragon. The asp is another instance of this unnatural generation. . . .

BENVENUTO CELLINI (1500–1571)
AUTOBIOGRAPHY

The belief that salamanders live in fire was affirmed as early as Aristotle. Even though Albertus Magnus deemed the story "completely false" and Marco Polo called it "fabulous nonsense," the fable lived on through the centuries. A well-known eyewitness account of a salamander in a fire is that of the Italian artist Benvenuto Cellini in his *Autobiography*. The goldsmith and sculptor's portrayal of his life and times was completed in 1562 and first printed in 1728.

Cellini is best known for his Perseus holding the head of Medusa and a gold and enamel salt cellar formed from mythological figures.

A Salamander in the Fire *

When I was about five years of age, my father happened to be in a little room in which they had been washing, and where there was a good fire of oak burning: with a fiddle in his hand he sang and played near the fire, the weather being exceedingly cold: he looked at this time into the flames, and saw a little animal resembling a lizard, which could live in the hottest part of that element; instantly

---

* Benvenuto Cellini, *The Life of Benvenuto Cellini: A Florentine Artist. Written by Himself*, vol. 16: *Autobiography*, trans. Thomas Nugent (London: Hunt and Clarke, 1828), 8–9.

Heraldic crest of a salamander in flames. From James Fairbairn's 1859 *Heraldic Crests* (rpt., New York: Dover, 1993). Courtesy of Dover Publications.

perceiving what it was, he called for my sister, and after he had shown us the creature, he gave me a box on the ear; I fell a crying, while he, soothing me with his caresses, spoke these words: "My dear child, I don't give you that box for any fault you have committed, but that you may recollect that the little creature in the fire is a salamander; such a one as never was beheld before, to my knowledge"; so saying, he embraced me, and gave me some money.

FRANÇOIS RABELAIS (C. 1495–1553)
GARGANTUA AND PANTAGRUEL

Traditional authorities, travelers' tales, and fabulous animals alike receive exuberantly nontraditional treatment in Rabelais's mock-heroic *Gargantua and Pantagruel* (1532–1564). Parody, satire, and burlesque transform them all on the fantastic island of Satinland.

Rabelais's book chronicles the adventures of a race of giants, namely, Gargantua, his son Pantagruel, Pantagruel's companion Panurge, and Friar John. In the fifth and final book, Pantagruel, Panurge, and the irreverent friar continue their global quest for the Oracle of the Holy Bottle, which will advise Panurge on whether or not to marry. The company sails across the top of the world to reach Cathay and stops at many islands, each giving the author opportunity for broad satire. At the end of the voyage, the message of the Holy Bottle is "Drink."

In the manner of travelers from classical times on, Pantagruel describes their visit to Satinland, where tapestry phoenixes, unicorns, and other fantastic creatures mix with a host of other animals. Rabelais's exaggerated catalogs, parodied composite descriptions, and scurrilous burlesque all emerge from a wealth of classical and medieval lore. Published after Rabelais's death, the fifth book is generally thought to have been completed by a different author.

Along with its extravagant play and its celebration of the senses and learning, *Gargantua and Pantagruel* satirically attacked contemporary social institutions, including the universities and the Church. The Sorbonne repeatedly condemned the work.

The first ellipsis in the following text is the editor's; all others are the translator's.

For the literary genre Rabelais satirizes here, see Chapter 7. For an earlier parody of the genre, see Lucian.

How We Visited the Land of Satin*

Happy at having been afforded an opportunity of seeing the new Order of Holy Demisemiquaver Friars, we sailed on for two days. On the third day, our skipper landed in the most beautiful and delightful island we had yet seen. It was called Isle of Frieze, for all the roads were of woolen cloth.

On this island lay the land of Satin, famed among pages at court. The trees and high grasses, which were of figured velvet and damask, never shed their leaves or flowers.

The beasts and birds were all of tapestry work. We had occasion to examine not a few beasts, birds and trees, which in shape, size and color, resembled ours at home. But they ate nothing, sang not at all and did not bite as ours do. We viewed many sorts of creatures we had never seen before, especially elephants. . . .

I saw thirty-two unicorns. These were extraordinarily vicious beasts, in every respect like thoroughbred horses, except that their heads were like a stag's, their feet like an elephant's, their tails like a boar's, and out of their foreheads, grew a sharp black horn, six or seven feet long. The latter usually dangled down like a turkey-cock's crest, but when the unicorn meant to fight or to use it for any other purpose, she thrust it out, straight and hard as an arrow. I watched one unicorn leading a throng of wild animals to a fountain, which she proceeded to purify, by dipping her horn into the water.

Panurge assured me that he, too, possessed a horn, growing out, not from the middle of his forehead, but somewhat lower down. It was comparable to the unicorn's, if not in length, at least in its virtues and properties. Hers cleaned the waters of marshes and fountains of all ordure and poison, enabling animals to drink there in safety. So, too, Panurge with his nervous horn, scoured out foul sewers and mephitic sumpholes, allowing others to slosh about after him, without risk of chancre, pox, clap, scaldstale, ulcer or gangrenous sores.

---

* François Rabelais, *The Complete Works of Rabelais: The Five Books of Gargantua and Pantagruel*, trans. Jacques Le Clercq (New York: Modern Library, 1936), 794–98.

"When you're married, we'll try this out on your wife," cried Friar John. "This for mere charity's sake, since you are gracious enough to give us such instructions."

"You try it," said Panurge, "and I'll feed you a pill that will bring you face to face with your Maker . . . a pill known as Caesarian, because it did for Julius of that name . . . a pill compounded of twenty-two stabs of the dagger."

"Thanks," said Friar John, "but I would prefer a draught of cool wine!"

I beheld other marvels in Satinland.

There was, for instance, the Golden Fleece conquered by Jason. Whoever states that Jason's spoil was a golden apple, not a fleece, arguing that the Greek μῆλον means both apple and sheep, is utterly mistaken, and must have visited Satinland with his eyes closed.

There was a chameleon, such as Aristotle describes, and such as Charles Marais, a famous physician in the noble city of Lyons on the Rhône, once showed me years ago. It lived exclusively on air, like the other.

There were three hydras—a sort of seven-headed snake—such as I had seen elsewhere in the past.

There were fourteen phoenixes. Now I have read in many authors that there was but one phoenix in the wide world in every century. In my humble opinion, these authors had never beheld a phoenix, save those woven in tapestries that hung on palace walls. This holds true of Firmianus Lactantius, the third-century rhetorician, too, even though he was known as the Christian Cicero.

There was the skin of Apuleius' Golden Ass. I recalled the satiric romance concerning the adventures of Lucian, who, while sojourning in Thessaly, was accidentally metamorphosed into an ass. I recalled how he fell into the hands of robbers, eunuchs, magistrates and others who treated him scurvily. I recalled how eventually he regained human form.

There were three hundred and nine pelicans. And six thousand six hundred seleucides. (The birds Jupiter sent to devour the locusts that were ravaging Mount Cesius.) That is exactly what they were doing to Satinland locusts, as they marched forward, row upon orderly row, across the fields.

What else did I see? Well, I saw cinnamologi, strange Arab birds . . . argathyles . . . caprimulgi or goatsuckers, a sort of raven that flies into goatsheds and milks the goats . . . tinnunculi, who defend pigeons against hawks . . . stymphalides, the cannibal birds slain by Hercules in his sixth labour . . . protonotaries! no, these are prelates: I mean onocrotaries or bitterns . . . harpies, winged monsters with the heads and breasts of women, fierce, starved and grasping creatures living in an atmosphere of filth and stench . . . panthers, so little known in France that some doubt their existence . . . dorcades or gazelles . . . cemades or fawns . . . cynocephali, great apes with heads like dogs . . . satyrs, with hindlegs, horns and ears like a goat's . . . cartasons or Indian unicorns . . . tarands, which resemble reindeer . . . uri or aurochs, wild oxen . . . monopodes or bonassi, which are like bison . . .

pephages, cepes and neares . . . stera, a sort of snake . . . cercopitheca or long-tailed monkeys . . . bugles or young bulls . . . musimons or Sardinian sheep . . . byturi, insects that devour the vines . . . ophyri, a deadly sort of serpent . . . stryges or screech dragons . . . and griffins, who had an eagle's head and wings on a lion's body . . .

I saw Mid-Lent on horseback, with Mid-August and Mid-March holding the stirrups. And I saw werewolves, centaurs, tigers, leopards, hyenas, camelopards or giraffes, and oryges, a variety of Egyptian unicorn with certain features of the antelope.

I saw a remora, a small fish named *echeinis* by the Greeks. Before it stood a tall ship, unable to budge an inch, despite a full complement of sails, a high wind and a strong current. I am convinced it was the vessel of Periander, the tyrant of Corinth, which, according to Pliny, was stopped by a denizen of the deep, despite wind and tide. Mutianus, Pliny's authority, beheld it in Satinland, and not elsewhere.

Friar John remarked that two kinds of fish used formerly to reign in the law courts, rotting the bodies and racking the souls of all plaintiffs, whether noble or base, rich or poor, exalted or humble. The first were April fish or mackerel. (Did not mackerel abound in April? Were not pimps called mackerel? Well, then, you found plenty of mackerel to bear false witness in court!) The second were remora, which, with their perpetual litigation, stayed the course of Justice.

I saw sphinxes, a sort of ape . . . raffes, a kind of jackal . . . ounces or lynxes . . . cephi, with forelegs like man's hands and hind-legs like man's legs . . . crocutas, half-hyena, half-lioness . . . eali, large as the hippopotamus, with a tail like an elephant's, jaws like a wild boar's, and horns as pliant as an ass' . . . .

There were also curcrocutes, very swift beasts about the size of our donkeys in Mirebelais, with neck, tail and chest like a lion's, legs like a stag's, snout split to the ears, and only two teeth, one upper and one lower. They spoke with human voice, but when I examined them, they were sulking in silence.

You have probably never seen an aerie of saker falcons. Let me hereby assure you that I saw no less than a dozen.

I saw some left-handed halberds, the first I had ever beheld.

I saw some manthicores, a strange sort of beast: the body a lion's, the coat red, face and ears like a man's, and three rows of teeth closed together, like joined hands with fingers interlocked. Their tails secreted a sting like a scorpion's; their voices were very melodious.

I saw some catoblepes, reptiles diminutive of body and huge of head, the latter so unwieldy as to be difficult to lift off the ground. So venemous were their eyes that, as with the basilisk, to face their glance spelled certain death.

I saw some two-backed beasts, marvellously happy and extraordinarily prolific at arseclicking; their dual rumps wagged more riotously than ever the most tail-wagging wagtail.

I also saw crawfish being milked, after which they paraded home in drill formation. You, too, would have watched them with delight.

LUDOVICO ARIOSTO (1474–1533)
ORLANDO FURIOSO

The hybrid creature called the hippogriff (literally "horse-griffin") is best known as a major figure in Ariosto's romance epic, *Orlando Furioso* (1532). Depicted in Greco–Roman and medieval art, the composite of two mortal enemies was not simply the Renaissance invention it has sometimes been said to be. Also, the beast's parts could have been inspired by Virgil's "Griffins now will be mated with horses," a proverbial line from the *Eclogues*, signifying impossibility.

While Ariosto did not create the hippogriff, he developed it as an essential character interwoven throughout the adventures of Charlemagne's paladins. At first the vehicle of the magician Atlante, the creature carries the knight Rogero to an enchanted isle and around the world. Bradamant is the knight's beloved. Later, near the end of the poem, another knight, Astolfo, rides the hippogriff around the globe to the Earthly Paradise and thereafter allows the animal to go free.

The griffin heritage of Ariosto's hippogriff is evident not only in its name and eagle elements but in the land from which it comes: "Ryfee." Both Mela and Solinus cite the northern Riphean Mountains as the home of the griffins. The creature is also a literary relative of Pegasus, the winged horse born of the blood of Medusa. Bellerophon rode the divine animal when he slew the Chimera, and in one version of the myth, Pegasus carries Perseus into battle against the sea-beast Cetus. After he passes over the known Renaissance world on the hippogriff, Rogero reenacts the Perseus tale by rescuing Orlando's beloved, Angelica, from the monstrous Orc. The hippogriff is not actually named in the particular translation excerpted below.

Orlando Furioso ("Roland Mad") was a continuation of Matteo Maria Boiardo's unfinished *Orlando Innamorato* ("Roland in Love"). Ariosto's massive poem of forty-six cantos was one of the most influential of Renaissance epics. The following excerpts are from John Harington's celebrated Elizabethan translation, *Orlando Furioso in English Heroical Verse*. Major modern illustrations of his hippogriff are those of Gustav Doré and N. C. Wyeth.

For fabulous beasts in other Renaissance romance epics, see Sir John Bourchier and Edmund Spenser.

The Hippogriff *

[ATLANTE AND THE HIPPOGRIFF]

. . . The host and other servants of the Inne
Came on the sodaine with a wofull crie,
And some did gaze without and some within
(As when men see a Comet in the skie):
The cause of this their wondring and
    their crying
Was that they saw an armed horseman flying,

      . . .

But yet the beast he rode was not of art
But gotten of a Griffeth and a Mare
And like a Griffeth had the former part,
And wings and head and clawes that
    hideous are
And passing strength and force and
    ventrous hart,
But all the rest may with a horse compare.
Such beasts as these the hils of Ryfee yeeld
Though in these parts they have bene seene
    but seeld.

This monster rare from farthest
    regions brought
This rare Magician ordred with such skill
That in one monthe or little more he
    tought
The savage monster to obey his will,
And though by conjurations strange
    he wrought
In other things his fancie to fulfill
(As cunning men stil trie each strange
    conclusion)
Yet in this Griffeth horse was no
    collusion.

*   *Ludovico Ariosto's Orlando Furioso: Translated into English Heroical Verse by Sir John Harington (1591)*, ed. Robert McNulty (Oxford: Clarendon , 1972), 49–50, 117 (4.3, 13–14, 10.58–60).

[Rogero's global flight]

Rogero mounted on the winged steed
Which he had learnd obedient now to make
Doth deeme it were a brave and noble deed
About the world his voyage home to take,
Forthwith beginneth Eastward to procede,
And though the thing were much to undertake,
Yet hope of praise makes men no travell shunne
To say another day: we this have donne;

And leaving first the Indian river Tana
He guides his journey to the great Catay;
From thence he passeth unto Mangiana
And came within the sight of huge Quinsay,
Upon the right hand leaving Sericana
And turning from the Scythians away,
Where Asia from Europa first doth draw
Pomeria, Russia, Prutina he saw.

His horse that hath the use of wings and feet
Did helpe with greater hast home to retire
And thoe with speed to turne he thought it meet
Because his *Bradamant* did so desire,
Yet having now of travell felt the sweet
(Most sweet to those to knowledge that aspire)
When Germanie and Hungrie he had past
He meanes to visit England at the last.

SIR JOHN BOURCHIER (1469–1533)
THE BOKE OF DUKE HUON OF BURDEUX

The medieval tale of griffins or rocs carrying people off to feed the birds' young forms a prominent adventure in the prose romance that introduced the fairy king Oberon to English literature.

The aerial journeys of Sindbad in *The Arabian Nights* and the anecdote Benjamin of Tudela recounts of griffins in the China Seas are only a few of many versions of a story that can be traced back at least to tenth-century Arabian narratives. *Huon of Bordeaux*, originally a thirteenth-century *chanson de geste* with epic characteristics, evolved over centuries into a prose romance filled with magic and the marvelous. During service to Henry VIII, Sir John Bourchier (Lord Berners), translated the French prose work into English. The story of Oberon in his *Boke of Duke Huon de Burdeux* (c. 1534) influenced Edmund Spenser and other Elizabethan poets.

One of the cycle of Charlemagne romances, the Huon tale begins with court treachery that leads to Huon's murder of the Emperor's son and Huon being sent on a mission to Babylon, from which he is not expected to return. Often aided by Oberon, the dwarf king of the fairies, Huon survives a series of adventures in the East and triumphantly returns to the court of Charlemagne. Among those adventures is his shipwreck on a magnetic island which draws the nails from passing ships. To escape from the castle of the Adamant, Huon, like Sindbad and Eastern sailors, uses deceit to be carried off by a gigantic bird. After battling and killing five young birds in the griffin's eyrie, Huon is attacked by the vengeful mother. Later in the romance, Huon presents to the King of France a foot of one of the griffins he slew, and it is hung for posterity in the holy chapel. Huon's shipwreck and ensuing griffin adventure may have been borrowed from a Bavarian folktale, *Herzog Ernst von Baiern.*

The Huon griffin episode is one of many medieval tales in which the creature is portrayed as rapacious. A demonic griffin attacks St. Brendan and his crew, and bestiary griffins are pictured grasping pigs and other animals in their claws. While often associated with Satan, the medieval griffin is sometimes symbolically linked with Christ. Griffin "claws," like unicorn horn, were reputed to have curative powers, and the beast's feathers were thought to restore sight.

Bourchier's sixteenth-century text, printed by Wynkyn de Worde, William Caxton's successor, has been retained in the following entry. The translation is inconsistent in capitalization of "Gryffon" and uses masculine pronouns for the griffin mother. Numbers in the text are lower-case Roman numerals.

For Duke Huon's griffin adventures and literary parallels, see also Sir Henry Yule.

Duke Huon and the Gryffons*

HOW HUON WAS BORNE BY A GRYFFON OUT OF THE CASTELL OF THE ADAMANT . . .

Thus as ye haue harde Huon past the tyme in the castel of the Adamant, and on a daye he lenyd and lokyd out at a wyndowe into the see warde / and he saw a farre of a great byrde come flyynge thethcrwarde / this byrd or fowle was bygger then any hors in the worlde / wherof he had great maruayle. Then he saw where it cam to the same porte, and lyghtyd in the maste of a great shyp, and sawe how

---

* *The Boke of Duke Huon of Burdeux*, trans. Sir John Bourchier, Lord Berners (1883; rpt., Millwood, N.Y.: Kraus Reprint, 1973), 425–33.

for the weyght of the fowle the mast had nere hand broke asonder. Then after he sawe the fowle a lyght downe into the shyp; and toke with his talantys one of the .x. men that dyed bycause they wolde not bileue fermely on god / they could not putrefye, but lay styll in the shype all hole and sounde; then the fowle lyfte hym vp into the ayre and caryed him awaye as lyghtly as a hauke wold carry a pegyon. Huon, who saw this, had great maruayle, and behelde the Gryffon whiche way he dyd flye; and as far of as he myght se he sawe to his semylytude a great rocke as whygt to the syght as Crystall / then he sayd to hymselfe "wold to god I were there, I thynke it be some place inhabytable"; then he thought to hymselfe to com thether agayne the next daye to se yf the Gryffon wolde come agayne to fech his praye: yf he dyd he thought yf he wolde be out of that castell, the gryffon myght bere hym armyd so suerly that he shuld do hym no hurte with his talantis / thinkynge to lye downe armyd with his sword in his hande amonge the dede men / and when the Gryffon had brought him wher his yonge byrdes were then to fyght with the Gryffon / . . .

when Huon sawe that the Gryffon was gone with his praye, he went to the bysshop and his company, and shewyd them all that he had sene and thought to do. . . . Then he departyd fro them and passyd out of the gate, and went downe the stayres and went in to the shyppe, and then he lokyd into the see and sawe where the gryffon was comynge / when he parseyued that he laye downe amonge the ded men withe his sword nakyd in his hande, and helde it on his thye by cause it shulde not fall in the see; and as sone as he was layd grouelynge a monge the dede men, the Gryffon came and restyd on a shyp maste as he was acustomyd to do / and he was so heuy that the mast bent nye asonder. when Huon saw that, he was in great fere, and callyd vp on our lorde Iesue chryste for ayde and socoure, and to saue hym fro ye fell Gryffon / & the Gryffon, lokynge for his pray, saw where Huon lay armyd / wherby he semyd more greatter then any of the other dede men / the Gryffon desyryd to haue hym to his nest to gyue hym to his yonge byrdis / so he cam downe into the shyppe and toke Huon in his clees, and straynyd hym so faste by bothe sydes that his clees enteryd into the flesshe for all his harnays, so that the blode issued out, and Huon was in that dystresse that all his body trymbelyd, & petuously he callyd vpon our lorde god for ayde / but he durst not stere for any payne that he felt, the Gryffon bare hym so hye and so far that in lesse then thre owres he bare hym to ye whyght rocke / and there layde hym downe. . . .

How Huon foughte with the great gryffon & slew her

When Huon saw that he had slayne the .v. yonge gryffons he thonkyd oure lorde god for the grase that he had sent hym as to ouercome suche .v. terryble beastis. then he sate downe to rest hym, and layd his sword by hym, thynkynge then to be in a suerty / but it was not longe but that the great Gryffon, who had brought hym fro the castel, came on hym with thre fete, and betynge with his wyngis / when she saw her yonge slayne, she cast out a great cry so that all the valey range therof / when Huon sawe her comynge he was in great fere, for he was sore wery with trauayle and losse of blode that it was payne to sustayne hymselfe / howbeit he sawe well it was nede to defende hymselfe / then he came to the Gryffon to haue stryken her, but he coude not, the gryffon was so nere hym betynge with her wyngis so fersly that Huon fell to the erthe, and his sworde fell out of his handys, wherof he had great fere / for he thought hymselfe in al hys lyfe neuer so nere dethe as he was then / he callyd then ryght petuously for ayde of our lorde Iesu chryste / and the Gryffon bet hym merueylusly with her beke / wyngis / and talouns / but the doble cotys of mayle that he had on were so strong that the gryffon coude not breke them / but yf the gryffon had not lost before one of his fete, and loste so moche blod as he had done, Huon coude neuer a scapyd without dethe / the Gryffon so sore defowlyd and bet hym that he could not ryse vp. Then he rememberyd hym selfe how he had by his syde a rych knyfe, the whyche he brought fro the castell of the Adamant / he drew it out and ther with strake the Gryffon on the brest .vi. great strokys, euery stroke as depe as the knyfe wold go / and as his hap was this knyfe was of two fote longe, and therwith ye Gryffon fell downe ded / then Huon arose and dyde of his helme, and lyfte vp his handis to the heuen & thankyd god of his vyctory. . . .

GUILLAUME DE SALLUSTE DU BARTAS (1544–1590)
THE DIVINE WEEKS

Traditional beasts soon to be rejected as fabulous were among the earth's animals born on the fifth and sixth days of Creation in *La Semaine ou Création du Monde* (1578). In his religious epic, the French Huguenot poet Du Bartas encompasses accepted science, including natural history and animal lore from the Bible, Pliny, the bestiaries, and the works of contemporary naturalists. Fabled creatures from the classical phoenix to the sixteenth-century "bishop fish" are all part of the poem's vast animal kingdom.

Du Bartas's account of the creation of fishes and birds on the fifth day of creation opens with the then-standard belief that all land creatures — including human beings — had their counterparts in the analogical universe of the sea. Like travelers' composite comparisons of parts of exotic beasts to well-known creatures, different species of marine life resembled cows, horses, sheep, and dogs. There were even mermen and mermaids (Pliny's Nereids) and sea-bishops, as illustrated in Guillaume Rondelet's *On Marine Fishes* (1554).

In *La Semaine*, the creation of birds begins with the phoenix. Among the host of birds that follow it in its flight is the griffin, a gold-guarding creature like the Dardane ants. Also in the flock are the ethereal "Mamuques," birds of paradise introduced to Europe earlier in the sixteenth century by the only ship to return from Magellan's ill-fated voyage. Reptiles and mammals are born on the sixth day, and all of animal creation ends with the barnacle goose, one of the forms of life thought to generate spontaneously, independent of others of its own kind.

La Semaine is an epic compilation of conventional material presented in highly ornate poetic diction. The popular work was a source of material for Elizabethan writers, and Joshua Sylvester's 1605 English translation, *The Divine Weeks and Works*, influenced the metaphysical poets. At first regarded as classics, Du Bartas's epics, traditional in thought, fell from favor due to the new intellectual climate in the late seventeenth century.

For the bird of paradise, see Antonio Pigafetta. For another commendation of the barnacle goose, see John Gerard.

Creation of the Wonders of the Seas *

In vaine had God stor'd Heav'n with glistring studs,
The Plaine with graine, the Mountain tops with woods,
Sever'd the Aire from Fire, the Earth from Water;
Had he not soone peopled this large Theater
With living Creatures: Therefore he began
(*This Day*) to quicken in the Ocean,
In standing pooles, and in the stragling Rivers
(Whose folding Channell fertile Champion severs)
So many Fishes of so many features,
That in the Waters one may see all Creatures;
And all that in this All is to be found;
As if the World within the Deepes were drown'd.

Seas have (as well as Skies) Sunne, Moone and Starres:
(As well as Aire) Swallowes, and Rookes, and Stares,
(As well as Earth) Vines, Roses, Nettles, Millions,
Pincks, Gilliflowers, Mushromes, and many millions
Of other Plants (more rare and strange then these)
As very Fishes living in the Seas:
And also Rammes, Calfes, Horses, Hares, and Hoggs,

---

* *The Divine Weeks and Works of Guillaume de Salluste Sieur du Bartas*, trans. Joshua Sylvester, ed. Susan Snyder (Oxford: Clarendon , 1979), vol. 1, pp. 232, 251, 253, 292–93.

Wolves, Lyons, Urchins, Elephants, and Doggs,
Yea Men and Maydes: and (which I more admire)
The Mytred Bishop, and the Cowled Fryer:
Whereof, Examples but a few yeeres since,
Were showne the *Norwayes*, and *Polonian* Prince.

Wondrous Birds

The Phoenix, cutting th'unfrequented Aire,
Forth-with is followed by a thousand paire
Of wings, in th'instant by th'Almighty wrought,
With divers Size, Colour, and Motion fraught. . . .

The rav'ning Kite, whose traine doth well supplie
A Rudders place; the Falcon mounting high,
The Marline, Lanar, and the gentle-Tercell,
Th'Ospray, and Saker, with a nimble Sarcell
Follow the *Phoenix*, from the Clouds (almost)
At once discovering many an unknowne Coast:
     In the swift Ranke of these fell Rovers, flies
The *Indian Griffin* with the glistring eyes,
Beake *Eagle-like*, backe sable, Sanguine brest,
White (Swan-like) wings, fierce tallents, alwaies prest
For bloody Battailes; for, with these he teares
Boares, Lyons, Horses, Tigres, Bulls, and Beares:
With these, our Grandames fruitfull panch he pulls,
Whence many an Ingot of pure Gold he culls,
To floore his proud nest, builded strong and steepe
On a high Rock better his thefts to keepe:
With these, he guards against an Armie bold,
The hollow Mines where first he findeth gold,
As wroath, that men upon his right should rove.
Or theevish hands usurp his *Tresor-trove*.
     O! ever may'st thou fight so (valiant Foule)
For this dire bane of our seduced soule,
And (with thee) may the *Dardane* ants, so ward
The Gold committed to their carefull Guard,
That hence-forth hope-less, mans fraile mind may rest-her
From seeking that, which doth it's Maisters maister. . . .
     But note we now, towards the rich *Moluques*,
Those passing strange and wondrous (birds) *Mamuques*,

(Wond'rous indeed, if Sea, or Earth, or Skie,
Saw ever wonder, swim, or goe, or flie)
Non knowes their nest, non knows the dam that breeds them,
Food-less they live, for th'Aire alonely feeds them,
Wing-lesse they flie, and yet their flight extends,
Till with their flight, their unknowne lyves-date ends.

Strange Transformations

God, not contented, to each Kind to give
And to infuse the Vertue Generative:
Made (by his wisedome) many Creatures breed
Of live-lesse bodies, without *Venus* deed.
　　So, the cold humour breeds the *Salamander*,
Who (in effect) like to her births-Commaunder,
With Childe with hundred Winters, with her touch
Quencheth the Fire though glowing ne'r so much.
　　So, of the Fire in burning furnace, springs
The Flie *Pyrausta* with the flaming wings:
Without the Fire, it dies; within it, joyes;
Living in that, which each thing else destroyed.
　　So, slow *Bootes* underneath him sees
In th'ycie *Iles*, those Goslings hatcht of Trees,
Whose fruitfull leaves falling into the Water,
Are turn'd (they say) to living Fowles soone after.
　　So, rotten sides of broken Shipps doo change
To *Barnacles*; O Transformation strange!
'Twas first a greene Tree, then a gallant Hull,
Lately a Mushrum, now a flying Gull.
So Morne and Evening the Sixth Day conclude,
And God perceav'd that All his Workes were good.

EDMUND SPENSER (c. 1522–1599)
THE FAERIE QUEENE

Medieval dragon lore culminates in what may be the most elaborate and sustained account of a dragon battle in literature: the climax of Book I of Edmund Spenser's allegorical epic romance, *The Faerie Queene* (1590–1596).

In his prefatory letter to Sir Walter Raleigh, Spenser reveals the intended meaning of his moral, religious, historical, and political allegories. He explains that his book is an allegory of the twelve moral virtues, intended "to fashion a gentleman"; the Red Cross Knight represents Holiness, and the Fairy Queen and her kingdom Queen Elizabeth I and England. Spenser later identifies the Red Cross Knight as St. George, the patron saint of England, and the poem itself equates goodness with Protestant England and evil with the country's Catholic enemies.

Beneath all these strata is a chivalric romance that opens *in medias res* with the Red Cross Knight being sent by Gloriana, the Fairy Queen, to free the parents of Una (Truth) from imprisonment by a dragon. Following his battle with an Echidna-like woman-serpent monster (Error) and a series of other adventures, the knight engages in a three-day combat with the "monstrous, horrible, and vaste" dragon. Following his victory, Red Cross is richly rewarded with ivory and gold, and he marries the fair Una.

Elsewhere in *The Faerie Queene*, Spenser relates in an extended simile (2.5.10) the lion and unicorn tale whose tradition extends from at least *The Letter of Prester John* to the present.

Spenser's uncompleted epic, written in what is now called the nine-line "Spenserian stanza" form he created for the work, earned him immediate honor as the preëminent English epic poet of his time. The Red Cross Knight's battle with the dragon, inspired by the St. George story, climaxed the literary dragon-slayer tradition, which faded in the following century, only to be revived in modern fantasy fiction.

For other dragon battles, see especially *Enuma Elish*, the *Hymn to Apollo*, *Beowulf*, Jacobus de Voragine, and J. R. R. Tolkien. For fabulous beasts in other Renaissance romance epics, see Ariosto and Sir John Bourchier.

Red-Crosse Knight and the Dragon *

The knight with that old dragon fights
    Two dayes incessantly:
The third, him overthrowes, and gayns
    Most glorious victory.

[THE DRAGON]

. . . they heard a roaring hideous sownd,
    That all the ayre with terror filled wyde,

* Edmund Spenser, *The Faerie Queene*, vol. 1 of *The Works of the English Poets*, ed. J. Aiken (London, 1802), 214–18, 230–31 (1.11.4, 8–15, 52–55).

A woodcut of the
Red Cross Knight
defeating the dragon.
Appeared in the first
edition of Spenser's
Faerie Queene (1590).

And seemd uneath to shake the stedfast ground.
Eftsoones that dreadful dragon they espyde,
Where stretcht he lay upon the sunny side
Of a great hill, himselfe like a great hill:
But all so soone as he from far descryde
Those glistring armes, that heven with light did fill,
He rousd himselfe full blyth, and hastned them untill.

.   .   .

By this, the dreadful beast drew nigh to hand,
Halfe flying, and halfe footing in his haste,
That with his largenesse measured much land,

And made wide shadow under his huge waste;
 As mountaine doth the valley overcaste.
 Approching nigh, he reared high afore
 His body monstrous, horrible, and vaste;
 Which, to increase his wondrous greatnes more,
Was swoln with wrath and poyson and with bloody gore;

And over all with brasen scales was armd,
 Like plated cote of steele, so couched neare
 That nought mote perce, ne might his corse bee harmd
 With dint of swerd, nor push of pointed speare:
 Which, as an Eagle, seeing pray appeare,
 His aery plumes doth rouze, full rudely dight;
 So shaked he, that horror was to heare:
 For, as the clashing of an armor bright,
Such noyse his rouzed scales did send unto the knight.

His flaggy winges, when forth he did display,
 Were like two sayles, in which the hollow wynd
 Is gathered full, and worketh speedy way:
 And eke the pennes, that did his pineons bynd,
 Were like mayne-yardes, with flying canvas lynd;
 With which whenas him list the ayre to beat,
 And there by force unwonted passage fynd,
 The cloudes before him fledd for terror great,
And all the hevens stood still amazed with his threat.

His huge long tayle, wownd up in hundred foldes,
 Does overspred his long bras-scaly back,
 Whose wreathed boughtes when ever he unfoldes,
 And thick-entangled knots adown does slack.
 Bespotted all with shieldes of red and blacke,
 It sweepeth all the land behind him farre,
 And of three furlongs does but litle lacke;
 And at the point two stinges infixed arre,
Both deadly sharp, that sharpest steele exceeden farre.

But stinges and sharpest steele did far exceed
 The sharpnesse of his cruel-rending clawes;
 Dead was it sure, as sure as death indeed,
 What ever thing does touch his ravenous pawes,
 Or what within his reach he ever drawes.

But his most hideous head my tongue to tell
Does tremble; for his deepe devouring iawes
Wide gaped, like the griesly mouth of hell,
Through which into his darke abysse all ravin fell.

And that more wondrous was, in either iaw
Three ranckes of yron teeth enraunged were,
In which yett trickling blood and gobbets raw
Of late devoured bodies did appeare,
That sight thereof bredd cold congealed feare;
Which to increase, and all at once to kill,
A cloud of smoothering smoke and sulphure seare,
Out of his stinking gorge forth steemed still,
That all the ayre about with smoke and stench did fill.

His blazing eyes, like two bright shining shieldes,
Did burne with wrath, and sparkled living fyre:
As two broad beacons, sett in open fieldes,
Send forth their flames far off to every shyre,
And warning give, that enemies conspyre
With fire and sword the region to invade;
So flam'd his eyne with rage and rancorous yre:
But far within, as in a hollow glade,
Those glaring lampes were sett, that made a dreadfull shade.

So dreadfully he towardes him did pas,
Forelifting up aloft his speckled brest,
And often bounding on the brused gras,
As for great ioyance of his new-come guest.
Eftsoones he gan advance his haughty crest;
As chauffed bore his bristles doth upreare;
And shoke his scales to battaile ready drest;
That made the red-crosse knight nigh quake for feare,
As bidding bold defyaunce to his foeman neare.

[THE THIRD DAY]

Then freshly up arose the doughty knight,
All healed of his hurts and woundes wide,
And did himselfe to battaile ready dight;
Whose early foe awaiting him beside
To have devourd, so soone as day he spyde,
When now he saw himselfe so freshly reare,

As if late fight had nought him damnifyde,
  He woxe dismaid, and gan his fate to feare;
Nathelesse with wonted rage he him advaunced neare:

And in his first encounter, gaping wyde,
  He thought attonce him to have swallowd quight,
  And rusht upon him with outragious pryde:
  Who him rencounting fierce, as hauke in flight,
  Perforce rebutted back. The weapon bright
  Taking advantage of his open iaw,
  Ran through his mouth with so importune might,
  That deepe emperst his darksom hollow maw,
And back retyrd, his life blood forth withall did draw.

So downe he fell, and forth his life did breath,
  That vanisht into smoke and cloudes swift;
  So downe he fell, that th' earth him underneath
  Did grone, as feeble so great load to lift;
  So downe he fell, as an huge rocky clift,
  Whose false foundacion waves have washt away,
  With dreadfull poyse is from the mayneland rift,
  And rolling downe, great Neptune doth dismay:
So downe he fell, and like an heaped mountaine lay.

The knight himselfe even trembled at his fall,
  So huge and horrible a masse it seemd;
  And his deare lady, that beheld it all,
  Durst not approch for dread, which she misdeemd,
  But yet at last, whenas the direfull feend
  She saw not stirre, off-shaking vaine affright
  She nigher drew, and saw that ioyous end:
  Then God she praysd, and thankt her faithfull knight,
That had atchievde so great a conquest by his might.

ROBERT CHESTER (FL. 1601)
LOVES MARTYR

Originally derived from the fable of the Arabian bird, the term "phoenix" became a common Elizabethan metaphor, first for the poet's mistress, and second for anyone of either sex possessing qualities considered rare. The epithet was also sometimes applied to Queen Elizabeth I, who selected the phoenix as a heraldic badge. One of the books emphasizing the phoenix theme was Robert Chester's *Loves Martyr* (1601), which contained a supplement of "Diverse Poeticall Essais" by William Shakespeare, Ben Jonson, George Chapman, and others. While his own poetry was later scorned, Chester's book is important in literary history as the first publication of a poem attributed to Shakespeare, *The Phoenix and the Turtle.*

Chester's allegory of love is a compilation of diverse materials, ending with a dialogue between the Turtle and the Phoenix. Within an earlier dialogue between Nature and the Phoenix—following a history of King Arthur—is a poetic natural history based on bestiary lore of both actual and fabulous animals.

For another verse catalog of animals, see Du Bartas.

Of Beasts and Birds*

> For the worlds blindnesse and opinion,
> I care not *Phoenix*, they are misbeleeuing,
> And if their eyes trie not conclusion,
> They will not trust a strangers true reporting.
>> With Beasts and Birds I will conclude my storie,
>> And to that All-in-all yeeld perfect glorie.

> . . .

> The *Mouse*, the *Mule*, the *Sow* and *Salamander*,
> That from the burning fire cannot live,
> The *Weasell*, *Cammell* and the hunted *Beauer*,
> That in pursute away his stones doth giue:
>> The *Stellio*, *Camelion* and *Unicorne*,
>> That doth expell hot poison with his Horne.

> . . .

> The *Onocentaur* is a monstrous beast;
> Supposed halfe a man and halfe an asse,
> That never shuts his eyes in quiet rest,
> Till he his foes deare life hath round encompast,

---

* Robert Chester, *Loves Martyr: or, Rosalins Complaint*, ed. Alexander B. Grosart (London: New Shakespeare Society, 1878), 107–8, 112–13, 119.

Such were the *Centaures* in their tyrannie,
That liv'd by humane flesh and villanie.

. . .

The labouring *Ant*, and the bespeckled *Adder*,
The *Frogge*, the *Tode*, and Sommer-haunting *Flie*,
The prettie *Silkeworme*, and the poisonous *Viper*,
That with his teeth doth wound most cruelly:
    The *Hornet* and the poisonous *Cockatrice*,
    That kills all birds by a most slie device.

. . .

The *Griffon* is a bird rich feathered,
His head is like a *Lion*, and his flight
Is like the *Eagles*, much for to be feared,
For why he kils men in the ugly night:
    Some say he keepes the *Smaragd* and the *Jasper*,
    And in pursute of Man is monstrous eager.

WILLIAM SHAKESPEARE (1564–1616)
PLAYS

Fabulous animals are referred to in nearly two-thirds of William Shakespeare's thirty-seven plays, the honored playwright's repeated use of their names assuring the creatures of a lasting place in English literature. As images that help define the speaker and his or her state of mind, the dragon, basilisk (cockatrice), and the phoenix appear more frequently than the others. They are evoked most often in the history plays, then with decreasing frequency in the tragedies, the comedies, and least of all in the romances. The barnacle goose, griffin, mermaids, and the unicorn, as well as other fantastic beings, are also referred to in the plays. Fabulous-animal imagery spans the entire Shakespeare canon, from the early *Henry VI* histories to *Henry VIII*.

Several of the scenes in which Shakespeare uses images of fabulous animals are dramatic turns or highlights of their respective plays, and some are among the most momentous in the canon.

The major fabulous animals take on a variety of verbal forms in the plays, from referential name to metaphor. Shakespeare's uses of the dragon range from allusions to St. George's battle with the monster to metaphorical dragons of the night. His dragon is a complex beast possessing qualities of both grandeur and evil. The "murd'ring," poisonous basilisk/cockatrice, with its lethal eyes, is a fitting image for bitter confrontations between characters. Uses of the name move between reference to the beast and identification of it with a person or thing, and "basilisk" is, besides, a term for deadly ordnance. The often bloody history plays and tragedies, and villains such as Richard III and Iachimo, appropriately generate dragon and basilisk/cockatrice imagery. The monstrous Richard III is naturally drawn to such beasts, and it is totally in character that he distort to his own ends not only the St. George story, but the phoenix fable as well. The popular Elizabethan "phoenix" has several references, including the Arabian bird, a person of rare character, and Queen Elizabeth I.

Shakespeare's work is rich in observed natural history, but his animal lore, as T. H. White points out in his *Book of Beasts*, consists of what could be considered common knowledge of the time. The playwright's fabulous animals are, overall, elemental: the basilisk kills with its glance, and the phoenix eternally renews itself. "That unicorns may be betrayed with trees," from *Julius Caesar*, and the unicorn reference in *Timon of Athens* derive from lion-and-unicorn lore established in the fourteenth-century *Letter of Prester John* and previously used by Shakespeare's older contemporary, Edmund Spenser, in *The Faerie Queene*. The most mythically complex and fluid of the beasts, the dragon, is the most multifaceted in the plays as well. Basic as they are, these animals are at the service of drama, transformed through character and dramatic situation into the texture of dramatic language.

Shakespeare the playwright nowhere directly reveals his own estimate of fabulous animals, leaving the audience to evaluate the speeches of individual characters, such as Hotspur's scorn of "skimble-skamble stuff" and Sebastian's astonished anything-is-possible affirmation of the unicorn and phoenix, now that he's seen the wonders of Prospero's island.

Barnacles*

[CALIBAN TO THE JESTER TRINCULO]

We shall lose our time
And all be turned to barnacles or to apes
With foreheads villainous low.

> *The Tempest* (4.1.246–248)

---

* *William Shakespeare: The Complete Works,* general ed. Alfred Harbage (Baltimore, Md.: Penguin Books, 1969).

Basilisks and Cockatrices

[HENRY VI TO THE DUKE OF SUFFOLK]

Upon thy eyeballs murderous tyranny
Sits in grim majesty to fright the world.
Look not upon me, for thine eyes are wounding.
Yet do not go away. Come, basilisk,
And kill the innocent gazer with thy sight;
For in the shade of death I shall find joy —
In life but double death, now Gloucester's dead.

2 Henry VI (3.2.49–55)

[THE DUKE OF SUFFOLK TO QUEEN MARGARET]

Poison be their drink!
Gall, worse than gall, the daintiest that they taste;
Their sweetest shade a grove of cypress trees,
Their chiefest prospect murd'ring basilisks. . . .

2 Henry VI (3.2.321–324)

[RICHARD OF GLOUCESTER TO KING EDWARD]

Why, I can smile, and murder whiles I smile,
And cry "Content!" to that which grieves my heart,
And wet my cheeks with artificial tears,
And frame my face to all occasions;
I'll drown more sailors than the mermaid shall;
I'll slay more gazers than the basilisk. . . .

3 Henry VI (3.2.182–187)

[LADY ANNE AND RICHARD, DUKE OF GLOUCESTER, LATER TO BE RICHARD III]

ANNE
Out of my sight! Thou dost infect mine eyes.

Fantastic creatures from an early
Tudor manuscript. MS Ashmole
1504. By permission of Bodleian
Library, Oxford.

Cockatrice

RICHARD

Thine eyes, sweet lady, have infected mine.

ANNE

Would they were basilisks to strike thee dead!

Richard III (1.2.148–150)

[THE DUCHESS OF YORK TO THE EARL OF DERBY]

O my accursèd womb, the bed of death!
A cockatrice hast thou hatched to the world,
Whose unavoided eye is murderous.

Richard III (4.1.53–55)

[JULIET TO THE NURSE]

Hath Romeo slain himself? Say thou but "I,"
And that bare vowel "I" shall poison more
Than the death-darting eye of cockatrice.
I am not I, if there be such an "I"
Or those eyes' shot that makes the answer "I."

Romeo and Juliet (3.2.45–49)

[ISABEL, QUEEN OF FRANCE, TO HENRY V, KING OF ENGLAND.
A "BASILISK" WAS ALSO A CANNON, NAMED AFTER THE BEAST.]

So happy be the issue, brother England,
Of this good day and of this gracious meeting
As we are now glad to behold your eyes —
Your eyes which hitherto have borne in them,
Against the French that met them in their bent,
The fatal balls of murdering basilisks.

Henry V (5.2.12–17)

[SIR TOBY BELCH TO FABIAN AND MARIA, SERVANT AND WOMAN
TO THE COUNTESS OLIVIA]

This will so fright them both that they will kill one another
by the look, like cockatrices.

Twelfth Night (3.4.181–182)

[Posthumus, husband of Imogen, the daughter of King Cymbeline,
relinquishing to Iachimo the ring he has lost in a wager over
her fidelity]

It is a basilisk unto mine eye,
Kills me to look on't.

Cymbeline (2.4.107–108)

[Polixenes, King of Bavaria, to Camillo, a lord of Sicilia]

Make me not sighted like the basilisk.
I have looked on thousands who have sped the better
By my regard, but killed none so. . . .

The Winter's Tale (1.2..386–388)

Dragons

[The Duke of Gloucester to the Duke of Bedford,
describing King Henry V]

England ne'er had a king until his time.
Virtue he had, deserving to command;
His brandished sword did blind men with his beams;
His arms spread wider than a dragon's wings. . . .

1 Henry VI (1.1. 8–11)

[Chatillion, ambassador of France, to Philip, King of France]

Rash, inconsiderate, fiery voluntaries,
With ladies' faces and fierce dragons' spleens,
Have sold their fortunes at their native homes. . . .

King John (2.1.67–69)

[Philip the Bastard to company]

Saint George, that swinged the dragon, and e'er since
Sits on's horseback at mine hostess' door,
Teach us some fence!

King John (2.1.288–290)

Dragons

[PUCK TO OBERON, KING OF THE FAIRIES]

My fairy lord, this must be done with haste,
For night's swift dragons cut the clouds full fast,
And yonder shines Aurora's harbinger. . . .

A Midsummer Night's Dream (3.2.378–380)

[RICHARD III TO THE DUKE OF NORFOLK DURING THE
BATTLE AT BOSWORTH FIELD]

A thousand hearts are great within my bosom!
Advance our standards, set upon our foes.
Our ancient word of courage, fair Saint George,
Inspire us with the spleen of fiery dragons!
Upon them! Victory sits on our helms.

Richard III (5.3.348–352)

[ACHILLES AFTER KILLING HECTOR]

The dragon wing of night o'erspreads the earth,
And, stickler-like, the armies separates.
My half-supped sword, that frankly would have fed,
Pleased with this dainty bait, thus goes to bed.

Troilus and Cressida (5.8.17–20)

[KING LEAR TO THE EARL OF KENT, AND THEN TO CORDELIA,
THE KING'S YOUNGEST DAUGHTER]

Peace, Kent!
Come not between the dragon and his wrath.
I loved her most, and thought to set my rest
On her kind nursery.—Hence and avoid my sight!—

King Lear (1.1.121–124)

[EDMUND SOLILOQUIZES ON THE CONSTELLATION DRACO AND OTHER STARS]

My father compounded
with my mother under the Dragon's Tail, and my nativity was under Ursa Major,
so that it follows I am rough and lecherous. Fut! I should have been that I am,
had the maidenliest star in the firmament twinkled on my bastardizing.

King Lear (1.2.124–129)

[THE THREE WITCHES]

   ALL
Double, double, toil and trouble,
Fire burn and cauldron bubble.

   3. WITCH
Scale of dragon, tooth of wolf,
Witch's mummy, maw and gulf
Of the ravined salt-sea shark. . . .

            Macbeth (4.1.20–24)

[ANTIOCHUS, KING OF ANTIOCH, INTRODUCES HIS DAUGHTER
TO PERICLES, PRINCE OF TYRE]

Before thee stands this fair Hesperides,
With golden fruit, but dangerous to be touched;
For death-like dragons here affright thee hard.

               Pericles (1.1.28–30)

[CORIOLANUS TO HIS MOTHER, VOLUMNIA]

        . . . — though I go alone,
Like to a lonely dragon, that his fen
Makes feared and talked of more than seen —. . . .

             Coriolanus (4.1.29–31)

[MENENIUS SPEAKS OF HIS FRIEND CORIOLANUS
TO THE TRIBUNE SICINIUS]

        This Marcius is grown from man
to dragon. He has wings; he's more than a
creeping thing.

             Coriolanus (5.4.12–14)

[IACHIMO, AFTER STEALING THE BRACELET OF THE SLEEPING IMOGEN,
DAUGHTER OF KING CYMBELINE, WIFE OF POSTHUMUS]

Swift, swift, you dragons of the night, that dawning
May bare the raven's eye.

             Cymbeline (2.2.48–49)

Griffins

[HELENA TO BELOVED DEMETRIUS, THE SUITOR OF HERMIA]

The story shall be changed:
Apollo flies and Daphne holds the chase,
The dove pursues the griffon, the mild hind
Makes speed to catch the tiger — bootless speed,
When cowardice pursues, and valor flies.

A Midsummer Night's Dream (2.1.230–234)

[HENRY PERCY, "HOTSPUR," TO EDMUND MORTIMER,
REFERRING TO MORTIMER'S FATHER-IN-LAW, OWEN GLENDOWER]

Sometimes he angers me
With telling me of the moldwarp and the ant,
Of the dreamer Merlin and his prophesies,
And of a dragon and finless fish,
A clip-winged griffin and a moulten raven,
A couching lion and a ramping cat,
And such a deal of skimble-skamble stuff
As puts me from my faith.

1 Henry IV (3.1.146–153)

Mermaids

[KING OBERON TO PUCK]

My gentle Puck, come hither. Thou rememb'rest
Since once I sat upon a promontory
And heard a mermaid on a dolphin's back,
Uttering such dulcet and harmonious breath
That the rude sea grew civil at her song,
And certain stars shot madly from their spheres
To hear the sea-maid's music.

A Midsummer Night's Dream (2.1.148–154)

Griffin

The Phoenix

[Sɪʀ Wɪʟʟɪᴀᴍ Lᴜᴄʏ ᴛᴏ Cʜᴀʀʟᴇs, ʟᴀᴛᴇʀ Cʜᴀʀʟᴇs VII ᴏF Fʀᴀɴᴄᴇ, ᴜᴘᴏɴ ʙᴇɪɴɢ
ɢʀᴀɴᴛᴇᴅ ᴘᴇʀᴍɪssɪᴏɴ ᴛᴏ ʀᴇᴛᴜʀɴ ᴛʜᴇ ʙᴏᴅɪᴇs ᴏF sʟᴀɪɴ sᴏʟᴅɪᴇʀs ᴛᴏ Eɴɢʟᴀɴᴅ]

I'll bear them hence; but from their ashes shall be reared
A phoenix that shall make all France afeard.

1 Henry VI (4.7.92-93)

[Rɪᴄʜᴀʀᴅ Pʟᴀɴᴛᴀɢᴇɴᴇᴛ, Dᴜᴋᴇ ᴏF Yᴏʀᴋ, ᴛᴏ Lᴏʀᴅ CʟɪFFᴏʀᴅ]

My ashes, as the phoenix, may bring forth
A bird that will revenge upon you all. . . .

3 Henry VI (1.4.35–36)

[Rɪᴄʜᴀʀᴅ III ᴀɴᴅ Eʟɪᴢᴀʙᴇᴛʜ, Qᴜᴇᴇɴ ᴛᴏ Eᴅᴡᴀʀᴅ IV,
ᴍᴏᴛʜᴇʀ ᴏF ᴛʜᴇ ᴘʀɪɴᴄᴇs Rɪᴄʜᴀʀᴅ ᴍᴜʀᴅᴇʀᴇᴅ ᴀɴᴅ ᴏF Eʟɪᴢᴀʙᴇᴛʜ,
ᴛʜᴇ ᴏʙᴊᴇᴄᴛ ᴏF Rɪᴄʜᴀʀᴅ's ᴄᴏᴜʀᴛsʜɪᴘ]

QUEEN ELIZABETH
Yet thou didst kill my children.

KING RICHARD
But in your daughter's womb I bury them,
Where, in that nest of spicery, they will breed
Selves of themselves, to your recomforture.

Richard III (4.4.422–425)

[Rᴏsᴀʟɪɴᴅ, ᴅɪsɢᴜɪsᴇᴅ ᴀs ᴀ ᴍᴀɴ, ᴛᴏ Sɪʟᴠɪᴜs, ᴀ sʜᴇᴘʜᴇʀᴅ,
ᴜᴘᴏɴ ʀᴇᴄᴇɪᴠɪɴɢ ᴀ ʟᴇᴛᴛᴇʀ Fʀᴏᴍ Pʜᴇʙᴇ, ᴀ sʜᴇᴘʜᴇʀᴅᴇss]

She says I am not fair, that I lack manners,
She calls me proud, and that she could not love me,
Were man as rare as phoenix.

As You Like It (4.3.16–18)

[Hᴇʟᴇɴᴀ, ᴀ ᴘʜʏsɪᴄɪᴀɴ's ᴏʀᴘʜᴀɴᴇᴅ ᴅᴀᴜɢʜᴛᴇʀ, ᴛᴏ Pᴀʀᴏʟʟᴇs,
Fᴏʟʟᴏᴡᴇʀ ᴏF Bᴇʀᴛʀᴀᴍ, Cᴏᴜɴᴛ ᴏF Rᴏssɪʟʟɪᴏɴ]

There shall your master have a thousand loves,
A mother, and a mistress, and a friend,
A phoenix, captain, and an enemy. . . .

All's Well That Ends Well (1.1.160–162)

[A Senator, to Caphis, a servant]

        . . . for I do fear,
When every feather sticks in his own wing,
Lord Timon will be left a naked gull,
Which flashes now a phoenix.

                Timon of Athens (2.1.29–32)

[Cranmer, Archbishop of Canterbury, christening Henry VIII's infant daughter Elizabeth, later Queen]

Nor shall this peace sleep with her; but as when
The bird of wonder dies, the maiden phoenix,
Her ashes new create another heir
As great in admiration as herself,
So shall she leave her blessedness to one
(When heaven shall call her from this cloud of darkness)
Who from the sacred ashes of her honor
Shall starlike rise, as great in fame as she was,
And so stand fixed. . . .

                Henry VIII (5.5.39–47)

Unicorns

[Decius to Cassius, a fellow conspirator who fears augurers will dissuade Julius Caesar from going to the Capitol]

Never fear that. If he be so resolved,
I can o'ersway him; for he loves to hear
That unicorns may be betrayed with trees
And bears with glasses, elephants with holes,
Lions with toils, and men with flatterers. . . .

            Julius Caesar (2.1.202–206)

[Timon to the philosopher Apemantus]

Wert thou the unicorn, pride and wrath would
confound thee and make thine own self the conquest
of thy fury.

Timon of Athens (4.3.333–335)

[Prospero, the rightful Duke of Milan, prepares a banquet
for the noblemen shipwrecked on his island:]

*Solemn and strange music; and Prospero on the top
(invisible). Enter several strange Shapes, bringing in a banquet;
and dance about it with gentle actions of salutation;
and, inviting the King & c. to eat, they depart.*

ALONSO
What harmony is this? My good friends, hark!

GONZOLO
Marvellous sweet music!

ALONSO
Give us kind keepers, heavens! What were these?

SEBASTIAN
A living drollery. Now I will believe
That there are unicorns; that in Arabia
There is one tree, the phoenix' throne; one phoenix
At this hour reigning there.

ANTONIO
                          I'll believe both;
And what does else want credit, come to me,
And I'll be sworn 'tis true. Travellers ne'r did lie,
Though fools at home condemn 'em.

The Tempest (3.3.18–27)

SAMUEL PURCHAS (C. 1577–1626)
HAKLUYTUS POSTHUMUS OR *PURCHAS HIS PILGRIMES*

Two English clergymen who traveled very little compiled accounts of voyages and discoveries to convey knowledge and to inspire British expansion and colonization. The first and now the better known and more highly regarded of the two works was Richard Hakluyt's *Principall Navigations, Voiages, and Discoveries of the English Nation* (1589–1600). Following Hakluyt's death in 1616, his manuscripts were passed on to Samuel Purchas, who expanded them more than twice over to produce *Hakluytus Posthumus or Purchas His Pilgrimes; Contayning a History of the World in Sea voyages & lande Travells by Englishmen & others. . . .* (1625). Purchas's four-million-word epic, beginning with Noah's Ark, was the largest English book to be printed up to its time. Within Purchas's massive collection is a description of the fabled kingdom of Prester John and an eyewitness account of a strange sea creature.

Between *The Letter of Prester John* and the Age of Exploration, Prester John's legendary kingdom moved from India to Ethiopia. The Portuguese explorer Juan Bermudez describes the wonders of Ethiopia in the spirit of *The Letter of Prester John* and Mandeville's *Travels*. Purchas's note indicates he is skeptical of Bermudez's tale—and of the phoenix in particular—but he does grant the possibility of "Incredibilities" being true in that exotic country. In 1505, Bermudez discovered the Caribbean island named after him. As Captain Richard Whitbourne acknowledges, his 1610 account of what he thought might be a mermaid was one of many such recorded encounters. Descriptions of the entries are from Purchas's contents pages.

Purchas's book was the third of his Pilgrim series, following compilations on the world's religions and human history. It was one of Purchas's earlier works that Samuel Taylor Coleridge said he was reading when he slipped into an opium-induced sleep and dreamed of the pleasure dome of Kubla Khan. Prepared for the general public, *Hakluytus Posthumus* lacked the careful scholarship and editing of Hakluyt's work, but it was immediately successful and remained popular for centuries.

The Ethiopian Kingdom of Presbyter John *

A briefe Relation of the Embassage which the Patriarch Don John Bermudez brought from the Emperour of Ethiopia, vulgarly called Presbyter John, to the most Christian and zealous of the Faith of Christ, Don John, the third of this Name, King of Portugal.

---

* Samuel Purchas, *Hakluytus Posthumus, or Purchas His Pilgrimes*, 20 vols. (Glasgow: James MacLehose, 1905–7), vol. 7, pp. 363–64; vol. 19, pp. 439–40.

... There is neere to Damute, a Province of women without men: which doe live after the manner of the ancient Amazones of Scythia, which in certaine time of the yeere permitted the companie of some men that were their Neighbours, and of the children which they bare, they sent the men-children to their Fathers, and the women they kept with themselves, and brought them up in their customes and stile. In the same manner doe these of Aethiopia, and they burne also their left paps, as those did for to shoot more readily with their Bow, which they use in their Warres, and in Hunting. The Queene of these Women knoweth no man, and for that act is worshipped among them for a Goddesse. They are permitted and preserved, because they say, that they were instituted by the Queene of Saba, which went to see King Salomon. In this Province of the Women there be Grif-fons, which are Fowles so bigge that they kill the Buffes, and carrie them in their clawes as an Eagle carryeth a Rebbet. They say, that here in certaine Mountaines very rough, and desert, there breedeth and liveth the Bird *Phenix, which is one alone in the World, and it is one of the wonders of nature. So doe the Inhabitors of those Countries affirme, that this Bird is there, and they do see it and know it, and that it is a great and faire Bird. There be other Fowles so bigge, that they make a shadow like a Cloud.

A Strange Sea Creature in New-found-land

Captaine Richard Whitbournes voyages to New-found-land, and observations there, and thereof; taken out of his printed booke.
Now also I will not omit to relate something of a strange Creature that I first saw there in the yeer 1610. In a morning early as I was standing by the water side, in the Harbour of Saint Johns, which I espied verie swiftly to come swimming towards me, looking cheerefully, as it had beene a woman, by the Face, Eyes, Nose, Mouth, Chin eares, Necke and Forehead: It seemed to be so beautifull, and in those parts so well proportioned, having round about upon the head, all blew strakes, resembling haire, downe to the Necke (but certainly it was haire) for I beheld it long, and another of my companie also, yet living, that was not then farre from me; and seeing the same comming so swiftly towards mee, I stepped

---

* [*Samuel Purchas Note*] Monstrous huge fowles, or foule monstrous fooles & lies, which happly the cunning and bragging Natives reported and we had need of their faith of Miracles to beleeve. For how did God create first and after bring into the Arke all Creatures Male and Female, if this Phenix bee sole? Qui Bavium non odit, amet tua carmina Maevi. He which beleeveth this Phenix, and these Griffons, &c. may beleeve 'Gamas Miracles. Which I speake not to disgrace the whole storie (which is usefull) but to make the Reader warie where things are told upon report, or are advantagious to Rome or Portugall. Much of this Chapter seemeth to mee Apocrypha, but I leave libertie of Faith to the most licentious Credulitie, which shall thinke fitter to beleeve then to goe and see. And yet may Africa have a Prerogative in Rarities, and some seeming Incredibilities be true.

backe, for it was come within the length of a long Pike. Which when this strange Creature saw that I went from it, it presently thereupon dived a little under water, and did swim to the place where before I landed; whereby I beheld the shoulders and backe downe to the middle, to be as square, white and smooth as the backe of a man, and from the middle to the hinder part, pointing in proportion like a broad hooked Arrow; how it was proportioned in the forepart from the necke and shoulders, I know not; but the same came shortly after into a Boat, wherein one William Hawkridge, then my servant, was, that hath bin since a Captaine in a Ship to the East Indies, and is lately there imploied againe by Sir Thomas Smith, in the like Voyage; and the same Creature did put both his hands upon the side of the Boate, and did strive to come in to him and others then in the said Boate: whereat they were afraid; and one of them strooke it a full blow on the head; whereat it fell off from them: and afterwards it came to two other Boates in the Harbour; the men in them, for feare fled to land: This (I suppose) was a Mermaide. Now because divers have written much of Mermaides, I have presumed to relate, what is most certaine of such a strange Creature that was seene at New-found-land: whether it were a Mermaide or no, I know not; I leave it for others to judge, &c.

R. W.

Unnatural History

10

OLAUS MAGNUS (1490–1557)
HISTORY OF THE GOTHS, SWEDES, & VANDALS

During the Age of Exploration, the varieties of sea monsters multiplied in tales sailors brought back from voyages in strange waters. The major chronicler of such creatures was Olaf Storr, a Catholic priest who left his native Sweden following the Reformation and took up residence in Rome, where he inherited from his brother the position of Archbishop of Uppsala and became known as Olaus Magnus. He published one of the first maps of Scandinavia (1539), its ocean teeming with sea beasts, and a chapter in his history of the Scandinavian peoples (*Historia de gentibus septentrionalibus*, 1555) details marine life in the Northern seas. Olaus's verbal descriptions — most of them of actual creatures from the walrus to the narwhal (the sea unicorn) — are no less fanciful than his art. Among these monsters of the deep, the two most celebrated and controversial are the giant squid and the sea serpent, both of them gigantic, terrifying creatures that crush ships and engorge crews. Olaus also repeats as natural history the traditional story of mariners mistaking a whale for an island.

Olaus's squid is a "Whale" with "horns" like "a Tree rooted up by the Roots." In his later *Natural History of Norway* (1752–53), the Norwegian bishop Eric Pontoppidan calls the creature *kraken*, a beast a mile and a half in circumference that causes whirlpools when

Not these onely, but many other Fables haue been written by those of auncient tyme, that haue as it were set down their owne imaginations for vndoubted truthes. . . .

—Robert Norman
The newe Attractiue

it submerges. Defended at the beginning of the nineteenth century by Pierre Denys de Montfort, the giant squid was nonetheless dismissed as fabulous until 1861, when the crew of a French warship, the *Alecton*, encountered and killed such a creature. That incident inspired the battle between Captain Nemo's *Nautilus* and the giant octopus in Jules Verne's *Twenty Thousand Leagues Under the Sea*. Homer's many-headed Scylla has often been identified as a mythological form of a giant squid, and Scylla is associated with the whirlpool Charybdis as the legendary kraken was with whirlpools off the coast of Norway.

Olaus's description of the whale is derived not only from sailor lore but from entries in medieval bestiaries. In *Paradise Lost*, Milton echoes Olaus's detail of the anchor fastened in the monster's back.

Olaus's account of the Norway Serpent is repeated in the sixteenth-century natural histories of Conrad Gesner, Ulisse Aldrovandi, and others. Many sightings of sea serpents were claimed in following centuries, and the Loch Ness Monster is still a subject of speculation. In his book of fishes, Gesner used Olaus's illustrations, and variations of them appeared in other natural histories. The sea monsters depicted on Abraham Ortelius's 1585 map of Iceland are reminiscent of those on Olaus's map of Scandinavia.

Elsewhere in Olaus's chapter on marine life of the Northern seas is a description of the sea-unicorn, the narwhal, whose spiraled tusk "can penetrate and destroy the ships in his way, and drown multitudes of men." Narwhal tusks were one of the sources of what was sold as alicorn (unicorn horn).

The Vast Ocean *

The vast Ocean in its Gulph offers all Nations an admirable spectacle, and shews divers sorts of Fish; and these not onely wonderful for magnitude, as the Stars are compared one with another, as they are terrible in shape; so that there is nothing in the Ayr nor Earth, nor Bowels of it, or in domestique Instruments that may seem to lye hid, that is not found in the depth of the Sea. . . .

Of the Horrible Monsters of the Coast of Norway

There are monstrous fish on the Coasts or Sea of Norway, of unusual Names though they are reported a kind of Whales, who shew their cruelty at first sight, and make men afraid to see them; and if men look long on them, they will fright and amaze

* Olaus Magnus, *A Compendious History of the Goths, Swedes, & Vandals and Other Northern Nations* (1658; Ann Arbor, Mich.: University Microfilms, 1975). Microfilm Wing M257, wing reel 541:1, pp. 222–23, 225, 231, 235.

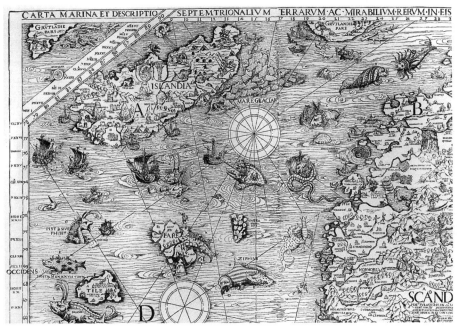

Detail from Olaus Magnus's 1539 *Carta Marina*, a map of the Northern regions. Many of the sea beasts were later reproduced in the natural histories of Conrad Gesner and others. The following illustrations in the Olaus Magnus entry and the "sea-swine" in the Ambroise Paré entry are all variations of figures on the *Carta Marina*. Also on the map (*far left*) is the horned head of the sea-unicorn (narwhal). By permission of Uppsala University Library, Uppsala, Sweden.

A version of the giant squid, first described by Olaus Magnus. From Konrad Gesner, *Curious Woodcuts of Fanciful and Real Beasts* (New York: Dover, 1971). Courtesy of Dover Publications.

them. Their Forms are horrible, their Heads square, all set with prickles, and they have sharp and long Horns round about, like a Tree rooted up by the Roots: They are ten or twelve Cubits long, very black, and with huge eyes: the compass whereof is above eight or ten cubits: the Apple of the Eye is of one Cubit, and is red and fiery coloured, which in the dark night appears to Fisher-men afar off under Waters, as a burning fire, having hairs like Goose-Feathers, thick and long, like a Beard hanging down; the rest of the body, for the greatness of the head, which is square, is very small, not being above 14 or 15 Cubits long; one of these Sea-Monsters will drown easily many great ships provided with many strong Marriners. . . .

Of Anchors Fastned upon the Whales Back

The Whale hath upon his Skin a Superficies, like the gravel that is by the Sea-side: so that oft-times, when he raiseth his back above the waters, Saylors take it to be nothing else but an Island and sayl unto it, and go down upon it, and they strike in piles unto it, and fasten them to their ships: they kindle fires to boyl their meat; until at length the Whale feeling the fire, dives down to the bottome; and such as are upon his back, unless they can save themselves by ropes thrown forth of the ship, are drown'd. . . .

Of the Greatness of the Norway Serpent

They who in Works of Navigation, on the Coasts of Norway, employ themselves in fishing or Merchandise, do all agree in this strange story, that there is a Ser-

A pictorial version of the traditional tale of mariners mistaking a whale for an island. From Konrad Gesner, *Curious Woodcuts of Fanciful and Real Beasts* (New York, Dover, 1971). Courtesy of Dover Publications.

The Great Norway Serpent. Olaus Magnus's description of this monster of the sea was followed by centuries of sightings of the fabled beast. From Charles Gould, *Mythical Monsters* (London: W. H. Allen, 1886).

pent there which is of a vast magnitude, namely 200 foot long, and more — over 20 feet thick; and is wont to live in Rocks and Caves toward the Sea-coast about Berge: which will go alone from his holes in a clear night, in Summer, and devour Calves, Lambs, and Hogs, or else he goes into the Sea to feed on Polypus, Locusts, and all sorts of Sea-Crabs. He hath commonly hair hanging from his neck a Cubit long, and sharp Scales, and is black, and he hath flaming shining eyes. This Snake disquiets the Shippers, and he puts up his head on high like a pillar, and catcheth away men, and he devours them; and this hapneth not, but it signifies some wonderful change of the Kingdom near at hand; namely that the Princes shall die, or be banished; or some Tumultuous Wars shall presently follow. There is also another Serpent of an incredible magnitude in a Town, called *Moos*, or the Diocess of *Hammer*; which, as a Comet portends a change in all the World, so, that portends a change in the Kingdom of *Norway*, as it was seen, *Anno 1522*. That lifts himself high above the Waters, and rouls himself round like a sphere. This Serpent was thought to be fifty Cubits long by conjecture, by sight afar off: there followed this the banishment of King Christiernus, and a great persecution of the Bishops; and it shew'd also the destruction of the Countrey.

Ambroise Paré (1510-1590)
On Poysons, Of Monsters and Prodigies

Considered one of the greatest surgeons of the Renaissance and "the Father of French surgery," Ambroise Paré was one of several authors of his time to question the widespread belief in the powers of alicorn (unicorn horn) to prevent or cure disease. This independent and courageous thinker, living in a transitional age, also compiled contemporary descriptions of monstrous animal forms.

In the earliest account of the unicorn, Ctesias (late fifth century B.C.) wrote that anyone drinking from a cup fashioned from the beast's horn was safe from poison and disease. Aelian, Philostratus, and others repeated the tale, although Philostratus recorded that Apollonius of Tyana wryly said, "I will believe it, if I find the king of the Indians hereabout to be immortal." The unicorn of the Middle Ages purified contaminated pools by dipping its horn into the water. By the time of the Renaissance, powdered alicorn could cost many times its weight in gold. Royalty, popes, and others of wealth treasured the magical substance. Queen Elizabeth I's "Horn of Windsor" was reputedly valued at 100,000 British pounds. Value led to charlatanism and to tests distinguishing *unicornum verum* ("true alicorn") from *unicornum falsum*. Such tests ranged from drawing a circle of powdered alicorn around a spider to see if the poisonous creature could cross the line, to administering treatments to poisoned subjects.

Andrea Marini and others had already been skeptical of the efficacy of alicorn when Paré wrote a discourse on mummies, unicorns, poisons, and the plague (1582). The commoner had risen from a barber's apprentice to a battle surgeon and then to physician to kings of France. Among his accomplishments was eliminating the standard practice of cauterizing wounds with boiling oil. In his treatise on poisons, he first reviews accounts of unicorns from Pliny to Ludovico de Varthema; he then systematically questions the existence of unicorns and the curative properties of horns attributed to them and impugns the ethics of other skeptical physicians who prescribed such treatment when it was requested by their royal patients. Although alicorn was eventually revealed as parts of actual animals, from rhinoceros "horn" to narwhal tusk, apothecaries continued to sell "unicorn horn" into the eighteenth century, and French royalty tested food with alicorn as late as the 1780s.

The following Paré treatise is from Thomas Johnson's 1634 English translation from the Latin collected works, themselves translated from the original French.

Later in the omnibus volume, in *Of Monsters and Prodigies*, are passages and illustrations of a variety of strange and beautiful creatures compiled from the works of Olaus Magnus, Guillaume Rondelet, Conrad Gesner, and others. The illustrations are all variations of woodcuts that appeared in the natural histories of Conrad Gesner.

*Of the Unicornes Horne**

There are very many at this day who thinke themselves excellently well armed against poyson and all contagion, if they be provided with some powder of Unicornes horne, or some infusion made therewith. Therefore I have thought it good to examine more diligently how much truth this inveterate, and grounded opinion hath. . . .

. . . I thinke that beast that is vulgarly called & taken for an Unicorn, is rather a thing imaginary than really in the world. I am chiefly enduced to beleeve thus, by these conjectures. Because of those who have travelled over the world, there is not one that professeth that ever he did see that creature. . . .

. . . Grant there be Unicornes, must it therefore follow that their hornes must be of such efficacy against poysons? If we judge by events, and the experience of things, I can protest thus much, that I have often made tryall thereof, yet could I never find any good successe in the use thereof against poisons, in such as I have had in cure. If the matter must bee tryed by witnesses and authorities, a great part of the Physitians of better note have long since bid it adieu, and have detracted from the divine and admirable vertues for which it formerly was so much desired. And this they have done, moved thereto by many just, but two especiall reasons. The first is of Rondeletius, who in this case affirmes that horns are endued with no taste nor smell; and therefore have no effect in physicke, unlesse it bee to dry. Neither (saith he) am I ignorant that such as have them, much predicate their worth, so to make the greater benefit and gaine by them, as of the shavings or scrapings of Unicornes horne, which they sell for the weight in gold, as that which is singular good against poysons and wormes, which things I thinke Harts-horne and Ivory doe no lesse effectually performe, which is the cause why for the same disease, and with the like successe, I prescribe Ivory to such as are poor, and Unicornes horn to the rich, as that they so much desire. This is the opinion of Rondeletius, who without any difference was wont for Unicornes horne to prescribe not onely Harts-horn or Ivory, but also the bones of Horses and Dogges, and the stones of Myrabalanes [ed., plumlike fruit]. Another reason is, that whatsoever resists poyson is cordiall, that is, fit to strengthen the heart, which is chiefly assailed by poysons; but nothing is convenient to strengthen the heart, unlesse it bee by laudible blood or spirit, which two are onely familiar to the heart, as being the work-house of the arterious blood and vitall spirits. For all things are preserved by their like, as they are destroyed by their contraries; for all things that generate, generate things like themselves. But Unicornes horne, as it conteines no smell, so neither hath it any aery parts, but is wholly earthy and dry; neither can it bee converted into blood by the digestive faculty, for as it is with-

---

* *The Collected Works of Ambroise Paré,* trans. Thomas Johnson (1634; facsimile ed., Pound Ridge, N.Y.: Milford House, 1968), *Of Poysons,* 813–15; *Of Monsters and Prodigies,* 1000–1005, 1016.

out juice, so is it without flesh. For as it cannot bee turned into Chylus, so neither is it fit to become Chymus (that is) juice or blood. Therefore it is joyned to the heart by no similitude nor familiarity. Furthermore, there is not a word in Hippocrates and Galen concerning the Unicornes horne, who notwithstanding have in so many places commended Harts-horne. Therefore D. Chapelaine, the chiefe Physitian of King Charles the ninth, often used to say, that hee would very willingly take away that custome of dipping a piece of Unicorns horn in the Kings cup, but that he knew that opinion to be so deeply ingrafted in the minds of men, that he feared, that it would scarce be impugned by reason. Besides (he said) if such a superstitious medicine do no good, so certainely it doth no harme. . . . This is my opinion of Unicornes horne, which if any doe not approve of, hee shall doe mee a favour, if for the publicke good, hee shall freely oppose his; but in the interim take this in good part which I have done.

Monsters and Prodigies

OF THE WONDROUS NATURE OF SOME MARINE THINGS, AND OTHER LIVING CREATURES.

[Ed., These creatures] which follow, though they be not wonderfull of themselves, as those that consist of their owne proper nature, and that working well and after an ordinary manner; yet they are wondrous to us, or rather monstrous, for that they are not very familiar to us. For the rarity and vastnesse of bodies, is in some sort monstrous. Of this sort there are many, especially in the Sea, whose secret corners and receptacles are not pervious to men. . . .

In our times, saith Rondeletius, in Norway was a monster taken in a tempestuous sea, the which as many as saw it, presently terms a Monk, by reason of the shape which you may see here set forth.
The figure of a fish resembling a Monke.

Anno Dom. 1531. there was seene a sea-monster in the habite of a Bishop, covered over with scailes: Rondeletius and Gesner have described it.
The figure of a fish in the habite or shape of a Bishop.

Creatures from *Of Monsters and Prodigies*, in *The Collected Works of Ambroise Paré*. The engravings appear with their corresponding texts, as they did in the 1634 edition.

Not long before the death of Pope Paul the third, in the midst of the Tyrrhene sea, a monster was taken, and presented to the sucessour of this Paul: it was in shape and bignesse like to a Lion, but all scaily, and the voice was like a mans voice. It was brought to Rome to the

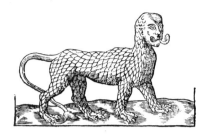

great admiration of all men, but it lived not long there, being destitute of its own naturall place and nourishment, as it is reported by Philip Forrest.

The effigies of a Lion-like scaily Sea-monster.

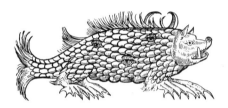

Olaus Magnus writes that this monster was taken at Thyle an Iland of the North, Anno Dom. 1538. it was of a big-nesse almost incredible, as that which was seventy two foot long, and four-teene high, and seven foot betweene the eyes: now the liver was so large that therewith they filled five hogsheads, the head resembled a swine, having as it were a half moone on the backe, and three eyes in the midst of his sides, his whole body was scaily.

The effigies of a monstrous Sea-swine.

Jerome Cardane in his booke De subtili-tate, writes that in the Ilands of the Molucca's, you may sometimes find lying upon the ground, or take up in the waters, a dead bird called a Manucodiata, that is in Hebrew, the bird of God, it is never seene alive. It lives aloft in the aire, it is like a Swallow in body and beake, yet distinguished with divers coloured feath-

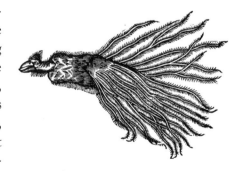

ers: for those on the toppe of the head are of a golden colour, those of the necke like to a Mallard, but the taile and wings like Peacocks; it wants feet: Wherefore if it is become weary with flying, or desire sleepe, it hange up the body by twining the feathers about some bough of a tree. It passeth through the aire, wherein it must remaine as long as it lives, with great celerity, and lives by the aire and dew onely. The cocke hath a cavity deprest in the backe, wherein the hen laies and sits upon her egges. I saw one at Paris which was presented to King Charles the ninth.

The effigies of a Manucodiata, or bird of Paradise.

John Gerard (1545–1612)
Herball

The animal that crowns the sixth day of creation in *The Divine Weeks* (1578) of Du Bartas is again eulogized in the final chapter of John Gerard's *Herball* (1597). In the thirteenth century, Albertus Magnus had scorned the story of geese generating from either trees or driftwood, but the eyewitness testimonies of Giraldus Cambrensis, Gerard, and others and acceptance of the tale in the natural histories of Conrad Gesner and Ulisse Aldrovandi maintained belief in the miraculous birth of these birds at least until the eighteenth century.

Gerard was a surgeon and botanist, and superintendent of the gardens of Queen Elizabeth I's secretary of state. His catalog of plants was based on a work by Rembert Dodoens. The following text and woodcut are from Thomas Johnson's revised 1636 edition. Johnson's translation of the works of Ambroise Paré (see immediately previous entry in this volume) was published two years earlier.

*Of the Goose tree, Barnacle tree, or the tree bearing Geese**

The Description

Having travelled from the Grasses growing in the bottome of the fenny waters, the Woods, and mountaines, even unto Libanus it selfe; and also the sea, and bowels of the same, wee are arrived at the end of our History; thinking it not impertinent to the conclusion of the same, to end with one of the marvels of this land (we may say of the World). The history whereof to set forth according to the worthinesse and raritie thereof, would not only require a large and peculiar volume, but also a deeper search into the bowels of Nature, than my intended purpose will suffer me to wade into, my sufficiencie also considered; leaving the History thereof rough hewen, unto some excellent man, learned in the secrets of nature, to be both fined and refined: in the meane space take it as it falleth out, the naked and bare truth, though unpolished. There are found in the North parts of Scotland and the Islands adjacent, called Orchades, certaine trees whereon do grow certaine shells of a white colour tending to russet, wherein are contained little living creatures: which shells in time of maturity doe open, and out of them grow those little living things, which falling into the water do become fowles, which we call Barnacles; in the North of England, bran Geese; and in Lancashire, tree Geese: but the other that do fall upon the land perish and come to nothing. Thus much by the writings of others, and also from the mouthes of people of those parts, which may very well accord with truth.

* *Gerard's Herball*, ed. Marcus Woodward (1636; rpt., London: Spring Books, 1964), 282–85.

But what our eies have seene, and hands have touched we shall declare. There is
a small Island in Lancashire called the Pile of Foulders, wherein are found the broken pieces of old and bruised ships, some whereof have beene cast thither by ship-
wracke, and also the trunks and bodies with the branches of old and rotten trees,
cast up there likewise; whereon is found a certaine spume or froth that in time
breedeth unto certain shells, in shape like those of the Muskle but sharper pointed,
and of a whitish colour; wherein is contained a thing in forme like a lace of silke
finely woven as it were together, of a whitish colour, one end whereof is fastned
unto the inside of the shell, even as the fish of Oisters and Muskles are: the other
end is made fast unto the belly of a rude masse or lumpe, which in time commeth to
the shape and forme of a Bird: when it is perfectly formed the shell gapeth open,
and the first thing that appeareth is the foresaid lace or string; next come the legs of
the bird hanging out, and as it groweth greater it openeth the shell by degrees, til at
length it is all come forth, and hangeth onely by the bill: in short space after it commeth to full maturitie, and falleth into the sea, where it gathereth feathers, and
groweth to a fowle bigger than a Mallard, and lesser than a Goose, having blacke
legs and bill or beake, and feathers black and white, spotted in such manner as is
our Magpie, called in some places a Pie-Annet, which the people of Lancashire call
by no other name than a tree Goose: which place aforesaid, and all those parts
adjoyning do so much abound therewith, that one of the best is bought for three
pence. For the truth hereof, if any doubt, may it please them to repaire unto me,
and I shall satisfie them by the testimonie of good witnesses.

Moreover, it should seeme that there is another sort hereof; the History of
which is true, and of mine owne knowledge: for travelling upon the shore of our
English coast betweene Dover and Rumney, I found the trunke of an old rotten
tree, which (with some helpe that I procured by Fishermens wives that were there
attending their husbands returned from the sea) we drew out of the water upon
dry land: upon this rotten tree I found growing many thousands of long crimson
bladders, in shape like unto puddings newly filled, before they be sodden, which
were very cleere and shining; at the nether end whereof did grow a shell fish,
fashioned somewhat like a small Muskle, but much whiter, resembling a shell fish
that groweth upon the rockes about Garnsey and Garsey, called a Lympit: many
of these shells I brought with me to London, which after I had opened I found in
them living things without forme or shape; in others which were neerer come to
ripenesse I found living things that were very naked, in shape like a Bird: in others, the Birds covered with soft downe, the shell halfe open, and the Bird ready to
fall out, which no doubt were the Fowles called Barnacles. I dare not absolutely
avouch every circumstance of the first part of this history, concerning the tree
that beareth those buds aforesaid, but will leave it to a further consideration;
howbeit, that which I have seene with mine eies, and handled with mine hands, I
dare confidently avouch, and boldly put downe for verity. Now if any will object
that this tree which I saw might be one of those before mentioned, which either

Barnacles from Gerard's *Herball*.

by the waves of the sea or some violent wind had beene overturned as many other trees are; or that any trees falling into those seas about the Orchades, will of themselves beare the like Fowles, by reason of those seas and waters, these being so probable conjectures, and likely to be true, I may not without prejudice gainesay, or indeavour to confute.

The Place

The bordes and rotten plankes whereon are found these shels breeding the Barnakle, are taken up in a small Island adjoyning to Lancashire, halfe a mile from the main land, called the Pile of Foulders.

The Time

They spawn as it were in March and Aprill; the Geese are formed in May and June, and come to fulnesse of feathers in the moneth after.

And thus having through Gods assistance discoursed somewhat at large of Grasses, Herbes, Shrubs, Trees, and Mosses, and certaine Excrescences of the earth, with other things moe, incident to the historie thereof, we conclude and end our present Volume, with this wonder of England. For the which Gods Name be ever honored and praised.

EDWARD TOPSELL (1572–1625)
THE HISTORIE OF FOURE-FOOTED BEASTES

A culmination of Western animal lore from antiquity up to its own time, the Rev. Edward Topsell's early seventeenth-century natural histories represent the final stage of belief in fabulous beasts before such creatures were rejected by the New Science. *The Historie of Foure-Footed Beastes* first appeared in 1607, *The Historie of Serpents* in 1608, and both were reissued, along with Thomas Mouffet's *Theater of Insects*, in 1658.

Unlike Conrad Gesner (1516–1565) and other sixteenth-century naturalists who were also physicians, Edward Topsell was a minister of the Church of England and published religious books in addition to his natural histories. Topsell translated the mammal volume of Conrad Gesner's Latin *Historia Animalium* and based his book of serpents largely on Gesner's posthumous reptile treatise. His uncompleted *Fowles of Heauen; or, History of Birdes*, a translation of the ornithology of Ulisse Aldrovandi (1552–1605), remained unpublished until 1972.

Following Gesner, Topsell generally arranged animals in each volume alphabetically, his order of English names differing from Gesner's Latin names. Also like Gesner, he usually includes several areas of information in each entry: the animal's names in various languages; according to multiple authorities, a description of the animal, its habitat, habits, and usefulness to man; and depiction of the animal in human art and culture. Topsell often writes in his own voice, adding his own opinions, observations, and religious views to the original material. As he states in the "Epistle Dedicatory" to *Foure-Footed Beastes*, he followed Gesner as closely as he could, "yet I have gathered up that which he let fall and have added many pictures and stories." Most of the illustrations were reengraved from Gesner's works. Variations of many appear in other sixteenth- and seventeenth-century natural histories and have been reproduced ever since.

A devout author who believes that "the knowledge of beasts is divine" and that all creatures represent "reproof and instruction to man," Topsell is a moralistic writer in the tradition of the bestiarists. His ultimate authority is scriptural. Like Gesner before him, he attempts to distinguish fable and the work of poets from "truth," and he cites recent and contemporary naturalists, but the quadruped and serpent books are nonetheless steeped in tradition and present as actual many animals soon to be rejected as fabulous. While the early editions of Topsell's natural histories were immensely popular, the posthumous 1658 edition was already outdated in its traditional, moralistic approach to animals.

In the 1658 edition, Topsell's 200-plus entries on quadrupeds and serpents fill more than 800 folio pages. His book-length chapter on the horse alone is 120 pages long. Given his expansive style and his comprehensive treatment of most of his animal subjects, the following are only brief excerpts describing a variety of fantastic creatures and highlights of his famous treatise on the unicorn. No excerpts can do Topsell justice; his thoroughness can be fully appreciated only by a reading of his complete chapters. Topsell's "Gorgon" is the catoblepas, a confusion probably derived from Mela and Pliny. Mela had said the beast lived near the Gorgon Isles, and Pliny juxtaposed descriptions of the catoblepas (perhaps the gnu) and the basilisk (later cockatrice), the lethal stare of the two naturally associated with the mythological Gorgons. Topsell identifies the manticore as a species of hyena rather than the usual tiger, and his "Leucrocuta" is actually a different beast altogether, even though he states the two are the same with different names. Topsell's survey of unicorn lore supports his outspoken belief in the animal. In his account of the curative powers of unicorn horn (alicorn), he personalizes material he translates from Gesner. The winged dragon entry is the beginning of Topsell's twelve-page discourse on the creature. Along with a host of other fantastic creatures, the "Eal" (yale), Olaus Magnus's sea serpent, the cockatrice, the barnacle goose, and the phoenix (which he rejects) also appear in his books.

Topsell's "Gorgon" appears on the title page of the 1607 edition; the other woodcuts accompanied corresponding texts.

Of the Gorgon or Strange Lybian Beast *

Among the many old and divers sorts of Beasts which are bred in Africk, it is thought that the Gorgon is brought forth in that Countrey. It is a fearful and terrible beast to behold, it hath high and thick eye-lids, eyes not very great, but much like an Oxes or Bugils, but all fiery-bloudy, which neither look directly forward, nor yet upwards, but continually down to the earth, and therefore are called in Greek, Catobleponta. From the crown of their head down to their nose they have a long hanging mane, which make them to look fearfully. It eateth deadly and poysonful herbs, and if at any time he see a Bull or other creature whereof he is afraid, he presently causeth his mane to stand upright, and being so lifted up, opening his lips, and gaping wide, sendeth forth of his throat a certain sharp and horrible breath, which infecteth and poysoneth the air above his head, so that all living creatures which draw in the breath of that air are grievously afflicted thereby, losing both voyce and sight, they fall into lethal and deadly Convulsions. It is bred in Hesperia and Lybia.

* Edward Topsell, *The History of Four-footed Beasts and Serpents* (1658; Ann Arbor, Mich.: University Microfilms, 1962), Microfilm Wing G624, wing reel 70:1, pp. 206, 343–45, 551–52, 558–59, 705.

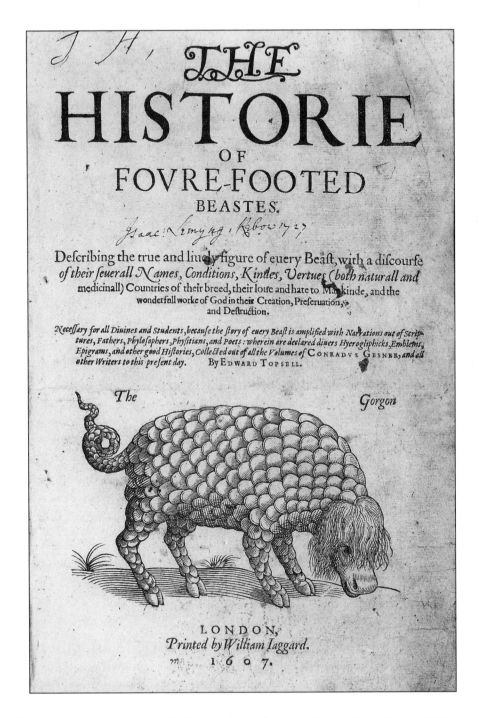

THE
HISTORIE
OF
FOVRE-FOOTED
BEASTES.

Isaac: Lemyng: Rebow 1727

Describing the true and liuely figure of euery Beaſt, with a diſcourſe
of their ſeuerall *Names, Conditions, Kindes, Vertues* (both naturall and
medicinall) Countries of their breed, their loue and hate to Mankinde, and the
wonderfull worke of God in their Creation, Preſeruation,
and Deſtruction.

Neceſſary for all Diuines and Students, becauſe the ſtory of euery Beaſt is amplified with Narrations out of Scriptures, Fathers, Phyloſophers, Phyſitians, and Poets: wherein are declared diuers Hyerogliphicks, Emblems, Epigrams, and other good Hiſtories, Collected out of all the Volumes of CONRADVS GESNER, *and all other Writers to this preſent day.* By EDWARD TOPSELL.

The   *Gorgon*

LONDON,
Printed by William Iaggard.
1607.

The facsimile title page, with Gorgon (catoblepas), of the 1607 edition of Edward
Topsell's *Historie of Foure-Footed Beastes*. Reproduced by permission of the Houghton
Library, Harvard University.

Manticore. From Konrad Gesner, *Curious Woodcuts of Fanciful and Real Beasts* (New York, Dover, 1971). Courtesy of Dover Publications.

The Manticora

This beast or rather Monster (as Ctesias writeth) is bred among the Indians, having a treble row of teeth beneath and above, whose greatness, roughness, and feet are like Lyons, his face and ears like unto a man, his eyes gray, and colour red, his tail like the tail of a Scorpion, of the earth, armed with a sting, casting forth sharp pointed quils. . . . This also is the same Beast which is called Leucrocuta about the bigness of a wilde Ass, being in legs and Hoofs like a Hart, having his mouth reaching both sides to his ears, and the head and face of a female like unto a Badgers. It is called also Martiora, which in the Persian tongue signifieth a devourer of men; and thus we conclude the story of the Hyena for her description, and her several kindes. . . .

Of the Unicorn

We are now come to the history of a beast, whereof divers people in every age of the world have made great question, because of the rare vertues thereof; therefore it behoveth us to use some diligence in comparing together the several testimonies that are spoken of this beast, for the better satisfaction of such as are now alive, and clearing of the point for them that shall be born hereafter, whether there be a Unicorn; for that is the main question to be resolved.

Unicorn. From Konrad Gesner, *Curious Woodcuts of Fanciful and Real Beasts* (New York, Dover, 1971). Courtesy of Dover Publications.

Now the vertues of the horn, of which we will make a particular discourse by itself, have been the occasion of this question, and that which doth give the most evident testimony unto all men that have ever seen it or used it, hath bred all the contention; and if there had not been disclosed in it any extraordinary powers and vertues, we should as easily believe that there was a Unicorn in the world, as we do believe there is an Elephant although not bred in Europe. . . .

Likewise in the City Zeila of Aethiopia, there are Kine of a purple colour, as Ludovicus Romanus [ed., Ludovico de Varthema] writeth, which have but one horn growing out of their heads, and that turneth up towards their backs. Caesar was of opinion that the Elk had but one horn, but we have shewed the contrary. It is said that Pericles had a Ram with one horn, but that was bred by way of prodigy, and not naturally. Simeon Sethi writeth, that the Musk-cat hath also one horn growing out of the fore-head, but we have shewed already that no man is of that opinion but himself. Aelianus writeth, that there be Birds in Aethiopia having one horn on their fore-heads, and therefore are called Unicornes: and Albertus saith, there is a fish called Monoceros, and hath also one horn. Now our discourse of the Unicorn is of none of these beasts, for there is not any vertue attributed to their horns, and therefore the vulgar sort of Infidel people which scarcely believe any herb but such as they see in their own Gardens, or any beast but such as is in their own flocks, or any knowledge but such as is bred in their own brains, or any birds which are not hatched in their own nests, have never made question of these, but of the true Unicorn, whereof there were more proofs in the world, because of the nobleness of his horn, they have ever been in doubt: by which distraction it appeareth unto me that there is some secret enemy in the inward degenerate nature of man, which continually blindeth the eyes of God his people, from beholding and believing the greatness of God his works.

But to the purpose, that there is such a beast, the Scripture it self witnesseth, for David thus speaketh in the 92. Psalme: *Et erigetur cornu meum tanquam Monocerotis*. That is, my horn shall be lifted up like the horn of a Unicorn; whereupon all Divines that ever wrote, have not only collected that there is a Unicorn, but also affirm the similitude to be betwixt the Kingdom of David and the horn of the Unicorn, that as the horn of the Unicorn is wholesome to all beasts and creatures, so should the Kingdom of David be in the generation of Christ; And do we think that David would compare the vertue of his Kingdom, and the powerful redemption of the world unto a thing that is not, or is uncertain or fantastical, God forbid that ever any man should so despight the holy Ghost. For this cause also we read in Suidas, that good men which worship God and follow his laws are compared to Unicorns, whose greater parts as their whole bodies are unprofitable and untamable, yet their horn maketh them excellent: so in good men, although their fleshy parts be good for nothing, and fall down to the earth, yet their grace and piety exalteth their souls to the heavens.

. . . In the 39. of Job, the Lord speaketh in this manner to Job: *Numquid acquiescet Monoceros ut serviat tibi, aut ut moretur juxta praesepia tua? Numquid ligabis Monocerotem fune suo pro sulco faciendo, aut complanabit glebas vallium post te?* That is to say, will the Unicorn rest and serve thee, or tarry beside thy cratches? Canst thou binde the Unicorn with a halter to thy plough to make furrows, or will he make plain the clots of the Vallies? Likewise in the prophesie of Esa. the 34. chap. and in many other places of Scripture, whereby God himself must needs be traduced, if there be no Unicorn in the world. . . .

THE MEDICINES ARISING FROM THE UNICORN

The horns of Unicorns, especially that which is brought from new Islands, being beaten and drunk in water, doth wonderfully help against poison: as of late experience doth manifest unto us, a man, who having taken poison and beginning to swell was preserved by this remedy. I myself have heard of a man worthy to be believed, that having eaten a poisoned cherry, and perceiving his belly to swell, he cured himself by the marrow of this horn being drunk in Wine, in very short space.

The same is also praised at this day for the curing of the Falling sickness, and affirmed by Aelianus, who called this disease cursed. The ancient Writers did

Winged dragon. From Konrad Gesner, *Curious Woodcuts of Fanciful and Real Beasts* (New York, Dover, 1971). Courtesy of Dover Publications.

attribute the force of healing to cups made of this horn, Wine being drunk out of them: but because we cannot have cups, we drink the substance of this horn, either by itself or with other medicines. I happily sometime made this Sugar of the horn, as they call it, mingling with the same Amber, Ivory dust, leaves of gold, coral, & certain other things, the horn being included in silk, and beaten in the decoction of Raisins and Cinnamon, I cast them in water, the rest of the reason of healing in the meantime not being neglected. . . . The horn of a Unicorn being beaten and boiled in Wine hath a wonderful effect in making the teeth white or clear, the mouth being well cleansed therewith. And thus much shall suffice for the medicines and virtues arising from the Unicorn.

The Winged Dragon

There be some dragons which have wings and no feet, some again have both feet and wings, and some neither feet nor wings, but are only distinguished from the common sort of Serpents by the comb growing upon their heads, and the beard under their cheeks.

JOHN SWAN (FL. 1635)
SPECULUM MUNDI

Even while presenting traditional lore, John Swan's encyclopedic *Speculum Mundi; Or, A Glasse Representing the Face of the World* (1635) reflects early seventeenth-century doubts about the existence of certain creatures. A compilation of authors from Pliny to Topsell, the clergyman's catalog of the six days of creation is, overall, weighted on the side of time-honored authority. Swan believes in the powers of unicorn horn, accepts mermaids and mermen as marine animals, and repeats the standard accounts of the manticore and others, but in keeping with the growing skepticism of his time, he reasons from biblical authority that the phoenix story is fable, and he is ambivalent about the griffin. He writes that belief in such creatures "shall be left to every mans liberty." Each succeeding edition of *Speculum Mundi*, up through 1670, appeared in a cultural climate increasingly more skeptical of received, traditional knowledge.

For rejection of the phoenix, see also Samuel Purchas, Sir Thomas Browne, and George Caspard Kirchmayer.

The Feathered Fowls *

From fishes I must come to birds, from the water to the air, and teach my pen to flie a while with the feathered fowls, as before it was swimming with the fearfull silent fish. . . .

The Phoenix, saith Munster, is a noble bird, and is but one in the World. Cornelius Valerius (whom Pliny mentioneth) doth witness that when Quintus Plautius and Sex. Papinius were Consuls, one was seen to fly into Aegypt. And Tacitus also writeth, that when Lucius Vitellius and Paulus Fabius were consuls, another was likewise seen to fly thither: and yet not another, but the same rather; for there was not above two years difference in the time of this appearance . . . but our Countreyman Mr. Lydiat rather thinketh, that it pointed out the time when Christ, that true Phoenix, did both die and rise again. . . .

Howbeit many think that all this is fabulous: for (besides the differing reports which go of this bird) what species or kind of any creature can be rehearsed, whereof there is never but one? and whereas the Lord said to all his creatures, Increase and multiply, this benediction should take no place in the Phoenix which multiplieth not. And again, seeing all creatures which came into the Ark, came by two and two, the male and female, it must needs follow that the Phoenix

---

* John Swan, *Speculum Mundi: or, A Glasse Representing the Face of the World*, 3rd ed. (1665; Ann Arbor, Mich.: University Microfilms, 1971), Microfilm Wing S6239, wing reel 401:1, pp. 347, 349–51.

by this means perished. And so saith one, As for the Phoenix, I (and not I alone) think it is a fable, because it agreeth neither to reason nor likelihood, but plainly disagrees to the history of the creation and of Noahs floud, in both which God made all male and female, and commanded them to increase and multiply.

The Griffon is a creature (if there be any such, for many doubt it) which whether I may reckon amongst the birds or beasts, I cannot tell. Howbeit as I find him marked by Aelianus, he is thus described; namely that he is a kind of beast with four feet, keeping most of all in India, being as mighty in strength as a lion: he hath wings and crooked talons, black on the back, and in the forepart purple. His wings be somewhat white, his bill and mouth like an eagles bill, his eyes fiery; he is hard to be taken except he be young, he maketh his nest in the high mountains, and fighteth with every kind of beast, saving the Lion and Elephant: he diggeth up gold in desert places, and giveth repulse to those that come near him. But (as I said) some doubt whether there be any such creature or no: which, for my part, shall be left to every mans liberty.

BATTLE OF THE BOOKS

Over the course of two millennia, belief in the existence of animals we now consider fabulous was dependent in large part on written authority and the transmission of that authority through writings that included classical histories and geographies, scriptural texts, bestiaries, encyclopedias, and travelers' tales. The only way the creatures could ultimately be discredited was through the discrediting of the authors who—along with artists—gave them cultural life in the first place. These authors included Herodotus, Aristotle, Pliny, and ultimately the writers of Holy Writ.

Isolated objections had little effect on the vast body of authority and popular belief. It wasn't until the sixteenth-century inception and development of modern zoology that questions about the validity of these creatures began to multiply. While Conrad Gesner accepted the unicorn, the footless bird of paradise, and the mysterious generation of the barnacle goose, he was cautious in his treatment of such creatures as the phoenix, griffin, and siren. In his ornithological volume, Ulisse Aldrovandi includes the siren, harpy, griffin, and others in a chapter on birds of fable. Ambroise Paré and others challenged the curative powers of alicorn.

Early in the sixteenth century, Paracelsus rejected the authority of Galen and Avicenna in medicine, and at the end of the century, Francis Bacon ushered in the New Philosophy with his revolutionary rejection of authority and establishment of observation and experimentation as the only valid sources of knowledge.

In this new intellectual climate, the literary English physician Sir Thomas Browne confronted classical and medieval authorities with his *Pseudodoxia Epidemica* (1646). While honoring "excellent and useful" earlier authors, Browne cautions that "they write from others, as later pens from them." Among those are writers important in the history of fabulous animals: Herodotus, Ctesias, Pliny, Aelian, and Solinus. Browne praises Pliny's *Natural History* (a compilation of some 2000 classical sources) as an immortal achievement but adds that "there is scarce a popular error passant in our days, which is not either directly expressed, or diductively contained in this Work." By using the scholastic review of authorities against itself, Browne's reasoned book refutes much traditional learning and exposes as fallacious many commonly held beliefs. Among Browne's targets is time-honored lore regarding animals, including the griffin, basilisk, unicorn, and phoenix.

Shortly after the second edition of the *Pseudodoxia* appeared, a Scots schoolmaster, churchman, and prolific author, Alexander Ross, answered Browne's book and the works of other proponents of the New Philosophy with his confrontational *Arcana Microcosmi*. The now obscure Ross was renowned in his own time as the Champion of the Ancients, a staunch defender of traditional knowledge against the charges of the new science. The *Arcana*, true to its subtitle, directly confronts the *Pseudodoxia*.

The two books together represent the seventeenth-century Battle of the Books between the Ancients and the Moderns. Encapsulating major controversies of the age, the *Pseudodoxia* and the *Arcana* embody the literary clash of the new scientific spirit with traditional authority. In terms of fabulous animals, they are scholastic culminations of lore from the Bible and Herodotus up to their own time.

The *Arcana Microcosmi* was not reprinted again, but Thomas Browne's expanded *Pseudodoxia* saw six more printings in the author's lifetime. Another subject of Ross's wrath, John Wilkins, helped found the Royal Society of London for Improving Natural Knowledge (1662). The first group of its kind in England and one of the first in Europe, the Royal Society has ever since devoted itself to the advancement of science.

Alexander Ross and others who defended classical and medieval authority had lost the battle, and creatures considered for so long members of the animal kingdom became "fabulous" and "mythical," embarrassing products of fallacious thinking and superstition.

SIR THOMAS BROWNE (1605–1682)
PSEUDODOXIA EPIDEMICA

More than any other single book, Sir Thomas Browne's *Pseudodoxia Epidemica; or, Enquiries into Very Many Received Tenents and Commonly Presumed Truths*

(1646, commonly known as "Vulgar Errors") represents the end of literal belief in traditional animals shaped by the imagination and sustained over millennia by literary authority.

Browne was a physician of wide learning, educated at Oxford and continental universities. Simultaneously attracted to traditional learning and skeptical of it, Browne joined the new scientific movement of his time by challenging received knowledge. His *Pseudodoxia* is in the tradition of compilation that developed from Pliny's *Natural History* through the thirteenth-century encyclopedias to the sixteenth-century natural histories. Browne gathers into his book a vast amount of learning from earlier writers, but by subjecting their work to the tests of experience and reason, he exposes errors that contributed to a vast body of fallacious knowledge. One of his primary targets is Pliny himself.

The most popular portions of both Pliny's and Browne's books may well be those on animals. Browne's Book 3 is entitled, "Of divers popular and received Tenets concerning Animals, which examined, prove either false or dubious." In it, he rejects the venerable fables about actual animals and devotes entire chapters to the centaur, griffin, basilisk, unicorn, amphisbaena, and the phoenix. In the following excerpts, Browne first establishes his position on knowledge and truth. He then rejects the griffin and the phoenix outright and is skeptical of the power of unicorn horn.

T. H. White contended that Browne was the first since Aristotle "to raise the subject of biology to a scientific level." That achievement earned Browne the dubiously distinctive position at the bottom of White's chart of the bestiary's "Family Tree."

For Alexander Ross's responses to Sir Thomas Browne's charges against the animals, and his defense of traditional learning, see the next entry. For the "Family Tree" diagram, see T. H. White in Chapter 12.

On Truth *

Would Truth dispense, we could be content, with Plato, that knowledge were but Remembrance; that Intellectuall acquisition were but Reminiscentiall evocation, and new impressions but the colourishing of old stamps which stood pale in the soul before. For, what is worse, knowledge is made by oblivion; and to purchase a clear and warrantable body of Truth, we must forget and part with much wee know. Our tender Enquiries taking up Learning at large, and together with true and assured notions, receiving many wherein our renewing judgements doe finde no satisfaction; and therefore in this Encyclopaedie and round of knowledge, like

* Sir Thomas Browne, *Pseudodoxia Epidemica; or, Enquiries into Very Many Received Tenents and Commonly Presumed Truths* (1646; Ann Arbor, Mich.: University Microfilms, 1978), Microfilm Wing B5159, wing reel 158:12, pp. A2, 129–31, 169, 131–33.

the great and exemplary wheeles of heaven, wee must observe two Circles: that while we are daily carried about, and whirled on by the swindge and rapt of the one, wee may maintaine a naturall and proper course, in the slow and sober wheele of the other. And this wee shall more readily performe, if we timely survey our knowledge; impartially singling out those encroachments, which junior compliance and popular credulity hath admitted. Whereof at present wee have endeavoured a long and serious *Adviso*; proposing not onely a large and copious List, but from experience and reason, attempting their decisions.

The Griffon

That there are Griffons in Nature, that is a mixt and dubious animall, in the forepart resembling an Eagle, and behinde the shape of a Lion, with erected eares, foure feet, and a long taile, many affirme, and most I perceive deny not; the same is averred by Aelian, Solinus, Mela, and Herodotus, countenanced by the name sometimes found in Scripture, and was an Hieroglyphick of the Egyptians.

Notwithstanding wee finde most diligent enquirers to be a contrary assertion, for beside that Albertus and Pliny have disallowed it, the learned Aldrovand hath in a large discourse rejected it; Mathias Michovius who writ of those Northerne parts wherein men place these Griffons, hath positively concluded against it, and if examined by the doctrine of animals, the invention is monstrous, not much inferiour unto the figment of Sphynx, Chimaera, and Harpies; for though some species there be of a middle and participating natures, that is, of bird and beast, as we finde the Bat to be, yet are their parts so conformed and set together that we cannot define the beginning or end of either, there being a commixtion of both in the whole, rather than an adaptation or cement of the one unto the other.

Now for the word γρύψ or Gryps, sometimes mentioned in Scripture, and frequently in humane Authors, properly understood, it signifies some kinde of Eagle or Vulture, from whence the Epithite Grypus for an hooked or Aquiline nose. Thus when the Septuagint makes use of this word in the eleventh of Leviticus, Tremellius and our Translation hath rendred it the Ossifrage, which is one kinde of Eagle, although the Vulgar translation, and that annexed unto the Septuagint retaine the word *Grips*, which in ordinary and schoole construction is commonly rendred a Griffin . . . .

As for the testimonies of ancient Writers, they are but derivative and terminate all in one Aristeus a Poet of Proconesus; who affirmed that neere the Arimaspi, or one eyed Nation, Griffins defended the mines of gold: but this as Herodotus delivereth, he wrote by heresay; and Michovius who hath expresly written of those parts plainly affirmeth, there is neither gold nor Griffins in that countrey, nor any such animall extant. . . .

Lastly, concerning the Hieroglyphicall authority, although it neerest approacheth the truth, it doth not inferre its existency; the conceit of the Griffin properly taken being but a symbolicall phancy, in so intollerable a shape including allowable morality. So doth it well make out the properties of a Guardian, or any person entrusted; the eares implying attention, the wings celerity of execution, the Lion-like shape, courage and audacity, the hooked bill, reservance and tenacity. It is also an Embleme of valour and magnanimity, as being compounded of the Eagle and the Lion, the noblest animals in their kinds; and so it is applyable unto Princes, Presidents, Generals, and all heroick Commanders, and so is it also borne in the Coat armes of many noble Families of Europe.

Unicorn Horn

Since therefore there be many Unicornes, since that whereto wee appropriate a horne is so variously described, that it seemeth either never to have beene seene by two persons, or not to have beene one animall; Since though they agreed in the description of the animall, yet is not the horne wee extoll the same with that of the Ancients; Since what hornes soever they be that passe among us, they are not the hornes of one but severall animals; Since many in common use and high esteeme are no hornes at all; Since if they were true hornes, yet might their vertues be questioned; Since though we allowed some virtues, yet were not others to be received, with what security a man may rely on this remedy, the mistresse of fooles hath already instructed some, and to wisdome (which is never too wise to learne) it is not too late to consider.

The Phaenix

That there is but one Phaenix in the world, which after many hundred yeares burneth it selfe, and from the ashes thereof ariseth up another, is a conceit not new or altogether popular, but of great Antiquity; not onely delivered by humane Authors, but frequently expressed by holy Writers, by Cyrill, Epiphanius, and others, by Ambrose in his Hexameron, and Tertul. in his Poem *de Iudicio Domini*, but more agreeably unto the present sence in his excellent Tract, *de Resur. carnis.* . . .

All which notwithstanding we cannot presume the existence of this animall, nor dare we affirme there is any Phaenix in Nature. For, first there wants herein the definitive confirmator and test of things uncertaine, that is, the sense of man: for though many Writers have much enlarged hereon, there is not any ocular describer, or such as presumeth to confirme it upon aspection; and therefore Herodotus that led the story unto the Greeks, plainly saith, he never attained the sight of any, but onely in the picture.

Againe, primitive Authors, and from whom the streame of relations is derivative, deliver themselves very dubiously, and either by a doubtfull parenthesis, or a
timorous conclusion overthrow the whole relation: Thus Herodotus in his
Euterpe, delivering the story hereof, presently interposeth, ἐμοὶ μὲν οὐ πιστὰ
γέγοντες; that is, which account seemes to me improbable; Tacitus in his Annals
affordeth a larger story, how the Phaenix was first seene at Heliopolis in the
reigne of Sesostris, then in the reigne of Amasis, after in the dayes of Ptolomy, the
third of the Macedonian race; but at last thus determineth, *Sed Antiquitas
obscura, & nonnulli falsum esse hunc Phoenicem, neque Arabum è terris credidere*.
Pliny makes a yet fairer story, that the Phaenix flew into Aegypt in the Consulship of Quintus Plancius, that it was brought to Rome in the Censorship of
Claudius, in the 800. yeare of the City, and testified also in their records; but after
all concludeth, *Sed quae falsa esse nemo dubitabit*, but that this is false no man will
make doubt. . . .

Lastly, many Authors who have made mention hereof, have so delivered themselves, and with such intentions we cannot from thence deduce a confirmation:
For some have written Poetically as Ovid, Mantuan, Lactantius, Claudian, and
others: Some have written mystically, as Paracellsus in his booke *de Azoth*, or *de
ligno & linea vitae*; and as severall Hermeticall Philosophers, involving therein the
secret of their Elixir, and enigmatically expressing the nature of their great worke:
Some have written Rhetorically, and concessively, not controverting but assuming
the question, which taken as granted advantaged the illation: So have holy men
made use hereof as farre as thereby to confirme the Resurrection; for discoursing
with heathens who granted the story of the Phaenix, they induced the Resurrection from principles of their owne, and positions received among themselves. Others have spoken Emblematically and Hieroglyphically, and so did the Aegyptians,
unto whom the Phaenix was the Hieroglyphick of the Sunne; and this was probably the ground of the whole relation, succeeding ages adding fabulous accounts,
which laid together built up this singularity, which every pen proclaimeth.

ALEXANDER ROSS (1591–1654)
ARCANA MICROCOSMI

After Sir Thomas Browne's *Pseudodoxia Epidemica* (1646, "Vulgar Errors") discredited many traditional beliefs, Alexander Ross, "Champion of the Ancients," came
to the defense of classical and medieval authorities with his *Arcana Microcosmi . . .
With a Refutation of Doctor Brown's Vulgar Errors, The Lord Bacon's Natural History,
And Doctor Harvy's Book De Generatione, Comenius, and Others* (1652). One of the

areas Ross passionately defends is animal lore, from the habits of actual animals to the existence or attributes of others that Browne considered fabulous.

A schoolmaster and chaplain of Charles I, Alexander Ross was the prolific author of about thirty books on a wide range of subjects, from a verse history of the Jews to a continuation of Sir Walter Raleigh's *History of the World*. He was best known, though, for his literary attacks on prominent advocates of the New Philosophy.

Arcana Microcosmi was Ross's second confrontation with Thomas Browne, following his *Medicus Medicatus*, a response to Browne's *Religio Medici*. In the *Arcana*, Ross refutes Browne point for point, doggedly defending tradition and authority by any means of argument possible, from textual evidence to personal experience. He ends his book with a resigned but moving defense of Aristotelian learning.

An ultraconservative voice in the major philosophical debate of his age, Ross died wealthy and renowned. A century later, Samuel Johnson wrote in his essay on Browne that Ross's *Medicus Medicatus* was "universally neglected by the world." Ross has been remembered primarily through a satirical couplet in Samuel Butler's *Hudibras* (Canto 2):

> There was an ancient sage philosopher
> That had read Alexander Ross over.

All bracketed statements in the text are Ross's own.

The Griffin *

WHAT THE ANCIENTS HAVE WRITTEN OF GRIFFINS MAY BE TRUE. GRIFFINS MENTIONED IN SCRIPTURE. GRYPI AND GRYPHES, PERES AND OSSIFRAGE.

The Doctor [denies there be Griffins, that is, dubious animals in the fore part resembling an Eagle, and behind a Lion, with erected ears, foure feet, and a long tail, being averred by Aelian, Solinus, Mela, and Herodotus.] (Answ.) Aelian tells us, That Griffins are like Lions in their pawes and feet, and like Eagles in their wings and head. Solinus saith onely, that they are very fierce fowls; Mela, that they are cruell and stubborn animals; Herodotus onely mentions their names, when hee shewes the Arimaspi takes away their gold from them: So Philostrates shewes, That in strength and bignesse they are like Lions; So Pausanius speaks of them; but neither he, nor the others named, tell us in plain terms, that they are like Lions behind, and Eagles in the fore-part: For Pliny and some others doubt of this as fabulous. 2. Suppose they had thus described Griffins, as

---

* Alexander Ross, *Arcana Microcosmi* (1652; Ann Arbor, Mich.: University Microfilms, 1964), Microfilm Wing R1947, wing reel 158:12, pp. 199–200, 129–30, 201, 204–5, 207.

mixt and dubious animals, yet this is not sufficient to prove them fabulous: for divers such animals there are in the World. . . . Neither is it fabulous that these Griffins are greedy of gold, which they preserve & hide in the earth: for I have seen Mag-pies doe the like: I have observed one which stole money, and hid it in a hole; and perhaps it may be from this that Plautus calls Griffins Mag-pies. . . . Besides, though some fabulous narrations may be added to the story of the Griffins, as of the one-ey'd Arimaspi with whom they fight, yet it follows not that therefore there are no Griffins. If any man say, That now such animals are not to be seen; I answer, It may be so, and yet not perished: for they may be removed to places of more remotenesse and security, and inaccessible to men: for many such places there are in the great and vast Countries of Scythia, and Tartaria, or Cathaia, whither our Europeans durst never, nor could venture.

Unicorn Horn

If the Ancients adscribed no vertue to this horn, why was it of such account among them? Why did the Indian Princes drink out of them, and make Cups and Rings of them, which either they wore on their fingers, or applied to their breasts, but that they knew there was in them an antidotal vertue against poison, as Andreth Baccius [l. *de Unicor.*] sheweth, and the Doctor denieth not [an Antidotall efficacy, and such as the Ancients commended in this Horn] and yet two lines before, [he denies that the Ancients adscribed any vertue to it.] But sure it is apparent, that not only there is an occult quality in it against poison, as in the Elks Hoof against the falling sicknesse, but also by manifest qualities it works; for Baccius proves it to be of an excessive drying quality, and therefore good against worms and putrefaction. And that Riccius the Physitian did use sometimes the weight of a scruple, sometimes of ten grains thereof in burning fevers with good successe. 3. That it can resist Arsnick, the same Baccius proves, by the experiment which the Cardinal of Trent made upon two Pigeons, [l. *de Unic.*] to which he caused some Arsenick to be given: shortly after he gave som scrapings of his Unicorns horn to one of them, which after some symptomes recovered and lived, the other died two hours after it had eaten the Arsenick: The same Horn cured divers pestilential Fevers, and such as were poisoned. Hence then it appears, that this Horn was both commended by the Ancients, namely, by Aelian, Philostrates, and divers others, as also by modern Physitians, as Ficinus, Brasavolus, Matthiolus, Mandella, and many more. . . .

The Phoenix

Because the Doctor following the opinion of Pererius, Fernandus de Cordova, Francius, and some others, absolutely denies the existence of the Phoenix, I will in some few positions set down my opinion concerning this bird. . . .

10. Though Aristotle and some others make no mention of the Phoenix, it will not follow that therefore there is no such bird extant; for there are many kinds of creatures of which they write not. 11. It is likely that the bird Semenda in the Indies, which burneth her self to ashes, out of which springs another bird of the same kind, is the very same with the old Phoenix. 12. The testimony of so many Writers, especially of the Fathers, proving by the Phoenix the incarnation of Christ, and his Resurrection, and withall our resuscitation in the last day, doe induce me to believe there is such a bird, else their Arguments had been of small validity among the Gentiles, if they had not believed there was such a bird. What wonder is it, saith Tertullian, for a virgin to conceive, when the Eastern bird is generated without copulation, *Peribunt homines, avibus Arabiae de resurrectione sua securis.* Shall men utterly perish (saith he) and the birds of Arabia be sure of their resurrection? The existence of this bird is asserted by Herodotus, Seneca, Mela, Tacitus, Pliny, Solinus, Aelian, Lampridius, Aur. Victor, Laertius, Suidas, and others of the Gentile-Writers. The Christian Doctors who affirm the same, are, Clemens, Romanus, Tertullian, Eusebius, Cyril of Jerusalem, Epiphanius, Nazianzenus, Ambrose, Augustine, Hierom, Lactantius, and many others.

Now out of what we have spoken, we can easily answer the Doctors objections which he hath collected out of Pererius, Feriundes, Franzius, and others, as first, when he saith, That *none of those who have written of the Phoenix, are oculary describers thereof. Ans.* Neither was Aristotle, Gesner, Aldrovandus, and others, who have written largely of beasts, birds, and Fishes ocular witnesses of all they wrote: they are forced to deliver much upon hear-say and tradition: So those that write the later stories of American and Indian animals, never saw all they write of. Secondly when he saith, [That Herodotus, Tacitus, and Pliny, speak so dubiously, that they overthrow the whole relation of the Phoenix.] *Answ.* Herodotus doubteth not of the existency of the Phoenix, but onely of some circumstances delivered by the Heliopolitans, to wit, that the younger Phoenix should carry his Father wrapt up in Myrrh, to the Temple of the Sun, and there bury him; so Tacitus denieth not the true Phoenix, but onely saith, That some hold the Phoenix there described, which was seen in the dayes of Ptolomy in Aegypt, not the right Phoenix spoken of by the Ancients. The words of Pliny are falsified by the Doctor, who cites them thus: *Sed quae falsa esse nemo dubitabit*: whereas the words are, *Sed quem falsum esse nemo dubitabit*: So that he doth not say, That what is written of the Phoenix is false; but onely that this Phoenix which was brought to Rome in the Consulship of Claudius, was false, and not the right one. 3. He saith, *That they who discourse of the Phoenix, deliver themselves diversly, contrarily, or contradictorily. Answ.* There is no contradiction except it be (*ad idem*) most of them agree in the substance, that there is a Phoenix, they onely differ in the accidents and circumstances of age, colour, and place. We must not deny all simply that is controverted by Writers: for so we might deny most points both in Divinity and Philosophy. . . .

. . . I answer with Aristotle, speaking of Bees, that as they have a proper and peculiar kind of Nature differing from all other creatures, so it was fit they should have γενεσιν ἴδιον, a peculiar and proper kind of production. The like I say of the Phoenix, which is a miracle in nature, both in his longevity, numericall unity, and way of generation. And in this wonderfull variety the Creator manifests his wisdome, power and glory.

In Defense of Ancient Learning

Thus have I briefly and cursorily run over the Doctors elaborate book, *tanquam canis ad Nilum*, having stoln some hours from my universall History, partly to satisfie my self and desires of my friends, and partly to vindicate the ancient Sages from wrong and misconstruction, thinking it a part of my duty to honor and defend their reputation, whence originally I have my knowledge, and not with too many in this loose and wanton age, slight all ancient Doctrines and Principles, hunting after new conceits and whimzies, which though specious to the eye at the first view, yet upon neer inspection and touch, dissolve like the apples of Sodom into dust. I pitie to see so many young heads still gaping like Camelions for knowledge, and are never filled, because they feed upon airy and empty phansies, loathing the sound, solid and wholsome viands of Peripatetick wisdom, they reject Aristotles pure fountains, and digge to themselves cisternes that will hold no water; whereas they should stick close and adhere as it were by a matrimoniall conjunction to sound doctrine, they go a whoring (as the Scripture speaketh) after their own inventions. Let us not wander then any longer with Hagar in the wild desart where there is no water; for the little which is in our pitcher, will be quickly spent; but let us return to our Masters house, there we shal find pure fountains of ancient University learning. Let Prodigals forsake their husks, and leave them to swine, they will find bread enough at home: And as dutifull children let us cover the nakednesse of our Fathers with the Cloke of a favourable Interpretation.

GEORGE CASPARD KIRCHMAYER (1635–1700)
SIX ZOOLOGICAL DISPUTATIONS

Rejection of traditional animal lore became increasingly scornful in the later seventeenth century. George Caspard Kirchmayer, for one, called the phoenix tale "impossible, absurd, and openly ridiculous" and "a slander against Holy Writ, nature, and sound reason." In his mid-twenties when he published *Hexas desputa-*

tionum Zoologicarum (1661), the Wittenberg professor and fellow of the Royal Societies of London and Vienna vigorously discredits the fable of the immortal bird and even dismisses salamander lore for good measure. Following is the concluding segment of Kirchmayer's treatise.

Kirchmayer is one of three seventeenth-century German authors represented in Edmund Goldsmid's privately-printed *Un-Natural History, or Myths of Ancient Science* (1886). Subtitled a "Collection of Curious Tracts on the Basilisk, Unicorn, Phoenix, Behemoth or Leviathan, Dragon, Giant Spider, Tarantula, Chameleons, Satyrs, Homines Caudati, &c," the work is a valuable but difficult-to-find repository of arcane lore.

For other doubts about the phoenix, see Herodotus, Pliny, Albertus Magnus, Samuel Purchas, John Swan, and Sir Thomas Browne.

The Phoenix an Impossible Fiction*

This creature is quite a myth, and has never been seen except in pictures (I use the words of Herodotus). No man has ever seen it in true reality. Except a "'tis said," "'tis reported," "'tis a tale," or "so they say," no one can bring forward a clear statement in regard to the matter (Gesner, page 692). I regard as impossible, absurd, and openly ridiculous whatever, except in the way of a fiction, has been told of this creature. Such a belief as that in the Phoenix is a slander against Holy Writ, nature, and sound reason. We shall proceed regularly, and prove all our steps. Now, it is clear from the Scriptures that the creator made male and female in all the brute tribes. With this intention the task of procreation was committed to all. To all alike did the same command proceed—"Increase and multiply." The Phoenix cannot be exempted from this command. And at the flood, not only did the quadrupeds but all the winged tribes go in with Noah, two by two of the unclean, and seven couples of the clean. The Phoenix is to be referred to the clean, nay to the most clean, class of animals, if any is. But where can we now discover either a male, a female, or seven couples?

Nature herself supplies us with arguments to defeat the defenders of the Phoenix. From death she declares there is no natural regress to life. The Phoenix, once dead, has entered on a stage of total extinction. This is the fiat of death. Nature declares that whatever is born into the world is born from what is similar to itself. In this work an equivocal birth has no place. If from a worm there springs a Phoenix, its birth would be doubtful, nay, the bird *itself* would be under a cloud of grave doubt. Nature says: "Birds are born from eggs, not from ashes."

* George Caspard Kirchmayer, *Hexas disputationum Zoologicarum*, from *Un-Natural History, or Myths of Ancient Science*, ed. and trans. Edmund Goldsmid (Edinburgh: privately printed, 1886), chapter 2, pp. 41–47.

Birds likewise are oviparous, not viviparous. From the ashes of a fowl no one looks for a fowl, nor from those of a pheasant do we expect a pheasant. The same thing applies to the Phoenix. Nature tells us that without the fecundation and parturition of the female, no kind of creature can be preserved on the earth. Nature, too, teaches that no animal can be born from fire, nay, nor even be preserved in such great heat as is spoken of in the story of the Phoenix.

The statement made about the Salamander, to the effect that it can remain in the midst of flame without receiving any harm, is false. . . .

The Phoenix introduces the thinking mind to many and inexplicable difficulties. We shall relate some of the absurd stories. It is said that death is its life. When it dies it arises, and when dissolving away it is born again. Such nonsense! This bird is said to be of no sex. Our common sense tells us this is false. It is declared to be a solitary creature, and the only specimen of its kind. Sober philosophy demands that this philosophy be relegated to the regions of the absurd. . . .

. . . we shall make it a special point to speak freely what we think on those passages which relate to a matter which is obscure and covered with the veil of enigma. Next to the Hebrews, the Egyptians were the first to make use of and discover the liberal arts and sciences, as they were the first to employ various figures, paintings, and hieroglyphics. They were all kept secret, and lest they might come to be known among the common people, every effort was made to keep them hid. That age which we call ἄδηλον, that is uncertain and obscure, was a long one. The age that followed next we may consider the mythic or fabulous. In this, Poetry, especially that of Greece, and through her that of Rome, produced widespread traditions. We can the more freely pardon this art the crime of creating these fables, the more we remember the license poetry is allowed in whatever she touches. This is the source of the Phoenix story. It was by a hieroglyphic that the ancients wished to indicate nothing more or less than the constitution of this mundane machine, and the end of everything sublunary. We have the words of Laurembergius. . . .

. . . "I believe it has never been a real bird; there is a secret meaning hidden under this fable. Namely, this bird called the Phoenix is a token of the whole world; the golden head indicates the heaven with its stars, the bright body the earth, the blue breast and tail, the water and air. The Phoenix or world, however, will exist so long as the heaven and stars stand at that place where they were at the creation. When that ends the Phoenix will be dead, and if the old world renews its course everything will begin again."

. . . To our mind the Phoenix is a pure figment and nonentity. Long ago this was the belief of such great men as Herodotus, Pliny, Gesner, Aldrovandus, Franzius, and Sperlingius. To God alone be glory!

JOHN MILTON (1608–1674)
PARADISE LOST

Outside the discrediting of certain animals as fabulous, Milton retained traditional animal lore in the work generally regarded as the greatest epic in English. Along with mythological monsters, the sea beast thought to be an island, the griffin, the phoenix, the dragon, and the amphisbaena all have their memorable places in the sonorous blank verse of *Paradise Lost* (1667). While phoenix imagery is associated with the angel Raphael, the other creatures are related to Satan, either figuratively or dramatically.

The poem that concerns "Man's first disobediance" and sets out to "justify the ways of God to Man" moves, overall, from Lucifer's fall from Heaven to Adam and Eve's expulsion from the Garden of Eden. A Christian humanist work, Milton's epic is rich in literary tradition, encompassing both the body of holy scripture and works from Homer to Du Bartas. Joshua Sylvester's 1605 English translation of Du Bartas's *Divine Weeks* was, overall, a major influence on Milton's poem. Specific passages, like those below, contain multiple literary echoes. See other entries in this anthology for particular references.

Modeled on the epic form and conventions of Homer and Virgil, *Paradise Lost* opens *in medias res* with Satan (the former Lucifer) and his army of rebellious angels in the burning lake of Hell. Satan's vast size is compared to that of classical giants and the biblical Leviathan. The great sea beast that mariners believe to be an island is a widespread tale, from Sindbad to St. Brendan to Olaus Magnus. Like the medieval bestiaries and Pope Gregory I, Milton equates the monster with Satan. The poet's references to both Norway and the "fixed anchor in his skaly rind" echo Olaus's Norwegian whale with "Anchors Fastned" on its back.

Satan rouses his legions with promises of regaining Heaven. While their master sets off to the new Earth to avenge himself on God by guile, his minions explore their infernal domain, one area of which is infested with mythological monsters. Milton's "Gorgons, and Hydras, and Chimaeras dire" is a well-known phrase that hearkens back to catalogs of monsters in descriptions of Hell in Virgil's *Aeneid* and Torquato Tasso's *Jerusalem Delivered* and is varied to "Dragons and griffins and monsters dire" by John Greenleaf Whittier in the opening of his *Double-Headed Snake of Newbury*.

Meanwhile, Satan hurries on to Earth, his movement compared in an epic simile to a griffin pursuing the one-eyed Arimaspi who stole its gold. Milton's description of the griffin's movement as "half on foot, Half fly'ing" is an apparent variation of Edmund Spenser's dragon "Halfe flying, and halfe footing in his haste."

Seeing Satan's flight through chaos toward the Earthly Paradise, God sends the angel Raphael to warn Adam and Eve of the Arch-Fiend's coming. Raphael's flight is like that of the phoenix in that he is joined by flocks of birds.

Later, following the temptation in the Garden, Satan returns to Hell in triumph, only to be transformed by God into a dragon and his followers into serpents. The noxious reptiles born of the blood from Medusa's severed head are cataloged in Lucan's *Pharsalia*. Milton's "Huge Python" alludes to the beast in the *Hymn to Apollo*.

Satan as Leviathan*

> Thus Satan talking to his nearest mate
> With head up-lift above the wave, and eyes
> That sparkling blaz'd, his other parts besides
> Prone on the flood, extended long and large
> Lay floting many a rood, in bulk as huge
> As whom the fables name of monstrous size,
> Titanian, or Earth-born, that warr'd on Jove,
> Briareos or Typhon, whom the den
> By ancient Tarsus held, or that sea-beast
> Leviathan, which God of all his works
> Created hugest that swim th' Ocean stream:
> Him haply slumb'ring on the Norway foam
> The pilot of some small night-founder'd skiff,
> Deeming some iland, oft, as sea-men tell,
> With fixed anchor in his skaly rind
> Moors by his side under the lee, while night
> Invests the sea, and wished morn delays:
> So stretch'd out huge in length the Arch-Fiend lay
> Chain'd on the burning lake . . .

Gorgons, and Hydras, and Chimaeras Dire

> . . . Thus roving on
> In confus'd march forlorn, th' adventrous bands
> With shudd'ring horror pale, and eyes aghast,
> View'd first their lamentable lot, and found
> No rest: through many a dark and dreary vale
> They pass'd, and many a region dolorous,

* John Milton, *Paradise Lost*, 6th ed., ed. Thomas Newton (London, 1763), vol. 1, pp. 27–29, 138–39, 164–66, 371–72; vol. 2, pp. 261–64. (1.192–210, 2.614–28, 2.943–50, 5.266–74, 10.511–33).

O'er many a frozen, many a fiery Alp,
Rocks, caves, lakes, fens, bogs, dens, and shades of death,
A universe of death, which God by curse
Created ev'il, for evil only good,
Where all life dies, death lives, and nature breeds,
Perverse, all monstrous, all prodigious things,
Abominable, inutterable, and worse
Than fables yet have feign'd, or fear conceiv'd,
Gorgons, and Hydras, and Chimaeras dire.

As When a Gryphon

. . . nigh founder'd on he fares,
Treading the crude consistence, half on foot,
Half fly'ing; behoves him now both oar and sail.
As when a gryphon through the wilderness
With winged course, o'er hill or moory dale,
Pursues the Arimaspian, who by stealth
Had from his wakeful custody purloin'd
The guarded gold: So eagerly the Fiend
O'er bog, or steep, through strait, rough, dense, or rare,
With head, hands, wings, or feet pursues his way,
And swims, or sinks, or wades, or creeps, or flies. . . .

Raphael's Phoenix Flight

. . . Down thither prone in flight
He speeds, and through the vast ethereal sky
Sails between worlds and worlds, with steddy wing,
Now on the polar winds, then with quick fan
Winnows the buxom air; till within soar
Of tow'ring eagles, to all the fowls he seems
A Phoenix, gaz'd by all, as that sole bird,
When to inshrine his reliques in the sun's
Bright temple, to Egyptian Thebes he flies.

Transformed into Serpents

His visage drawn he felt to sharp and spare,
His arms clung to his ribs, his legs intwining

Each other, till supplanted down he fell
A monstrous serpent on his belly prone,
Reluctant, but in vain, a greater power
Now rul'd him, punish'd in the shape he sinn'd
According to his doom: he would have spoke,
But hiss for hiss return'd with forked tongue
To forked tongue, for now were all transform'd
Alike, to serpents all as accessories
To his bold riot: dreadful was the din
Of hissing through the hall, thick swarming now
With complicated monsters head and tail,
Scorpion, and Asp, and Amphisbaena dire,
Cerastes horn'd, Hydrus, and Elops drear,
And Dipsas (not so thick swarm'd once the soil
Bedropt with blood of Gorgon, or the ile
Ophiusa) but still greatest he the midst,
Now Dragon grown, larger than whom the sun
Ingender'd in the Pythian vale on slime,
Huge Python, and his pow'r no less he seem'd
Above the rest still to retain; they all
Him followed issuing forth to th' open field. . . .

Thomas Boreman (fl. 1736–1744)
A Description of Three Hundred Animals

While most animals discredited as "fabulous" were either ignored or scorned in eighteeneth-century literature, a few lived on in a popular natural history produced expressly for children, A Description of Three Hundred Animals, viz., Beasts, Birds, Fishes, Serpents, and Insects. With a particular Account of the Manner of their Catching Whales in Greenland (1730). Intended for the "Instruction of Children," particularly to introduce them to the "Habit of Reading," the book was illustrated with engravings.

The major (unidentified) source of the children's animal book, "Extracted from the best Authors," was Edward Topsell's natural history. Boreman's manticore, for one, is virtually lifted from one part of Topsell's description. The illustration is derivative of those in the Topsell and Gesner natural histories.

The manticore, from the 1786 edition of Thomas Boreman's *A Description of Three Hundred Animals*, derived from Gesner and Topsell engravings. Reproduced with permission by Harcourt Brace.

Unlike serious natural histories of his own time, Boreman's book retains several animals by then generally rejected as fabulous: the unicorn, manticore, lamia, cockatrice, and dragon; he does, though, qualify their reality with such phrases as "tho' doubted of by many Writers."

Three Hundred Animals, which its publishers claimed to be the first animal book published for the entertainment of children, went through at least fifteen editions between 1730 and 1812. It is a forerunner of children's books in which fantastic creatures appear as characters.

The Manticora *

The MANTICORA, (or, according to the Persians, Mantiora) a Devourer, is bred among the Indians; having a triple Row of Teeth beneath and above, and in Bigness and Roughness like a Lion's; as are also his Feet; Face and Ears like a Man's; his Tail like a Scorpion's, armed with a Sting, and sharp-pointed Quills.

---

* Thomas Boreman, *A Description of Three Hundred Animals* (1786; facsimile, New York: Johnson Reprint, 1968), 19.

His Voice is like a small trumpet, or Pipe. He is so wild, that 'tis very difficult to tame him; and as swift as an Hart. With his Tail he wounds the Hunters, whether they come before or behind him. When the Indians take a Whelp of this Beast, they bruise its Buttocks and Tail, to prevent its bearing the sharp Quills; then it is tamed without Danger.

OLIVER GOLDSMITH (C. 1730–1774)
A HISTORY OF THE EARTH
AND ANIMATED NATURE

By the publication of Oliver Goldsmith's popular compilation of natural history, *A History of the Earth and Animated Nature* (1774), the monstrous dragon of the past could be regarded as a creation of the "capricious imagination," still believed in only by superstitious primitives. Goldsmith adds in a note that the basilisk, "so dreadful to the imagination of our ancestors," is "an inoffensive animal, a native of South America."

In his preface, Goldsmith distinguishes between two treatments of natural history: systematic naming, and descriptions of the "properties, manners, and relations" of animals. The ancients, he writes, emphasized the stories at the expense of the science. They "only dwelt upon what was new, great, and surprising, and sometimes even warmed the imagination at the expense of truth."

The best known of Goldsmith's prolific and diverse literary works are *The Deserted Village, The Vicar of Wakefield,* and *She Stoops to Conquer.* One of his several compilations, *Animated Nature* was published the last year of his life.

The Dragon *

To this class of lizards, we may refer the Dragon, a most terrible animal, but most probably not of nature's formation. Of this death-dealing creature all people have read; and the most barbarous countries, to this day, paint it to the imagination in all its terrors, and fear to meet it in every forest. It is not enough that nature has furnished those countries with poisons of various malignity; with serpents forty

---

* Oliver Goldsmith, *A History of the Earth and Animated Nature* (New York, 1825), 721–22.

feet long; with elephants, lions, and tigers; to make their situation really dangerous, the capricious imagination is set at work to call up new terrors; and scarce a
savage is found that does not talk of winged serpents of immoderate length, flying
away with the camel or the rhinoceros, or destroying mankind by a single glare.
Happily, however, such ravages are no where found to exist at present; and the
whole race of dragons is dwindled down to the Flying Lizard, a little harmless
creature, that only preys upon insects, and even seems to embellish the forest
with its beauty.

Part

Recurring
Images

IV

Phoenix illustration, from *The Letters of D. H. Lawrence* by D. H. Lawrence. Introduction by Aldous Huxley. Copyright 1932 by the Estate of D. H. Lawrence. Used by permission of Viking Penguin, a division of Penguin Books USA Inc.

After being discredited by seventeenth-century science, fabulous animals were largely dismissed throughout the Age of Reason as products of fallacious thinking and superstition. But by the early nineteenth century, a Romantic hunger for what rationalism had discarded leads to interest in the faculty of the human imagination, generating the collection and study of folklore, mythology, and the Indo–European roots of myth and language. Now no longer members of the animal kingdom, fabulous animals reappear in literature on the other side of belief — in the company of mythological monsters. While some expository writers treat the creatures condescendingly, as quaint reminders of earlier ignorant eras, others speculate about the figures' natural prototypes, their global imaginary relatives, their possible existence in former times, their literary histories, and even their continued existence in remote areas of the world. Fabulous creatures begin to appear in children's fantasy as eccentric anthropomorphized animals.

In the increasingly technological and materialistic twentieth century, animals of the imagination multiply in symbolic meanings and commercial forms. Elemental shapes of human consciousness, fears and spiritual longings, they are now thriving in children's literature, adult fantasy, popular nonfiction, and specialized scholarship. They have become their own distinct area of study, and their images are scattered throughout contemporary culture.

Myths and Fallacies

Jacob and Wilhelm Grimm
(1785–1863, 1786–1859)
Fairy Tales

Apart from learned controversy and rejection by the New Science of the seventeenth century, some animals of the imagination lived on in folklore as well as in art and heraldry. Ancient lore of the dragon and others resurfaced in print in tales gathered from oral tradition and written down.

The most important and still the best known of these collections, the major source of the scientific study of folklore, is the *Kinder- und Hausmärchen* (1812–1815) of Jacob and Wilhelm Grimm. Prefaces to later editions of the tales address the question of how stories from widely differing countries could have similar patterns of character and action, such as brothers undergoing a series of tests to acquire a kingdom and the hand of the princess. The folkloric and philological studies of the Grimm brothers led to their theories that such tales derived from a common body of Indo-European language and mythology. The literary scholar Wilhelm expressed his and Jacob's belief that German and other European fairy tales had their origin in Indo-European mythology, while philologist Jacob developed and established the consonant correspondences between Germanic and other Indo-European languages, the theory that came to be known as Grimm's Law.

Traditional creatures of the imagination appear in the tales as integral participants in the action while

> But you can read the
> Hieroglyphs on the great
> sand-stone obelisks,
> And you have talked with
> Basilisks, and you have
> looked on Hippogriffs.
>
> —Oscar Wilde, *The Sphinx*

303

still retaining ancient characteristics. The fierce unicorn the Little Tailor captures in order to win the King's daughter is the wild beast of ancient authors and
scripture, and the method of capture reiterates the lion and unicorn story in the
fourteenth-century *Letter of Prester John*. In *The Four Accomplished Brothers*, one
of countless dragon-capture tales, the maiden is confined on a rock in the sea,
similar to Andromeda in the Perseus story. Like numerous other figures of
mythology, legend, and folk tale, a prince and princess are transported by a giant
bird. Following a series of adventures involving quests, transformations, love,
loss, and magic spells, the two escape to happiness on the back of a griffin that,
phoenix-like, renews its energy in an Arabian nest. The entries are excerpts from
The Brave Little Tailor, *The Four Accomplished Brothers*, and *The Soaring Lark*.

The Brave Little Tailor and the Unicorn*

. . . Now the Tailor demanded his promised reward of the King; but he repented of
his promise, and began to think of some new scheme to get rid of the hero.
"Before you receive my daughter and the half of my kingdom," said he to him,
"you must perform one other heroic deed. In the forest there runs wild a unicorn,
which commits great havoc, and which you must first of all catch."

"I fear still less for a unicorn than I do for two Giants! Seven at one blow! that
is my motto," said the Tailor. Then he took with him a rope and an axe and went
away to the forest, bidding those who were ordered to accompany him to wait on
the outskirts. He had not to search long, for presently the unicorn came near and
prepared to rush at him as if it would pierce him on the spot. "Softly, softly!" he
exclaimed; "that is not done so easily"; and, waiting till the animal was close
upon him, he sprang nimbly behind a tree. The unicorn, rushing with all its force
against the tree, fixed its horn so fast in the trunk, that it could not draw it out
again, and so it was made prisoner. "Now I have got my bird," said the Tailor; and,
coming from behind the tree, he first bound the rope around its neck, and then,
cutting the horn out of the tree with his axe, he put all in order, and, leading the
animal, brought it before the King.

The King, however, would not yet deliver up the promised reward, and made a
third request, that, before the wedding, the Tailor should catch a wild boar which
did much injury. . . .

The Four Accomplished Brothers and the Dragon

. . . When his sons had done all these wonderful things, the Father said to them,
"Well, you have certainly used your time well, and learned what is very useful,
and for this I must praise you in green clover, as the saying goes; but I cannot tell

* *The Complete Illustrated Stories of the Brothers Grimm* (*Grimm's Household Stories*, 1853; rpt., London: Chancellor Press, 1984), 103–4, 589–91, 692–94, 383.

An 1853 illustration in *The Four Accomplished Brothers and the Dragon*. From *The Complete Illustrated Stories of the Brothers Grimm* (rpt., London: Chancellor Press, 1985).

which of you ought to have the preference, and so that must be left to be seen when an opportunity occurs of displaying your talents publicly."

Not long after this a great lamentation was made in the country because the King's daughter had been carried away by a Dragon. Her father was overcome with grief all day and night long, and caused it to be proclaimed that whoever should rescue the Princess should have her for his wife. The four Brothers thereupon thought this was the opportunity they needed, and agreed to go together and deliver the Princess, and show their talents. "I will soon discover where she is!" cried the Star-gazer, and peeping through his telescope, he said, "I can see her already; she is on a rock in the midst of the sea far away from here, and watched by the Dragon." Then he went to the King, and requested a ship for himself and his Brothers, in which they sailed over the sea till they came near the rock. The Princess observed their arrival, but the Dragon was fast asleep, with his head in her lap. "I dare not shoot!" said the Hunter, when he saw them, "for fear I should kill the Princess as well as the Dragon." "Then I will try my remedy!" said the Thief; and, slipping away, he stole the Princess out of the power of the Dragon, but so lightly and cunningly that the monster noticed nothing, but snored on. Full of joy, they hurried with her down to the ship, and steered away to the open sea; but the Dragon, soon awaking, missed the Princess, and came flying through the air full of rage in pursuit of her. Just as he was hovering above the ship, and was about to alight on it, the Huntsman took aim, fired, and shot the beast through the heart. The Dragon fell, but in his fall he crushed the whole ship to pieces, because of his great size and weight. Luckily they saved a couple of planks, and on these the four Brothers and the Princess floated about. They were now in a great strait, but the Tailor with his wonderful needle sewed together the two planks with great stitches, and then collected the remaining pieces of the ship. These he sewed together so cleverly that in a short time the whole vessel was as tight and complete as before, and they sailed home in her without further accident!

As soon as the King saw his dear daughter again he was very glad and said to the four Brothers, "One of you shall have my daughter to wife, but which you must settle amongst yourselves."

Thereupon a tremendous quarrel took place between them, for each pressed his own claims. The Star-gazer declared that if he had not seen the Princess all their doings would have been of no use, and so she was his. But the Thief exclaimed, "Of what use would your seeing have been if I had not stolen her away from the Dragon? the Princess is mine!" "But you would have been all torn in pieces by the Dragon had not my ball reached his heart!" interrupted the Huntsman; "and so she must be mine." "That is all very fine!" said the Tailor; "but if it had not been for my sewing the ship together again you would have been all drowned! no, the Princess is mine!" When they had all spoken thus, the King decided the question by saying: "You have all an equal claim; but since you cannot all have the Princess, not one of you shall have her, but I will give each of you instead the half of a province as a reward."

The decision pleased the Brothers, who said, "Yes, it will be better so, for then we shall remain united." Thereupon each received half the revenue of a province, as the King said; and in the enjoyment of this they lived happily with their Father to the end of their lives.

The Prince, the Princess, and the Griffin

. . . Then as quickly as possible they both went out of the palace, for they were afraid of the father of the Princess, who was an enchanter. They set themselves upon the griffin, who carried them over the Red Sea, and as soon as they were in the middle of it, the Princess let drop her nut. Thereupon a great nut-tree grew up, whereon the bird rested, and then it carried them straight to their home, where they found their child grown tall and handsome, and with him they ever afterwards lived happily to the end of their lives.

JOHANN WOLFGANG VON GOETHE (1749–1832)
FAUST

After seventeenth-century science separated dubious creatures from actual animals, some of the discredited figures earlier sanctioned by tradition became "mythical." In the "Classical Walpurgis-Night" sequence in Goethe's *Faust*, griffins, gold-digging ants, and the one-eyed Arimaspians (who are here, though, enemies of the ants rather than the griffins) mix with ancient sphinxes, sirens, and other beasts from Greek mythology.

The Classical Walpurgis-Night in the philosophical Part II (1833) of Goethe's poetic drama parallels the folk Witches' Sabbath in the more realistic Part I (1808). In Part I, Faust's pact with Mephistopheles in exchange for ultimate knowledge leads the Renaissance scholar to passion and depravity, climaxing with a satanic orgy on a mountain peak. Part I ends with the death and salvation of Margaret, the village girl Faust destroyed. In Part II, Mephistopheles and Faust are transported from the North to the Grecian plain of Pharsalia through the agency of the tiny being Homunculus. Faust is now in quest of ideal beauty, embodied in Helen of Troy. Disguised as the ugly Phorcys, sire of the brood of Gorgons, Scylla, and other monsters, Mephistopheles is the first of the two to come upon a group of mythological beasts.

Ill at ease in the formidable company, the Devil puns with the snarling and ironic griffins, who play etymologically with their name. The wise and riddling Sphinx matches wits with him. After Sirens arrive, Faust approaches, looking for Trojan Helen, and is immediately awed by the ancient ones. The Stymphalian birds, disembodied heads of the Hydra of Lerna, and the Lamia all join the pageant, which later moves to the sea and grows even greater with Nereids, Tritons, sea-horses and sea-dragons. The company eventually halts before the palace of Menelaus in Sparta, and Helen appears.

The legend of Dr. Faustus engaged Goethe throughout his lifetime. The first part of his dramatic poem appeared nearly twenty years after an early fragment on the theme. Part II, completed a year before his death, was published posthumously. Although the celebrated work contains both neoclassical and romantic elements and is difficult to categorize, it dramatizes the romantic striving to attain the unreachable. The Classical Walpurgis-Night has been said to represent the aesthetic and historical dimensions of the soul's journey. Goethe's granting of redemption to Faust departed from the tradition and has remained controversial since the publication of the book.

For classical monsters, see Homer and Hesiod. For giant ants, griffins, and Arimaspians, see Herodotus. For the Stymphalides, see Pausanias. For another collection of nightmarish beasts, see Flaubert.

The Beasts of Walpurgis-Night *

MEPHISTOPHELES (*prying around*).
And as among these fires I wander, aimless,
I find myself so strange, so disconcerted:

* Johann Wolfgang von Goethe. *Faust: A Tragedy*, trans. Bayard Taylor (1870; rpt. New York: Modern Library, 1950), part 2, pp. 84–87, 88–91.

Quite naked most, a few are only shirted;
The Griffins insolent, the Sphinxes shameless,
And what not all, with pinions and with tresses,
Before, behind, upon one's eyesight presses!—
Indecency, 't is true, is our ideal,
But the Antique is too alive and real;
One must with modern thought the thing bemaster,
And in the fashion variously o'erplaster:—
Disgusting race! Yet I, perforce, must meet them,
And as new guest with due decorum greet them.—
Hail, then, Fair Ladies! Graybeards wise, good cheer.

GRIFFIN (*snarling*).
Not graybeards! Graybeards? No one likes to hear
One call him *gray*. For in each word there rings
The source, wherefrom its derivation springs.
Gray, growling, grewsome, grinning, graves, and grimly
Etymologically accord, nor dimly,
And make us grim.

MEPHISTOPHELES.
And yet, why need you stiffen?
You like the *grif* in your proud title, "Griffin."

GRIFFIN.
(*as above, and continuously so*).
Of course! for this relation is found fit;
Though often censured, oftener praised was it.
Let one but *grip* at maidens, crowns, and gold:
Fortune is gracious to the Griper bold.

ANTS.
(*of the colossal kind*).
You speak of gold, much had ourselves collected;
In rocks and caverns secretly we trapped it:
The Arimaspean race our store detected,—
They're laughing now, so far away they've snapped it.

THE GRIFFINS.
We soon shall force them to confess.

THE ARIMASPEANS.
But not in this free night of jubilee.
Before the morrow all will squandered be;
This time our efforts will obtain success.

MEPHISTOPHELES.
(*who has seated himself between the* SPHINXES).
How soon I feel familiar here, among you!
I understand you, one and all.

SPHINX.
Our spirit-tones, when we have sung you,
Become, for you, material.
Now name thyself, till we shall know thee better.

MEPHISTOPHELES.
With many names would men my nature fetter.
Are Britons here? So round the world they wheel
To stare at battle-fields, historic traces,
Cascades, old walls, and classic dreary places;
And here were something worthy of their zeal.
Their Old Plays also testify of me;
Men saw me there as "Old Iniquity."

SPHINX.
How did they hit on that?

MEPHISTOPHELES.
I know not, verily.

SPHINX.
Perhaps! Hast thou in star-lore any power?
What say'st thou of the aspects of the hour?

MEPHISTOPHELES (*looking up*).
Star shoots on star, the cloven moon doth ride
In brilliance; in this place I'm satisfied:
I warm myself against thy lion's hide.
It were a loss to rise from out these shades:—
Propose enigmas, or at least charades!

SPHINX.
Express thyself, and 't will a riddle be.
Try once thine own analysis: 't were merry.
"To both Devout and Wicked necessary:
To those, a breast-plate for ascetic fighting;
To these, boon-comrade, in their pranks uniting;
And both amusing Zeus, the fun-delighting."

FIRST GRIFFIN (*snarling*).
I like not him!

SECOND GRIFFIN (*snarling more gruffly*).
What will the fellow here?

BOTH.
The Nasty One is not of us, 't is clear!

MEPHISTOPHELES (*brutally*).
Think'st thou, perhaps, thy guest has nails to scratch,
That with thy sharper talons cannot match?
Just try it once!

SPHINX (*gently*).
Stay, shouldst thou find it well;
But from our ranks thou wilt thyself expel.
In thine own land thou'rt wont thyself to pamper,
Yet here, I think, thy spirits feel a damper.

MEPHISTOPHELES.
Thine upper part entices; naught is fairer;
But, further down, the beast excites my terror.

SPHINX.
Bitter, False one, will be thy expiation;
Our claws are sound and worthy proof,
But thou with withered horse's-hoof,
Art ill at ease in our association

.　.　.

FAUST (*approaching*).
How strange! I, satisfied, behold these creatures,—
In the Repulsive, grand and solid features:
A fate propitious I behold advance.
Whither transports me now this solemn glance?
　　(*Pointing to the* SPHINXES.)
Once before these took Oedipus his stand:
　　(*Pointing to the* SIRENS.)
These made Ulysses write in hempen band:
　　(*Pointing to the* ANTS.)
By these the highest treasure was amassed:
　　(*Pointing to the* GRIFFINS.)
By these 't was held inviolate and fast:
Fresh spirit fills me, face to face with these—
Grand are the Forms, and grand the Memories!

MEPHISTOPHELES.
Once thou hadst cursed such crude antiques,
But now, it seems, they've comfort given;
For when a man his sweetheart seeks,
Welcome to him are monsters, even.

FAUST (*to the* SPHINXES).
Ye woman-forms, give ear, and say
Hath one of you seen Helena?

SPHINXES.
Before her day our line expired in Greece;
Our very last was slain by Hercules:
Yet ask of Chiron, if thou please.
He gallops round throughout this ghostly night,
And if he halt for thee, thy chance is bright.

SIRENS.
Thou art not to failure fated!
How Ulysses, lingering, learned us,
Nor, regardless passing, spurned us,
Manifold hath he narrated:
All to thee shall be confided,
Seekest thou our meads, divided
By the dark-green arms of Ocean.

SPHINX.
Let not thyself thus cheated be!
Not like Ulysses bound,— but we
Will with good counsel thee environ.
If thou canst find the noble Chiron,
Thou'lt learn what I have promised thee.
    [FAUST *goes away*.]

MEPHISTOPHELES (*ill-temperedly*).
What croaks and flaps of wings go past!
One cannot see, they fly so fast,
In single file, from first to last:
A hunter would grow tired of these.

SPHINX.
The storm-wind like, that winter harrows,
Reached hardly by Aleides' arrows,
They are the swift Stymphalides;
And not ill-meant their greetings creak,

With goose's foot and vulture's beak.
They fain would join us in our places,
And show themselves as kindred races.

MEPHISTOPHELES (*as if intimidated*).
Some other brute is hissing shrill.

SPHINX.
Be not afraid, though harsh the paean!
They are the hydra-heads, the old Lernaen,
Cut from the trunk, yet think they're something still.
But say, what means your air distressed?
Why show your gestures such unrest?
Where will you go? Then take your leave!
That chorus, there, I now perceive,
Turns like a weathercock your neck. Advance!—
Greet as you will each lovely countenance!
They are the Lamiae, wenches vile,
With brazen brows and lips that smile,
Such as the satyr-folk have found so fair:
A cloven foot may venture all things there.

MEPHISTOPHELES.
But stay you here, that I again may find you?

SPHINX.
Yes! Join the airy rabble there behind you!
From Egypt we, long since, with all our peers,
Accustomed were to reign a thousand years.
If for our place your reverence be won,
We rule for you the days of Moon and Sun.
    We sit before the Pyramids
    For the judgment of the Races,
    Inundation, War, and Peace,—
    With eternal changeless faces.

THOMAS BULFINCH (1796–1867)
THE AGE OF FABLE

Creatures rejected as fabulous during the seventeenth century received little literary attention for nearly two hundred years. One of the earliest modern treat-

ments of these discredited beasts as a subject in themselves is the "Modern Monsters" chapter of Thomas Bulfinch's popular retelling of classical and Scandinavian myths, *The Age of Fable* (1855). Handbooks of heraldry, such as John
Guillim's *Display of Heraldry*, had included the griffin, dragon, and other "monsters" in sections by themselves, but these creatures were distinguished from other
animals because they were considered freaks of nature, not because they did not
exist. Like the early heraldic writers, Bulfinch, too, regards them as monsters, but
monsters of fable, as the title of his book indicates.

In his introduction to the chapter, Bulfinch carefully separates this group of
fantastic beasts from the figures of classical mythology. He defines the phoenix,
basilisk, unicorn, and salamander as animals not associated with ancient deities
nor with mythological poetry, but made popular through prose since the beginning of the Christian era. This is a basic distinction between two kinds of imaginary animals.

Like the Renaissance writers, Bulfinch reviews authorities, but unlike most of
them, he writes outside the context of belief. Also, he cites far more poets than
earlier authors did. While somewhat condescending in tone, his small treatises
are essentially literary surveys of given beasts, similar in approach to later studies.

The chapter introduction, "Modern Monsters," is complete below. The
phoenix section is reprinted intact except for the quoted passages from Ovid,
Tacitus, and Milton, which can be found elsewhere in this anthology. The other
entries are excerpted explanations of the fables.

Thomas Bulfinch was an American teacher and accountant who retold classical myths and medieval legends for a general audience unable to read Greek or
Latin and desiring less than translations of full works.

Modern Monsters *

There is a set of imaginary beings which seems to have been the successors of the
"Gorgons, Hydras, and Chimeras dire" of the old superstitions, and having no
connection with the false gods of Paganism, to have continued to enjoy an existence in the popular belief after Paganism was superseded by Christianity. They
are mentioned perhaps by the classical writers, but their chief popularity and cur-
rency seem to have been in more modern times. We seek our accounts of them
not so much in the poetry of the ancients as in the old natural history books and
narrations of travellers. The accounts which we are about to give are taken
chiefly from the Penny Cyclopedia.

---

* *Bulfinch's Mythology* (New York: Modern Library, n.d.), 248–53.

The Phoenix

Ovid tells the story of the Phoenix as follows: "Most beings spring from other individuals; but there is a certain kind which reproduces itself. The Assyrians call it the Phoenix. . . ."

Such is the account given by a poet. Now let us see that of a philosophic historian. Tacitus says, "in the consulship of Paulus Fabius (A.D. 34) the miraculous bird known to the world by the name of the Phoenix, after disappearing for a series of ages, revisited Egypt. . . ." Other writers add a few particulars. The myrrh is compacted in the form of an egg, in which the dead Phoenix is enclosed. From the mouldering flesh of the dead bird a worm springs, and this worm, when grown large, is transformed into a bird. Herodotus *describes* the bird, though he says, "I have not seen it myself, except in a picture. Part of his plumage is gold-coloured, and part crimson; and he is for the most part very much like an eagle in outline and bulk."

The first writer who disclaimed a belief in the existence of the Phoenix was Sir Thomas Browne, in his "Vulgar Errors," published in 1646. He was replied to a few years later by Alexander Ross, who says, in answer to the objection of the Phoenix so seldom making his appearance, "His instinct teaches him to keep out of the way of the tyrant of the creation, *man*, for if he were to be got at, some wealthy glutton would surely devour him, though there were no more in the world."

Dryden in one of his early poems has this allusion to the Phoenix:

> "So when the new-born Phoenix first is seen
> Her feathered subjects all adore their queen,
> And while she makes her progress through the East,
> From every grove her numerous train 's increased;
> Each poet of the air her glory sings,
> And round him the pleased audience clap their wings."

Milton, in "Paradise Lost," Book V, compares the angel Raphael descending to earth to a Phoenix:

> ". . . Down thither, prone in flight
> He speeds. . . ."

The Cockatrice, or Basilisk

. . . The reader will, we apprehend, by this time have had enough of absurdities, but still we can imagine his anxiety to know what a cockatrice was like. The following is from Aldrovandus, a celebrated naturalist of the sixteenth century, whose work on natural history, in thirteen folio volumes, contains with much that is valuable a large proportion of fables and inutilities. In particular he is so ample on the subject of the cock and the bull that from his practice, all rambling, gossiping tales of doubtful credibility are called *cock and bull stories*. . . .

The Unicorn

. . . Modern zoologists, disgusted as they well may be with such fables as these, disbelieved generally the existence of the unicorn. Yet there are animals bearing on their heads a bony protuberance more or less like a horn, which may have given rise to the story. The rhinoceros horn, as it is called, is such a protuberance, though it does not exceed a few inches in height, and is far from agreeing with the descriptions of the horn of the unicorn. The nearest approach to a horn in the middle of the forehead is exhibited in the bony protuberance on the forehead of the giraffe but this also is short and blunt, and is not the only horn of the animal, but a third horn, standing in front of the two others. In fine, though it would be presumptuous to deny the existence of a one-horned quadruped other than the rhinoceros, it may be safely stated that the insertion of a long and solid horn in the living forehead of a horse-like or deer-like animal is as near an impossibility as anything can be.

The Salamander

. . . The foundation of the above fables is supposed to be the fact that the salamander really does secrete from the pores of his body a milky juice, which when he is irritated is produced in considerable quantity, and would doubtless, for a few moments, defend the body from fire. Then it is a hibernating animal, and in winter retires to some hollow tree or other cavity, where it coils itself up and remains in a torpid state till the spring again calls it forth. It may therefore sometimes be carried with the fuel to the fire, and wake up only time enough to put forth all its faculties for its defence. Its viscous juice would do good service, and all who profess to have seen it, acknowledge that it got out of the fire as fast as its legs could carry it; indeed, too fast for them ever to make prize of one, except in one instance, and in that one the animal's feet and some parts of its body were badly burned. . . .

W. Winwood Reade (1838–1875)
Savage Africa

"Is it not possible that some of those accounts which we still regard as fabulous may yet be cited against us by another generation?" Winwood Reade asks in his *Savage Africa* (1864). The explorer devotes an entire chapter of his book to reassessing traditional animal lore in light of contemporary discoveries. He proposes actual prototypes for fabled wonder people, mermaids, winged dragons, and others, and cites the famous fossilized Aepyornis egg as evidence for the roc; he also reviews both traditional and contemporary accounts of the unicorn to suggest that a single-horned quadruped other than the rhinoceros actually did exist in Africa. Omitted here is Reade's quotation of Ludovico de Varthema's description of unicorns in the Temple of Mecca, a passage reprinted elsewhere in this collection.

Three years before publication of Reade's book, Philip Henry Gosse reviewed African "unicorn" sightings in his *Romance of Natural History*. Reports of African unicorns continued to multiply, given possible credence by Dr. W. Franklin Dove's 1933 artificial unicornization of a day-old calf.

Monsters and Fabulous Animals of Africa*

It must be laid down as a certain principle that man can originate nothing; that lies are always truths embellished, distorted, or turned inside out. There are other facts beside those which lie on the surface, and it is the duty of the traveler and historian to sift and wash the gold-grains of truth from the dirt of fable.

It was a saying of the ancients that Africa is always affording something new. As in the days of Pliny and Herodotus, so now it still remains *par excellence* the land of mystery and romance. It is true that some of the ancient myths have been sobered down to natural beings. The men with dogs' heads, of whom Herodotus speaks, are the barking baboons which I saw in the Senegal; the men with their heads under their shoulders, their eyes in their breast, are the ill-formed negroes, whose shoulders are shrugged up, and whose heads drop on their breasts; the mermaids of the Arab tales are the sea-cows of the African rivers, which have feminine dugs, and a face almost human in expression; the huge serpent which opposed the army of Regulus is now well known as the python; the burning mountains which Hanno saw, and the sounds as of lutes which were believed to proceed from the strife of the elements, are only caused by the poor negroes burn-

---

* W. Winwood Reade, *Savage Africa: Being the Narrative of a Tour in Equatorial, Southwestern, and Northwestern Africa* (New York: Harper and Brothers, 1864), 369–75.

ing the grass on their hill-tops; the music being that of their flutes, as I have heard it often in those long and silent African nights far away.

But those who have studied African literature must confess that we know little more respecting the natural productions of this country than the ancients did. Many of the stories of Herodotus, which in the last century were ridiculed as absurd, have been endorsed by the experience of recent travelers. Is it not possible that some of those accounts which we still regard as fabulous may yet be cited against us by another generation?

Incredulity has now become so vulgar a folly, that one is almost tempted, out of simple hatred for a fashion, to run into the opposite extreme. However, I shall content myself with citing evidence respecting certain unknown, fabulous, and monstrous animals of Africa, without committing myself to an opinion one way or the other, preserving only my conviction that there is always a basis of truth to the most fantastic fables, and that, by rejecting without inquiry that which appears incredible, one throws away ore in which others might have found a jewel. A traveler should believe nothing, for he will find himself so often deceived; and he should disbelieve nothing, for he will see so many wonderful things: he should doubt; he should investigate; and then he may perhaps discover. . . .

The existence of the *roc* of Marco Polo and the "Arabian Nights" is now proved by the discovery of an immense egg in a semi-fossil state in Madagascar. . . .

Of all the animals which have been classed as fabulous, the unicorn is the most remarkable, since to this very day it is impossible for a careful writer to make a positive assertion respecting its existence.

The ancients compared their *monoceros* to a horse with a stag's head, which proves that they had seen an animal very different from the rhinoceros. They also distinctly name the *unicorn-ass*, an animal of great size, swift of foot, solitary in his habits, and having a horn striped with white, black, and brown.

Garcias, a writer of the sixteenth century, relates that the Portuguese navigators saw, between the Cape of Good Hope and Cape Corrientes, an animal having the head and mane of a horse, with one movable horn. In this same region Sparmann and Barrow saw representations of a one-horned animal. The rocks of Camdebo and Bambo are covered with them — a curious fact, setting zoology aside; for it proves the ancient connection of Caffraria with Asia; the unicorn, among the Persians and Hebrews, being the symbol of kingly power. It is with this meaning delineated on the monuments of Persepolis, and on the royal arms of great Britain.

The Dutch colonists also, according to Voight, affirmed that they had seen these animals alive, and that they resembled the quagga, while the horn adhered only to the skin.

According to Merolla, the real unicorn is extinct; though I shall quote better authority to prove that it is living than that upon which he makes his assertion. "Here," he says, writing of Angola, "is also the unicorn, called by the Congolans *abada*, whose medicinal virtue, being sufficiently known, needs not to be taken notice of. These unicorns are very different from those commonly mentioned by authors; and, if you will believe what I have heard say, there are none of that sort now to be found. . . ."

In the fifteenth century, Barthema, or Verdomanus, who preceded Burckhardt and Burton in a pilgrimage to Mecca, gives a minute account of two unicorns which he saw there. . . .

The next authority is that of a Portuguese who had lived some time in Abyssinia, and is quoted by Father Tellez.

"It is certain that the unicorn is not to be confounded with the *abada*, about which they usually dispute; this one may see by the difference of their names, as well as by the difference of their body and parts, and it would appear by the *abada* which we have seen, and by the unicorn which we have seen painted. The latter has a long straight horn of admirable virtue; the *abada* has two crooked horns, which are not so sovereign, although they will serve as antidotes against poison. The country of the unicorn, which is an animal of Africa, where only it is known, is the province of Agoa, in the kingdom of Damotes, although it is occasionally seen in more distant places. This animal is as large as a fine horse, is a dark bay color, the mane and tail black, short, and thin though in other parts of the province observed to be longer and thicker. On the forehead there is a beautiful horn five palms long, as they are usually painted, the color being nearly white. They live in woods and retired thickets, sometimes coming out into the plains, where they are not often seen, because they are timid animals, not numerous, and easily hidden in the wood. . . ."

The latest traveler who has spoken of the unicorn is Dr. Baikie, who, when I was in Africa, had started on an incursion after this animal, the existence of which he must therefore have credited, and could only have done so upon reliable authority. That such an animal has existed, there can, I think, be little doubt; it is possible that he is extinct; but more probable that, flying from firearms (which, it must always be remembered, are used by tribes whom white men have never visited), he has concealed himself in those vast forest-wastes of Central Africa which are uninhabited and unexplored.

J. G. WOOD (1827–1889)
BIBLE ANIMALS

Biblical authority was the major force that developed and maintained Western belief in certain animals from the beginnings of Christianity up to the seventeenth century. The Septuagint, the Vulgate, the Church Fathers, bestiaries, and the King James translation all helped establish the unicorn, cockatrice (basilisk), and others as part of the animal kingdom. In his *Bible Animals* (1870), the Rev. J. G. Wood scornfully attributes the biblical unicorn and cockatrice to earlier ages' lack of scientific knowledge and the fanciful theories of the "old writers" that served as natural history.

The compiler of "ludicrous tales" that Wood cites most frequently is Edward Topsell. Regardless of his own rationalistic approach, Wood enjoys telling the old stories. The exaggerations he accuses the Talmudic writers of indulging in when they describe animals with which they are unfamiliar could stand as one explanation of the creation of fabulous beasts in general.

Wood was the author of many works of popular natural history.

The Biblical "Unicorn" *

There are many animals mentioned in the Scriptures which cannot be identified with any certainty, partly because their names occur only once or twice in the sacred writings, and partly because, when they are mentioned, the context affords no clue to their identity by giving any hint as to their appearance or habits. In such cases, although the translators would have done better if they had simply given the Hebrew word without endeavouring to identify it with any known animal, they may be excused for committing errors in their nomenclature. There is one animal, however, for which no such excuse can be found, and this is the Reêm of Scripture, translated as Unicorn in the authorized version.

Now the word Reêm is mentioned seven times in the Old Testament, and is found, not in one, but several books, showing that it was an animal perfectly well known to those for whom the sacred books were written. It is twice mentioned in the Pentateuch, several times in the Psalms, once in the book of Job, once by Isaiah, and reference is once made to it in the historical books. In these various passages, abundant details are given of its aspect and habits, so that there is very little doubt as to the identity of the animal.

The Septuagint translates Reêm by the word Monoceros, or the One-horned, which has been transferred to the Vulgate by the term Unicornis, a word having the same signification.

In an age when scientific investigation was utterly neglected, such a translation would readily be accepted without cavil, and there is no doubt that the generality of those who read the passages in question accepted them as referring to the Unicorn of heraldry with which we, as Englishmen, are so familiar. I may per-

*   J. G. Wood, *Bible Animals; Being a Description of Every Living Creature Mentioned in the Scriptures from the Ape to the Coral* (New York: Charles Scribner, 1870), 121–30, 554–57.

haps mention briefly that such an animal is a physiological impossibility, and that the Unicorn of the fables was a mere compound of an antelope, a horse, and a narwhal. The tusks or teeth of the narwhal were in former days exhibited as horns of the Unicorn, and so precious were they that one of them was laid up in the cathedral of St. Denis, and two in the treasury of St. Mark's at Venice, all of which were exhibited in the year 1658 as veritable Unicorns' horns.

The physiological difficulty above mentioned seems to have troubled the minds of the old writers, who saw that an ivory horn had no business to grow upon the junction of the two bones of the skull, and yet felt themselves bound to acknowledge that such an animal did really exist. They therefore put themselves to vast trouble in accounting for such a phenomenon, and, in their determination to believe in the animal, invented theories nearly as wonderful as the existence of the Unicorn itself. . . .

In late years, after the true origin of the Unicorn's horn was discovered, and the belief in its many virtues abandoned, the Reêm, or Monoceros, was almost unhesitatingly identified with the rhinoceros of India, and for a long time this theory was the accepted one. It is now, however, certain that the Reêm was not the rhinoceros, and that it can be almost certainly identified with an animal which, at the time when the passages in question were written, was plentiful in Palestine, although, like the lion, it is now extinct. . . .

On turning to the Jewish Bible we find that the word Reêm is translated as buffalo, and there is no doubt that this rendering is nearly the correct one, and at the present day naturalists are nearly all agreed that the Reêm of the Old Testament must have been the now extinct Urus. A smaller animal, the Bonassus or Bison, also existed in Palestine, and even to the present day continues to maintain itself in one or two spots, though it will probably be as soon completely erased from the surface of the earth as its gigantic congener. . . .

A curious rabbinical legend of the Reêm is given in Lewysohn's "Zoologie des Talmus." When the ark was complete, and all the beasts were commanded to enter, the Reêm was unable to do so, because it was too large to pass through the door. Noah and his sons therefore were obliged to tie the animal by a rope to the ark, and to tow it behind; and, in order to prevent it from being strangled, they tied the rope, not round its neck, but to its horn.

The same writer very justly remarks that the Scriptural and Talmudical accounts of the Reêm have one decided distinction. The Scripture speaks chiefly of its fierceness, its untameable nature, its strength, and its swiftness, as its principal characteristics, while the Talmud speaks almost exclusively of its size. It was evidently the largest animal of which the writers had ever heard, and, according to Oriental wont, they exaggerated it preposterously. Whenever the Talmudical writers treat of animals with which they are personally acquainted, they are simple, straightforward, and accurate. But, as soon as they come to animals unknown to them except by hearsay, they go off into the wildest extravagances, such, for example, as asserting that the leopard is a hybrid between the wild boar and the lioness. The exaggerated statements concerning the Reêm show therefore that the animal must have been extinct long before the time of the writers.

The Biblical "Cockatrice"

Another name of a poisonous snake occurs several times in the Old Testament. The word is *tsepha*, or *tsiphôni*, and it is sometimes translated as Adder, and sometimes as Cockatrice. The word is rendered as Adder in Prov. xxiii.32, where it is said that wine "biteth like a serpent, and stingeth like an adder." Even in this case, however, the word is rendered as Cockatrice in the marginal translation. . . .

As to the old ideas respecting the origin of the Cockatrice, a very few words will suffice for them. This serpent was thought to be produced from an egg laid by a cock and hatched by a viper. "For they say," writes Topsel, "that when a cock groweth old, he layeth a certain egge without any shell. . . ."

In this curious history it is easy to see the origin of the notion respecting the birth of the Cockatrice. It is well known that hens, after they have reached an advanced age, assume much of the plumage and voice of the male bird. Still, that one of them should occasionally lay an egg is no great matter of wonder, and as the egg would be naturally deposited in a retired and sheltered spot, such as would be the favoured haunts of the warmth-loving snake, the ignorant public might easily put together a legend which, absurd in itself, is yet founded on facts. The small shell-less egg, so often laid by poultry, is familiar to every one who has kept fowls.

Around this reptile a wonderful variety of legends have been accumulated. The Cockatrice was said to kill by its very look, "because the beams of the Cockatrice's eyes do corrupt the visible spirit of a man, which visible spirit corrupted all the other spirits coming from the brain and life of the heart, are thereby corrupted, and so the man dyeth."

The subtle poison of the Cockatrice infected everything near it, so that a man who killed a Cockatrice with a spear fell dead himself, by reason of the poison darting up the shaft of the spear and passing into his hand. Any living thing near which the Cockatrice passed was instantly slain by the fiery heat of its venom, which was exhaled not only from its mouth, but its sides. For the old writers, whose statements are here summarized, contrived to jumble together a number of miscellaneous facts in natural history, and so to produce a most extraordinary series of legends. We have already seen the real origin of the legend respecting the egg from which the cockatrice was supposed to spring, and we may here see that some one of these old writers has in his mind some uncertain floating idea of the respiratory orifices of the lamprey, and has engrafted them on the Cockatrice.

"To conclude," writes Topsel, "this poyson infecteth the air, and the air so infected killeth all living things. . . ."

I should not have given even this limited space to such puerile legends, but for the fact that such stories as these were fully believed in the days when the Authorized Version of the Bible was translated. The ludicrous tales which have been occasionally mentioned formed the staple of zoological knowledge, and an untravelled Englishman had no possible means of learning the history of foreign animals, except from such books which have been quoted, and which were in those days the standard works on Natural History. The translators of the Bible believed most heartily in the mysterious and baleful reptile, and, as they saw that the Tsepha of Scripture was an exceptionally venomous serpent, they naturally rendered it by the word Cockatrice.

LEWIS CARROLL (1832–1898)
ALICE'S ADVENTURES IN WONDERLAND,
THROUGH THE LOOKING-GLASS

The griffin and the unicorn reappear in surprising new forms in the classic nonsense fantasies of Lewis Carroll (Charles Lutwidge Dodgson). While both creatures retain some of their traditional characteristics, Carroll reshapes them into original, eccentric creations, their characters played off against their cultural pasts.

In *Alice's Adventures in Wonderland* (1865), the Gryphon is introduced as a slumbering figure rudely awakened by the Queen. The hybrid beast's first words, appropriately spoken "half to itself, half to Alice," are comically out of traditional character, but fitting for the wild figure that soon after creates the "Lobster-Quadrille" with the Mock Turtle. Carroll's authorial direction to look at the accompanying illustration originally referred to his own pen and ink drawing in *Alice's Adventures Under Ground*, a manuscript gift he prepared in 1863 for the real-life prototype of his heroine. The most widely known rendering of Carroll's Gryphon is that of John Tenniel, illustrator of the first printed edition of the book.

Alice has further fantastic adventures in *Through the Looking-Glass* (1872), in which she comes upon the Lion and the Unicorn "fighting for the crown" and she and the Unicorn differ on what constitutes a fabulous monster. The enmity between the lion and the unicorn was recounted as early as the fourteenth-century *Letter of Prester John* and became widely known through the traditional rhyme alluding to the English lion and the Scottish unicorn. The two beasts are the heraldic supporters of the royal arms of Great Britain. Earlier in the chapter, Alice sings the rhyme upon which Carroll bases his comic skirmish between his animal antagonists:

John Tenniel's Gryphon from *Alice's Adventures in Wonderland.*

> The Lion and the Unicorn were fighting for the crown:
> The Lion beat the Unicorn all round the town.
> Some gave them white bread, some gave them brown:
> Some gave them plum-cake and drummed them out of town.

Alice and the Gryphon *

They very soon came upon a Gryphon, lying fast asleep in the sun. (If you don't know what a Gryphon is, look at the picture.) "Up, lazy thing!" said the Queen, "and take this young lady to see the Mock Turtle, and to hear his history. I must go back and see after some executions I have ordered"; and she walked off, leaving Alice alone with the Gryphon. Alice did not quite like the look of the creature, but on the whole she thought it would be quite as safe to stay with it as to go after that savage Queen; so she waited.

The Gryphon sat up and rubbed its eyes; then it watched the Queen till she was out of sight; then it chuckled. "What fun!" said the Gryphon, half to itself, half to Alice.

"What *is* the fun?" said Alice.

"Why, *she*," said the Gryphon. "It's all her fancy, that; they never executes nobody, you know. Come on!"

* Lewis Carroll, *Alice's Adventures in Wonderland* (rpt. New York: Random House, 1946), 109–10, 116–18; *Through the Looking-Glass* (rpt., New York: Random House, 1946), 112–15.

"Everybody says 'come on!' here," thought Alice, as she went slowly after it: "I never was so ordered about before, in all my life, never!"

The Gryphon and the Mock Turtle

The Mock Turtle sighed deeply, and drew the back of one flapper across his eyes. He looked at Alice and tried to speak, but, for a minute or two, sobs choked his voice. "Same as if he had a bone in his throat," said the Gryphon; and it set to work shaking him and punching him in the back. At last the Mock Turtle recovered his voice, and, with tears running down his cheeks, he went on again:—

"You may not have lived much under the sea —" ("I haven't," said Alice)— "and perhaps you were never even introduced to a lobster —" (Alice began to say "I once tasted —" but checked herself hastily, and said "No, never") "— so you can have no idea what a delightful thing a Lobster-Quadrille is!"

"No, indeed," said Alice. "What sort of a dance is it?"

"Why," said the Gryphon, "you first form into a line along the sea-shore ——"

"Two lines!" cried the Mock Turtle. "Seals, turtles, salmon, and so on: then, when you've cleared all the jelly-fish out of the way ——"

"*That* generally takes some time," interrupted the Gryphon.

"— you advance twice ——"

"Each with a lobster as a partner!" cried the Gryphon.

"Of course," the Mock Turtle said: "advance twice, set to partners —"

"— change lobsters, and retire in same order," continued the Gryphon.

"Then, you know," the Mock Turtle went on, "you throw the ——"

"The lobsters!" shouted the Gryphon, with a bound into the air.

"— as far out to sea as you can ——"

"Swim after them!" screamed the Gryphon.

"Turn a somersault in the sea!" cried the Mock Turtle, capering wildly about.

"Change lobsters again!" yelled the Gryphon at the top of its voice.

"Back to land again, and — that's all the first figure," said the Mock Turtle, suddenly dropping his voice; and the two creatures, who had been jumping about like mad things all this time, sat down again very sadly and quietly, and looked at Alice.

The Lion and the Unicorn

At this moment the Unicorn sauntered by them, with his hands in his pockets. "I had the best of it this time?" he said to the King, just glancing at him as he passed.

"A little — a little," the King replied, rather nervously. "You shouldn't have run him through with your horn, you know."

Lewis Carroll's own drawing of the Gryphon and the Mock Turtle dancing the Lobster-Quadrille, from *Alice's Adventures Under Ground*. Courtesy of Dover Publications.

John Tenniel's Lion and the Unicorn from *Through the Looking-Glass*.

"It didn't hurt him," the Unicorn said carelessly, and he was going on, when his eye happened to fall upon Alice: he turned round instantly, and stood for some time looking at her with an air of the deepest disgust.

"What — is — this?" he said at last.

"This is a child!" Haigha replied eagerly, coming in front of Alice to introduce her, and spreading out both his hands towards her in an Anglo-Saxon attitude. "We only found it to-day. It's as large as life, and twice as natural!"

"I always thought they were fabulous monsters!" said the Unicorn. "Is it alive?"

"It can talk," said Haigha solemnly.

The Unicorn looked dreamily at Alice, and said "Talk, child."

Alice could not help her lips curling up into a smile as she began: "Do you know, I always thought Unicorns were fabulous monsters, too? I never saw one alive before!"

"Well, now that we *have* seen each other," said the Unicorn, "if you'll believe in me, I'll believe in you. Is that a bargain?"

"Yes, if you like," said Alice.

"Come, fetch out the plum-cake, old man!" the Unicorn went on, turning from her to the King. "None of your brown bread for me!"

"Certainly — certainly!" the King muttered, and beckoned to Haigha. "Open the bag!" he whispered. "Quick! Not that one — that's full of hay!"

Haigha took a large cake out of the bag, and gave it to Alice to hold, while he got out a dish and carving-knife. How they all came out of it Alice couldn't guess. It was just like a conjuring-trick, she thought.

The Lion had joined them while this was going on: he looked very tired and sleepy, and his eyes were half shut. "What's this?" he said, blinking lazily at Alice, and speaking in a deep hollow tone that sounded like the tolling of a great bell.

"Ah, what *is* it, now?" the Unicorn cried eagerly. "You'll never guess! *I* couldn't."

The Lion looked at Alice wearily. "Are you animal — or vegetable — or mineral?" he said, yawning at every other word.

"It's a fabulous monster!" the Unicorn cried out, before Alice could reply.

"Then hand round the plum-cake, Monster," the Lion said, lying down and putting his chin on his paws. "And sit down, both of you," (to the King and the Unicorn): "fair play with the cake, you know!"

The King was evidently very uncomfortable at having to sit down between the two great creatures; but there was no other place for him.

Gustav Flaubert (1821–1880)
The Temptation of Saint Anthony

Fabulous animals, mythological beasts, and the monstrous races all pass through the vision of St. Anthony in a highly colored poetic novel by an author best known for his naturalistic fiction. Conceived as "the French *Faust*," Flaubert's *La Tentation de Saint Antoine* (1872) developed over a thirty-five-year period that encompassed most of his major work, including *Madame Bovary*. The translator, author Lafcadio Hearn, describes the climactic "Walpurgis-Night" in his introductory "Argument":

> Anthony in reveries meditates upon the monstrous symbols painted upon the walls of certain ancient temples. Could he know their meaning he might learn also something of the secret lien between Matter and Thought. Forthwith a phantasmagoria of monsters commence to pass before his eyes:—the Sphinx and the Chimera, the Blemmyes and Astomi, the Cynocephali and all creatures of mythologic creation. He beholds the fabulous beings of Oriental imagining,—the abnormities described by Pliny and Herodotus, the fantasticalities to be later adopted by heraldry,—the grotesqueries of future medieval illumination made animate;—the goblinries and foulnesses of superstitious fancy,—the Witches' Sabbath of abominations.

The excerpt below begins with the appearance of a fantastic stag — following the Sphinx and Chimera and monstrous people — and rises to a surreal frenzy of forms. Later, after the arrival and departure of the unicorn, St. Anthony beholds birds and sea creatures and experiences the mystical intermingling of all nature. When the vision fades with sunrise, the saint sees the face of Christ.

For another phantasmagoria of monsters, see Goethe.

Martin Schongauer's engraving of *The Temptation of St. Anthony* (c. 1480–90). A popular subject in Renaissance art. By permission of the Metropolitan Museum of Art, New York.

The Monsters of Saint Anthony*

(Anthony inhales the freshness of the green leaves. There is a movement among them, a clashing of branches; and all of a sudden appears a huge black stag, with the head of a bull, having between his ears a thicket of white horns.)

THE SADHUZAG

"My seventy-four antlers are hollow like flutes.

"When I turn me toward the wind of the South, there issue from them sounds that draw all the ravished animals around me. The serpents twine about my legs; the wasps cluster in my nostrils; and the parrots, the doves, the ibises, alight upon the branches of my horns.

*   Gustav Flaubert, *The Temptation of Saint Anthony*, trans. Lafcadio Hearn (New York: Boni and Liveright, 1911), 262–68.

"Listen!"

(He throws back his horns, whence issues a music of sweetness ineffable.

Anthony presses both hands upon his heart. It seems to him as though his soul were being borne away by the melody.)

THE SADHUZAG

"But when I turn me toward the wind of the North, my antlers, more thickly bristling than a battalion of lances, give forth a sound of howlings: the forests are startled with fear; the rivers remount toward their sources; the husks of fruits burst open; and the bending grasses stand erect on end, like the hair of a coward.

"Listen!"

(He bends his branching antlers forward; hideous and discordant cries proceed from them. Anthony feels as though his heart were torn asunder. And his horror augments upon beholding)—

THE MARTICHORAS

(A gigantic red lion, with human face, and three rows of teeth):

"The gleam of my scarlet hair mingles with the reflection of the great sands. I breathe through my nostrils the terror of solitudes. I spit forth plague. I devour armies when they venture into the desert.

"My claws are twisted like screws, my teeth shaped like saws; and my curving tail bristles with darts which I cast to right and left, before and behind!

"See! see!"

(The Martichoras shoots forth the keen bristles of his tail, which irradiate in all directions like a volley of arrows. Drops of blood rain down, spattering upon the foliage.)

THE CATOBLEPAS

(A black buffalo with a pig's head, falling to the ground, and attached to his shoulders by a neck long, thin, and flaccid as an empty gut.

He wallows flat upon the ground, and his feet entirely disappear beneath the enormous mane of coarse hair which covers his face):

"Fat, melancholy, fierce — thus I continually remain, feeling against my belly the warmth of the mud. So heavy is my skull that it is impossible for me to lift it. I roll it slowly all around me, open-mouthed; and with my tongue I tear up the venemous plants bedewed with my breath. Once, I even devoured my own feet without knowing it!

"No one, Anthony, has ever beheld mine eyes,— or at least, those who have beheld them are dead. Were I to lift my eyelids — my pink and swollen eyelids, thou wouldst forthwith die!"

Anthony: "Oh, that one! Ugh! As though I could desire it?—Yet his stupidity fascinates me! No, no! I will not!"

(*He gazes fixedly upon the ground.*

But the weeds take fire; and amidst the contortions of the flames, arises)—

THE BASILISK

(*A great violet serpent, with trilobate crest, and two fangs, one above, one below*):

"Beware, lest thou fall into my jaws! I drink fire. I am fire!—and I inhale it from all things: from clouds, from flints, from dead trees, the fur of animals, the surface of marshes. My temperature maintains the volcanoes: I lend glitter to jewels: I give colours to metals!"

THE GRIFFIN

(*A lion with a vulture's beak, and white wings, red paws and blue neck*):

"I am the master of deep splendours. I know the secrets of the tombs wherein the Kings of old do slumber.

"A chain, issuing from the wall, maintains their heads upright. Near them, in basins of porphyry, the women they loved float upon the surfaces of black liquids. Their treasures are all arrayed in halls, in lozenge-shaped designs, in little heaps, in pyramids;—and down below, far below the tombs, and to be reached only after long travelling through stifling darkness, there are rivers of gold bordered by forests of diamonds, there are fields of carbuncles and lakes of mercury.

"Addossed against the subterranean gate I remain with claws uplifted; and my flaming eyes spy out those who seek to approach. The vast and naked plain that stretches away to the end of the horizon is whitened with the bones of travellers. But for thee the gates of bronze shall open; and thou shalt inhale the vapour of the mines, thou shalt descend into the caverns. . . . Quick! quick!"

(*He burrows into the earth with his paws, and crows like a cock.*

A thousand voices answer him. The forest trembles.

And all manner of frightful creatures arise:—The Tragelaphus, half deer, half ox; the Myrmecoles, lion before and ant behind, whose genitals are set reversely; the python Askar, sixty cubits long, that terrified Moses; the huge weasel Pastinaca, that kills the trees with her odour; the Presteros, that makes those who touch it imbecile; the Mirag, a horned hare, that dwells in the islands of the sea. The leopard Phalmant burst his belly by roaring; the triple-headed bear Senad tears her young by licking them with her tongue; the dog Cepus pours out the blue milk of her teats upon the rocks. Mosquitoes begin to hum, toads commence to leap; serpents hiss. Lightnings flicker. Hail falls.

Then come gusts, bearing with them marvellous anatomies:—Heads of alligators with hoofs of deer; owls with serpent tails; swine with tiger-muzzles; goats with the crupper of an ass; frogs hairy as bears; chameleons huge as hippopotami; calves with two heads, one bellowing, the other weeping; winged bellies flitting hither and thither like gnats.

They rain from the sky, they rise from the earth, they pour from the rocks; everywhere eyes flame, mouths roar, breasts bulge, claws are extended, teeth gnash, flesh clacks against flesh. Some crouch; some devour each other at a mouthful.

Suffocating under their own numbers, multiplying by their own contact, they climb over one another; and move about Anthony with a surging motion as though the ground were the deck of a ship. He feels the trail of snails upon the calves of his legs, the chilliness of vipers upon his hands:—and spiders, spinning about him enclose him within their network.

But the monstrous circle breaks, parts; the sky suddenly becomes blue . . . .

ANGELO DE GUBERNATIS (1840–1913)
ZOOLOGICAL MYTHOLOGY

One of the earliest full-length studies of animals in comparative mythology is *Zoological Mythology: or, The Legends of Animals* (1872) by Angelo de Gubernatis. The Italian professor of Sanskrit and comparative literature, like the Grimm brothers, traces animal tales to Indo–European roots; he examines the roles of creatures of earth, sky, and sea in light of both Asian and European folklore and mythology. Like other nineteenth-century mythologists, de Gubernatis identifies animals with forces of the sky, characterizing them primarily as solar or lunar creatures. Max Müller pursued the nature theory to such extremes that the writer Andrew Lang satirically called Müller himself a solar myth.

Most of de Gubernatis's subjects are actual animals, the cow and the bull alone dominating more than a quarter of his two-volume work. The phoenix, griffin, and other avian creatures that never were are included in his chapter on birds of prey, and the mythological dragon later appears in the section on serpents.

Solar Birds*

The most heroic of birds is the bird of prey; the strength of its beak, wings, and claws, its size and swiftness, caused it to be regarded as a swift celestial messenger, carrier, and warrior.

---

* Angelo de Gubernatis, *Zoological Mythology: or, The Legends of Animals*, 2 vols. (1872; facsimile ed., Detroit, Mich.: Singing Tree Press, 1968), vol. 2, pp. 181, 199–201, 204–5.

The hawk, the eagle, and the vulture, three powerful birds of prey, generally play the same part in myths and legends; the creators of myths having from the first observed their general resemblance, without paying any regard to their specific differences.

The bird of prey, in mythology, is the sun, which now shines in its splendour, and now shows itself in the cloud or darkness by sending forth flashes of lightning, thunderbolts, and sunbeams. The flash, the thunderbolt, and the sunbeam are now the beak, now the claw of the bird of prey, and now, the part being sometimes taken for the whole, even the entire bird. . . .

Besides these royal birds of prey that become mythical, there are several mythical birds of prey that never existed, still to be noticed, such as the phoenix, the harpy, the griffon, the strix, the Seleucide birds, the Stymphalian birds, and the sirens. Popular imagination believed in their terrestrial existence for a long time, but it can be said of them all as of the Arabian Phoenix:—

> "All affirm that it exists;
> Where it is no one can tell."

In point of fact, no man has ever seen them; a few deities or heroes alone approached them; their seat is in the sky, where, according to their several natures and the different place occupied by the sun or the moon in the sky, they attract, ravish, seduce, enchant, or destroy.

[THE PHOENIX]

The phoenix is, beyond all doubt, the eastern and western sun; hence Petrarch was able to say with reason,

"Nè 'n ciel nè 'n terra è più d'una Fenice,"

as there is not more than one sun; and we, like the ancient Greeks, say of a rare man or object, that he or it is a phoenix. Tacitus, who narrates, in the fourteenth book, the fable of the phoenix, calls it *animal sacrum soli*; Lactantius says that it alone knows the secrets of the sun —

> "Et sola arcanis conscia Phoebe tuis,"

and represents it as rendering funereal honours to its father in the temple of the sun; Claudian calls it *solis avem* and describes its whole life in a beautiful little poem. . . .

In my opinion, no more proofs are required to demonstrate the identity of the phoenix with the sun of morning and of evening, and, by extension, with that of autumn and of spring. That which was fabled concerning it in antiquity, and by reflection, in the Middle Ages, agrees perfectly with the twofold luminous phenomenon of the sun that dies and is born again every day and every year out of its ashes, and of the hero or heroine who traverses the flames of the burning pyre intact.

The nature of the phoenix is the same as that of the burning bird (szar-ptitza) of Russian fairy tales, which swallows the dwarf who goes to steal its eggs (the evening aurora swallows the sun).

[THE GRIFFIN]

The gryphes are represented as of double nature, now propitious, now malignant. Solinus calls them, "Alites forocissimae et ultra rabiem saevientes." Ktesias declares that India possesses gold in mountains inhabited by griffins, quadrupeds, as large as wolves, which have the legs and claws of a lion, red feathers on their breasts and in their other parts, eyes of fire and golden nests. For the sake of the gold, the Arimaspi, one-eyed men, fight with the griffins. As the latter have long ears, they easily hear the robbers of the gold; and if they capture them, they invariably kill them. In Hellenic antiquity, the griffins were sacred to Nemesis, the goddess of vengeance, and were represented in sepulchres in the act of pressing down a bull's head; but they were far more celebrated as sacred to the golden sun, Apollo, whose chariot they drew (the hippogriff, which, in mediaeval chevaleresque poems, carries the hero, is their exact equivalent). And as Apollo is the prophetical and divining deity, whose oracle, when consulted, delivers itself in enigmas, the word *griffin*, too, meant enigma, logogriph being an enigmatical speech, and griffonnage an entangled, confused, and embarrassing handwriting.

SIR HENRY YULE (1820–1889)
THE BOOK OF SER MARCO POLO

Sir Henry Yule's note on the roc (rukh) in his standard *Book of Ser Marco Polo* (1875 edition) is a seminal study of gigantic-bird lore, a collection of worldwide accounts of birds of wondrous size.

Embracing the diffusionist theory that mythological images have a single place of origin and spread from culture to culture, Yule contends that tales of gigantic birds from New Zealand to Madagascar are variations of the roc fable. He cites contemporary findings of fossilized remains to suggest that the roc made known to the West through Marco Polo's account of the bird of Madagascar and Sindbad's adventures could have had a basis in natural history. Yule also refers to Benjamin of Tudela, Ibn Battuta, Antonio Pigafetta, and others who recounted tales of roc-like birds with other names.

Regardless of how difficult such claims of common origin and development are to substantiate, Yule's note is a rich gathering of sources—from fossils to early maps, mythology, and folklore to travelers' tales. At the very least, the lore establishes a group of wondrous birds so large their wings eclipse the sun and so strong they can carry off the largest beasts.

Omitted from the excerpt is Ibn Battuta's account of the roc, reprinted elsewhere in this collection.

For people being carried off by birds, see *The Arabian Nights*, Benjamin of Tudela, Antonio Pigafetta, and Sir John Bourchier. For fossilized bones as a possible source of fabulous creatures, see Peter Lum.

Note: Yule's extensive note, actually an essay, is cited or echoed in footnotes on the roc and other gigantic birds by Sir Richard Burton, in a Sindbad note in his *Book of the Thousand Nights and Night,* and by N. M. Penzer, in his edition of Somadeva's *Ocean of Story* (vol. 1, pp. 103–5). Penzer cites the notes of both Yule and Burton.

The Rukh*

The fable of the Rukh was old and widely spread, like that of the Male and Female Islands, and just as in that case, one accidental circumstance or another would give it a local habitation, now here now there. The *Garuda* of the Hindus, the *Simurgh* of the old Persians, the *Angka* of the Arabs, the *Bar Yuchre* of the Rabbinical legends, the *Gryps* of the Greeks, were probably all versions of the same original fable.

Bochart quotes a bitter Arabic proverb which says, "Good Faith, the Ghul, and the Gryphon ('Angka) are three names of things that exist nowhere." And Mas'udi, after having said that whatever country he visited he always found that the people believed these monstrous creatures to exist in regions as remote as possible from their own, observes: "It is not that our reason absolutely rejects the possibility of the existence of the *Nesnás* (see vol. i. p. 206) or of the *'Angka*, and other beings of that rare and wondrous order; for there is nothing in their existence incompatible with the Divine Power; but we decline to believe in them because their existence has not been manifested to us on any irrefragable authority."

The circumstances which for the time localized the Rukh in the direction of Madagascar was perhaps some rumour of the great fossil *Aepyornis* and its colossal eggs, found in that island. According to Geoffroy St. Hilaire, the Malagashes assert that the bird which laid those great eggs still exists, that it has an immense

* *The Travels of Marco Polo: The Complete Yule-Cordier Edition,* eds. Sir Henry Yule and Henri Cordier, 2 vols. (1903, 1920; rpt., New York: Dover, 1993), vol. 2, pp. 415–19.

The roc, after a Persian drawing. From Edward William Lane's *Arabian Nights' Entertainments*, reproduced in Sir Henry Yule's *Book of Ser Marco Polo*. Courtesy of Dover Publications.

power of flight, and preys upon the greater quadrupeds. Indeed the continued existence of the bird has been alleged as late as 1861 and 1863!

On the great map of Fra Mauro (1459) near the extreme point of Africa which he calls *Cavo de Diab*, and which is suggestive of the Cape of Good Hope, but was really perhaps Cape Corrientes, there is a rubric inscribed with the following remarkable story: "About the year of Our Lord 1420 a ship or junk of India in crossing the Indian Sea was driven by way of the Islands of Men and Women beyond the Cape of Diab, and carried between the Green Islands and the Darkness in a westerly and south-westerly direction for 40 days, without seeing anything but sky and sea, during which time they made to the best of their judgment 2000 miles. The gale then ceasing they turned back, and were seventy days in getting to the aforesaid Cape Diab. The ship having touched on the coast to supply its wants, the mariners beheld there the egg of a certain bird called *Chrocho*, which egg was as big as a butt. And the bigness of the bird is such that between the extremities of the wings is said to be 60 paces. They say too that it carries away an elephant or any other great animal with the greatest ease, and does great injury to the inhabitants of the country, and is most rapid in its flight." . . .

Sindbad's adventures with the Rukh are too well known for quotation. A variety of stories of the same tenor hitherto unpublished, have been collected by M. Marcel Devic from an Arabic work of the 10th century on the "*Marvels of Hind,*" by an author who professes only to repeat the narratives of merchants and mariners whom he had questioned. . . . The story takes a peculiar form in the travels of Rabbi Benjamin of Tudela. He heard that when ships were in danger of being lost in the stormy sea that led to China the sailors were wont to sew themselves up in hides, and so when cast upon the surface they were snatched up by great eagles called gryphons, which carried their supposed prey ashore, etc. It is curious that this very story occurs in a Latin poem stated to be *at least* as old as the beginning of the 13th century, which relates the romantic adventures of a certain Duke Ernest of Bavaria; whilst the story embodies more than one other adventure belonging to the History of Sindbad. . . . The Gryphon story also appears in the romance of Huon de Bordeaux, as well as in the tale called "Hasan of el-Basrah" in Lane's Version of the *Arabian Nights*.

It is in the China Seas that Ibn Batuta beheld the Rukh, first like a mountain in the sea where no mountain should be, and then "when the sun rose," says he, "we saw the mountain aloft in the air, and the clear sky between it and the sea. . . ." In this story we have evidently a case of abnormal refraction, causing an island to appear suspended in the air.

The Archipelago was perhaps the legitimate habitat of the Rukh, before circumstances localised it in the direction of Madagascar. In the Indian Sea, says Kazwini, is a bird of size so vast that when it is dead men take the half of its bill and make a ship of it! And there too Pigafetta heard of this bird, under its Hindu name of *Garuda*, so big that it could fly away with an elephant. Kazwini also says that the 'Angka carries off an elephant as a hawk flies off with a mouse; his flight is like the loud thunder. Whilom he dwelt near the haunts of men, and wrought them great mischief. But once on a time it had carried off a bride in her bridal array, and Hamd Allah, the Prophet of those days, invoked a curse upon the bird. Wherefore the Lord banished it to an inaccessible Island in the Encircling Ocean.

The Simurgh or 'Angka, dwelling behind veils of Light and Darkness on the inaccessible summits of Caucasus, is in Persian mysticism an emblem of the Almighty.

In Northern Siberia the people have a firm belief in the former existence of birds of colossal size, suggested apparently by the fossil bones of the great pachyderms which are so abundant there. And the compressed sabre-like horns of *Rhinoceros tichorinus* are constantly called, even by Russian merchants, *birds' claws*. Some of the native tribes fancy the vaulted skull of the same rhinoceros to be the bird's head, and the leg-bones of other pachyderms to be its quills; and they relate that their forefathers used to fight wonderful battles with this bird. Erman ingeniously suggests that the Herodotean story of the Gryphons, *from under which* the Arimaspians drew their gold, grew out of the legends about these fossils.

I may add that the name of our rook in chess is taken from that of this same bird; though first perverted from (Sansk.) *rath*, a chariot.

WILLIAM JONES (FL. C. 1880)
CREDULITIES PAST AND PRESENT

Disparagement of popular belief in the marvelous and strange takes Victorian form in William Jones's *Credulities Past and Present* (1880). Jones's exposure of commonly held fallacies is a nineteenth-century counterpart of Sir Thomas Browne's *Pseudodoxia Epidemica.*

One of the fallacies Jones examines is the centuries-long belief in the barnacle goose. Despite Albertus Magnus's debunking of the Northern legend in the thirteenth century, numerous eyewitness accounts established that a species of goose was born from either trees or barnacles. This belief had already been discredited by the time Jones reviews authors and poets who contributed to acceptance of the "singular fable."

Omitted from this excerpt are passages from Du Bartas and John Gerard, reprinted elsewhere in this collection.

See also the Old English Riddle and Giraldus Cambrensis.

The Singular Fable of the Barnacle Goose *

An extraordinary belief was long current that the *barnacle*, a well-known kind of shell-fish, which is found adhering to the bottom of ships, would, when broken off, become a species of goose. Several old writers assert this, and Holinshed gravely declares that with his own eyes he saw the feathers of these barnacles "hang out of the shell at least two inches." Giraldus Cambrensis gives similar ocular testimony. "Who," he said, "can marvel that this should be so? When our first parent was made of mud, can we be surprised that a bird should be born of a tree?"

The singular fable concerning the origin of these geese, so prevalent in the sixteenth century, and credited even by some generally well-informed naturalists, is at the present day retained in our memory principally by Isaac Walton's quotations from "The Divine Weekes and Workes" of Du Bartas. . . .

---

* William Jones, *Credulities Past and Present* (1880; facsimile ed., Detroit, Mich: Singing Tree Press, 1968), 17–19.

In a description of West Connaught, Ireland, by Roderic O'Flaherty (1684), the barnacle is thus mentioned: "There is a bird engendered by the sea, out of timber long lying in the sea. Some call these birds *clakes*, and soland geese, and some, puffins, others barnacles; we call them *girrinn*."

Butler tells us in "Hudibras" of those —

> "Who from the most refined of saints
> As naturally grow miscreants,
> As barnacles turn Soland geese
> In the Islands of the Orcades."

Gerard, author of the "Herbal" (1597), gives a minute account of this prodigy. . . .

Honest Gerard delighted in the marvellous, and found ready believers: indeed, this particular ground of discussion had been abundantly cropped already. The numerous tentacles or arms of the animal inhabiting the barnacle shell which are disposed in a semicircular form, and have a feathery appearance, seem to have been all that could reasonably have been alleged in favour of this strange supposition.

Henry Davenport Northrop (1836–1909)
Marvelous Wonders of the Whole World

The legend of the beautiful footless bird that came from paradise began in Indonesia, was introduced to Europe with the return of Magellan's remaining crew in the early sixteenth century, and was repeated in natural histories. By the latter nineteenth century, the highly colored story had been exposed as fable. One who explained reasons for the tale was Henry Davenport Northrop, an American compiler who extolled the marvels of nature in his *Marvelous Wonders of the Whole World* (1886).

For the bird of paradise, see Antonio Pigafetta and Ambroise Paré.

The Bird of Paradise *

None of the inhabitants of the bird world approach the Paradiseidae in elegance of shape and beauty of plumage; and there is something so superb, and at the

---

* Henry Davenport Northrop, *Marvelous Wonders of the Whole World* (Chicago: N. Juul, 1899), 620–21.

same time so unearthly, in their appearance, that it is hardly to be wondered at if the fancy of the early voyagers supposed them to be fit denizens of the Garden of Eden. The most extraordinary legends at one time prevailed about them. It was said that they lived wholly upon dew, and passed their lives in long aerial voyages; that they so spurned the earth as never to touch it until the moment of death approached; that they never rested except when suspending themselves from the branches of trees by the shafts of their two tail-feathers; and it is still a belief of the Malays that for raising their young they retire to the untroubled groves of Paradise. These fables partly arose in their peculiar habits, and partly in the Papuan custom of tearing off their legs before sending them to market, which led the European navigators to suppose that they were all wings and body. Then, again, owing to the singular looseness of their plumage, they always fly against the wind. Add to this, that they dwell in the recesses of the vast virgin forests, afar from the haunts of men, and that their song or cry is very characteristic, and it is not difficult to understand how they came to be invested with so many fabulous attributes, and made the subjects of so many romantic stories.

CHARLES GOULD (1834–1893)
MYTHICAL MONSTERS

Charles Gould's *Mythical Monsters* (1886) holds a special place in fabulous-animal literature as one of the earliest full-length studies of a collection of fabulous creatures. Gould, a geologist and son of the prominent nineteenth-century ornithologist John Gould, reassesses fabled beasts in light of contemporary science, concluding that some animals regarded as mythical had become extinct and others still existed. Granting that much of the lore associated with certain creatures is exaggeration and superstition, Gould seriously attempts to discover the animals' actual prototypes. Like the seventeenth-century Alexander Ross, Gould is an apologist for fabulous beasts, but instead of citing literary authority for their existence, he amasses the findings of contemporary science.

After reviewing nineteenth-century geology, paleontology, and principles of Darwinian evolution, Gould examines the Western and Eastern dragon and unicorn, the sea serpent, and the Chinese phoenix, analyzing traditional animal lore from the perspective of science. In his introduction, he refutes the solar school of mythology that explained myths in terms of celestial phenomena, and he later rejects the assumptions of Sir Henry Yule and others who held that world-wide tales of gigantic birds were all local versions of a single monomythical fable. He also believes the tradition of the Eastern phoenix is independent of Western influence.

Aside from its scientific claims, Mythical Monsters is a rich encyclopedic collection of both Western and Eastern fabulous-beast lore, enriched by Gould's first-hand familiarity with Far East literature and containing extensive notes and appendices. The book is regularly cited in bibliographies of fabulous beasts, and interest in it as an antiquarian work was revived in 1969, when the first of at least four late twentieth-century reprint editions appeared.

Mythical Monsters *

It would have been a bold step indeed for anyone, some thirty years ago, to have thought of treating the public to a collection of stories ordinarily reputed fabulous, and of claiming for them the consideration due to genuine realities, or to have advocated tales, time-honoured as fictions, as actual facts; and those of the nursery as being, in many instances, legends, more or less distorted, descriptive of real beings or events.

Now-a-days it is a less hazardous proceeding. The great era of advanced opinion, initiated by Darwin, which has seen, in the course of a few years, a larger progress in knowledge in all departments of science than decades of centuries preceding it, has, among other changes, worked a complete revolution in the estimation of the value of folk-lore; and speculations on it, which in the days of our boyhood would have been considered as puerile, are now admitted to be not merely interesting but necessary to those who endeavour to gather up the skeins of unwritten history, and to trace the antecedents and early migrations from parent sources of nations long since alienated from each other by customs, speech, and space.

Dragons and sea serpents from Charles Gould, Mythical Monsters (London: W. H. Allen, 1886)

I have, therefore, but little hesitation in gravely proposing to submit that many of the so-called mythical animals, which throughout long ages and in all nations have been the fertile subjects of fiction and fable, come legitimately within the scope of plain matter-of-fact Natural History, and that they may be considered, not as the outcome of exuberant fancy, but as creatures which really once existed, and of which, unfortunately, only imperfect and inaccurate descriptions have filtered down to us, probably very much refracted, through the mists of time.

*   Charles Gould, Mythical Monsters (London: W. H. Allen,) 1886, 1–5, 17.

I propose to follow, for a certain distance only, the path which has been pursued in the treatment of myths by mythologists, so far only, in fact, as may be necessary to trace out the homes and origin of those stories which in their later dress are incredible; deviating from it to dwell upon the possibility of their having preserved to us, through the

medium of unwritten Natural History, traditions of creatures once co-existing with man, some of which are so weird and terrible as to appear at first sight to be impossible. I propose stripping them of those supernatural characters with which a mysteriously implanted love of the wonderful has invested them, and to examine them, as at the present day we are fortunately able to do, by the lights of the

modern sciences of Geology, Evolution, and Philology.

For me the major part of these creatures are not chimeras but objects of rational study. The dragon, in place of being a creature evolved out of the imagination of Aryan man by the contemplation of lightning flashing through the caverns which he tenanted, as is held by some mythologists, is an animal which once lived and dragged its ponderous coils, and perhaps flew; which devastated herds, and on occasions swallowed their shepherd; which, establishing its lair in some cavern overlooking the fertile plain, spread terror and destruction around, and, protected from assault by dread or superstitious feeling, may even have been subsidised by the terror-stricken peasantry, who, failing the power to destroy it, may have preferred tethering offerings of cattle adjacent to its cavern to having it come down to seek supplies from amongst their midst.

To me the specific existence of the unicorn seems not incredible, and, in fact, more probable than that theory which assigns its origin to a lunar myth.

Again, believing as I do in the existence of some great undescribed inhabitant of the ocean depths, the much-derided sea-serpent, whose home seems especially to be adjacent to Norway, I

recognise this monster as originating the myths of the midgard serpent which the Norse Elder Eddas have collected, this being the contrary view to that taken by mythologists, who invert the derivation, and suppose the stories current among the Norwegian fishermen to be modified versions of this important element of Norse mythology.

I must admit that, for my part, I doubt the general derivation of myths from "the contemplation of the visible workings of external nature." It seems to me easier to suppose that the palsy of time has enfeebled the utterance of these oft-told tales until their original appearance is almost unrecognisable, than that uncultured savages should possess powers of imagination and poetical invention far beyond those enjoyed by the most instructed nations of the present day; less hard to believe that these wonderful stories of gods and demigods, of giants and dwarfs, of dragons and monsters of all descriptions, are transformations than to believe them to be inventions.

The author of *Atlantis*, indeed, claims that the gods and goddesses of the ancient Greeks, the Phoenicians, the Hindoos, and the Scandinavians were simply the kings, queens, and heroes of Atlantis, and the acts attributed to them in mythology a confused recollection of real historical events. Without conceding the *locus* of the originals, which requires much greater examination than I am able to make at the present time, I quite agree with him as to the principle. I believe that the mythological deities represent a confused chronology of far-distant times, and that the destruction of the Nemean lion, the Lernean hydra, and the Minotaur are simply the records of acts of unusual bravery in combating ferocious animals.

On the first landing of Pizarro the Mexicans entertained the opinion that man and horse were parts of one strange animal, and we have thus a clue to the explanation of the origin of the belief in centaurs from a distant view of horsemen, a view possibly followed by the immediate flight of the observer, which rendered a solution of the extraordinary phenomenon impossible. . . .

Surely a profound acquaintance with the different branches of natural history should render a man credulous rather than incredulous, for there is hardly conceivable a creature so monstrous that it may not be paralleled by existing ones in every-day life.

Continuing Transformations 12

E. NESBIT (1858–1924)
THE PHOENIX AND THE CARPET

The phoenix is fictionally reborn into the modern world in Edith Nesbit's *The Phoenix and the Carpet* (serialized in the *Strand Magazine*, 1903–1904). The prolific author of children's adventure stories transforms details from traditional phoenix lore into her own eccentric talking bird.

In the opening chapter of Nesbit's novel, her fictional Edwardian siblings dabble in magic in their London lodgings during school holidays. In the room is a replacement for a rug they had accidentally burned in earlier play, and on the mantlepiece is a golden egg they had found in the newly purchased Persian carpet. Nesbit varies the usual rebirth patterns of the phoenix by having her bird hatch in the fire from an egg centuries old. The bird later guides the children through a series of magic-carpet adventures before immolating itself in the nursery fireplace for another cycle of death and rebirth.

As in other Nesbit books, the fairy-tale magic in *The Phoenix and the Carpet* occurs within the context of everyday life, and a fantastic creature interacts with realistic characters. In the preceding book, *Five Children and It*, the same children discover Nesbit's own fantastic creation, the Psammead, an irascible Sand-fairy with a plump furry body, monkey-like hands and feet, bat-like ears and eyes on stalks. Nesbit also published a number of original dragon tales.

Biographer Julia Briggs records that Nesbit was given the idea for the phoenix and carpet story from

True myth may serve for thousands of years as an inexhaustible source of intellectual speculation, religious joy, ethical inquiry, and artistic renewal. The real mystery is not destroyed by reason.

—Ursula K. LeGuin
Myth and Archetype in Science-Fiction

Recurring images: fabulous creatures in modern logos, derived from heraldry.

(*left*) Griffin. Logo of Griffin Publishing Company, Inc. Reproduced by permission. (*center*) Dragon "tending the soul of the world." Seal of Pacifica Graduate Institute. Reproduced by permission. (*right*) Phoenix. Logo of the City of Phoenix, Arizona. Reproduced by permission.

Lawrence Housman, brother of poet A. E. Housman, and that H. G. Wells wrote in a letter to her: "The Phoenix is a great creation; he is the best character you ever invented—or anybody ever invented in this line."

In the following excerpt, "The Lamb" is the children's absent baby brother.

The Phoenix and the Carpet*

So they traced strange figures on the linoleum, on the part where the hearth-rug had kept it clean. They traced them with chalk that Robert had nicked from the top of the mathematical master's desk at school. You know, of course, that it is stealing to take a new stick of chalk, but it is not wrong to take a broken piece, so long as you only take one. (I do not know the reason of this rule, nor who made it.) And they chanted all the gloomiest songs they could think of. And, of course, nothing happened. So then Anthea said, "I'm sure a magic fire ought to be made of sweet-swelling wood, and have magic gums and essences and things in it."

"I don't know any sweet-smelling wood except cedar," said Robert; "but I've got some ends of cedar-wood lead pencil."

So they burned the ends of lead pencil. And still nothing happened.

"Let's burn some of the eucalyptus oil we have for our colds," said Anthea.

And they did. It certainly smelt very strong. And they burned lumps of camphor out of the big chest. It was very bright, and made a horrid black smoke, which looked very magical. But still nothing happened. Then they got some clean tea-cloths from the dresser drawer in the kitchen, and waved them over the magic chalk-tracings, and sang "The Hymn of the Moravian Nuns of Bethlehem," which is very impressive. And still nothing happened. So they waved more

* E. Nesbit, *The Phoenix and the Carpet* (facsimile ed., London: Octopus Books, 1979), 197–98.

E. Nesbit's phoenix appears
to children in the fireplace
of a London flat. Illustrated
by H. R. Millar.

The bird rose in its nest of fire

and more wildly, and Robert's tea-cloth caught the golden egg and whisked it off
the mantel-piece, and it fell into the fender and rolled under the grate.

"Oh, crikey!" said more than one voice.

And every one instantly fell down flat on its front to look under the grate, and
there lay the egg, glowing in a nest of hot ashes.

"It's not smashed, anyhow," said Robert, and he put his hand under the grate
and picked up the egg. But the egg was much hotter than any one would have
believed it could possibly get in such a short time, and Robert had to drop it with
a cry of "Bother!" It fell on the top bar of the grate, and bounced right into the
glowing red-hot heart of the fire.

"The tongs!" cried Anthea. But alas, no one could remember where they were.
Every one had forgotten that the tongs had last been used to fish up the doll's tea-
pot from the bottom of the water-butt, where the Lamb had dropped it. So the
nursery tongs were resting between the water-butt and the dustbin, and cook
refused to lend the kitchen ones.

"Never mind," said Robert, "we'll get it out with the poker and the shovel."

"Oh, stop," cried Anthea. "Look at it! Look! look! look! I do believe something *is* going to happen!"

For the egg was now red-hot, and inside it something was moving. Next
moment there was a soft cracking sound; the egg burst in two, and out of it came

a flame-coloured bird. It rested a moment among the flames, and as it rested there the four children could see it growing bigger and bigger under their eyes.

Every mouth was a-gape, every eye a-goggle.

The bird rose in its nest of fire, stretched its wings, and flew out into the room. It flew round and round, and round again, and where it passed the air was warm. Then it perched on the fender. The children looked at each other. Then Cyril put out a hand towards the bird. It put its head on one side and looked up at him, as you may have seen a parrot do when it is just going to speak, so that the children were hardly astonished at all when it said, "Be careful; I am not nearly cool yet."

They were not astonished, but they were very, very much interested.

SIR JAMES GEORGE FRAZER (1854–1941)
THE GOLDEN BOUGH

In his *The Golden Bough: A Study in Magic and Religion* (1890, enlarged 1907–1915), James George Frazer amasses ancient myths and primitive folklore, illustrating universal patterns in customs and beliefs. One such set of rituals developed to appease natural forces involves human sacrifices to water spirits. In the excerpt below, Frazer finds global correspondences to the dragon-battle tales of Perseus and St. George.

Frazer's comprehensive comparative study of primitive religion is generally regarded as the foundation of modern mythological inquiry. His thesis that belief evolves through magic to religion to science has been discredited by Bronislaw Malinowski and other anthropologists, but his connections between fertility myths and the death and resurrection of gods and kings had enormous influence throughout the century, on writers from Carl Jung to Joseph Campbell.

Sacrifices to Water-spirits*

Ibn Batutah's narrative of the demon lover and his mortal brides closely resembles a well-known type of folk-tale, of which versions have been found from Japan and Annam in the East to Senegambia, Scandinavia, and Scotland in the West. The story varies in details from people to people, but as commonly told it runs thus. A certain country is infested by a man-headed serpent, dragon, or

---

* Sir James George Frazer, *The Golden Bough* series, *The Magic Art and the Evolution of Kings* (New York: Macmillan, 1935), vol. 2, pp. 155–57, 163.

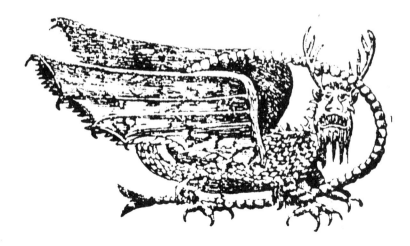

Sketch of a Piasa, a North American water monster. Inscribed by Native Americans on a cliff above a stretch of turbulent water at what is now Alton, Illinois. From G. Elliot Smith's 1918 *Evolution of the Dragon* (rpt., Albert Saifer, Watchung, N.J., 1990).

other monster, which would destroy the whole people if a human victim, generally a virgin, were not delivered up to him periodically. Many victims have perished, and at last it has fallen to the lot of the king's own daughter to be sacrificed. She is exposed to the monster, but the hero of the tale, generally a young man of humble birth, interposes in her behalf, slays the monster, and receives the hand of the princess as his reward. In many of the tales the monster, who is sometimes described as a serpent, inhabits the water of a sea, a lake, or a fountain. In other versions he is a serpent or dragon who takes possession of the springs of water, and only allows the water to flow or the people to make use of it on condition of receiving a human victim.

It would probably be a mistake to dismiss all these tales as pure inventions of the story-teller. Rather we may suppose that they reflect a real custom of sacrificing girls or women to be the wives of water-spirits, who are very often conceived as great serpents or dragons. Elsewhere I have cited many instances of this belief in serpent-shaped spirits of water; here it may be worth while to add a few more. Thus the Warramunga of Central Australia perform elaborate ceremonies to appease or coerce a gigantic, but purely mythical water-snake who is said to have destroyed a number of people. Some of the natives of western Australia fear to approach large pools, supposing them to be inhabited by a great serpent, who would kill them if they dared to drink or draw water there by night. The Indians of New Granada believed that when the mother of all mankind, named Bachue, was grown old, she and her husband plunged into the Lake of Iguague, where they were changed into two enormous serpents, which still live in the lake and sometimes shew themselves. The Oyampi Indians of French Guiana imagine that each waterfall has a guardian in the shape of a monstrous snake, who lies hidden under the eddy of the cascade, but has sometimes been seen to lift up its huge head. To see it is fatal. Canoe and Indians are then dragged down to the bottom, where the monster swallows all the men, and sometimes the canoe also. Hence the Oyampis never name a waterfall till they have passed it, for fear that the snake at the bottom of the water might hear its name and attack the rash intruders. The Huichol Indians of Mexico adore water. Springs are sacred and the gods in them are mothers or serpents, that rise with the clouds and descend as fructifying rain. The Tarahumares, another Indian tribe of Mexico, think that every river, pool, and spring has its serpent, who causes the water to come up out of the earth. All these water-serpents are easily offended; hence the Tarahumares place their houses some little way from the water, and will not sleep near it when they are on a journey. Whenever they construct weirs to catch fish, they take care to offer fish to the water serpent of the river; and when they are away from home and are making pinole, that is, toasted maize-meal, they drop the first of the pinole into the water as an offering to the serpents, who would otherwise try to seize them and chase them back to their own land. In Basutoland the rivers Ketane and Maletsunyane tumble, with a roar of waters and a cloud of iridescent spray, into vast chasms hundreds of feet deep. The Basutos fear to approach the foot of these huge falls, for they think that a spirit in the shape of a gigantic snake haunts the seething cauldron which receives the falling waters. . . .

. . . Among civilised peoples these customs survive for the most part only in popular tales, of which the legend of Perseus and Andromeda, with its mediaeval counterpart of St. George and the Dragon, is the most familiar example. . . .

D.H. LAWRENCE (1885–1930)
APOCALYPSE, PHOENIX

"What we want," D. H. Lawrence wrote at the end of *Apocalypse* (1927), "is to destroy our false, inorganic connections, especially those related to money, and re-establish the living organic connections, with the cosmos, the sun and earth, with mankind and nation and family. Start with the sun, and the rest will slowly, slowly happen." The man who adopted the phoenix as his personal emblem infused ancient mythic forms with poetic power. Among the symbols he reinterprets in expressing his individualistic ideas are the dragon and the phoenix.

Directly confronting the reader with his vision of creative life within debilitating society, Lawrence is also one of the most controversial of modern writers. With the conviction of a prophet, he passionately and poetically attacks conventional thought, attempting in his fiction, essays, and poetry to realign human consciousness with elemental life forces. Lawrence rejected the psychoanalytical approaches of both Sigmund Freud and Carl Jung as mechanical and limiting.

Apocalypse (1927) is a summing up of Lawrence's conviction that the full realization of modern men and women can be achieved only through identification with primal cosmic forces. Basing his book on the Revelation of St. John the Divine, Lawrence rejects Christian dogma, instead seeking out St. John's mother and dragon symbols in the most ancient mythologies.

Phoenix (1930) presents the symbol of regeneration that Lawrence adopted as his own: the emblem later imprinted on his books, the figure depicted above the entrance and inside the Taos, New Mexico, shrine housing his ashes.

In an early philosophical essay, *The Crown* (1915), Lawrence used the unicorn and the lion to represent forces warring within the human soul.

The Dragon of the Stars *

The woman is one of the "wonders." And the other wonder is the Dragon. The dragon is one of the oldest symbols of the human consciousness. The dragon and serpent symbol goes so deep in every human consciousness, that a rustle in the grass can startle the toughest "modern" to depths he has no control over.

First and foremost, the dragon is the symbol of the fluid, rapid, startling movement of life within us. That startled life which runs through us like a serpent, or coils within us potent and waiting, like a serpent, this is the dragon. And the same with the cosmos.

From earliest times, man has been aware of a "power" or potency within him—and also outside him—which he has no ultimate control over. It is a fluid, rippling potency which can lie quite dormant, sleeping, and yet be ready to leap out unexpectedly. Such are the sudden angers that spring upon us from within ourselves, passionate and terrible in passionate people: and the sudden accesses of violent desire, wild sexual desire, or violent hunger, or a great desire of any sort, even for sleep. . . .

And man "worshipped" the dragon. A hero was a hero, in the great past, when he had conquered the hostile dragon, when he had the power of the dragon *with him* in his limbs and breast. When Moses set up the brazen serpent in the wilderness, an act which dominated the imagination of the Jews for many centuries, he was substituting the potency of the good dragon for the sting of the bad dragon, or serpents. That is, man can have the serpent with him or against him. When his serpent is with him, he is almost divine. When his serpent is against him, he is stung and envenomed and defeated from within. The great problem, in the past,

* D. H. Lawrence, *Apocalypse* (New York, 1971), 142–48; *The Complete Poems of D. H. Lawrence*, eds. Vivian de Sola Pinto and Warren Roberts (New York: Viking, 1971), vol. 2, p. 728.

was the conquest of the *inimical* serpent and the liberation within the self of the gleaming bright serpent of gold, golden fluid life within the body, the rousing of the splendid divine dragon within a man, or within a woman.

What ails men today is that thousands of little serpents sting and envenom them all the time, and the great divine dragon is inert. We cannot wake him to life, in modern days. He wakes on the lower planes of life: for a while in an airman like Lindbergh or in a boxer like Dempsey. It is the little serpent of gold that lifts these two men for a brief time into a certain level of heroism. But on the higher planes, there is no glimpse or gleam of the great dragon.

The usual vision of the dragon is, however, not personal but cosmic. It is in the vast cosmos of the stars that the dragon writhes and lashes. We see him in his maleficent aspect, red. But don't let us forget that when he stirs green and flashing on a pure dark night of stars it is he who makes the wonder of the night, it is the full rich coiling of his folds which makes the heavens sumptuously serene, as he glides around and guards the immunity, the precious strength of the planets, and gives lustre and new strength to the fixed stars, and still more serene beauty to the moon. His coils within the sun make the sun glad, till the sun dances in radiance. For in his good aspect, the dragon is the great vivifier, the great enhancer of the whole universe.

So he persists still to the Chinese. The long green dragon with which we are so familiar on Chinese things is the dragon in his good aspect of life-bringer, life-giver, life-maker, vivifier. There he coils, on the breasts of the mandarins' coats, looking very horrific, coiling round the centre of the breast and lashing behind with his tail. But as a matter of fact, proud and strong and grand is the mandarin who is within the folds of the green dragon, lord of the dragon.—It is the same dragon which, according to the Hindus, coils quiescent at the base of the spine of a man, and unfolds sometimes lashing along the spinal way: and the yogi is only trying to set this dragon in controlled motion. Dragon-cult is still active and still potent all over the world, particularly in the east.

But alas, the great green dragon of the stars at their brightest is coiled up tight and silent today, in a long winter sleep. Only the red dragon sometimes shows his head, and the millions of little vipers. The millions of little vipers sting us as they stung the murmuring Israelites, and we want some Moses to set the brazen serpent aloft: the serpent which was "lifted up" even as Jesus later was "lifted up" for the redemption of men.

The red dragon is the kakodaimon, the dragon in his evil or inimical aspect. In the old lore, red is the colour of *man's* splendor, but the colour of evil in the cosmic creatures or the gods. The red lion is the sun in his evil or destructive aspect. The red dragon is the great "potency" of the cosmos in its hostile and destructive activity.

The agathodaimon becomes at last the kakodaimon. The green dragon becomes with time the red dragon. What was our joy and our salvation becomes with time, at the end of the time-era, our bane and our damnation. What was a

creative god, Ouranos, Kronos, becomes at the end of the time-period a destroyer
and a devourer. The god of the beginning of an era is the evil principle at the end
of that era. For time still moves in cycles. What was the green dragon, the good
potency, at the beginning of the cycle has by the end gradually changed into the
red dragon, the evil potency. The good potency of the beginning of the Christian
era is now the evil potency of the end.

This is a piece of very old wisdom, and it will always be true. Time still moves
in cycles, not in a straight line. And we are at the end of the Christian cycle. And
the Logos, the good dragon of the beginning of the cycle, is now the evil dragon
of today. It will give its potency to no new thing, only to old and deadly things. It
is the red dragon, and it must once more be slain by the heroes, since we can
expect no more from the angels.

Phoenix

Are you willing to be sponged out, erased, cancelled,
made nothing?
Are you willing to be made nothing?
dipped into oblivion?

If not, you will never really change.

The phoenix renews her youth
only when she is burnt, burnt alive, burnt down
to hot and flocculent ash.
Then the small stirring of a new small bub in the nest
with strands of down like floating ash
Shows that she is renewing her youth like the eagle,
immortal bird.

Phoenix illustration, from *The Letters of D. H. Lawrence* by D H. Lawrence. Introduction
by Aldous Huxley. Copyright 1932 by the Estate of D. H. Lawrence. Used by permission
of Viking Penguin, a division of Penguin Books USA Inc.

Unicorn drawing at head of final chapter of Odell Shepard, *The Lore of the Unicorn* (1930; rpt., New York: Dover, 1993). Courtesy of Dover Publications.

ODELL SHEPARD (1884–1967)
THE LORE OF THE UNICORN

Odell Shepard's *The Lore of the Unicorn* (1930) is one of the first full-length works to trace the complex history of the mysterious single-horned creature. Shepard begins his quest for the unicorn with an alicorn on his desk and explores all aspects of the evolution of the legend, from its ancient beginnings through nineteenth-century sightings and mythological lunar theories. The book is a model modern study of a single fabulous animal.

The concluding chapter is Shepard's personal summing up of the meaning and value of the legend to the human imagination, leaving no doubt as to where his sympathies lie in a rationalistic age.

*Reflections on the Unicorn**

. . . For the most part we have made the beasts of fancy in our own image — far more cruel and bloodthirsty, that is to say, than the actual "lower animals." The dragons of the Western world do evil for evil's sake; the harpy is more terrible than the vulture, and the were-wolf is far more frightful than the wolf. Almost the only beast that kills for the pure joy of killing is Western civilized man, and he has attributed his own peculiar trait to the creatures of his imagination. There are a few exceptions, however, to this rule that our projection of ourselves is lower than the facts of Nature, and the unicorn — noble, chaste, fierce yet beneficent, altruistic though solitary, strangely beautiful — is the clearest exception of all. The unicorn was not conceived in fear. Our early sense of Nature's majesty and mystery is revealed in him. If he came from Ur of the Chaldees, where the moon was a friend to man always contending against the demoniacal sun and the powers of darkness alike, his constant benevolence is more readily understood; but whatever may have been his first local habitation and whatever was his origi-

* Odell Shepard, *The Lore of the Unicorn* (1930; rpt. New York: Dover, 1993), 273–75, 277–78.

nal name, this "airy nothing" was born and bred in the human mind. There are times when one takes hope and comfort in remembering the fact. . . .

The legend of the unicorn is so old and it has been since its dim beginnings so close to human hearts and bosoms that it illustrates vividly Auguste Comte's three stages of intellectual "progress": the theological, the metaphysical, and the positivistic. Tracing it through the centuries, we have seen it remodelled again and again by the changing *Zeitgeist* or adjusting itself anew to the time-climates into which it has strayed. The historian of thought might find this legend, indeed, a serviceable thread upon which to arrange his generalizations, and it would save him from Comte's error, and ours, of supposing that the successive stages of human thought are stages of progress in the sense of amelioration. We do not think better about the unicorn than the men who made the myth of the three-legged ass; we think differently.

Although the conception of the unicorn does us credit, the total history of the animal's legend does not flatter our modern pride. In the beginnings, wherever and whatever they may have been, the unicorn was a symbol of beneficent power inhabiting the poetic imagination. The symbol expanded into myth and this myth was debased into fable. The unicorn next became an *exemplum* of moral virtues, then an actual animal, then a thaumaturge, then a medicine, then an article of merchandise, then an idle dream, and, last stage of all, an object of antiquarian research. Relics of the earlier stages are discoverable in the later, but what is most apparent is the steady intrusion of fact upon fancy and the invasion of what was once a sanctuary by the positivistic temper. We are accustomed to regard the growth of this temper as unqualified gain, and it has indeed brought us many advantages that no sensible man or woman would forgo, but it has not been good for unicorns or for the many holy and beautiful things that unicorns may be taken to represent. There are some quite sober moods in which one may sum up all the unquestionable advantages of modernity and calmly decide that he would "rather be a pagan suckled in a creed outworn. . . ."

Is there no choice possible, then, except that between a docile and unquestioning acceptance of authority on the one hand and a world of physicists and mathematicians on the other? Because Ole Wurm has demonstrated that alicorns are really the teeth of whales, must we abandon the unicorn altogether? I do not see the necessity.

The higher and the enduring values of a belief—the faiths that we call religious provide the best examples—do not depend at all upon its congruity with actual fact, but upon its sway over the human heart and mind. They are grounded not upon fact, but upon what even we may perhaps still call "the truth." The question of historicity and actuality with regard to gods and unicorns is a relatively trifling matter which may be left to antiquarians and biologists, for both the god and the unicorn had a business to perform greater than any mere existence in the flesh could explain or provide a basis for. We wrong ourselves when we insist that if they cannot make good their flesh-and-blood actuality on our level we will have none of them.

The unicorn came to stand for Christ, and for that reason if for no other we can scarcely avoid passing in thought from the symbol to the symbolized. Here are two great and beautiful legends, to say no more than that, neither of which could have lived so long in the world if it had not contained a truth far higher than any historic or zoological fact could help us to understand. But legends and truths of this kind are in grave danger in a world increasingly adjusted to the requirements of physicists and mathematicians; there is question whether they can hold out against our tendency to accept no truths except those the senses seem to warrant—which is to say, no truths whatever, but only facts. The legend of the unicorn was assailed three centuries ago on the side of fact, and it gradually withered because there was no longer any sufficient capacity for a faith unsustained by the senses. That attack could never have been made if the unicorn had not first been dragged from the fastnesses of the imagination to take his chances in the mob of animals whose only claim upon our attention is that they happen to exist. Three centuries from now, if we continue to make the question of fact decisive where it should have least weight, the legend of Christ may be as outworn as that of the beast that was once His appropriate symbol. For the decline of the unicorn began with the affirmation that the animal must exist in nature, and just so, as Matthew Arnold saw with painful clearness, religion is declining because it has based its claim upon fact, or supposed fact, which is now crumbling. Our best hope seems to lie in the faith expressed by Arnold himself that in the years coming on poetry will be an ever surer and surer stay.

J. R. R. TOLKIEN (1892–1973)
THE HOBBIT

"Fantasy is a natural human activity. It certainly does not destroy or even insult Reason; and it does not either blunt the appetite for, nor obscure the perception of, scientific verity. On the contrary. The keener and the clearer is the reason, the better fantasy will it make."

So did professor, philologist, and fantasist J. R. R. Tolkien defend maligned literary fantasy in his 1938 lecture, *On Fairy-Stories*. Both as practitioner and critic, Tolkien was a major figure in the evolution of a vast popular genre. While discredited animals of the imagination were becoming subjects of nonfiction books, adult fantasy fiction offered yet another literary area in which such creatures could thrive.

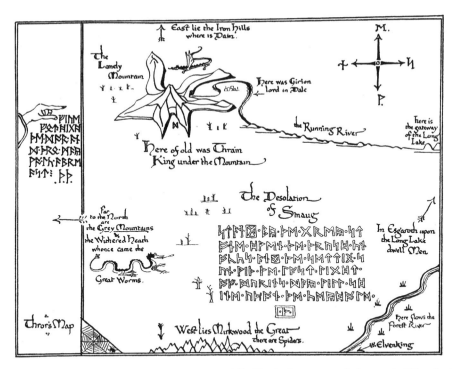

J. R. R. Tolkien's *Thror's Map*, depicting Middle Earth dragons and the runic "Desolation of Smaug." From *The Hobbit* (New York: Ballantine Books, 1965). Reprinted by permission of Houghton Mifflin.

Tolkien differentiated between the "primary" real world in which we live and the "secondary" fictional world created by the writer of fantasy, a "sub-creator." The professor of medieval studies created his own "Elvish" world in *The Hobbit* (1937), the following *Lord of the Rings* trilogy, and the posthumous "prequel," *The Simarillion.* Achieving immense popularity decades after their initial publication, the influential Middle Earth novels are now accepted as exemplars of the fantasy genre.

A major character in the prologue volume is the dragon Smaug, a flying, fire-breathing descendent of medieval monsters. "A dragon is no idle fancy," Tolkien states in his essay *Beowulf: The Monsters and the Critics.* "Whatever may be his origins, in fact or invention, the dragon in legend is a potent creation of men's imagination, richer in significance than his barrow is in gold."

Smaug*

The men of the lake-town Esgaroth were mostly indoors, for the breeze was from the black East and chill, but a few were walking on the quays, and watch-

* J. R. R. Tolkien, *The Hobbit* (New York: Ballantine Books, 1965), 234–36.

ing, as they were fond of doing, the stars shine out from the smooth patches of the lake as they opened in the sky. From their town the Lonely Mountain was mostly screened by the low hills at the far end of the lake, through a gap in which the Running River came down from the North. Only its high peak could they see in clear weather, and they looked seldom at it, for it was ominous and drear even in the light of morning. Now it was lost and gone, blotted in the dark.

Suddenly it flickered back to view; a brief glow touched it and faded.

"Look!" said one. "The lights again! Last night the watchmen saw them start and fade from midnight until dawn. Something is happening up there."

"Perhaps the King under the Mountain is forging gold," said another. "It is long since he went north. It is time the songs began to prove themselves again."

"Which king?" said another with a grim voice. "As like as not it is the marauding fire of the Dragon, the only king under the Mountain we have ever known."

"You are always foreboding gloomy things!" said the others. "Anything from floods to poisoned fish. Think of something cheerful!"

Then suddenly a great light appeared in the low place in the hills and the northern end of the lake turned golden. "The King beneath the Mountain!" they shouted. "His wealth is like the Sun, his silver like a fountain, his rivers golden run! The river is running gold from the Mountain!" they cried, and everywhere windows were opening and feet were hurrying.

There was once more a tremendous excitement and enthusiasm. But the grim-voiced fellow ran hotfoot to the Master. "The dragon is coming or I am a fool!" he cried. "Cut the bridges! To arms! To arms!"

Then warning trumpets were suddenly sounded, and echoed along the rocky shores. The cheering stopped and the joy was turned to dread. So it was that the dragon did not find them quite unprepared.

Before long, so great was his speed, they could see him as a spark of fire rushing towards them and growing ever huger and more bright, and not the most foolish doubted that the prophecies had gone rather wrong. Still they had a little time. Every vessel in the town was filled with water, every warrior was armed, every arrow and dart was ready, and the bridge to the land was thrown down and destroyed before the roar of Smaug's terrible approach grew loud, and the lake rippled red as fire beneath the awful beating of his wings.

Amid shrieks and wailing and the shouts of men he came over them, swept towards the bridges and was foiled! The bridge was gone, and his enemies were on an island in deep water—too deep and dark and cool for his liking. If he plunged into it, a vapour and a steam would arise enough to cover all the land with a mist for days; but the lake was mightier than he, it would quench him before he could pass through.

Roaring he swept back over the town. A hail of dark arrows leaped up and snapped and rattled on his scales and jewels, and their shafts fell back kindled by his breath burning and hissing into the lake. No fireworks you ever imagined equalled the sights that night. At the twanging of the bows and the shrilling of the trumpets the dragon's wrath blazed to its height, till he was blind and mad with it. No one had dared to give battle to him for many an age; nor would they have dared now, if it had not been for the grim-voiced man (Bard was his name), who ran to and fro cheering on the archers and urging the Master to order them to fight to the last arrow.

Fire leaped from the dragon's jaws. He circled for a while high in the air above them lighting all the lake; the trees by the shores shone like copper and like blood with leaping shadows of dense black at their feet. Then down he swooped straight through the arrow-storm, reckless in his rage, taking no heed to turn his scaly sides towards his foes, seeking only to set their town ablaze.

Fire leaped from thatched roofs and wooden beam-ends as he hurtled down and past and round again, though all had been drenched with water before he came. Once more water was flung by a hundred hands wherever a spark appeared. Back swirled the dragon. A sweep of his tail and the roof of the Great House crumbled and smashed down. Flames unquenchable sprang high into the night. Another swoop and another, and another house and then another sprang afire and fell; and still no arrow hindered Smaug or hurt him more than a fly from the marshes.

JAMES THURBER (1894–1961)
FABLES FOR OUR TIME

A creature whose existence was seriously debated for centuries becomes the focus of a domestic dispute in James Thurber's *The Unicorn in the Garden*, a modern fable of the ongoing battle between the sexes. Both Rabelais and Lewis Carroll had treated the unicorn in fantastic settings, the one bawdily, the other as a comic figure. Thurber places the animal within a realistic context. Like E. Nesbit's phoenix emerging from a fireplace in a London residence, Thurber's unicorn appears within a modern garden. In one tradition of unicorn lore, the creature was one of the animals in the Garden of Eden. Thurber's story, accompanied by his own drawing, was collected in *Fables for Our Time* (1940).

An American humorist whose writings and cartoons appeared for decades in the *New Yorker* magazine, Thurber is probably best known for *The Secret Life of Walter Mitty*, another story in which the individual imagination is at odds with the world around it. One of Thurber's most popular cartoons depicts a seal peering over the headboard of a bed, above a wife scornfully saying to her resigned husband: "All right, have it your way—you heard a seal bark."

James Thurber's drawing accompanying his *Unicorn in the Garden*. Copyright © 1940 James Thurber. Copyright © 1968 Helen Thurber and Rosemary A. Thurber. Reprinted by arrangement with Rosemary A. Thurber and the Barbara Hogenson Agency.

The Unicorn in the Garden *

Once upon a sunny morning a man who sat in a breakfast nook looked up from his scrambled eggs to see a white unicorn with a gold horn quietly cropping the roses in the garden. The man went up to the bedroom where his wife was still asleep and woke her. "There's a unicorn in the garden," he said. "Eating roses." She opened one unfriendly eye and looked at him. "The unicorn is a mythical beast," she said, and turned her back on him. The man walked slowly downstairs and out into the garden. The unicorn was still there; he was now browsing among the tulips. "Here, unicorn," said the man, and he pulled up a lily and gave it to him. The unicorn ate it gravely. With a high heart, because there was a unicorn in his garden, the man went upstairs and roused his wife again. "The unicorn," he said, "ate a lily." His wife sat up in bed and looked at him, coldly. "You are a booby," she said, "and I am going to have you put in the booby hatch." The man, who had never liked the words "booby" and "booby-hatch," and who liked them even less on a shining morning when there was a unicorn in the garden, thought for a moment. "We'll see about that," he said. He walked over to the door. "He has a golden horn in the middle of his forehead," he told her. Then he went back to the garden to watch the unicorn; but the unicorn had gone away. The man sat down among the roses and went to sleep.

As soon as the husband had gone out of the house, the wife got up and dressed as fast as she could. She was very excited and there was a gloat in her eye. She telephoned the police and she telephoned a psychiatrist; she told them to hurry

* James Thurber, *Fables for Our Time*, in *The Thurber Carnival* (New York: Delta, 1964), 268–69.

to her house and bring a strait-jacket. When the police and the psychiatrist arrived they sat down in chairs and looked at her, with great interest. "My husband," she said, "saw a unicorn this morning." The police looked at the psychiatrist and the psychiatrist looked at the police. "He told me it ate a lily," she said. The psychiatrist looked at the police and the police looked at the psychiatrist. "He told me it had a golden horn in the middle of its forehead," she said. At a solemn signal from the psychiatrist, the police leaped from their chairs and seized the wife. They had a hard time subduing her, for she put up a terrific struggle, but they finally subdued her. Just as they got her into the strait-jacket, the husband came back into the house.

"Did you tell your wife you saw a unicorn?" asked the police. "Of course not," said the husband. "The unicorn is a mythical beast." "That's all I wanted to know," said the psychiatrist. "Take her away. I'm sorry, sir, but your wife is as crazy as a jay bird." So they took her away, cursing and screaming, and shut her up in an institution. The husband lived happily ever after.

Moral: Don't count your boobies until they are hatched.

CARL JUNG (1875–1961)
PSYCHOLOGY AND ALCHEMY

To analytical psychologist Carl Jung, individuals share a "collective unconscious" which is expressed in the form of "archetypal" images. These symbolic motifs in dreams and fantasies, he believed, are similar or identical to those of myths, folklore, ancient religions, and cults. His *Psychology and Alchemy* (1944) explores the correspondences between two disciplines, proposing that the symbols of alchemy express the part of the mind identified as the unconscious. Jung parallels the alchemical transmutation of base metals from the *prima materia* (prime matter) into gold and the self-realizing integration of the unconscious with the conscious area of the self. One of his major symbols is the unicorn.

The concluding chapter of *Psychology and Alchemy* is "The Paradigm of the Unicorn." Following is the first of nine subsections that also include the figure of the unicorn in Christian, Gnostic, Indian, Persian, Jewish and Chinese religious and mythological traditions. In "The Unicorn in Alchemy," the unicorn is one of the many symbols of Mercurius, which represents the *prima materia*. The entry is complete.

Jung was closely associated with Sigmund Freud, the founder of psychoanalysis, before Jung expanded Freud's theories about individual sexuality to encompass the universality of the collective unconscious. Jung's ideas, like those of

James George Frazer, have greatly influenced the later development of comparative mythology.

For alchemy, see Paracelsus.

The Unicorn in Alchemy*

I have chosen the example of the unicorn in order to show how the symbolism of
Mercurius is intermingled with the traditions of pagan Gnosticism and of the
Church. The unicorn is not a single, clearly defined entity but a fabulous being
with a great many variations: there are, for instance, one-horned horses, asses,
fish, dragons, scarabs, etc. Therefore, strictly speaking, we are more concerned
with the theme of the single horn (the alicorn). In the *Chymical Wedding* of
Rosencreutz, a snow-white unicorn appears and makes his obeisance before the
lion. Lion and unicorn are both symbols of Mercurius. A little farther on in the
book the unicorn gives place to a white dove, another symbol of Mercurius, who,
in his volatile form of *spiritus*, is a parallel of the Holy Ghost. At least ten out of
the fifteen figures in Lambspringk's symbols are representations of the dual nature
of Mercurius. Figure III shows the unicorn facing a stag. The latter, as *cervus fugi-
tivus*, is also a symbol of Mercurius. Mylius illustrates the opus by a series of seven
symbols, of which the sixth is the unicorn couched under a tree, symbolizing the
spirit of life that leads the way to resurrection. Penotus gives a table of symbols
where the unicorn, together with the lion, the eagle, and the dragon, is the co-
ordinate of gold. The *aurum no vulgi*, like the lion, eagle and dragon, is a synonym
for Mercurius. The poem entitled "Von der Materi und Prattick des Steins" says:

> I am the right true Unicorn.
> What man can cleave me hoof from horn
> And join my body up again
> So that it no more falls in twain?

Here I must refer once again to Ripley, where we meet the "green lion lying in
the queen's lap with blood flowing from his side." This image is an allusion on the
one hand to the Pietà, on the other to the unicorn wounded by the hunter and
caught in the lap of a virgin, a frequent theme in medieval pictures. True, the
green lion has replaced the unicorn here, but that did not present any difficulty
to the alchemist since the lion is likewise a symbol of Mercurius. The virgin represents his passive, feminine aspect, while the unicorn or the lion illustrates the
wild, rampant, masculine, penetrating force of the *spiritus mercurialis*. Since the

---

* C. G. Jung, *Psychology and Alchemy*, trans. R. F. C. Hull (Princeton, N.J.: Princeton University
Press, 1993), pp. 435–38.

symbol of the unicorn as an allegory of the Christ and of the Holy Ghost was current all through the Middle Ages, the connection between them was certainly known to the alchemists, so that there can be no question that Ripley had in his mind, when he used this symbol, the affinity, indeed the identity, of Mercurius with Christ.

PETER LUM (1911–)
FABULOUS BEASTS

Peter Lum (Bettina Lum Crowe) offers a number of possible origins of imaginary animals in her *Fabulous Beasts* (1951), one of the first books devoted to the study of such creatures and a standard listing in bibliographies on the subject.

The author ranges through global mythology and folklore, citing many kinds of fantastic beings from creation myths to the distorted descriptions of travelers. Among the many theories she presents, Lum echoes Charles Gould's thesis in *Mythical Monsters* that some animals we regard as fabulous were once actual creatures that have since become extinct, and she cites the nature myth explanation of nineteenth-century comparative mythologists. Later in the chapter, she categorizes the beasts as unmixed variations of actual animals, composites of parts of different animals, and animal-human hybrids. An earlier chapter treats animals in fable, and later chapters focus on individual creatures.

*The Creation of Imaginary Animals**

. . . granted that until quite recently man had no reason for denying the existence of certain animals that we now know to have been imaginary, there remains the question of what caused him to believe in the existence of these particular animals in the first place. Why, if no creature with the forepart of an eagle and the hindquarters of a lion, or with the head of a cock and the tail of a serpent, ever lived, did it occur to anyone to invent the gryphon or the cockatrice? Why, if there has never been a dragon, did the thought of it strike terror into civilizations already old when Abraham was born? Each beast has its own history of myth and error and exaggeration to account for the form in which we know it, and in some cases we can at least guess at the idea that might have been responsible for it. But

* Peter Lum, *Fabulous Beasts* (New York: Pantheon, 1951), 23–30.

there are certain characteristics shared by more than one fabulous beast, and some influences that may have encouraged the development of them.

For one thing, it is possible that certain legendary animals are based on creatures which did actually once exist, but are now extinct. A number of animals have become extinct even in historic times, either as the result of changing climate, some shift in the balance of nature, or simply the predatory habits of man. . . .

But there is another way in which the gigantic reptilian monsters who existed in earth's infancy may have influenced the formation of the dragon and other non-existent creatures, and that is by their skeletons. The finding of bones and fossils unlike those of animals with which he was familiar would naturally persuade man of the existence of creatures unknown to him, especially when the bones were of a size to suggest that they belonged to some huge and therefore terrifying monster. The tusks of an extinct Siberian rhinoceros were long accepted in Europe as being the claws of the huge bird called the gryphon, while in the Middle Ages the finding on remote Arctic islands of occasional single, slender ivory tusks (actually the tooth of the narwhal) revived the waning belief in the existence of the unicorn. In Japan the headbones of a particular fish were believed to be the skulls of the "tengu," a fabulous bird demon, and stone age weapons sometimes found nearby provided the claws for these same creatures. Even if the finding of such horns and tusks and skeletons did not of itself shape particular mythological animals, it certainly provided powerful evidence in favor of their existence. Faced with bones that were clearly those of some animals, yet unrelated to any identifiable animal, even the sceptic must hesitate.

Two other possible elements in the creation of imaginary animals have already been mentioned as operating equally on both the real and the unreal. One is that, with the coming of human and superhuman gods, the original animal gods that had once been worshiped by mankind became degraded into creatures of myth and fable. The other is that in very early times men tried to express natural phenomena by describing them in terms of bird or animal and that, when this had been forgotten, the creatures so described took on a life of their own and lingered in the mythology of races who had no idea of their original significance. The giant bird that was the sun becomes the fabulous phoenix, the wind becomes personified as a horse, or the equally swift "son of the wind" becomes a monkey: rain is worshiped as a rain-bringing dragon, and the starry sky becomes the hundred-eyed Argus, whose eyes eventually come to decorate the tail of Juno's peacock. In the same way certain monstrous and unnatural beasts, such as the Persian "senmurv," half mammal and half bird, may have resulted from an attempt to symbolize the union of different elements of earth and heaven, or earth and sea. Mermaids and other sea-monsters are probably relics of some such effort to find a connecting link between the creatures of dry land and those of water. Equally, for some reason unknown to us, the Sphinx and other creatures which combine the lion and the human form were evolved as a symbol of death.

Some supernatural animals may have come into being as supposedly taking part in the creation or preservation of the universe. The Chinese believe that when the first man, P'an Ku, began his work of creation he was attended by the four auspicious animals: the dragon, the unicorn, the tortoise and the phoenix. Together they worked away at the universe with mallet and chisel for some eighteen thousand years, and every day that they worked P'an Ku increased six feet in height. But it was not until P'an Ku himself died that the task could be finished, for it was the body of P'an Ku (like that of the Chaldean Tiamat and the Indian Prajapati) which provided the earth: his blood flowed and became the rivers, his flesh was the soil, his bones the rock, and his hair the tangled forest. . . .

All these are creatures not only fabulous but remote, and creatures of which there existed but a single one. When we come to the more modern fabulous beasts, those catalogued in natural histories as regular species, examples of which might be found almost anywhere, the basilisks, the unicorns, the antholops with their two horns protruding so awkwardly that they were always catching them in thickets, or the catoblepas with his head so heavy that he could never lift it off the ground, the main source of these was undoubtedly the stories brought back by credulous travelers. Often the tales were told in good faith, and were the result either of misunderstandings or of faulty observation. The slim-horned antelope seen at a distance seemed to have but a single horn; the mounted horseman observed by those who had not learned to ride appeared to be a centaur (when Pizarro first landed in the New World the Mexicans fled from his soldiers in the belief that they and their horses were a breed of unknown and terrible monsters), and in a world filled with things far more strange and wonderful than these there was no reason for a traveler to doubt what he believed to be the evidence of his eyes. The home of most of the marvels reported in Europe and the Mediterranean countries was India, or later Abyssinia, and as the tales were passed on by word of mouth they grew more fantastic, and at the same time more difficult to deny by those who had never been East and had no reason to believe that anything might not exist on that rim of the world.

Wishful thinking also played its part. Man was constantly seeking some secret that would render him immortal, or invisible, or proof against injury, or cure him of his illnesses. . . .

. . . Language adds its difficulty; in translating the unfamiliar one must use familiar words, and this may lead to the confusion either of a real with a fabulous beast or of one fabulous creature with another.

T. H. WHITE (1906–1964)
THE BOOK OF BEASTS*

The bestiaries were a major part of the histories of many fabulous beasts, even though fantastic creatures comprised only a small fraction of the animals represented in those medieval natural histories. In the afterword of his *Book of Beasts* (1954) are diagrams T. H. White adapted from P. Ansel Robin's *Animal Lore in English Literature* to trace major literary sources and later influence of the bestiaries. White's charts, while focusing on bestiaries in particular, are broadly applicable to the literary transmission of animal lore in general. Because animals we now call fabulous are a relatively small but nonetheless integral part of that literary tradition, the diagrams necessarily apply to them as well. Most of the authors listed on White's charts are represented in this collection; those whose works are not represented here are referred to in editorial text.

White's *Book of Beasts* is the first complete English translation of a Latin prose bestiary. Along with his engaging notes throughout and his extensive afterword, the book is an essential work on animal lore, frequently reprinted since its initial publication. In the beginning, middle, and end of his book, White quotes Alexander Ross's "And as dutifull Children let us cover the Nakednesse of our Fathers with the Cloke of a favourable Interpretation," expressing his own approach to the bestiaries.

Excerpts from *The Book of Beasts* appear in the "Latin Prose Bestiary" entry earlier in this volume. White's diagrams appear facing this page and overleaf.

JORGE LUIS BORGES (1899–1986)
THE BOOK OF IMAGINARY BEINGS

Perhaps the earliest and most popular fabulous-beast book in encyclopedia format is *The Book of Imaginary Beings* (1957), by Jorge Luis Borges, compiled in collaboration with Margaritta Guerro. The collection covers fantastic creatures from the Malaysian "A Bao Qu" to the Arabian "Zaratan."

In the preface to the first edition of their fantastic bestiary (below), Borges and Guerro contrast the relatively small number of fantastic creations of the human imagination with the richness and variety of nature's animal kingdom. Nonethe-

---

* T.H. White, *The Book of Beasts* (New York: G. P. Putnam's Sons, 1954; rpt. New York: Dover Publications, 1984.), pp. 233, 263.

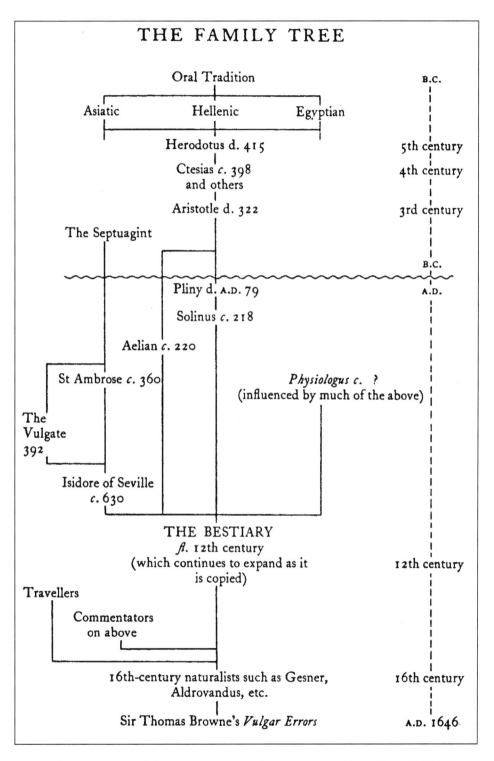

THE FAMILY TREE

Oral Tradition   B.C.

Asiatic   Hellenic   Egyptian

Herodotus d. 415   5th century

Ctesias *c.* 398
and others   4th century

Aristotle d. 322   3rd century

The Septuagint

B.C.

Pliny d. A.D. 79   A.D.

Solinus *c.* 218

Aelian *c.* 220

St Ambrose *c.* 360   *Physiologus c.* ?
(influenced by much of the above)

The
Vulgate
392

Isidore of Seville
c. 630

THE BESTIARY
fl. 12th century
(which continues to expand as it
is copied)   12th century

Travellers

Commentators
on above

16th-century naturalists such as Gesner,   16th century
Aldrovandus, etc.

Sir Thomas Browne's *Vulgar Errors*   A.D. 1646

T. H. White's diagram of the literary origins of bestiary animal lore. From T. H. White, *The Book of Beasts*. Courtesy of Dover Publications.

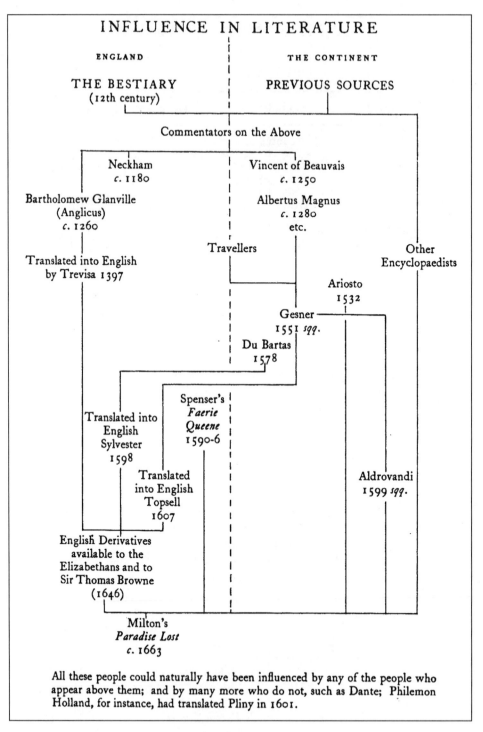

INFLUENCE IN LITERATURE

ENGLAND   THE CONTINENT

THE BESTIARY
(12th century)

PREVIOUS SOURCES

Commentators on the Above

Neckham
c. 1180

Vincent of Beauvais
c. 1250

Bartholomew Glanville
(Anglicus)
c. 1260

Albertus Magnus
c. 1280
etc.

Travellers

Other
Encyclopaedists

Translated into English
by Trevisa 1397

Ariosto
1532

Gesner
1551 sqq.

Du Bartas
1578

Spenser's
*Faerie
Queene*
1590-6

Translated into
English
Sylvester
1598

Translated
into English
Topsell
1607

Aldrovandi
1599 sqq.

English Derivatives
available to the
Elizabethans and to
Sir Thomas Browne
(1646)

Milton's
Paradise Lost
c. 1663

All these people could naturally have been influenced by any of the people who
appear above them; and by many more who do not, such as Dante; Philemon
Holland, for instance, had translated Pliny in 1601.

T. H. White's diagram of the literary influence of bestiary animal lore. From T. H. White,
The Book of Beasts. Courtesy of Dover Publications.

less, "there is a kind of lazy pleasure in useless and out-of-the-way erudition," the editors write in a later preface, and they hope the reader will share the enjoyment they had "ransacking the bookshelves of our friends and the mazelike vaults of the Biblioteca Nacional in search of old authors and abstruse references."

A major twentieth-century fiction writer, poet, and essayist, Borges, an Argentinian, is renowned for his labyrinthine tales incorporating philosophical concepts and arcane scholarship.

The Zoo of Reality and the Zoo of Mythologies*

A small child is taken to the zoo for the first time. This child may be any one of us or, to put it another way, we have been this child and have forgotten about it. In these grounds — these terrible grounds — the child sees living animals he has never before glimpsed; he sees jaguars, vultures, bison, and — what is still stranger — giraffes. He sees for the first time the bewildering variety of the animal kingdom, and this spectacle, which might alarm or frighten him, he enjoys. He enjoys it so much that going to the zoo is one of the pleasures of childhood, or is thought to be such. How can we explain this everyday and yet mysterious event?

We can, of course, deny it. We can suppose that children suddenly rushed off to the zoo will become, in due time, neurotic, and the truth is there can hardly be a child who has not visited the zoo and there is hardly a grown-up who is not a neurotic. It may be stated that all children, by definition, are explorers, and that to discover the camel is in itself no stranger than to discover a mirror or water or a staircase. It can also be stated that the child trusts his parents, who take him to this place full of animals. Besides, his toy tiger and the pictures of tigers in the encyclopedia have somehow taught him to look at the flesh-and-bone tiger without fear. Plato (if he were invited to join in this discussion) would tell us that the child had already seen the tiger in a primal world of archetypes, and that now on seeing the tiger he recognizes it. Schopenhauer (even more wondrously) would tell us that the child looks at the tigers without fear because he is aware that he is the tigers and the tigers are him or, more accurately, that both he and the tigers are but forms of that single essence, the Will.

Let us pass now from the zoo of reality to the zoo of mythologies, to the zoo whose denizens are not lions but sphinxes and griffons and centaurs. The population of this second zoo should exceed by far the population of the first, since a monster is no more than a combination of parts of real beings, and the possibilities of permutation border on the infinite. In the centaur, the horse and man are blended; in the Minotaur, the bull and man (Dante imagined it as having the face

* Jorge Luis Borges, *The Book of Imaginary Beings,* with Margaritta Guerro, trans. Norman Thomas di Giovanni (1957; rpt., New York: Avon, 1970), 15–17.

of a man and the body of a bull); and in this way it seems we could evolve an endless variety of monsters—combinations of fishes, birds, and reptiles, limited only by our own boredom or disgust. This, however, does not happen; our monsters would be stillborn, thank God. Flaubert has rounded up, in the last pages of his *Temptation of Saint Anthony*, a number of medieval and classical monsters and has tried—so say his commentators—to concoct a few new ones; his sum total is hardly impressive, and but few of them really stir our imaginations. Anyone looking into the pages of the present handbook will soon find out that the zoology of dreams is far poorer than the zoology of the Maker.

We are as ignorant of the meaning of the dragon as we are of the meaning of the universe, but there is something in the dragon's image that appeals to the human imagination, and so we find the dragon in quite distinct places and times. It is, so to speak, a necessary monster, not an ephemeral or accidental one, such as the three-headed chimera or the catoblepas. . . .

Barbara Wersba (1932–)
The Land of Forgotten Beasts

The cultural distance fabulous animals have traveled over time can be measured by placing Pliny's *Natural History*, for example, beside a modern children's book in which such creatures appear. Barbara Wersba's *The Land of Forgotten Beasts* (1964) is particularly representative of the latter in that the American author provides the still-existing animals of the imagination with their own habitat outside the unbelieving world.

In Wersba's book, a scientific-minded boy who scorns imaginary things fantastically enters a Book of Beasts, in which he encounters animal creations of the past. At the climactic banquet attended by all the creatures, the griffin sings (off-key) about his mythological and fabulous friends.

The "Mushrush" (mushussu) is a Babylonian dragon, one of the demonic brood of the primordial goddess Tiamat.

*The Land of Forgotten Beasts**

Oh the world is filled with strangeness and delight.
There are fish that fly and birds that walk on land,
There are swans that sing and insects that do dances,
So why we're off I'll never understand.

* Barbara Wersba, *The Land of Forgotten Beasts* (New York: Atheneum, 1964), 77–79.

We're courteous, unusual, and charming,
We're thoughtful and amazingly sincere.
We only need a little admiration
To fill our lives with happiness and cheer.

I will admit we're rather odd to look at,
Our heads and tails are sometimes out of place,
Occasionally we breathe a little fire,
But that should be no reason for disgrace.

The Cockatrice, for instance, is quite useful,
Though small, he has a mortifying glance.
If a mountain's in your way, he'll make it crumble,
His life is filled with danger and romance.

The Unicorn, by contrast, is so gentle
His horn can sweeten clouded pools and springs.
He lives on flowers and cannot be captured
By errant knights, or emperors, or kings.

The Manticore is equally appealing,
He jumps about and has a prickly tail.
Three rows of teeth and two superb mustaches,
You'll find him leaping over hill and dale.

Our country is incredibly exciting,
You'd never see a Mushrush back at home,
You couldn't grow a Goose Tree in Chicago,
You'd never find a Hippocamp in Rome.

Where else do serpents have two heads, or seven?
Where else are Centaurs quite so fancy-free?
Would you ever find a Griffin in your garden?
Do your Bishops ever frolic in the sea?

Your zoos are filled with simple things like Tigers,
Menageries like ours are more unique.
We have Ant-Lions, Phoenixes, and Dragons,
Our Mermaids are mysterious and chic.

We'll show you flying horses from the heavens,
We'll give you rides on monsters from the sea,

We'll take your hand and walk with you through fables,
Through legends filled with charm and poetry.

Though quite unreal, we're still the best beasts ever,
The fact that we're forgotten makes us weep.
The world that dreamed us cares for us no longer,
Its eyes are dim, its visions are asleep.

But some day Unicorns will be remembered,
And Griffins will again be brave and strong,
A Phoenix will be seen on the horizon
And all forgotten creatures shall belong.

HEINZ MODE (1913–)
FABULOUS BEASTS AND DEMONS

The most systematic study of fabulous beings in global art and literature is Heinz Mode's *Fabeltier und Damonen* (1973). After scrupulously defining terms in his opening treatise on fantastic creatures in general, Mode traces the geographical spread of "monsters" from their Middle Eastern origins, explains the beasts' development from actual prototypes, and classifies them according to five major hybrid families. These categories encompass far more varieties than simply "fabulous beasts." Individual chapters group the subjects according to: Bull-men and Satyrs, Angels and Devils; Sphinxes, Centaurs and Sirens; Dragons, Griffins and Other Winged Animals; Unicorns and Divinities with Multiple Heads; and Boat-man, Winged Sun and Marching Drum. Containing more than 500 illustrations, notes, a glossary of beasts, and an extensive bibliography, the book is a comprehensive resource. It is listed in most bibliographies of books about fabulous creatures.

The Birthplace and Migration of Monsters *

. . . It may at first appear surprising that monsters had not already received their visual shape in the imaginations of the earliest human communities but that the conscious creation of such creatures is a product of the earliest known civilizations, as far as we can now tell, in the period around 3,000 B.C. The first

---

* Heinz Mode, *Fabulous Beasts and Demons* (London: Phaidon Press, 1975), 12–13, 17–29.

pictorial records of monsters are to be found in that period in Egypt and Mesopotamia and perhaps a little later, in India, in the civilizations of what is called the ancient Near East. The representation of monsters was later to reach its most flourishing period in classical Greece, in ancient Italy and to a lesser extent in the Roman period, after two thousand years, during which the Hittite, Syrian, Iranian and also Cretan-Mycenaean civilizations kept the monsters alive.

Monsters spread farther towards Southeast Asia via India and towards the Far East not only by that route but also via Iran. It was roughly during the florescence of classical antiquity that China, like India, became a center of monster-creation. Thus the westward spread is matched by an eastward one, and both proceeded from the same centre in the Near East. The further diffusion in westerly and North European directions runs chronologically parallel to the spread of ancient civilization and can be roughly placed during the last two thousand years.

In Europe a new peak is later reached in Romanesque and Gothic art of France, Germany, Italy, Spain and England. Older monster types are to be found in Celtic civilization, and also in the Slavonic East of Europe. Here the ancient oriental images penetrated the North and West through the mediation of Central Asiatic nomadic tribes, as a tributary to the main stream, which started in classical times and flowed from East to West and from South to North. The peoples of the Eastern Mediterranean and of Iran, who had been converted to Islam, played an important intermediary role in this. While Buddhism confined itself essentially to Asia, and Christianity at first conquered Europe alone, Islamic culture became an important connecting link between these continents and also between them and Africa.

The Natural Sources of Monsters

. . . The shapes of monsters are always based, ultimately, upon observation of nature, and it is this fact, in turn, that accounts for their astonishing vitality. On the other hand, what is characteristic is the exaggeration and mixing of shapes, the combination of the qualities, abilities and powers of various natural beings into one composite figure, a process which can only be achieved in the human imagination. In it the most impressive parts of various animals were those that were most widely used. That is why the mighty pinions of birds of prey, the horns of wild bulls, the fangs and claws of the great cats, and the sting of the scorpion are so often found as conspicuous components of these monsters. The ruling castes of early times often adopted similar power symbols: the ancient oriental ruler claimed a crown of horns for his headpiece or mounted a lion-throne. At times he is shown surrounded by monsters, which are looked upon as the embodiments of his attributes.

A Classification of Monsters in Art

. . . A judicious use of formal criteria suggests a division into five categories, which can themselves be further subdivided.

I. Monsters with a human body or with an animal body in a markedly human posture, with an animal head or some other features of animal origin. This category can be termed "animal-man." It comprises devils, angels, satyrs and minotaurs, and also the many animal-men of the ancient Near East which show the same characteristics. . . .

II. Monsters with an animal body, or in unmistakable animal posture, combined with a human head, a human chest or other purely human features. For this category we propose the term "man-animal." It includes some of the best-known types such as the sphinx, the centaur, and the siren with the body of a bird or of a fish. In the ancient Near East and in South, South-East and East Asia this category was popular, particularly in the Naga and Innara figures, which have snake and bird bodies but a human chest and head. . . .

III. Monsters made up of parts (body and head) taken from different animal species or with other animal features added. Into this category come the griffin, the dragon, Pegasus and numerous other winged animals, and also the marine creatures with fish-tail and animal-body. This category can be put under the heading "animal-monsters." Most figures of this type have repeatedly been said either to occur in the world of nature or to result from a slight error of observation. The essential feature is the absence of human components.

IV. This category includes monstrous figures and combinations with deliberate reduplication or simplification, and also those with exaggerated enlargement or reduction of physical features, of limbs, heads and bodies. In some cases animal and human parts are combined, in others the natural shapes are merely modified. . . .

V. This is the smallest but perhaps the most interesting category. Natural phenomena or man-made objects are given human or animal features and turned into new entities, often with only small, symbolic changes. From the ancient Near East we know water-men, mountain-men and tree-men, and also the sword in the shape of a man and the ship in the form of either a man or an animal. . . .

JULIAN BARNES (1946–)
A HISTORY OF THE WORLD IN 10½ CHAPTERS

In paintings of the Creation and of animals boarding the Ark, the unicorn is commonly included along with actual members of the animal kingdom, even though the beast is not named in either Genesis event. Folklore explains the beast's later extinction by concluding it had perished in the Flood. According to various legends, the unicorn, too proud to mix with other creatures, remained on land or swam behind the vessel, or it was so unmanageable on the ship that Noah drove it into the sea. With serious overtones, English novelist Julian Barnes satirically proposes yet another explanation for extinction of the unicorn and other fabulous animals in his *History of the World in 10½ Chapters* (1989).

The following excerpt, narrated by a stowaway woodworm, is from the opening segment of the novel, whose first line announces the mixed nature of Noah's cargo: "They put the behemoths in the hold along with the rhinos, the hippos and the elephants." The novel is composed of a collection of stories loosely connected by the Noah voyage.

*Leaps in the Spectrum of Creation**

Put it another way: what the hell do you think Noah and his family ate in the Ark? They ate *us*, of course. I mean, if you look around the animal kingdom nowadays, you don't think this is all there ever was, do you? A lot of beasts looking more or less the same? I know you've got some theory to make sense of it all — something about relationship to the environment and inherited skills or whatever — but there's a much simpler explanation for the puzzling leaps in the spectrum of creation. One fifth of the earth's species went down with Varadi; and as for the rest that are missing, Noah's crowd ate them. . . .

. . . As far as Noah and his family were concerned, we were just a floating cafeteria. Clean and unclean came alike to them on the Ark; lunch first, then piety, that was the rule. And you can't imagine what richness of wildlife Noah deprived you of. Or rather, you can, because that's precisely what you do: you imagine it. All those mythical beasts your poets dreamed up in former centuries: you assume, don't you, that they were either knowingly invented, or else they were alarmist descriptions of animals half-glimpsed in the forest after too good a hunting lunch? I'm afraid the explanation's more simple; Noah and his tribe scoffed them. At the start of the Voyage, as I said, there was a pair of behemoths in our hold. I didn't

---

*   Julian Barnes, *A History of the World in 10½ Chapters* (New York: Vintage International, 1990), 13–16.

get much of a look at them myself, but I'm told they were impressive beasts. Yet Ham, Shem or the one whose name began with J apparently proposed at the family council that if you had the elephant and hippopotamus, you could get by without the behemoth; and besides — the argument combined practicality with principle — two such large carcases would keep the Noah family going for months.

Of course, it didn't work out like that. After a few weeks there were complaints about getting behemoth for dinner every night, and so — merely for a change of diet — some other species was sacrificed. There were guilty nods from time to time in the direction of domestic economy, but I can tell you this: there was a lot of salted behemoth left over at the end of the journey.

The salamander went the same way. The real salamander, I mean, not the unremarkable animal you still call by the same name; our salamander lived in fire. That was a one-off beast and no mistake; yet Ham or Shem or the other one kept pointing out that on a wooden ship the risk was simply too great, and so both the salamanders and the twin fires that housed them had to go. The carbuncle went as well, all because of some ridiculous story Ham's wife had heard about it having a precious jewel inside its skull. She was always a dressy one, that Ham's wife. So they took one of the carbuncles and chopped its head off; split the skull and found nothing at all. Maybe the jewel is only found in the female's head, Ham's wife suggested. So they opened up the other one as well, with the same negative result.

I put this next suggestion to you rather tentatively; I feel I have to voice it, though. At times we suspected a kind of system behind the killing that went on. Certainly there was more extermination than was strictly necessary for nutritional purposes — far more. And at the same time some of the species that were killed had very little eating on them. What's more, the gulls would occasionally report that they had seen carcases tossed from the stern with perfectly good meat thick on the bone. We began to suspect that Noah and his tribe had it in for certain animals simply for being what they were. The basilisk, for instance, went overboard very early. Now, of course it wasn't very pleasant to look at, but I feel it my duty to record that there was very little eating underneath those scales, and that the bird certainly wasn't sick at the time.

In fact, when we came to look back on it after the event, we began to discern a pattern, and the pattern began with the basilisk. You've never seen one, of course. But if I describe a four-legged cock with a serpent's tail, say that it had a very nasty look in its eye and laid a misshapen egg which it then employed a toad to hatch, you'll understand that this was not the most alluring beast on the Ark. Still, it had its rights like everyone else, didn't it? After the basilisk it was the griffon's turn; after the griffon, the sphinx; after the sphinx, the hippogriff. You thought they were all gaudy fantasies, perhaps? Not a bit of it. And do you see what they had in common? They were all crossbreeds. We think it was Shem — though it could well have been Noah himself — who had this thing about the purity of the species. Cock-eyed, of course; and as we used to say to one another, you only had to look at Noah and his wife, or at their three sons and their three wives, to realize what a genetically messy lot the human race would turn out to be. So why should they start getting fastidious about cross-breeds?

Still, it was the unicorn that was the most distressing. That business depressed us for months. Of course, there were the usual sordid rumours — that Ham's wife had been putting its horn to ignoble use — and the posthumous smear campaign by the authorities about the beast's character; but this only sickened us the more. The unavoidable fact is that Noah was jealous. We all looked up to the unicorn, and he couldn't stand it. Noah — what point is there in not telling you the truth? — was bad-tempered, smelly, unreliable, envious and cowardly. He wasn't even a good sailor: when the seas were high he would retire to his cabin, throw himself down on his gopher-wood bed and leave it only to vomit out his stomach into his gopher-wood wash-basin; you could smell the effluvia a deck away. Whereas the unicorn was strong, honest, fearless, impeccably groomed and a mariner who never knew a moment's queasiness. Once, in a gale, Ham's wife lost her footing near the rail and was about to go overboard. The unicorn — who had deck privileges as a result of popular lobbying — galloped across and stuck his horn through her trailing cloak, pinning it to the deck. Fine thanks he got for his valour; the Noahs had him casseroled one Embarkation Sunday. I can vouch for that. I spoke personally to the carrier-hawk who delivered a warm pot to Shem's ark.

You don't have to believe me, of course; but what do your own archives say? . . .

Epilogue

LEWIS THOMAS (1913–93)
THE LIVES OF A CELL

The hybrid nature of many fabulous animals was a major cause of the discrediting of such creatures. This composite makeup is the very characteristic of fantastic beasts that twentieth-century microbiologist Lewis Thomas parallels to the structural behavior of cells. In his *The Lives of a Cell* (1974), a winner of the National Book Award, Thomas reassesses the nature of mythical animals. He juxtaposes two sets of subjects as unlike as parts of bird, beast, serpent, and fish, identifying fabulous constructs with living organisms. At one point in the "Some Biomythology" chapter near the end of his book, Thomas cites intertwined serpents in ancient art as representing the double helix symbol of the origin of life. The serpent image and the meaning circles back to Marduk's creation of the world from the body of the primal dragoness Tiamat.

Some Biomythology*

The mythical animals catalogued in the bestiaries of the world seem, at a casual glance, nothing but exotic nonsense. The thought comes that Western civilized, scientific, technologic society is a standing proof of human progress, in having risen above such imaginings. They are as obsolete as the old anecdotes in which they played their puzzling, ambiguous roles, and we have no more need for the beasts than for the stories. The Griffon, Phoenix, Centaur, Sphinx, Manticore, Ganesha, Ch'i-lin, and all the rest are like recurrent bad dreams, and we are well rid of them. So we say.

The trouble is that they are in fact like dreams, and not necessarily bad ones, and we may have a hard time doing without them. They may be as essential for society as mythology itself, as loaded with symbols, and as necessary for the architecture of our collective unconscious. If Levi-Strauss is right, myths are constructed by a universal logic that, like language itself, is as characteristic for human beings as nest-building is for birds. The stories seem to be different stories, but the underlying structure is always the same, in any part of the world, at any

* Lewis Thomas, *The Lives of a Cell; Notes of a Biology Watcher* (New York: Bantam Books, 1975), 141–44, 147–48.

time. They are like engrams, built into our genes. In this sense, bestiaries are part of our inheritance.

There is something basically similar about most of these crazy animals. They are all unbiologic, but unbiologic in the same way. Bestiaries do not contain, as a rule, totally novel creatures of the imagination made up of parts that we have never seen before. On the contrary, they are made up of parts that are entirely familiar. What is novel, and startling, is that they are mixtures of species.

It is perhaps this characteristic that makes the usual bestiary so outlandish to the twentieth-century mind. Our most powerful story, equivalent in its way to a universal myth, is evolution. Never mind that it is true whereas myths are not; it is filled with symbolism, and this is the way it has influenced the mind of society. In our latest enlightenment, the fabulous beasts are worse than improbable — they are impossible, because they violate evolution. They are not species, and they deny the existence of species.

The Phoenix comes the closest to being a conventional animal, all bird for all of its adult life. It is, in fact, the most exuberant, elaborate, and ornamented of all plumed birds. It exists in the mythology of Egypt, Greece, the Middle East, and Europe, and is the same as the vermilion bird of ancient China. It lives for five hundred triumphant years, and when it dies it constructs a sort of egg-shaped cocoon around itself. Inside, it disintegrates and gives rise to a wormlike creature, which then develops into the new Phoenix, ready for the next five hundred years. In other versions the dead bird bursts into flames, and the new one arises from the ashes, but the worm story is very old, told no doubt by an early biologist.

There are so many examples of hybrid beings in bestiaries that you could say that an ardent belief in mixed forms of life is an ancient human idea, or that something else, deeply believed in, is symbolized by these consortia. They are disturbing to look at, nightmarish, but most of them, oddly enough, are intended as lucky benignities. The Ch'i-lin, for instance, out of ancient China, has the body of a deer covered with gleaming scales, a marvelously bushy tail, cloven hooves, and small horns. Whoever saw a Ch'i-lin was in luck, and if you got to ride one, you had it made.

The Ganesha is one of the oldest and most familiar Hindu deities, possessing a fat human body, four human arms, and the head of a cheerful-looking elephant. Prayers to Ganesha are regarded as the quickest way around obstacles.

Not all mythical beasts are friendly, of course, but even the hostile ones have certain amiable redeeming aspects. The Manticore has a lion's body, a man's face, and a tail with a venomous snake's head at the end of it. It bounds around seeking prey with huge claws and three rows of teeth, but it makes the sounds of a beautiful silver flute.

Some of the animal myths have the ring of contemporary biologic theory, if you allow for differences in jargon. An ancient idea in India postulates an initial Being, the first form of life on the earth, analogous to our version of the earliest prokaryotic arrangement of membrane-limited nucleic acid, the initial cell, born of lightning and methane. The Indian Being, undefined and indefinable, finding itself alone, fearing death, yearning for company, began to swell in size, rearranged itself inside, and then split into two identical halves. One of these changed into a cow, the other a bull, and they mated, then changed again to a mare and stallion, and so on, down to the ants, and thus the earth was populated. There is a lot of oversimplification here, and too much shorthand for modern purposes, but the essential myth is recognizable.

The serpent keeps recurring through the earliest cycles of mythology, always as a central symbol for the life of the universe and the continuity of creation. There are two great identical snakes on a Levantine libation vase of around 2000 B.C., coiled around each other in a double helix, representing the original generation of life. They are the replicated parts of the first source of living, and they are wonderfully homologous. . . .

Bacteria are the greatest of all at setting up joint enterprises, on which the lives of their hosts are totally dependent. The nitrogen-fixing rhizobia in root nodules, the mycetomes of insects, and the enzyme-producing colonies in the digestive tracts of many animals are variations of this meticulously symmetrical symbiosis.

The meaning of these stories may be basically the same as the meaning of a medieval bestiary. There is a tendency for living things to join up, establish linkages, live inside each other, return to earlier arrangements, get along, whenever possible. This is the way of the world.

The new phenomenon of cell fusion, a laboratory trick on which much of today's science of molecular genetics relies for its data, is the simplest and most unbiologic of all phenomena, violating the most fundamental myth of the last century, for it denies the importance of specificity, integrity, and separateness in living things. Any cell—man, animal, fish, fowl, or insect—given the chance and under the right conditions, brought into contact with any other cell, however foreign, will fuse with it. Cytoplasm will flow easily from one to the other, the nuclei will combine, and it will become, for a time anyway, a single cell with two complete, alien genomes, ready to dance, ready to multiply. It is a Chimera, a Griffon, a Sphinx, a Ganesha, a Peruvian god, a Ch'i-lin, an omen of good fortune, a wish for the world.

A Glossary of Fabulous Beasts

Nearly all the imaginary animals described below appear in this collection in early expository works that assumed the creature either did exist or might exist. Some of these animals, such as the dragon and the sirens, were among the monsters in earlier mythological poetry. While a few are included in only a single entry in this book, most are referred to by writers in different epochs, and the major figures appear repeatedly throughout the entire Western literary tradition. Readers wishing to seek out references to a particular animal through this collection should, of course, consult the index. Also in the index are many mythological monsters not included here and creatures mentioned by name but not described in detail. For groups of imaginary animals, see especially Pliny's beasts of Ethiopia and the selections from Rabelais, Goethe, and Flaubert.

Amphisbaena (Greek, "one that goes both ways"): A classical and bestiary reptile with a head at each end of its body. A worm lizard of the genus of the same name.

Ant-Lion (Greek, *mermicoleon*; Latin, *formicoleon*): A *Physiologus* animal generated by mistranslation. A word that literally means "lion among ants" became the name of a fearsome composite of the two. Insects of the family *Myrmeleontidae*.

Barnacle goose (Bernaca, bernicle, etc.; also, tree goose): Differs from the actual barnacle goose (*Branta leucopsis*) in its attested generation from barnacles on rotted wood or from fruit on trees. Denounced by papal authority. Eyewitness descriptions helped perpetuate the tale from the Middle Ages to the Age of Reason.

Basilisk (Greek *basiliskos*, "little king"; Latin *regulus*, "prince"; also cockatrice): Regarded as the king of serpents for the crown-like spot on its head. Its petrifying stare and poisonous breath are fatal to most living things, but it can be killed by cockcrows, weasels, and by seeing its own reflected image. The first major authoritative account of the beast was by Pliny the Elder. The basilisk is in translations of the Old Testament, is a bestiary creature, and from the late Middle Ages onward was generally known as a cockatrice, born from a cock's egg hatched by a toad. It is a heraldic monster and was the subject of seventeenth-century controversy. *Basiliscus* is the genus name of a tropical American lizard.

Bird of paradise (Malay, *manucodiata*, "bird of the gods," Mamuque, etc.): An East Indies bird of brilliant plumage thought to have come from Paradise and never land on earth. Specimens of the birds, skinned by natives, were introduced in Europe during the Age of Exploration. Described in natural histories.

Bishop fish: A fish resembling a bishop, described and illustrated in sixteenth-century natural histories. Authors commonly paired it with the monk fish, another creature that appeared to be wearing a habit.

Caladrius (Charadrius): *Physiologus* and bestiary bird, pure white, prized for its diagnosis of sick kings. It turns away from someone beyond cure, or if the patient can recover, it gathers the sickness into itself and spreads it into the air while in flight toward the sun.

Caristae (Carystiae): In Albertus Magnus from Solinus, birds that fly through flame unharmed, but Albertus debunked the story.

Catoblepas (Greek, "that which looks downwards"; Catoplepe, also Gorgon): A beast having an oversized head so heavy it always hangs close to the ground, but the animal's Gorgon-like gaze, like that of the basilisk, can kill. In writings from classical times. Often identified with the gnu.

Cinnamon bird ("Cinomolgus" in the bestiaries): A classical and bestiary bird whose nest of cinnamon is the object of hunters. Pliny considered it fabulous. The bird is similar to the phoenix in that, in one version of the story, it builds a nest of spices in tall trees.

Dragon (Greek *drakon*, "sharp-sighted," "to see clearly," a large serpent; Latin *draco*): The most ancient, mythologically complex, and universal of all animals of the imagination. In Babylonian art, it is a horned and footed serpent, often associated with the primal goddess Tiamat. To the Greeks and Romans, dragon simply meant a large snake, both in mythology, as in the Apollo and Python myth, or in natural histories, in which it is presented as a large constrictor that entangles elephants. Christian art and literature depict it as a scaly monster with claws, wings, and fiery breath, a representation of Satan and evil. Natural history compiler Edward Topsell presents dragons both with wings and without. A grand heraldic figure with two legs (wivern) or four (as in the Red Dragon of Wales). The most popular and widespread imaginary creature in contemporary fantasy. A major figure throughout the Far East; one of the four Celestial Animals of China. *Draco* is the name of both a constellation and a genus of lizards.

Echeneis (Greek, "ship-detaining"; Latin *remora*, "delay," "hindrance"): A classical and bestiary fish that can stop a ship under full sail by attaching itself to the hull.

Ercinee: A bird of the Hercynian Forest, whose feathers glow so brightly in the dark that travelers carry the creature with them to light their way. In classical and bestiary writings.

Garuda bird: A gigantic bird that Antonio Pigafetta heard about during the Magellan voyage around the world. One of the global family of large fabulous birds that includes the roc, griffin, simurgh, and angka. In the mythology of India, Garuda is the vehicle of the god Vishnu.

Giant ants: Ants of India that dig up from the desert gold that men try to steal. Described by Herodotus as larger than a fox and smaller than a dog. Later identified with human miners and with marmots.

Griffin (Greek *gryps*, "curved, having a hooked beak"; griffon, gryphon, etc.): A composite animal with the body of a lion and the forelegs, wings, and head of an eagle. One of the oldest and most majestic of imaginary beasts, it was depicted in ancient art centuries before classical accounts of one-eyed Arimaspians attempting to steal its treasure. The "griffin" of the Bible is the griffon vulture. The creature is usually portrayed as evil in the bestiaries, but is also associated with Christ in medieval literature and art. Renowned for its strength and vigilance, it is a major heraldic figure, the fabulous equivalent of the lion. In contemporary culture, it is widespread as a character in fantasy fiction and as an image in business logos. The griffon vulture is a raptor of the genus *Gyps*.

Harpy (Greek, "snatcher"): A ravenous mythological monster with the body of a bird and the head of a woman. Similar to sirens. It is included in bestiaries and is a heraldic monster.

Hercynian stag: From the same forest as the ercinee, the single-horned stag described by Julius Caesar is cited by later authors as an example of a unicorn animal.

Hippogriff ("horse-griffin"; hippogryph): An unlikely hybrid comprised of the griffin and its natural enemy, the horse. Horse-griffin figures are depicted in classical and medieval art. The creature is best known as a character in Ariosto's *Orlando Furioso*.

Hydrippus (sea horse): In the Greek *Physiologus*, a fish whose front half resembles a horse. Similar to the mythological figure commonly depicted in heraldry and the other arts. A marine creature of the genus *Hippocampus*.

Leucrota (Leukrokotta; Greek, "white wolf-dog"): An Ethiopian creature Pliny described as being the size of ass, with cloven hooves, the haunches of a stag, the neck and tail of a lion, the head of a badger, and a mouth that extends to the ears; it imitates the sound of the human voice. Derived from the *krokottas* of Ctesias, Pliny's animal is thought to be based on the hyena. It appears in the bestiaries and in later natural histories. Edward Topsell confused it with the manticore.

Manticore (Old Persian, "man-eater"; martikhora, martichoras, etc.): A beast of India having a man's face, a triple row of teeth, a lion's body, and the tail of a scorpion. First described by Ctesias, whose account has been paraphrased ever since.

Mermaid: A sea creature with the head and torso of a woman and the tail of a fish, depicted in art and mythology since ancient times. In the bestiaries, often interchangable with the siren. Since the Age of Exploration, men and women of the sea have generally been regarded as the imagination's version of marine mammals.

Ness monster: A man-eating water beast of the River Ness, driven off by St. Columba. The tale is often cited as the earliest account of the controversial Loch Ness Monster.

Odontotyrannos (Greek, literally "tooth-king"): A gigantic one-horned beast in the Alexander romance. After soldiers slay the creature, it takes 1300 men to drag it away.

Onocentaur: In the *Physiologus*, the ass-centaur is usually paired with the siren, both being of a double nature and signifying duplicity.

Pegasies: In Mela's geography, Ethiopian birds with ears like horses. Pliny believed them to be fabulous.

Phoenix (Greek, the bird, "purple-red," "date palm," and "Phoenicia"; corresponding to the Egyptian *benu*): The eternal bird is said to appear at periodic intervals at the Temple of the Sun in Heliopolis, Egypt. It comes from Arabia and other regions of the East, where it dies in its nest of spices and is reborn from its own ashes. Herodotus is credited with introducing the story to the West, where it has been perpetuated through repetition and variation ever since. A Christian allegory of resurrection, a heraldic emblem of renewal, a symbol of the alchemical process, the phoenix was one of the animals rejected as fabulous in the seventeenth century. The bird reappears in modern literature, in children's fantasy, scholarship, and poetry. As the Feng-Huang, one of the Celestial Animals of China. *Phoenix raptor* is the scientific name of a red dragonfly. *Phoenix* is a constellation in the southern hemisphere.

Roc (rukh, ruc): A fabled Eastern bird of colossal size, large enough to blot out the sun in its flight and strong enough to carry off elephants in its talons. Marco Polo heard about the "rukh" birds of Madagascar, creatures with feathers twenty to thirty feet long. The bird carried Sindbad above the earth in *The Arabian Nights*. One of the oriental "wonder birds."

Salamander: A lizard said to be impervious to fire. Sanctioned in Aristotle's writings, salamander lore was challenged by Albertus and others. The salamander is heraldically depicted in flames and is an alchemical symbol of fire.

Sadhuzag: In Flaubert's *Temptation of St. Anthony*, a black stag with hollow white antlers that make flute-like sounds in the wind: soft, enchanting music from a south wind and a violent howling sound in wind from the north.

Sea Monster: Olaus Magnus's map of Scandinavia contains a major pictorial collection of sea monsters. Illustrations based on the map were reproduced in natural histories. Olaus is regarded as the first author to describe the modern sea serpent and the giant squid.

Serra: A sawfish, swordfish, or flying fish that in the bestiaries flies ahead of a sailing ship, tires and dives into the sea like the faithful who fall into sin. In Philippe de Thaun's *Bestiary*, the serra is a bird-lion-fish composite similar to the Lion of the Sea.

Siren: One of a group of mythological sea nymphs that lure mariners to their deaths with their sweet singing. Sirens are depicted in Greek art as birds with women's faces. In *Physiologus*, they are maidens from the waist up, birds from the waist down. In bestiaries, often interchangable with mermaids.

Sphinx: In natural histories, a kind of ape, not the mythological human–lion composites of the Egyptians and the Greeks.

Tragopomone: In Mela, a horned bird of Ethiopia. Pliny, calling it the bearded eagle, declared it fabulous. *Tragopan* (Greek, "goat" plus "Pan") is a genus of Asian pheasants with erect fleshy "horns."

Unicorn (Greek *monoceros*; Latin *unicornis*): Of all fabulous creatures, one of the least fantastic in appearance: a horse or goat-like figure with a single long spiraling horn projecting from its forehead. Ctesias is credited with being the first to describe the creature and the medicinal properties of its horn (*alicorn*). Ctesias's fierce beast and the wild *rêem* of the Bible prefigure the medieval legend of the hunting of the unicorn and its capture only by a virgin. In homilies of the Church Fathers and in the *Physiologus* and the bestiaries, the beast represents Christ; in Christian art, the virgin is often identified with the Virgin Mary. Ludovico de Varthema wrote an influential eyewitness account of the animal, and the creature was accepted in most natural histories. Powdered horns and tusks of actual animals were for centuries sold as alicorn. Following challenges to the beast's authenticity, tales of one-horned beasts in remote areas continued to spread, and artificial unicornization of young animals helped confirm the stories. The unicorn is a major heraldic animal; in alchemy, it is a symbol of prime matter. The animal has enjoyed an ever-increasing popularity both in children's literature and adult fantasy and is now one of the best-known and most commercialized of fabulous beasts. As the Ki-Lin, one of the Celestial Animals of China. *Monoceros* is a constellation, and *Rhinoceros unicornis* is the Indian rhinoceros with which the animal has often been identified.

Vegetable lamb: In the journal of Friar Odoric of Pordenone, a little lamb-like beast produced in gourds, like fabled barnacle geese growing from trees.

Whale: Also Aspido Delone (Greek, "asp turtle"); Jasconius (Latinized "fish," from the Irish); and bestiarist Philippe de Thaun named it Cetus, after the sea monster slain by Perseus. A symbol of the Devil in the *Physiologus* and the bestiaries, the sea beast drowns mariners that land upon it, thinking it an island. A well-known legend of the sea.

Yale (Eale): Pliny is credited with being the first to describe this hippopotamus-sized black beast with an elephant tail, boar jaws, and horns that point forward for battle and backward when at ease. A heraldic animal.

Yllerion (Allerion, Ilerion, Ylerion): Just as there was said to be a single phoenix in the world at any one time, there are only two living Yllerion. The fictitious Prester John writes in his letter that after the male and female birds live sixty years, they build a nest and the female lays two eggs. Following the hatching of the young, the parents—followed by a flock of others, as in the phoenix story—fly to the sea and drown themselves. The other birds raise the orphaned young.

Bibliography

As ancient as many imaginary creatures are, it is primarily since the latter nineteenth century that fabulous animals have become a subject of study all their own. Thomas Bulfinch discussed several of the creatures in the "Modern Monsters" section in his *Age of Fable* (1855). Angelo de Gubernatis included some in his *Zoological Mythology: or The Legends of Animals* (1872), and more appeared in Edmund Goldsmid's *Un-Natural History: Myths of Ancient Science* (1886) and Charles Gould's *Mythical Monsters* (also 1886). Among the many works that are at least in part devoted to one or more fabulous creatures are important twentieth-century books that have appeared in several editions since their first printings, namely: Odell Shepard's *Lore of the Unicorn* (1930), T. H. White's *Book of Beasts* (1954), and Jorge Luis Borges's *Book of Imaginary Beings* (1957). In addition to an ever-expanding body of writings in which fabulous creatures are either characters in fantasy fiction or subjects of study, glossy treatments of dragons, unicorns, and other imaginary beings have enjoyed recent commercial success. Margaret Robinson's *Fictitious Beasts* (1961) has been the only annotated bibliography on the subject. With its wealth of information by multiple writers and its extensive bibliographies, Malcolm South's *Mythical and Fabulous Creatures: A Source Book and Research Guide* (1987) is an invaluable resource. The Library of Congress category is "Animals, Mythical."

Primary sources reprinted in this collection are cited within individual entries. Only those works which also served as research are included in this bibliography of secondary sources used or consulted.

Adams, H. C. *Travellers' Tales: A Book of Marvels*. New York: Boni and Liveright, 1927.

Allen, Judy, and Jeanne Griffiths. *The Book of the Dragon*. London: Orbis, 1979.

Armour, Peter. *Dante's Griffin and the History of the World*. Oxford: Clarendon Press, 1989.

Barber, Richard W., and Anne Riches. *A Dictionary of Fabulous Beasts*. London: Macmillan, 1971.

Baring-Gould, S. *Curious Myths of the Middle Ages*. London: Longmans, Green, 1901.

——— . *The Lives of the Saints*. London: John C. Nimmo, 1897.

Bedingfeld, Henry, and Peter Gwynn-Jones. *Heraldry*. Leicester, England: Magna Books, 1993.

Beer, Rüdiger Robert. *Unicorn: Myth and Reality*. Trans. Charles M. Stern. New York: Van Nostrand Reinhold, 1972.

Bell, David N. *Wholly Animals: A Book of Beastly Tales*. Kalamazoo, Mich.: Cistercian Publications, 1992.

Bennett, J. A. W., and G. V. Smithers, eds. *Early Middle English Verse and Prose*. Oxford: Clarendon, 1968.

Benton, Janetta Rebold. *The Medieval Menagerie: Animals in the Art of the Middle Ages*. New York: Abbeville Press, 1992.

Burkert, Walter. *Greek Religion*. Cambridge: Harvard University Press, 1985.

Best, Michael R., and Frank H. Brightman, eds. *The Book of Secrets of Albertus Magnus*. New York: Oxford University Press, 1974.

Blake, N. F., ed. *The Phoenix*. Manchester, England: Manchester University Press, 1964.

Block, Laurie. *An Odd Bestiary*. Chicago: University of Illinois Press, 1986.

Bolton, J. D. P. *Aristeas of Proconnesus*. Oxford: Clarendon, 1962.

Borges, Jorge Luis, with Margaritta Guerro. *The Book of Imaginary Beings*. Trans. Norman Thomas di Giovanni. 1957. Reprint. New York: Avon, 1970.

Bradford, Ernle. *Ulysses Found*. New York: Harcourt, Brace and World, 1963.

Branston, Brian. *Gods of the North*. New York: Thames and Hudson, 1980.

——— . *The Lost Gods of England*. New York: Thames and Hudson, 1984.

Breasted, J. H. *Development of Religion and Thought in Ancient Egypt*. New York: Harper and Row, 1959.

Brieger, Peter, Millard Meiss, and Charles S. Singleton, eds. *Illustrated Manuscripts of the Divine Comedy*. 2 vols. Princeton, N.J.: Princeton University Press, 1969.

Briggs, Julia. *A Woman of Passion: The Life of E. Nesbit, 1859-1924*. New York: New Amsterdam Books, 1987.

Brockway, Robert W. *Myth from the Ice Age to Mickey Mouse*. Albany: State University of New York Press, 1993.

Brown, Lloyd A. *The Story of Maps*. Boston: Little, Brown, 1949.

Bulfinch, Thomas. *Bulfinch's Mythology*. New York: Modern Library, n.d.

Burton, Sir Richard F. *Personal Narrative of a Pilgrimage to Al-Madinah & Meccah*. New York: Dover, 1964.

Buzurg ibn Shahriyar. *The Book of the Marvels of India*. Trans. Peter Quennell. New York: Dial, 1929.

Byrne, M. St. Clare, ed. *The Elizabethan Zoo: A Book of Beasts Both Fabulous and Authentic*. 1926. Reprint. Boston: David R. Godine, 1979. Excerpts from Edward Topsell and Philemon Holland's 1601 translation of Pliny the Elder. Also contains Abraham Ortelius's 1585 map of the sea monsters of Iceland.

Campbell, Joseph. *The Hero of a Thousand Faces*. New York: Meridian Books, 1960.

Cary, George. *The Medieval Alexander*. Cambridge: Cambridge University Press, 1956.

Casson, Lionel. *Travel in the Ancient World*. London: George Allen and Unwin, 1974.

Charbonneau-Lassay, Louis. *The Bestiary of Christ*. Trans. D. M. Dooling. New York: Parabola, 1991.

Cherry, John, ed. *Mythical Beasts*. San Francisco: Pomegranate Artbooks in association with British Museum Press, 1995.

Cirlot, J. E. *A Dictionary of Symbols*. New York: Philosophical Library, 1962.

Clair, Colin. *Unnatural History: An Illustrated Bestiary*. New York: Abelard-Schuman, 1967.

Clark, Anne. *Beasts and Bawdy*. New York: Taplinger, 1975.

Clark, Willene B., and Meradith T. McMunn, eds. *Beasts and Birds of the Middle Ages: The Bestiary and Its Legacy*. Philadelphia: University of Pennsylvania Press, 1989.

Cohen, Daniel. *A Modern Look at Monsters*. New York: Tower, 1970.

Conniff, Richard. "Healthy Terror." *Atlantic Monthly* (March 1994):18–20. Solinus and his monsters.

Cooper, J. C. *Symbolic and Mythological Animals*. London: Harper Collins, 1992.

Costello, Peter. *The Magic Zoo: The Natural History of Fabulous Animals*. New York: St. Martin's, 1979.

Dance, S. Peter. "The Illustrated Beast." *Portfolio* (Aug./Sept. 1979):58–67. Fabulous animals in early natural histories.

———. *The Art of Natural History*. New York: Arch Cape, 1990.

De Gubernatis. *Zoological Mythology: or, The Legends of Animals*. 2 vols. 1872. Reprint. Detroit, Mich.: Singing Tree Press, 1968.

De Voragine, Jacobus. *The Golden Legend: Readings on the Saints*. Trans. William Granger Ryan. 2 vols. Princeton, N.J.: Princeton University Press, 1995.

Dennis, Jerry. "Pliny's World: All the Facts—And Then Some." *Smithsonian* (Nov. 1995):152–62.

Dennys, Rodney. *The Heraldic Imagination*. New York: Clarkson N. Potter, 1975.

Dent, James. *World of Shakespeare: Animals and Monsters*. Reading Berkshire, England: Osprey, 1972.

Desmond, Ray. *The Wonders of Creation: Natural History Drawings in the British Library*. London: British Library, 1986.

Dove, W. Franklin. "Artificial Production of the Fabulous Unicorn: A Modern Interpretation of an Ancient Myth." *Scientific Monthly* 42 (1936):431–36.

Dyer, T. F. Thiselton. *Folk-Lore of Shakespeare*. New York: Harper and Brothers, 1884.

Eden, Richard, ed. and trans. *The First Three English Books on America*. Ed. Edward Arber, Birmingham, England: n.p., 1885. Contains sixteenth-century abridgment of *The Letter of Prester John*.

Fabricius, Johannes. *Alchemy: The Medieval Alchemists and Their Royal Art*. Northamptonshire, England: Aquarian Press, 1976.

Fairbairn, James. *Heraldic Crests: A Pictorial Archive of 4,424 Designs for Artists and Craftspeople.* New York: Dover, 1993.

Flaum, Eric. *Discovery: Exploration Through the Centuries.* New York: W. H. Smith, 1990.

Finch, Jeremiah S. *Sir Thomas Browne: A Doctor's Life of Science and Faith.* New York: Collier, 1961.

Fontenrose, Joseph. *Python: A Study of Delphic Myth and Its Origins.* Berkeley: University of California Press, 1980.

Fox-Davies, A. C. *A Complete Guide to Heraldry.* London: Thomas Nelson and Sons, 1961.

———. *Heraldry: A Pictorial Archive for Artists and Designers.* New York: Dover, 1991.

France, Peter. *An Encyclopedia of Bible Animals.* London: Croom Helm, 1986.

Franklyn, Julian. *Shield and Crest.* New York: Sterling, 1961.

Gesner, Konrad. *Curious Woodcuts of Fanciful and Real Beasts.* New York: Dover, 1971.

———. *Beasts and Animals in Decorative Woodcuts of the Renaissance.* Ed. Carol Belanger Grafton. New York: Dover, 1983.

Goldsmid, Edmund. *Un-Natural History, or Myths of Ancient Science.* Edinburgh: Privately printed, 1886.

Gosse, Philip Henry. *The Romance of Natural History.* Boston: Gould and Lincoln, 1861.

Gould, Charles. *Mythical Monsters.* 1886. Reprint. New York: Crescent Books, 1989.

Harting, James Edmund. *The Birds of Shakespeare.* Chicago: Argonaut, 1965.

Hathaway, Nancy. *The Unicorn.* New York: Viking, 1980.

Hargreaves, Joyce. *Hargreaves New Illustrated Bestiary.* Glastonbury, England: Gothic Image, 1990.

Heffernan, Carol Falvo. *The Phoenix at the Fountain: Images of Woman and Eternity in Lactantius's Carmen de Ave Phoenice and the Old English Phoenix.* Newark: University of Delaware Press, 1988.

Heidel, Alexander. *The Babylonian Genesis.* Chicago: University of Chicago Press, 1942.

Hesiod, *Theogony.* Ed. M. L. West. Oxford: Clarendon, 1966.

Heuvelmans, Bernard. *In the Wake of the Sea Serpents.* New York: Hill and Wang, 1968.

Holmgren, Virginia C. *Bird Walk Through the Bible.* New York: Seabury, 1972.

Hoult, Janet. *Dragons: Their History and Symbolism.* Glastonbury, England: Gothic Image, 1987.

Huber, Richard. *Treasury of Fantastic and Mythological Creatures: 1,087 Renderings from Historic Sources.* New York: Dover, 1981.

Huxley, Francis. *The Dragon: Nature of the Spirit, Spirit of Nature.* New York: Thames and Hudson, 1992.

Ingersoll, Ernest. *Birds in Legend, Fable and Folklore.* New York: Longmans, 1923.

Iversen, Erik. *The Myth of Egypt and Its Hieroglyphs in European Tradition.* Princeton, N.J.: Princeton University Press, 1993.

Jones, Richard Foster. *Ancients and Moderns: A Study of the Rise of the Scientific Movement in Seventeenth-Century England.* 1961. Reprint. New York: Dover, 1982.

Kennedy, Charles W. *The Earliest English Poetry.* New York: Oxford University Press, 1943.

King, L. W. *The Seven Tablets of Creation.* London: Luzac, 1902.

Lane, Edward William. *Arabian Nights' Entertainments—or the Thousand and One Nights.* New York: Tudor, 1927.

Larousse Encyclopedia of Mythology. London: Paul Hamlyn, 1966.

Leach, Maria. *Funk and Wagnall's Standard Dictionary of Folklore, Mythology and Legend.* New York: Funk and Wagnalls, 1949.

Le Guin, Ursula K., "Myth and Archetype in Science Fiction." *Parabola* (Fall 1976):42–47. reprinted in *The Language of the Night: Essays on Fantasy and Science Fiction.* Ed. Susan Wood. New York: G. P. Putnam's Sons, 1979.

Lehner, Ernst, and Johanna Lehner. *A Fantastic Bestiary: Beasts and Monsters in Myth and Folklore.* New York: Tudor, 1969.

Letts, Malcolm. *Sir John Mandeville: The Man and His Book.* London: Batchworth, 1949.

Lewinsohn, Richard. *Animals, Men and Myths.* New York: Harper and Brothers, 1954.

Ley, Willy. *Willy Ley's Exotic Zoology.* New York: Viking, 1959.

———. *Dawn of Zoology.* Englewood Cliffs, N.J.: Prentice-Hall, 1968.

London, H. Stanford. *The Queen's Beasts*. London: Newnan Neame, n.d.

Lum, Peter. *Fabulous Beasts*. New York: Pantheon, 1951.

McCulloch, Florence. *Mediaeval Latin and French Bestiaries*. Chapel Hill, N.C.: University of North Carolina Press, 1960.

McCrindle, J.W., trans. *Ancient India: As Described by Megasthenes and Arrian*. Ed. Ramchandra Jain. 1877. Reprint. New Delhi: Today and Tomorrow's Printers, 1972.

Mayor, Adrienne. "Guardians of the Gold." *Archeology* (Nov./Dec. 1994):52–59. Aristeas and Scythian griffins.

Mead, G. R. S. *Apollonius of Tyana: The Philosopher Explorer and Social Reformer of the First Century* A.D. 1901. Reprint. Chicago: Ares, 1980.

Megged, Matti. *The Animal That Never Was: In Search of the Unicorn*. New York: Lumen, 1992.

Mode, Heinz. *Fabulous Beasts and Demons*. London: Phaidon, 1975.

Møller-Christensen, V., and K. E. Jordt Jørgensen. *Encyclopedia of Bible Creatures*. Trans. Arne Unhjem. Philadephia, Pa.: Fortress, 1965.

Mora, George, ed. *Witches, Devils, and Doctors in the Renaissance: Johann Weyer, De praestigiis daemonum*. Binghamton, N.Y.: Medieval and Renaissance Texts and Studies, 1991.

Moseley, C. W. R. D. *The Travels of Sir John Mandeville*. London: Penguin, 1983.

Nebenzahl, Kenneth. *Rand McNally Atlas of Columbus and the Great Discoveries*. Chicago: Rand McNally, 1990.

Neubecker, Ottfried. *Heraldry: Sources, Symbols and Meaning*. London: Macdonald, 1988.

Newby, Eric. *A Book of Travellers' Tales*. New York: Viking Pengiun, 1986.

Newman, Erich. *The Great Mother*. Princeton, N.J.: Princeton University Press, 1974.

Newton, Alfred. *Dictionary of Birds*. London: Adam and Charles Black, 1893.

Newton, Arthur Percival. *Travel and Travellers of the Middle Ages*. New York: Alfred A. Knopf, 1926.

Nigg, Joe. *The Book of Gryphons*. Cambridge, Mass.: Apple-wood Books, 1982.

———. *A Guide to the Imaginary Birds of the World*. Cambridge, Mass.: Apple-wood Books, 1984.

———. *Wonder Beasts: Tales and Lore of the Phoenix, the Griffin, the Unicorn and the Dragon*. Englewood, Colo.: Libraries Unlimited, 1995.

Parmelee, Alice. *All the Birds of the Bible*. New York: Harper and Brothers, 1959.

Peissel, Michel. *The Ants' Gold: The Discovery of the Greek El Dorado in the Himalayas*. London: Harvill, 1984.

Pigafetta, Antonio. *Magellan's Voyage: A Narrative Account of the First Navigation*. Trans. and ed. R. A. Skelton. London: Folio Society, 1975.

Planche, J. R. *The Pursuivant of Arms*. London: Chatto and Windus, 1873.

Randall, Richard L., Jr., ed. *A Cloisters Bestiary*. New York: Metropolitan Museum of Art, 1960.

Rawson, Jessica. *Animals in Art*. London: British Museum, 1977.

Robin, P. Ansell. *Animal Lore in English Literature*. London: John Murray, 1932.

Robinson, Margaret W. *Fictitious Beasts: A Bibliography*. London: Library Association, 1961.

Roob, Alexander. *Alchemy & Mysticism*. Trans. Shaun Whiteside. Köln, Germany: Taschen, 1997.

Rose, H. J. *Handbook of Greek Literature*. New York: E. P. Dutton, 1960.

Ross, D. J. A. *Illustrated Medieval Alexander Books in Germany and the Netherlands: A Study in Comparative Iconography*. Cambridge: Modern Humanities Research Association, 1971.

Rowland, Beryl. *Animals with Human Faces: A Guide to Animal Symbolism*. Knoxville: University of Tennessee Press, 1973.

Shepard, Odell. *The Lore of the Unicorn*. 1930. Reprint. New York: Dover, 1993.

Sevrin, Tim. *The Brendan Voyage*. New York: McGraw-Hill, 1978.

———. *The Ulysses Voyage: Sea Search for the Odyssey*, New York: E. P. Dutton, 1987.

Shuker, Dr. Karl. *Dragons: A Natural History*. New York: Simon and Schuster, 1995.

Silverberg, Robert. *The Realm of Prester John*. Garden City, N.Y.: Doubleday, 1972.

Smith, George. *The Chaldean Account of Genesis*. 1876. Reprint. San Diego: Wizard's Bookshelf, 1994. Earliest English translation of *Enuma Elish*.

Somadeva, *The Ocean of Story*. Ed. Norman Penzer, trans. C. H. Tawney. Vol. 1. Delhi: Motilal Barrarsidass, 1968.

Smith, G. Elliot. *The Evolution of the Dragon*. 1919. Reprint. Wachung, N.J.: Albert Saifer, 1990.

South, Malcolm, ed. *Mythical and Fabulous Creatures: A Sourcebook and Research Guide*. 1987. Reprint. New York: Peter Bedrick Books, 1988.

Swinfen, Ann. *In Defence of Fantasy: A Study of the Genre in English and American Literature since 1945*. London: Routledge and Kegan Paul, 1984.

Thompson, Stith. *The Folktale*. 1946. Reprint. Berkeley: University of California Press, 1977.

Tolkien, J. R. R. *The Monsters and the Critics and Other Essays*. Ed. Christopher Tolkien. Boston: Houghton Mifflin, 1984.

Tolstoy, Nikolai. *The Quest for Merlin*. Boston: Little, Brown, 1985.

Topsell, Edward. *History of Four-footed Beasts, Serpents, and Insects*. 3 vols. Introduction by Willy Ley. New York: De Capo, 1967.

——— . *Fowles of Heauen; or, History of Birdes*. Eds. Thomas P. Harrison and F. David Hoeniger. Austin: University of Texas Press, 1972.

——— . *Topsell's Histories of Beasts*. Ed. Malcolm South. Chicago, Ill.: Nelson Hall, 1981.

Ullendorff, Edward, and C. F. Beckingham. *The Hebrew Letters of Prester John*. New York: Oxford University Press, 1982.

Van Den Broek, R. *The Myth of the Phoenix*. Leiden: E. J. Brill, 1972. The definitive study of the classical and early Christian Phoenix.

Vinycomb, John. *Fictitious and Symbolic Creatures in Art: With Special Reference to Their Use in British Heraldry*. London: Chapman and Hall, 1906.

Watson, Foster. "Alexander Ross: Pedant Schoolmaster of the Age of Cromwell." *Gentleman's Magazine* 279 (1895): 459–474.

Wendt, Herbert. *Out of Noah's Ark: The Story of Man's Discovery of the Animal Kingdom*. Boston: Houghton Mifflin, 1959. Chapters on the roc, bird of paradise, others.

White, T. H. *The Book of Beasts*. 1953. Reprint. New York: Dover, 1984.

Whitfield, Peter. *The Image of the World: 20 Centuries of World Maps*. San Francisco, Calif.: Pomegranate Press Books in association with the British Library, 1994.

——— . *The Charting of the Oceans: Ten Centuries of Maritime Maps*. Rohnett Park, Calif.: Pomegranate Press Books in association with the British Library, 1996.

Williams, Margaret. *Word-Hoard*. London: Sheed and Ward, 1946.

Wirtjes, Hanneke, ed. *The Middle English Physiologus*. Published for the Early English Text Society by Oxford University Press, 1991.

Wittkower, Rudolf. *Allegory and the Migration of Symbols*. London: Thames and Hudson, 1977.

Acknowledgments

The editor and publisher are grateful for permission to reproduce the following copyright textual material. Illustration acknowledgments are incorporated in the illustration captions.

Aelian: Reprinted by permission of the publishers and the Loeb Classical Library from Aelian, *On Animals*, vols. 1 and 2, translated by A. F. Scholfield, Cambridge, Mass.: Harvard University Press, 1972.

Albertus Magnus: *Albert the Great: Man and the Beasts; de animalibus (Books 22-26)*, translated with introduction and notes by James J. Scanlan, M.D. Medieval & Renaissance Texts & Studies, vol. 47 (1987). Copyright Center for Medieval & Early Renaissance Studies, State University of New York at Binghamton, 1987.

The Anglo-Saxon Chronicle: Translated for this volume by Raymond P. Tripp, Jr. Copyright © 1997 by Raymond P. Tripp, Jr.

Julian Barnes: From *A History of the World in 10½ Chapters* by Julian Barnes. Copyright © 1989 by Julian Barnes. Reprinted by permission of Alfred A.Knopf, Inc., and the Peters Fraser and Dunlop Group Ltd.

Ibn Batutta: *Ibn Batutta: Travels in Asia & Africa*, translated by H. A. R. Gibb, Routledge, © 1929.

Beowulf: From *Beowulf: An Edition and Literary Translation, In Progress*, edited and translated by Raymond P. Tripp, Jr., The Society for New Language Study, copyright © 1990.

The Boke of Duke Huon of Burdeux, translated by Sir John Bourchier, edited by S. L. Lee. Reprinted with acknowledgment to the Council of the Early English Text Society.

Jorge Luis Borges: "Preface to the 1957 Edition," from *The Book of Imaginary Beings* by Jorge Luis Borges with Margarita Guerrero, translated by Norman Thomas di Giovanni. Translation copyright © 1969 by Jorge Luis Borges and Norman Thomas di Giovanni. Used by permission of Dutton Signet, a division of Penguin Books USA Inc.

Thomas Boreman: *A Description of Three Hundred Animals*. London, 1730; facsimile edition © 1968 by Johnson Reprint Corp., New York. Reprinted by courtesy of Harcourt Brace.

Julius Caesar: *Commentaries of Caesar on the Gallic War*, David McKay Co. Copyright 1952 by David McKay.

Claudian: Reprinted by permission of the publishers and the Loeb Classical Library from *Claudian*, vol. 2, translated by Maurice Platnauer, Cambridge, Mass.: Harvard University Press, 1922.

Leonardo da Vinci: *The Notebooks of Leonardo da Vinci*, edited and translated by Edward MacCurdy, London: Jonathan Cape.

Pierre de Beauvais: *A Medieval Book of Beasts: Pierre de Beauvais' Bestiary*, translated by Guy R. Mermier. Edwin Mellen Press, copyright © 1992 by Guy R. Mermier.

Richard de Fournival: *Master Richard's Bestiary of Love and Response*, translated by Jeanette Beer, the University of California Press. Copyright 1986 by the Regents of the University of California.

Ludovico di Varthema: *The Travels of Ludovico di Varthema*, translated by John Winter Jones, edited by George Percy Badger, the Hakluyt Society, 1863. Reprinted with acknowledgment and thanks to the Hakluyt Society, original publisher of the material.

Enuma Elish: Myths from Mesopotamia, translated by Stephanie Dalley, Oxford: Oxford University Press. Copyright © Stephanie Dalley 1989. Reprinted by permission of Oxford University Press.

James George Frazer: Reprinted with the permission of Simon & Schuster from *The Golden Bough: A Study in Magic and Religion* by James George Frazer. Copyright © 1922 by Macmillan Publishing Company, renewed 1950 by Barclays Bank Ltd.

The Greek Alexander Romance, translated by Richard Stoneman (Penguin Classics, 1991), copyright © Richard Stoneman, 1991. Reproduced by permission of Frederick Warne & Co.

Hesiod and the *Hymn to Apollo*: Reprinted by permission of the publishers and the Loeb Classical Library from *Hesiod, The Homeric Hymns and Homerica*, translated by H. G. Evelyn-White, Cambridge, Mass.: Harvard University Press, 1982.

Hildegard of Bingen: Translated for this volume by Mary Margolies DeForest. Copyright © 1997 by Mary Margolies DeForest.

Horapollo: *The Hieroglyphics of Horapollo*, translated by George Boas, Princeton University Press, © 1950.

Carl Jung: *Psychology and Alchemy*, Princeton University Press, 1993. Copyright 1953 by the Bollingen Foundation.

Lactantius: Reprinted by permission of the publishers and the Loeb Classical Library from Lactantius, *Phoenix*, from *Minor Latin Poets*, translated by J. Wight Duff and Arnold M. Duff, Cambridge, Mass.: Harvard University Press, 1961.

The Latin *Physiologus*: *Physiologus*, translated by Michael J. Curley, copyright © 1979. By permission of the University of Texas Press.

D. H. Lawrence: *Apocalypse* by D. H. Lawrence, Introduction by Richard Aldington. Copyright © 1931 by the Estate of D. H. Lawrence, renewed © 1959 by the Estate of Frieda Lawrence Ravagli. Used by permission of Viking Penguin, a division of Penguin Books USA Inc. "Phoenix" by D. H. Lawrence, from *The Complete Poems of D. H. Lawrence* by D. H. Lawrence, edited by V. de Sola Pinto and F. W. Roberts. Copyright © 1964, 1971 by Angelo Ravagli and C. M. Weekley, Executors of the Estate of Frieda Lawrence Ravagli. Used by permission of Viking Penguin, a division of Penguin Books USA Inc.

The Letter of Prester John: From *Prester John: The Letter and the Legend*, translated by Vsevolod Slessarev, the University of Minnesota Press. Copyright © 1956, University of Minnesota.

Lucan: Reprinted by permission of the publishers and the Loeb Classical Library from *Lucan*, translated by J. D. Duff, Cambridge, Mass.: Harvard University Press, 1928.

Lucian: Reprinted by permission of the publishers and the Loeb Classical Library from *Lucian*, vol. 1, translated by A. M. Harmon, Cambridge, Mass.: Harvard University Press, 1991.

Lucretius: *On the Nature of the Universe*, translated by Ronald Latham (Penguin Classics, 1951). Copyright © R. E. Latham, 1951. Reproduced by permission of Frederick Warne & Co.

Peter Lum: *Fabulous Beasts*, Pantheon Books. Copyright © 1951 by Peter Lum. The editor and publisher, working through the author's agent, Curtis Brown, were unable to reach the author's estate for reprint permission.

Heinz Mode: *Fabulous Beasts and Demons* (London: Phaidon Press, 1975). Reprinted by permission of Phaidon Press.

The Old English *Phoenix*: Translated for this volume by Raymond P. Tripp, Jr. Copyright © 1997 by Raymond P. Tripp, Jr.

Old English Riddle: Translated for this volume by Gregory K. Jember. Copyright © 1997 by Gregory K. Jember.

Ovid: *The Metamorphoses* by Publius Ovidius Naso, translated by Horace Gregory. Translation copyright © 1958 by The Viking Press, Inc., renewed 1986 by Patrick Bolton Gregory. Used by permission of Viking Penguin, a division of Penguin Books, Inc.

Antonio Pigafetta: *The First Voyage Round the World*, edited and translated by Lord Stanley of Alderley, the Hakluyt Society, 1874. Reprinted with acknowledgment and thanks to the Hakluyt Society, original publisher of the material.

Pliny: Reprinted by permission of the publishers and the Loeb Classical Library from Pliny, *Natural History*, vols. 2, 3, 4, and 8, translated by H. Rackham, Cambridge, Mass.: Harvard University Press, 1983.

Pausanias: Reprinted by permission of the publishers and the Loeb Classical Library from Pausanias, *Description of Greece*, vol. 3, translated by W. H. S. Jones, Cambridge, Mass.: Harvard University Press, 1978.

Philostratus: Reprinted by permission of the publishers and the Loeb Classical Library from Philostratus, *The Life of Apollonius of Tyana; The Epistles of Apollonius and the Treatise of Eusebius*, vol. 1, translated by F. C. Conybeare, Cambridge, Mass.: Harvard University Press, 1960.

François Rabelais: *The Complete Works of Rabelais: The Five Books of Gargantua and Pantagruel*, translated by Jacques LeClercq, Modern Library, 1944. The editor and publisher, working through Random House, were unable to reach the most recent copyright owner for reprint permission.

St. Adamnan: *St. Adoman's Life of Columba*, translated by Alan Orr Anderson and Marjorie Ogilvie Anderson, Thomas Nelson & Sons Ltd., 1961. The editor and publisher, working through Thomas Nelson & Sons, were unable to reach the copyright owner for reprint permisson.

St. Ambrose: From *Saint Ambrose: Hexameron, Paradise and Cain and Abel*, translated by John J. Savage, The Catholic University of America Press © 1961 by Fathers of the Church, Inc.

St. Basil: *Saint Basil: Exegetic Homilies*, translated by Sister Agnes Clare Way, The Catholic University of America Press, © 1963 by the Catholic University of America Press.

St. Bernard: Conrad Rudolph, The *"Things of Greater Importance": Bernard of Clairvaux's Apologia and the Medieval Attitude Toward Art*, the University of Pennsylvania Press. Copyright 1990 by the University of Pennsylvania Press.

St. Brendan: *The Voyage of Saint Brendan: Journey to the Promised Land*, translated by John J. O'Meara, Colin Smythe Ltd. Copyright 1976, John J. O'Meara. Reprinted by permission of Colin Smythe on behalf of John J. O'Meara.

St. Clement: *The Apostolic Fathers*, translated by Francis X. Glimm, The Catholic University of America, 1948.

Strabo: Reprinted by permission of the publishers and the Loeb Classical Library from *The Geography of Strabo*, vol. 1, translated by Horace Leonard Jones, Cambridge, Mass.: Harvard University Press, 1969.

Snorri Sturluson: Section XLVIII, *The Prose Edda*, translated by Arthur Gilchrist Brodeur, The American-Scandinavian Foundation, 1960. Reprinted courtesy of The American-Scandinavian Foundation.

Theobaldus: *Theobaldi "Physiologus,"* translated by P. T. Eden, E. J. Brill. Copyright © 1972 by E. J.Brill.

Lewis Thomas: "Some Biomythology," from *The Lives of a Cell* by Lewis Thomas. Copyright © 1974 by Lewis Thomas; copyright © 1971 by The Massachusetts Medical Society. Used by permission of Viking Penguin, a division of Penguin Books USA Inc.

James Thurber: "The Unicorn in the Garden," from *Fables for Our Time*. Copyright © 1940 James Thurber. Copyright © 1968 Helen Thurber and Rosemary A. Thurber. Reprinted by arrangement with Rosemary A. Thurber and the Barbara Hogenson Agency.

J. R. R. Tolkien: Excerpt from *The Hobbit*. Copyright © 1966 by J. R. R. Tolkien. Reprinted by permission of Houghton Mifflin Company. All rights reserved.

Barbara Wersba: Copyright © 1964 Barbara Wersba, from the book *The Land of Forgotten Beasts*, published by Atheneum. Reprinted by permission of McIntosh & Otis, Inc.

In addition, the works of Sir Thomas Browne, Olaus Magnus, Pomponius Mela, Alexander Ross, John Swan, and Edward Topsell are here reprinted courtesy of University Microfilms International, Ann Arbor, Mich., with acknowledgments to the British Library, Harvard University Library, the Huntington Library, and Yale University for holdings reproduced on microfilm. The editor also wishes to acknowledge Dover Publications, a major source of reprinted material.

Index

Italic page numbers indicate illustrations.

A NOTE ON THE TYPE

The text and titling faces used in this book are from the Goudy family of typefaces, designed by Frederic Goudy (1865–1947), an American. In 1915, American Type Founders issued Goudy Old Style. For the rest of his prolific career, Goudy continued to issue variants of this original design. The extraordinary range of the Goudy family contribute to its continued popularity among designers.

Book design by Jeff Hoffman